A HOUSE OF GOLD AND SHADOWS

USA TODAY BESTSELLING AUTHOR

GENEVIEVE JACK

A House of Gold and Shadows: His Dark Charms, Books 1 & 2

Copyright © Genevieve Jack 2022, 2023

Published by Carpe Luna Ltd, Bloomington, IL 61704

First Edition: October 2022

ISBN: 978-1-962757-00-3

eISBN: 978-1-940675-92-3

Paperback: 978-1-940675-93-0

V 1.0

INDIGENOUS FAE IN THE AMERICAS

An excerpt from:
Our American Heritage
US History: Sixth Grade

Fairies, or the fae, as they've come to be called, were thought to be mythical creatures for most of American history. It wasn't until 1863, when the seelie king Kieran made himself known to Union Major General George Meade, that fae existence appears in any historical documents. Meade's journals describe the fae as "...seeming entirely human but demonstrating strange and little-understood powers." At Meade's request, Kieran and his fae army assisted Union forces during the second day of the Battle of Gettysburg. The fae neutralized eleven confederate brigades without lifting a single weapon, changing the course of the Civil War. Without their intervention, General Lee might have succeeded with his offensive attack on the North.

For a short time following the end of the Civil War, the fae were lauded as heroes and lived among humans. But with their arrival came the discovery of Devashire, a portion of the Appalachian

Mountains on the border between North Carolina and Tennessee, previously hidden from and unknown to humans. The United States government, wishing to claim these lands for expansion, invoked the 1851 Indian Appropriations Act and attempted to move the fae to a reservation west of the Mississippi as they had done numerous other native peoples.

Kieran refused, and his army proved too much for Reconstruction-era troops to best. In a historic accord, President Andrew Johnson designated Devashire a self-contained and self-governed territory completely independent of the United States. In exchange, Kieran agreed that no fairies would be permitted to reside outside Devashire. Although it is generally acknowledged that the US federal government occasionally pays handsomely for the help of the fae under special circumstances, it remains illegal for the fae to live among humans.

Today, American citizens can visit a village in Devashire called Dragonfly Hollow where visitors can learn about the fae for a daily fee. A theme park, casino, and education center have been erected in Dragonfly and are popular with tourists. Devashire now generates revenue approximately equal to the gross national product of Germany.

Back in 1863, fae powers were never fully understood. Even the human brigades involved directly had no explanation for why their mere presence seemed to change the course of the war. Although many hypothesized fae *magic* was to thank, according to the experts at Dragonfly Hollow, fairies wield one thing and one thing only—*luck*.

Part I
His Dark Charms

CHAPTER
ONE

There are only three times in life when everyone is equal: the moment we're born, the moment we die, and the moment we sit down at the poker table. Poker is the great equalizer. The cards don't give a shit what you look like. They don't care where you started from. All that matters is the hand you're dealt and how you play the game.

I love poker, but then you might say I'm lucky.

Luck is something I've been intimately familiar with since I was three and I learned that with a little focus I could make an ice cream cone drop from a human's hand into my own. My mother was furious that day. I licked that mint-chocolate-chip miracle so fast the human didn't want it back.

Since then, I've discovered I'm not the luckiest fae in existence or the smartest, but I know how to make the most of what I've got. I'm living proof that sometimes the hand we're dealt isn't the whole story.

Sometimes we can bluff.

Not that I prefer to lie. It would be a relief to have the privilege to be myself if doing so didn't come with grave consequences. Out of necessity, I've been living a lie for sixteen years now, from the time I got knocked up by a human man and left my fairy homeland. Living as an undocumented fae among humans can be a bitch, but it's taught me how to make the best of a raw deal.

Today the player across the poker table fits that description. He's a vexation, a thorn in my side. For the course of this game, I've referred to him as Mr. Fidget in my head. Mr. Fidget has a name, but I keep forgetting it because until this moment I would have bet my left tit he'd run out of chips long before this.

Fidget is a newbie. None of the regulars have ever heard of him. He's young, maybe thirty, and dressed more like an accountant than a poker pro, in a pair of khakis and a checkered dress shirt straight off a clearance rack. He never stops bobbing his knee or riffling his chips. It's annoying as hell.

It's one in the afternoon, and the room I'm in reeks of billowy floral cologne, stale smoke, and the sickly sweet essence of spilled liquor. I'm experiencing a stomach-clenching, throat-constricting anxiety that flails inside me like a trapped octopus. No one would ever know. From the outside, I maintain a carefully curated impassivity, as cool and collected as one of the marble statues in front of Caesar's Palace. Nothing to see here. Just a human woman holding a few cards, ordinary as can be. I'm no threat at all. Focus on the other players.

I need this win.

The pot could finally buy my daughter the life she deserves, the life I left Devashire to give her. A normal human life, free of lies. Free of constantly looking over her shoulder.

Casually, I toy with Kiko, the shiny gold maneki-neko (aka Japanese lucky cat) who sits atop my chips. I relish the bubbly rush of luck she feeds me and direct it at the deck shuffler beside the dealer. It's a fae thing. Wielding luck is a talent each of us possesses at varying levels. As a pixie, I'm certainly not as powerful as others of my kind, but you might say I've made the most of my talents.

The machine whirs, spits out a deck, and the dealer flicks out the cards with crisp precision. I turn up the corners of my two and find that the luck I've spent on the shuffle has paid off: pocket aces.

Mr. Fidget's eyes dart wildly between his cards and my face. He swallows hard. He has the small blind, which means he was a C-note in before we even saw our cards. Action folds to me, and I raise. He calls. The big blind, not wanting to get mixed up in things, smartly folds. The dealer rakes our chips into the pot, and now it's heads-up, just him and me.

I school my features as the flop is dealt. Ace of clubs, ten of clubs, nine of spades. And just like that, my pocket aces become three of a kind. Across from me, Mr. Fidget is sweating bullets and generally looks like his heart might fail at any moment.

He mops his brow with a cocktail napkin. "All in," he mumbles.

At the moment, I have what we call in poker terms the stone-cold nuts, the strongest hand given the situation, but I know a flush and a gut-shot straight draw are possibilities. Is he all in with a draw? Any decent player knows I've got great odds... and with my luck, I call. Here we go. Let's say goodbye to Mr. Fidget.

The turn drops. Ace of clubs. Four of a kind. It takes effort not to grin like a cat with a mouse between its paws. Mr. Fidget holds his breath as the dealer flips the river.

The jack of clubs. Interesting. I've dosed the deck with a heavy amount of luck, and it's a good thing because if I didn't know better, I might be worried. The makings of a royal flush lay on the table.

It's time to show our cards. When I tip my four of a kind, I can no longer hold back a self-satisfied grin, but Mr. Fidget doesn't react as expected. He goes perfectly still, no longer moving or sweating. He's transformed into someone older, cooler, and somehow smoother. A man who belongs in a Lexus commercial. A player in nerd clothing.

Without breaking eye contact, he flips his cards and my heart stops. All the tiny hairs on my body stand on end. King and queen of clubs. Royal flush. He wins.

As the dealer rakes my chips and the crowd applauds, Mr. Fidget makes eye contact and smiles for the first time. Warning bells ring inside my head, and fear stabs an icy tendril into my heart. His teeth gleam with the slightest hint of blue.

I snatch Kiko from the table and storm for the exit, trying to look like a disappointed pro rather than a terrified illegal alien. I drain the last morsels of luck from Kiko's belly and pray this isn't what I fear it is.

People call out to me. Faces blur in my haste for the exit. As fast as my muscles will move, I weave through the crowd and out onto the Strip. I want to deny it. I want to be wrong. But there is only one thing that can turn a human's teeth that shade of indigo: blue iron. And there's only one department whose agents drink it regularly for its luck-neutralizing effects, the Fairy Immigration and Rehabilitation Enforcement agency (FIRE).

Mr. Fidget explodes out the door behind me, and I pour on the speed, no longer even attempting to move at the same pace as the humans around me. He's gaining on me anyway. Damn, the man is in great shape for a human. I push my luck again, and a gaggle of scantily clad dancers in tall headdresses flood out of the nearest doorway and into the space between us. The distraction buys me precious distance. I duck into the Venetian, thinking I've lost him, but seconds later he's barreling through the doors, a cruel blue smile turning his lips. He's enjoying this.

I push my luck again and hear a grunt as an exceedingly large man slips on a discarded bag of chips and lands in front of him. That shot of luck was meant for Mr. Fidget, but the blue iron in his blood makes him immune. He steps over the man and relentlessly continues his pursuit.

My breath comes in huffs as I speed walk deeper into the casino and spend what remains of my luck to change my appearance. I go from brunette to blond and add a few pounds. Only I've used most of my luck on the game. I don't have enough juice to change my clothing, and I won't be able to hold the illusion for long. *Fuck!* He's drawn me down to almost nothing. I realize in full Technicolor horror that was his aim all along. Fidget's erratic play was meant to bottom me out the entire time.

I zig and zag through a dense cluster of gamblers and duck into the nearest restroom. A group of women celebrating a bachelorette party crowds the mirror. Without calling attention to myself, I rush into the last stall, lock the door, and draw my feet up so that they can't be seen from the outside.

This better work. I am dry, as is Kiko. If I push again, I'll overdraw my reserves, and for a fae, being overdrawn is deadly. Luck is a force. It's limited, like energy. A marathon runner can pour on the adrenaline and force themselves to use more than they actually have, but just like Pheidippides, who died when he reached his destination, fairies who overspend their luck welcome disaster. My father used to say, "An empty bucket can be filled with anything, Sophia. Never completely empty your bucket." It's one of the few ways fae can be seriously injured or killed.

I huddle, perched on the toilet, sure I've lost him, until the screams of the bachelorette party fill the bathroom.

"Get out," Fidget orders, his voice laced with malice. A few of the girls curse and threaten to call security, but their voices fade as they rush out the door. I hold perfectly still, taking slow, steady breaths.

Fidget slams the door of the first stall open.

I shiver. Out of the corner of my eye, my blond hair changes back to dark brown. My illusion fizzles like a burnt-out match. I'm out of luck. Closer, another door bangs open and then another. Maybe two more to get to mine. I have to act.

Crashing out my stall, I bolt, slip past his grabbing hands, and dash back into the casino. I don't make it. He tackles me from behind, and my face slaps the floor. His boot stomps on my back before I even have a chance to register the pain.

"Stay down," he orders. Like I have a choice. He twists my arms behind my back. Blue-iron cuffs snap onto my wrists. Then Fidget pokes a needle into my arm and through a dangerous smile says, "Nighty night."

CHAPTER

TWO

The moment I become conscious again, it's clear I'm in a world of shit. I'm naked, strapped facedown on a cold metal table in what looks like a surgical suite. Machines beep. A tray of needles rests near my head. Blue-iron cuffs clamped on my wrists and ankles keep me drained of all luck, leaving my head throbbing and my stomach nauseated.

Every part of me wants to panic. Anyone would in this situation. My heart races, and my palms sweat. But I know that how I handle the next several minutes could mean the difference between deportation and freedom. The stakes are too high for me to fuck this up, and the surest way to do that is by going on tilt—that's the poker term for when emotions cause a player to act illogically. It's something I'm practiced at avoiding, and I call on that skill now.

I don't struggle or scream. Neither will do any good anyway. Steadying my breath, I close my eyes and pretend to be asleep. A human would suffer the effects of anesthesia far longer than a fae, and my only hope right now is to introduce a sliver of doubt that I am anything but human.

"Might as well open your eyes," Fidget says. "I can tell by your heartbeat you're awake."

Fuck! I open my eyes.

"Name?" he commands.

"Soho Lane," I say immediately. "All my papers are in my purse. I am an American citizen."

He casts his gaze to the side as if my answer deeply disappoints him. "Let's try this again. I'm Agent Andrew Donovan of the Fairy Immigration and Rehabilitation Enforcement agency. You are an undocumented fae whom I've caught defrauding unsuspecting humans under the guise of human poker pro Soho Lane. We both know Soho Lane isn't real."

"It's the only name I have," I insist, and the lie comes so easily that in the moment I believe it.

"Tell me your real name now and admit what you are, or I'll have Dr. Pain prove it the hard way. Just so you know, Dr. Pain isn't his real name either, but he's earned the right to the pseudonym."

I almost wet myself when a masked man in scrubs steps into view. I've never been inside a rehabilitation facility before, but I've heard stories. Despite the name, no rehabilitation happens here. This is a place where the government uses fairies for their own ends. This is a place where fae like me disappear.

I lick my parched lips. Whatever Dr. Pain is going to do to me, nothing I'm willing to say is going to change it. Donovan is a bully, and bullies feed off getting under your skin. I refuse to give him the satisfaction. I decide then that if I'm going down, I'm going down swinging.

I reach for the only weapon at my disposal, my words. "What's *your* nickname, Agent Donovan? Does it start with tiny and end with prick? I know it's not your real name, but *you've earned it.*"

A low chuckle comes from somewhere in the room but is

muffled quickly. Donovan's eyes narrow into slits. "Tell me your name," he demands again.

"What type of man has to chain a woman to a table to get what he wants?" I grind out.

Donovan's expression rearranges into a sinister tableau, and he comes closer, crouching down until our faces are level. His cold and empty eyes remind me of a crocodile's. "The type of man I am...," he mumbles, then gives a breathy laugh. "I'll tell you a secret. I'm the type of man who wants to see a woman chained naked to a steel table. I'm the type of man who gets off on hearing her scream. Really does it for me."

I can't help it. He rattles me. I blink twice. I can't keep my voice from trembling as I say, "I am an American citizen. It's against the law for you to hold me here."

A brittle laugh hits me in the face. "Time's up. Looks like we're doing this the fun way." Those reptilian eyes flick up to Dr. Pain. "Do it."

Icy metal touches my bottom rib and scrapes across the skin of my back. I realize too late what he plans to do. A metal hook jabs under my wing flap. How does he even know it's there? Wings retracted, I look exactly like a human! "No... no, no, no!" I scream.

Anatomically, I am in the wrong position to spread my wings. Terror grips me in its razor-sharp claws as I realize this is intentional. The table is designed to arch my back and force my scapulae together, a position that makes it impossible to naturally spread my wings. This isn't about Donovan proving I'm a pixie. This is about torture. It's about forcing the truth from me in the most humiliating and painful way possible.

I scream myself hoarse while Dr. Pain forces my upper left wing out from under my wing flap with his metal hook. Agony sears along my spine, causing my stomach to lurch. I force the contents back down. My scream cuts off, more because I'm out of breath than anything else. Blood splatters the stainless steel beside my face, and I realize with bone-deep horror it's already stained with tiny dots of someone else's dried blood. He unhooks his implement, and shredded gossamer droops limply over my shoulder. I'm just relieved that the wing is still attached to my body.

Agent Donovan grunts. "It always surprises me when they bleed red. You'd think it would be green or purple."

"Yeah," Pain chimes in.

My back aches. I've never experienced this kind of suffering before, this sort of *torture*. But the pain itself isn't enough to crack me; it's what that limp gossamer wing represents. There's no going back now. No lie, trick, or story will make this better. Donovan knows what I am. He has cause to investigate further. And if I don't find a way to distract him, he'll keep digging deeper into my identity.

Soho Lane has an address on her passport. That address is owned by another identity that owns another property. And if he keeps digging, he'll eventually discover my daughter's existence. That can't happen. Not until she has a chance to run. The chips are down. My options are few. The best way I know to keep him focused on me and not on my papers is to cooperate.

"Sophia Larkspur," I blurt. My real name feels strange in my mouth but then it's been sixteen years since anyone has called me by it.

Donovan lowers his ear toward me. "Hmmm? What's that?"

"My name is Sophia Larkspur. I'm a pixie," I say through gritted teeth, my face wet with snot and tears.

He rolls his lips. "Disappointing. Just when things were getting interesting, you cave. Ah well, I guess we'll have to play another day." He turns his head and commands some worker outside my field of vision, "Get her cleaned up and bring her to my office. We start tonight."

AN HOUR LATER, I'M SITTING ON A METAL FOLDING CHAIR beside Agent Donovan's desk. I've never been a religious fairy, but if the goddess does exist, I pray she protects my daughter. I've done everything in my power to protect her myself. We've prepared for this event. Our home is rented under an alias, and the last name she uses for school is a different one altogether. But there are ways, undoubtedly, for them to find her. Things I've missed. I comfort myself by remembering she's a smart girl and I've taught her exactly what to do in this situation. All she has to do is follow through.

I can't take my eyes off Kiko. Donovan's set my lucky cat on top of a stack of file folders like a paperweight. Does he intend to keep her? I frown at the thought. As far as I know, she's one of a kind. The little arm that beckons you is made of blue iron, the only element on earth that can drain a fairy of their luck. But unlike Donovan's cuffs, designed of solid blue iron to both drain and neutralize a fairy's luck, the rest of Kiko is jade, a gem exceptionally suited for storing luck. Normally, I use the arm to siphon off a small amount throughout the day and store it inside Kiko for later use, when my own reserves are low.

I know she's empty at the moment, but my fingers still itch to steal her back, if only for the comfort of having something familiar in my hand. She's been with me a long time. My personal good luck charm, figuratively and literally.

"I'm going to take the cuffs off," Donovan says. "I need you to have a little juice for what we're going to do tonight. Just know that if you direct any of that luck toward anything other than the task at hand, I'll gladly put you back on that table. Every agent in this building has enough blue iron in their blood to take you down five times over. Understood?"

Poker makes you an expert at reading people. Donovan isn't bluffing. The reason I had trouble reading him at the table is precisely because he's a psychopath with zero empathy and a penchant for violence. I see now that his nervous newbie act was believable because he's a hunter who's mastered baiting his prey. He knew it would make me uncomfortable and cause me to spend my luck to try to force him out of the game. He did it on purpose to drain me. Make me easier to catch. I could respect it if he wasn't such a twisted twatwaffle.

I nod. "Understood."

He removes the heavy blue-iron manacles. As soon as they are off me, I draw a deep breath in relief as my luck bubbles in my veins again, weak but there. I close my eyes at the pleasure of it.

"Let's start with pictures. I'm going to show you a crime scene. You will answer my questions. We'll go from there."

What now? Pictures? Crime scenes? He grabs a manila folder from under Kiko and flips through it. With the hint of luck in my veins, my thoughts race for a means of escape. My gaze lands on the gun hanging from Donovan's hip.

"Iron bullets," he says, not looking up from the contents of the folder. "Don't even think about it, Ms. Larkspur. I've been doing this a long time. It won't work."

I fold my arms over the scratchy material covering my chest. "What is this, burlap?" I squirm uncomfortably. The orange jumpsuit chafes, especially against my back. I've managed to retract my wing, but the wound hasn't healed.

"I ask for barbed wire, but they keep sending me these," Donovan says heartlessly. Goddess, he's a prick.

"Why do you hate fae so much?"

"Who says I hate fae?"

"If this is how you treat people you like, I don't want to know how you treat those you don't."

He leans back in his chair and straightens his tie. "First of all, you're not people. You're fae. A creature. Not human."

"Creatures are people too," I mumble.

"Second, you are not just fae. I happen to like fae as an occasional diversion. I've spent a few weekends at the Dragonfly."

The Dragonfly is a club in Dragonfly Hollow, the part of Devashire open to humans. Total meat market. Humans who go there are typically hoping for an exotic sexual experience with a pixie or satyr, which means Donovan likes to get freaky. Gross. "Then why the torture?"

He bobs his eyebrows. "I like the torture."

I swallow and feel the blood rush from my face.

"You know what I *do* hate? When a fae such as yourself thinks the law doesn't apply to them and takes advantage of hapless humans." He opens the file again. "I did a little research while they were cleaning you up. Soho Lane has cheated humans out of hundreds of thousands of dollars over the past decade."

More like 2.4 million over the past sixteen years. I keep that thought to myself.

"Poker is eighty percent skill," I say. "I might have used luck occasionally to gain an advantage, but most of those games I won fair and square."

He snorts. "Sure you did." He pulls a pack of gum out of his desk drawer and folds a stick into his mouth. He doesn't offer me any. "Answer me this. If you weren't intentionally preying on human vulnerabilities, why did you leave Dragonfly Hollow? It's not like you don't have a casino there."

I roll my lips together. I don't like to talk about why I ran away. It's humiliating, and I was only seventeen at the time. A lifetime ago. "Domestic issue," I say vaguely. Not a complete lie. Gambling is prohibited for fae in Dragonfly, but I keep that information to myself. I doubt it would help my case.

"Hmm." Donovan chews his gum. "Well then, you'll be happy to know I've decided not to send you back there."

"I'm not being deported?" I can't believe the luck. But I also can't believe Donovan would let me go. There isn't a sliver of kindness or compassion behind those eyes.

He gives me a long, hard look, his gaze wandering the length of my jumpsuit. When he speaks again, his voice is menacingly soft, and his smile matches his crocodile eyes. "Nope, I've decided to keep you."

His tone sends a chill through me. It's like he's picked out a puppy at a pet store—a puppy he plans to permanently chain in his yard. "Wh-why?" I hate the way my voice breaks, but I'm losing my battle to remain strong. If he finds out my real secret... If he finds Arden... *Come on, Sophia. Be brave. Stay sharp.*

Again his gaze rakes down my body. I keep my arms folded protectively across my chest. When he reaches my knees, he spins the folder around to face me. "Look at these pictures."

Huh? I furrow my brow. He slides the folder closer, and I look down at the contents. It's an eight-by-ten photo of a bloody, twisted corpse, limbs splayed at odd angles in the middle of a crime scene. I have no idea how the person died except that it was obviously a violent death. Blood stains the pavement, splattered everywhere. "Why do you think I can help with this?"

"Because the murderer is fae."

I scoff. "Why would you think a fae did this?" Seelie fae are rarely violent. Even under extreme conditions, most seelie would avoid hurting humans outside Devashire for the simple fact of not wanting to get caught being outside Devashire.

Donovan studies me for a moment. "All his teeth are missing."

Hmm. That is strange but not necessarily fae. "Your Tooth Fairy is mythology," I say. "I'd guess this is a human-on-human crime, and the murderer didn't want his victim to be identified."

"That's what we thought too until we found his wallet in his pocket and his wife confirmed his identity. Why would a human pull the guy's teeth but then leave a big fat wallet in his pocket?"

"I have no idea."

Donovan rubs his chin. "The answer is a human wouldn't." He shuffles the picture to the bottom of the stack, revealing another. A footprint, definitely not human. "Can you tell me what creature made this?"

I study the print, wickedly uncomfortable. It looks like it was made by an eight-foot-tall skeleton. Each bone of the foot is clearly visible and is set deep in the mud. "I don't think that's a footprint, Donovan. It's much too large." The secret to a good lie is to tell a partial truth and concentrate on the true part. The footprint isn't human, but it also *isn't* seelie, which means that if it is fae at all, the human world has bigger problems than one dead man.

"Sophia... what made this?" he asks again through his teeth.

"I told you I don't know. Pixies and leprechauns have the same feet as humans." I stick my foot out to show him. "Satyrs also have human-looking feet most of the time. They can shift, but in their natural form, they have hooves. That's definitely not a hoofprint. Which means, whatever made that, it wasn't one of us."

"You know something more. I saw it on your face when you

first looked at this picture. Tell me." He has that psycho look in his eye, the same one as in the torture room. If I'm not careful, I'm going to end up strapped to that table again. Only I can't share what trotted through my mind when I saw that footprint. There are things humans don't know about Devashire, things they can never know.

What I need is a distraction. I lean forward, allowing the vee neck of my orange jumpsuit to reveal some skin. I'm not striking or voluptuous in my natural form, but I look young and cute by human standards. My sable shoulder-length hair and large chocolate-brown eyes give me the coloring of someone who could fit in among multiple cultures under the right conditions. I'm often mistaken as Asian, although in an indistinct way. People assume my ethnicity is mixed, maybe Japanese/Italian or Korean/Irish. I've heard it all. No way can I flirt my way out of answering his questions, but I hope I can accentuate that part of me that's approachable and sweet, that thing that made human men in my past tell me I was the type of girl they wanted to take home to mama.

"What made this print?" Donovan asks again, chewing his gum more vigorously.

"I don't know," I answer sweetly, genuinely. Even I believe me, and I know I'm lying.

"Is it true that pixies can make their boobs bigger anytime they want to?" he asks abruptly.

What the fuck? Maybe I *could* flirt my way out of this. "If you've been to the Dragonfly Club, you know the answer to that."

He nods slowly, that crocodile smile making an appearance again. "When you're rested, you can look any way you want. You can be Megan Fox or Kim Kardashian."

Is that why he's keeping me? To make me his personal, shape-shifting sex doll? I shudder.

"I bet you can even become the monster who made this footprint." He waves the folder, and I swallow as I understand that it isn't sex he's interested in but pinning a murder on a fae. *Fuck.*

"No," I say quickly. "We can't change our overall mass by that much. And we're a nonviolent community."

He snaps his gum. "I think you're lying."

"I'm not."

He opens his drawer and withdraws a set of blue-iron cuffs. "Tell me what could have made that footprint. Or don't tell me, and we'll play the torture game again." He jingles the blue cuffs. When I instinctively jerk away, he leans toward me and whispers, "Oh, and for the record, honey, I wouldn't change a single thing about your appearance except to see you in chains."

My throat constricts and my blood runs cold. He reaches for my wrist.

That's when the fire alarm goes off.

CHAPTER

THREE

In seconds, Donovan's office fills with thick smoke, and I use the distraction to put space between me and the blue cuffs. The chair rattles as I slip out of it, but Donovan ignores me. He's squinting at the lights blinking steadily above us as the alarm repeats a deafening blare. I cough into my hand.

He sneers and points a finger at me. "Stay right there."

The door to the hall pops open, and a panicked man appears. "Donovan, we need your help. The whole bloody place is on fire! The override system is opening cell doors."

"Fuck!" Donovan runs after him muttering something about why the sprinkler system isn't working. I hear him lock me in the office. Panicked, I search the room but there's no other exit.

The smoke thickens. My lungs sting and I cough repeatedly into my hand, hunching to keep myself low. Does he expect me to burn alive in this room? Fuck, he probably does. I try to sense my luck. I have a little, but I'm not sure it's enough. Maybe enough to get out of this room?

I snatch Kiko off Donovan's desk and rush for the door.

When I twist the knob, it's clear immediately that I don't need luck. It swings open easily. The lock is engaged, but Donovan must not have fully closed the door. It never latched. Bully for me.

The smoke is a dense cloud that blankets the ceiling as I stick my head into the hall and look both ways. Empty. At the end of the hall, an emergency exit hangs open. What a break! The override system must have popped that door too. I dash for the exit, holding my breath and crouched low.

Every part of me expects to meet Donovan outside. Where else would he go but out? But as I spill into the night, my assumptions prove incorrect. Gunshots ring out to my left, and I turn to see the rehabilitation center from the outside. I'm in the yard of a building that looks like a prison, sirens blaring behind a wall topped with barbed wire. On the far side of the yard from me, dozens of fae are flooding out of two double doors and agents are trying their best to round them up. Of course, that's what Donovan's counterpart had said—the fire caused their cell doors to open. Every agent in the vicinity is engaged in keeping the mob of fae under control.

I'm alone on my side of the yard... until suddenly I'm not. A helicopter appears above me, the thump-thump of its blades growing louder as it lands, blowing back my hair and forcing me to block my face with my arm. My mouth drops open as a familiar face leans out the side.

"Mom! Hurry!" My sixteen-year-old daughter, Arden—my heart, my reason for breathing—extends her hand from the door. I sprint toward her and dive into the helicopter's belly, scrambling into the seat beside her and strapping myself in.

"Go, go, go!" I scream to the human pilot. He nods, and we lift off. As the chopper banks left, I see Agent Donovan running into the space where I was just standing, his face a mask of rage. He draws the gun from his holster. I turn and pull

Arden into my arms, shielding her with my body, my back to Donovan. Six shots fire in rapid succession. I hold my breath but none of the bullets hit us. We're moving too fast. Too far away.

Only when the rehabilitation center is completely out of sight do I back off and look Arden in the eye. She's a beautiful, intelligent spark plug of a young woman. She's adaptable and clever as a fox. But she's human, the product of a one-night stand with a human man sixteen years ago. The fire, the door, the distraction, the helicopter, the fact that she was in exactly the right place at the right time means she had help. This is too much for a teenager to pull off on her own. Deep down I understand that some serious luck was involved in my rescue, which could only mean one thing.

"*How*, Arden?"

She tucks a strand of caramel-colored hair behind her ear and blinks wide green eyes at me. "When I found out what happened to you, I called Grandma and Grandpa."

"Noooo!" I direct my anger toward the heavens and punch the seat beside my leg. "Damn it, Arden! I gave that number to you to use only in case of emergency!"

She grimaces. "This is an emergency, Mom! FIRE had you!"

"Me, yes, but you were still safe. Why didn't you follow the protocol we talked about?"

The sigh she heaves toward me tells me exactly how she feels about my emergency plan. "No way was I going to empty your bank account and go on the run while you rotted in a rehabilitation center, Mom! It's stupid."

"You're human. You could have gone anywhere. You might have been free of this." I thump my chest. *You might have been free of me*, I think. It's too much to say it, but I'm sure she can read it in my eyes because she winces.

"I'm half fae. Just because the fae part is dormant doesn't mean FIRE wouldn't have caught up to me. There are pictures on the internet of us together. I wouldn't just have to run. I'd have to keep running. I don't want to live like that."

My brain sends me a disturbing vision of Arden strapped to a metal table, and I hold my head. I blow out a deep breath. She's right. After so many years establishing ourselves as human and living in a suburb of Las Vegas, her identity wouldn't have remained secret for long. That wasn't the life I'd wanted for her.

I nod and hug her again. It's done. The call has been made. There's nothing to do but to face the consequences. "I'm sorry," I yell over the blades. "You did the right thing."

I lean back in my seat knowing there is only one place my parents could arrange for us to be taken. Only one place where we'd both be safe from Agent Donovan and others like him: Devashire. And when we arrive, I'll have a price to pay, one that might make Donovan's table appealing.

WE LAND IN A PRIVATE AIRPORT, AND THE PILOT DIRECTS us to transfer to a personal jet. I cringe when I notice the four-leaf clover painted on the tail of the plane. Lucky Enterprises. My parents can't afford this. I hate to think what they must have done to get the money. I'll owe them big time. Considering how long I've been gone and how little contact we've had over the years, I wouldn't blame them for leaving me to rot in that rehabilitation center. I'm both grateful and dreading what this all means.

As I exit the helicopter, Arden shoves a carry-on in my direction. My brilliant daughter had the forethought to pack me a bag. I kiss her on the cheek, thankful for an option to the smoke-scented orange jumpsuit I'm wearing. We board the plane, and a few hours later, I've changed into a pair of jeans, a cami, and a dark cardigan in time to land in Asheville, North Carolina. A human in a Jeep picks us up on the tarmac.

Forty minutes later, we wind our way into the mountains, my heart jackhammering harder with every mile closer to Dragonfly. When I recognize the route the driver is taking, I slap her shoulder. "Hey, the front gate is that direction." I point at the access road we should have taken.

"My orders are to bring you the back way," she states, never taking her eyes off the road. Her platinum hair swings just under her ears and I notice a bulge I'm sure is a gun under her vest.

"Orders?" I shake my head. Who was giving her orders? *Fuck.* Whoever was helping my parents must not know our situation. "Arden is human," I tell her. "She can't get through the moon gate. You need to take us to the front entrance."

The driver presses her finger to her earpiece and relays what I've told her. A few uh-huhs later and she addresses me again. "Someone will meet you. It's taken care of, ma'am."

"Taken care of?" I don't understand. A human can't find or enter the fairy portal to Devashire. I shake my head, panic growing and sending my stomach tumbling. "I won't leave her behind!" I warn. "I'll die before I let them separate us."

"Ma'am," the driver says sternly. "Relax. No one is leaving anyone behind, and absolutely no one is dying. If the boss says it's taken care of, it's taken care of."

"But the only one with the power to let her through is—" My breath catches in my throat. Oh no. I thought my parents might have leveraged their business to pay for my rescue. I hadn't considered they might've gone to Godmother.

My pulse accelerates, and I hyperventilate until I have no

choice but to put my head between my knees to keep from being ill. This is a disaster.

"Mom? Are you okay?" Arden asks from the back seat. She pats my back and hands me her water bottle. "Drink something."

Just like Arden to be worried about me when her entire world has been turned upside down. She's always been precocious. I suppose she's had to be, considering our circumstances. I sip the water and nod to her as I hand it back. I need to stay strong... for her.

Godmother is our most powerful ruler. Humans always assume it's the king—a mistake made by creatures who've been conditioned toward patriarchy. Fae have a king, but he's a recluse. He hasn't been involved in Devashire's politics since the Civil War when he botched things royally. Godmother, on the other hand, plays an active role in leading the seelie. She's the real power. But she's not a queen or anything like it. The closest human equivalent is the Godfather, like the character from the movie. A mob boss. A power no one would ever mess with.

Godmother runs Devashire with magic and might. Unlike all other seelie, Godmother is so saturated with luck that she's capable of true magic. Some say she's a mage. Others that she learned her powers from a secret society of fae lost to time. One thing I know is that she is positively ancient. My grandmother tells me that her mother's grandmother remembered her looking exactly the same as she does today. Fae live long lives: three hundred years on average. Godmother is older—some say thousands of years old—and more powerful than any creature I've ever heard of. She can make things happen. She's also scary as fuck and deals in favors and bargains. If my parents went to her for help getting me back, I will owe a debt, one far greater than money could ever settle.

By the time the Jeep reaches the end of the dirt road and the driver parks at the edge of a dark forest, I'm a ball of nerves thinking about it.

"Where are we supposed to go?" Arden asks. She grabs the bags out of the back and jumps down from the Jeep. She hands me mine. The driver looks at me and touches the brim of her cap as she nods, then she backs up and pulls away.

"Mom?" For the first time, Arden seems genuinely afraid. The Jeep's headlights fade, and we're alone. I have a fleeting thought that we could run, but where would we go? There isn't another place on earth that's safe for us right now.

"We have to go through the woods," I say. "You'll be okay. Just follow me." I lift my suitcase and start walking. The wheels are useless where we are going. There is no path here.

"Follow you? I can't even see you!" Arden's anxiety makes her voice tremble, and it breaks my heart.

I set down my suitcase and remove my cardigan, tying the arms around my waist. It's cold, even for a fae, but it can't be helped. "I know this is scary for you. You've only ever been in the city and the desert. I'm sure the forest feels ominous. But this is where I'm from. I won't let anything happen to you." I grunt in pain as I spread my wings. My back is still sore from Donovan's torture. But with a little luck, I make myself glow.

"Oh... Mom." Her voice is full of wonder. She's seen my wings before but never at night. Never when my light was so clearly visible. The moment grabs me by the lapels and shakes. Pulling back this curtain for her, showing her what I am, it reminds me of our differences and the implications. Arden isn't fae, and where we have no choice but to go things might not be easy for her.

My voice is thick as I say, "Let's go." I lead her into the woods, thankful that she remembered her coat. We travel at a snail's pace so that she can pick her way through the underbrush at human speed. It's positively frustrating.

The forest is a pixie's natural habitat. I could fly through these trees and make it to the portal in minutes, but Arden doesn't have the benefit of my sixth sense. She has to see where she's walking before she takes a step, and the luggage slows both of us down. It takes over an hour to travel a mile.

"How much farther?" she whines, head tipped back. Arden never complains. I can count how many times we've argued about anything on one hand. She's always been a ray of sunshine and a real trooper. Not now. Now in her exhaustion, she reminds me of when she was six and would hold her hands skyward, wanting to be picked up. Only she's much too big to carry anymore, and there's nowhere to carry her to. I can see she's exhausted. I've asked too much of her tonight. But the truth is we should have been there by now. Either I've forgotten the way or the portal has been moved in my absence. The only other possibility, and this is what I'd been afraid of, is that Arden's human presence is keeping me from finding it.

"Let's rest for a moment," I say in a strained voice. I sit on my suitcase and watch her do the same. My glow flickers and burns out.

"Mom? What's wrong? What happened to your light?"

"Tired. I just need to rest." True but not the entire truth. The entire truth is I'm not sure where to go next and I need to preserve my luck. I take a few deep breaths. Worst-case scenario, we can wait here until the sun comes up, then make our way back to the main gate. At least we're in the woods. I always feel better in the woods. Well, except for the one time that changed everything. Being here again, I remember it like it was yesterday.

CHAPTER

FOUR

16 YEARS AGO

No bigger event existed in Dragonfly Hollow than the Yule Ball. It was the event of the season, and almost every high-profile couple in Devashire had announced their engagement on the magical night. Kicked off by an enchanting parade of traditional sleighs pulled by reindeer, young fae couples dressed in formal attire rode through the Winter Wood to the town square where they danced the night away under gently falling snow and twinkling lights.

Human tourists booked tickets over a year in advance to watch the event that ushered in the holiday season at the parks. Some lined up along the parade route days before, desperate for the best view. For fae teens near the end of their school-age years, attending the ball was a rite of passage, the closest thing to prom fairies celebrated.

In sum, the Yule Ball was a big fucking deal, and I was going. Never mind that I personally couldn't have afforded the sleigh I was sitting in. My boyfriend, Seven, could. We'd dated in secret for two long years. I was as surprised as anyone when he asked me to go and tied the traditional red ribbon around my wrist marking me as his date. It shone crisp and new against my tan skin. I stared at it, repeating to myself that he wouldn't have tied it on or rented the sleigh if he hadn't meant to come.

The reindeer shook in its harness, velvety horns rocking back and forth in front of me.

"I don't think he's coming, Soph. You know... leprechauns...," Penelope Hawthorne said softly, her wings fluttering. The fact that there wasn't a hint of derision in her voice made her message all the worse. She wasn't trying to humiliate me; she was my good friend and a fellow pixie who was trying to warn me. I pivoted in my seat to see her and her boyfriend in the sleigh behind me. Her frothy pink gown was perfect for her fair skin and platinum hair. Flick, her boyfriend, sat on the bench behind their reindeer, reins in hand, right where he was supposed to be. My sleigh's driver's seat was still empty. My eyes fell on the worn red ribbon around Penelope's wrist. She and Flick had been dating forever.

"I think... I think he's just late. Something must have come up." I flashed her a wobbly smile.

She shook her head. "Sophia, I tell you this as a friend and fellow pixie. He was never coming. No leprechaun would be seen in public dating a pixie. I know you thought you two were different, but it has never happened, and it never will."

"You don't know what you're talking about," I said more firmly, although a heaviness had started in my stomach. I looked at my watch. We were scheduled to parade through Winter Wood in five minutes. If he didn't get here soon...

Penelope fluttered her wings, her expression empathetic. "I'm sorry, Sophia. Someone should have stopped this." Flick turned around and smacked her shoulder and Penelope blurted, "I'm sorry." Then she said no more.

I checked my watch again. I knew in my heart that Seven would come. This wasn't just a dance for us. This was the night we were going to go public with our long-standing relationship. We'd professed our love for each other months ago and spent countless nights in the woods or on the beach whispering sweet promises. Tonight we planned to blaze a trail and break the unspoken rule that leprechauns couldn't date pixies. Us against the world.

Maybe he got scared and decided not to come? No. I shook my head at the thought. It wasn't just about going public. We'd promised each other that we'd find a place in the woods after the dance and be each other's first. Losing our virginity to each other was something Seven would never miss out on, even if he wasn't ready for the dance and public outing. We'd waited so long. We were almost eighteen. We'd be graduating from Bailiwick's in the spring. He would have sent a message if he'd changed his mind. Something had happened. Something was wrong.

With a sigh, I took one last glance at Penelope and stood, resolved to disembark from the sleigh and take refuge in my room until Seven explained himself. But a hand blocked my path. Mrs. Harper frowned at me over her clipboard. The satyr and mother of three had organized this event, and she lowered her chin so that I was face-to-face with her horns.

"What do you think you're doing?" she said through a tight scowl.

"My date didn't come," I whispered. "Something must have happened to him. I'm going home."

Mrs. Harper shook her graying head. "Oh no, dear. I'm sorry, but that's not possible. It's too late to remove your sleigh from the lineup. Had I known fifteen minutes ago, I might have found someone else to drive it, but I couldn't possibly in the next three minutes. You don't want to ruin the Yule Ball for everyone else, do you?"

My cheeks blazed with embarrassment. "No, but—"

"I'm very sorry. I realize this must be hard for you, my dear, but I have to ask you to be brave tonight. You are going to have to drive this sleigh yourself. Thankfully, it's just a matter of holding the reins. The reindeer are trained to follow the sleigh in front of them. Just wave and smile. I promise you can head home as soon as we park in the square." She sighed and clutched the clipboard against her chest, but there wasn't an ounce of give in her expression.

"But—" Wasn't it obvious how humiliating it would be to ride through the woods alone? The parade route was lined with fae and humans alike. Most of Dragonfly Hollow would see that I'd been stood up.

I gaped at the woman, speechless. But as I glanced at the couples behind and in front of me, I knew she was right. The sleighs were packed in tight. Mine would have to be lifted and turned to be removed from the line. True, once everyone started moving, I might be able to coax the reindeer to pull off route and let the people behind me move forward, but reindeer were very unpredictable when asked to do something they weren't trained to do. Not to mention, the sides of my sleigh were decorated to work with the others. I was the *u* in Merry Yule. Pulling out now would ruin everything.

Gods, everyone was staring. Even if I pushed past Mrs. Harper and ran for home, I wouldn't escape ridicule. I'd ruin the night for the rest of these couples, and I'd never hear the end of it.

"I can drive it if you want," a low, familiar voice said from just out of sight.

I leaned forward to see that a scrawny boy in a green apron had sidled up to Mrs. Harper. River Foxwood. I'd been friends with the young satyr I'd met in Alchemy class for years. In fact, we'd had to be separated on more than one occasion for disrupting the class with our laughter. His big brown eyes smiled up at me.

"There you go," Mrs. Harper said. "Problem solved." She sped busily away.

"I brought you this from our booth." He pointed his thumb at the Foxwood's concession stand, which was unmanned and had a lengthy line forming behind it.

My hands trembled a bit as I took the hot cocoa from him and savored a sip. It was so tempting to accept River's generous offer. I appreciated the gesture more than he'd ever know, but I was going to have to turn it down, and it was taking every ounce of bravery I had in me to do it.

"River, you can't abandon your parents' booth. Your dad would kill you."

His throat bobbed, and a flash of pity flitted through his expression. "He'd understand given the circumstances. He knows what it's like."

I realized exactly what he meant. His dad knew what it was like to be messed with by a leprechaun. In our world, there were leprechauns and then there was everyone else. Leprechauns were lucky as sin. Wealth magnets. Beautiful beyond compare. And sometimes... *often*, really... the rest of us got caught up in the gears of their empires.

I sighed. "Go back to your booth, River. I am going to drive this sleigh into the town square, and then I'm going to come back here, drink this chocolate, and cry on your shoulder, okay?" I handed him back the hot beverage.

"Deal." He took the mug and backed toward his booth. I fluffed my plum-colored skirt and climbed onto the driver's bench, lifting the reins.

"Oh my gods, is she actually going to drive?" I heard

someone say. A chorus of whispers clouded the night around me.

I would not cry. No way. I was a Larkspur. We didn't have much, but we were brave, and I was raised to do the right thing. When my grandmother was my age, she'd been an archer in the Goblin Wars. She'd faced off against an unseelie uprising and seen death and destruction from the front lines. Tonight I was going to live up to the name.

The lead whip cracked, and the orchestra started to play. Mrs. Harper wasn't lying; I didn't even have to slap the reins. Without any effort on my part, my reindeer pulled me into the forest. I sat up straighter, smiling and waving, shoving all my insecurities to the back of my brain.

At first, it seemed like things would be okay. People clapped and yelled, "Happy Yule!" as we slid by. But then I noticed a few fae children pointing and laughing. Mothers whispered to each other. Humans boldly asked why I was alone in voices loud enough for me to hear, ignorant to the shame of it.

It was the longest ride of my life.

I begged the gods to make the parade go faster, but it took the entirety of an hour to reach our destination. Seeing the square decked out in yuletide splendor made my heart give a painful squeeze. Seven was supposed to jump down from the driver's seat, then help me from the sleigh before sweeping me into the center of the square. A band of the best musicians in Devashire would accompany an evening of dancing, holiday-themed cocktails, and gourmet hors d'oeuvres. Godmother's magic would make it snow all night, but no one would feel cold. There would be no wind. No slush. And sometime during the evening, Seven would lead me to the central gazebo where he would kiss me, then whisk me away to somewhere private.

My eyes blurred with tears. It wasn't going to happen, and I had no idea why.

As soon as a volunteer guided my reindeer to a halt, I moved to flee, knowing my tears had flooded the dam of my lower lids and I could no longer hold back the deluge of my grief. I had to get out of there and fast.

But there was a reason the boys always drove the sleighs. My skirts tangled around my legs as I tried to descend, and my heel caught in the hem. I tripped off the step. It happened so fast I didn't have time to use my wings to break my fall. I landed on my stomach and elbows in the frozen grass.

Two leather shoes appeared in front of me, and I stared up into a leprechaun's pitiless, laughing face. Mr. Delaney's face. Seven's father.

"Pity it came to this, but Seven did you a favor tonight," he said. "Now you know your place, pixie. You'd do well to remember it."

He left without helping me up.

CHAPTER

FIVE

I snap out of my reverie when a firefly ignites between Arden and me, the horrific, humiliating memory fading with its phosphorescent glow. My heart leaps. All is not lost. "Keep your eyes open, Arden. You're in for a show."

"Huh?" She blinks tiredly at me.

Flash. Thousands of fireflies ignite at once, turning night into day. I pop off the suitcase and whirl. There it is! The circular stone gate was right behind me all along. How had I missed it before?

The fireflies fade, and everything goes dark again. The gate blends away into the night.

"What the hell?" Arden gasps. "Those little guys give off serious wattage! Is that normal?"

"For these fireflies it is. They're a rare synchronous variety that feed on fairy energy." I point in the direction of the circle of stones. "We're here. The portal is through the moon gate."

She sidles up to me, suitcase in hand. "Where? I don't see anything."

"I can't either. It's invisible in the darkness, but it's there. Wait for it..."

The fireflies ignite again, bathing the forest in their warm golden light. The gate appears again. "Come!" I take her hand and step forward but stop short when Arden squeezes tighter, her hand partially slipping from mine.

"I... *can't*," she says. "It feels like there's something in front of me. I can't move forward."

The light fades into velvety midnight blue again, and I back up to her. I was afraid this would happen. Fuck that driver. I thought she said someone was coming to help us.

Flash! Like a lightning strike, the forest glows again.

We are not alone.

No, no no no. Not *him*. My breath hitches. Of all the people Godmother might have sent to meet us, why oh why did it have to be *him*?

Spotlighted by a thousand fireflies, Seven Delaney is casually leaning against the stone arch of the moon gate as if he's been waiting for us the entire time. His legs are crossed at the ankle, and the crooked grin he shoots my way is heart-stopping and oh so infuriating. How dare he smile at me after what he did? How dare he come within striking distance?

This man is as close to a nemesis as I've ever had and as much the reason for me fleeing Devashire as anything else. On the outside, he's wrapped in a scrumptious package of long, lean muscle and uncanny grace. His shoulders strain the material of his dark dress shirt, and corded forearms, scandalous in their musculature, extend beyond his pushed-up sleeves. With a hand resting lightly on abs as tight as chiseled marble beneath the material, he winks one emerald eye at me, the other twinkling in the moonlight as if he finds our circumstances amusing. His perfectly tailored trousers are a work of art, as are his hand-crafted leather loafers.

In one word, Seven is stunning. I'm stunned. Arden is stunned. Likely at least half the fireflies flitting around us are stunned (at least the female ones). He is overtly sexual, undeniably handsome, and as charming as they come. In other words, a dangerous menace to all womankind.

Leprechauns have a reputation for being short and ugly in the human world. I laughed the first time I saw the University of Notre Dame's mascot. Nothing could be further from the truth. Jealous rivals and political enemies started those rumors to tarnish the reputations of the leprechaun dynasties they hated, anything to get a jab in at the luckiest fae. I can understand the sentiment. Of any of our kind, they have the most inherent luck. That translates into all aspects of their existence, including their physical forms. Leprechauns are beautiful —*always beautiful.*

Pixies like me, we're designed to blend with nature in our natural forms, but leprechauns stand out. They sparkle. And if their physical perfection weren't enough to make you hate them, they are also rich—the type of rich that's only possible through generations of wealth—a wealth that almost always leads to a power and a superiority complex.

In short, a leprechaun is a caramel-covered Adonis in couture. They're almost irresistible. Even knowing that Seven's soul is as rotten as a maggot-infested peach, his physical presence leaves me breathless.

"Seven." His name hisses through my teeth.

"Sophead," he says playfully. "I wasn't sure I'd ever see you again."

I cringe at the pet name he used to use when we were children. "Don't call me that! You have no right to call me that."

He snorts. "I didn't know rights were necessary to use a nickname."

"Mom?" Arden peers around me curiously. Without even realizing it, I've placed myself protectively between them.

"Who's this?" Seven pushes off the moon gate and approaches Arden to get a better look at her. No, he doesn't just look. He studies her like she's a specimen on a microscope slide. I move more fully in front of Arden, blocking his view.

"This is my *daughter*." I emphasize the word in a way that reminds him she's a child and off-limits. I don't trust him within an inch of her.

"I can see that," he says around a lopsided grin. "She's practically a miniature version of you."

Arden shoves around me and extends her hand before I can stop her. "I'm Arden."

I slap her hand down. "Arden, no!"

Arden flashes me an injured look.

"Never offer your hand to a fae, Arden," Seven says. "A handshake among fairies binds a magical agreement. As a human, you can't be sure the shake is just a shake. It's too dangerous for you. Keep your hands to yourself when you greet someone."

"Oh." She slides her hands into her pockets, a faint blush of embarrassment warming her cheeks.

Fury grips me in its shaking fist. "She doesn't need *you* of all people lecturing her on fairy etiquette. *I'll* teach her what she needs to know." I have taught her a thing or two about fairy culture, but who could blame her for not remembering? It's been years since we discussed it. I'd never planned for her to come back here. After sixteen successful years living among humans, I never thought she'd need to.

He ignores my tirade and smiles charmingly at Arden. "I'm Seven, by the way."

"Like the number?" she asks.

"Exactly like the number." He winks at her.

Gah! He's incorrigible. "Enough with the introductions." I slash a hand through the air between us. "Can you get her through the portal or not? You might as well know she's human."

He's still studying Arden in a way that fills me with unease. "How old are you, Arden?"

"Sixteen," she says. She'll be seventeen at the end of September. I can almost hear him doing the math. Arden came along soon after I left Dragonfly—nine months to be exact. Only my parents know the truth about my pregnancy. Did they tell anyone? If they did, I'll know soon enough. Fairies adore gossip and speculation.

It's none of his fucking business.

"Have you ever visited Dragonfly Hollow before?" he asks Arden, charismatic and steady, like he's trying to put her at ease.

"Stop it!" I grit out.

He glances uneasily in my direction. "Stop what?"

Trying to endear yourself to her, I almost say, but I halt the words before they come out of me. He's the only one with enough luck to walk us through the gate, and Arden is shivering and exhausted. I take a deep breath and blow it out, stuffing the memories of what he did to me in a dark closet at the back of my brain. I place my hand on Arden's shoulder. "We've been traveling all night. Please show us through."

His eyes crinkle at the corners. "Of course. You haven't changed a bit, Sophia. All business."

"I've changed," I snap, then narrow my eyes. "I'm far less naive."

Our eyes lock, and challenge sparks between us.

"Take my hand," he commands, holding one out to each of us. "I'll walk you through."

The last thing I want to do is to touch him, but there's no

other way. *I might be able to get through the gate without him, but I'd risk being separated from Arden.* Reluctantly I slip my fingers into his. My stomach gives an annoying flutter at his touch, my internal workings betraying a lingering desire for this man. I grind my teeth and thank the stars that my will and my mind are stronger than my libido. It's times like these that having a poker face comes in handy.

Arden takes his other hand and smiles warmly up at him, her eyes filled with stars. *Fuck.* We're overdue for a long talk.

Seven faces the moon gate and takes a deep breath. The fireflies glow again, lighting up the night. I notice the strain on his face as beneath our feet, the ground begins to rumble. *What is he doing? He couldn't be...* My eyes widen.

Luck is different than magic. A creature with magic can create something out of nothing and command the elements to do their bidding. True magic users are rare. Seven isn't a magic user, but the luck he's wielding is more powerful than any I've known before. Luck can't create something out of nothing, but it can influence the world around it to make something that could happen on its own happen right then.

The wards protecting Dragonfly are grounded in earth. Seven is disrupting their anchor, causing slabs of rock to shift deep beneath our feet. It's a natural phenomenon, but its occurrence now, at this moment, is all his doing. The amount of luck it takes to cause a minor earthquake like this is staggering, and I can't help but gape in awe of his abilities. This level of control could stop a beating heart. It could cause a bird to fall from the sky beak first and kill an enemy.

He's stronger now than when I left. Stronger, and far more dangerous.

"Now," he says and ushers us both forward. Arden and I shuffle through the moon gate at his side. I feel the wards nipping at my heels as they close again behind me. I breathe a sigh of relief when Seven releases my fingers, and I rub the tingle from my palm that lingers after his touch.

Seven cracks his neck, then his knuckles, the tension in his body relaxing once more.

I set my bag down and orient myself. We're near the back of Wonderland, one of five theme parks that make up the Dragonfly Hollow world. My parents live two blocks from here. This subdivision is called Enchantment and is one of three residential areas within Dragonfly Hollow and the only one inside Wonderland.

"Thanks for your help," I say to Seven, anxious to leave his presence. "We can make it from here."

"I'd better escort you." He starts walking toward my old place, gesturing for us to follow.

"Really, it's not necessary," I insist.

He doesn't acknowledge my protest. I grumble as Arden falls into step behind him and I'm forced to follow along. Arden's gaze drifts to the colorful mushroom-shaped houses that line the streets. Crimson, emerald, and royal purple caps top homes with matching shutters and circular doors. It's as if we've all been shrunk down into a cartoon village, a fantastical neighborhood designed to play into human misconceptions.

"Wow, this is wild," Arden says, spinning in place to take it all in.

"Fairies don't actually live in mushrooms," I tell her. "Outside the Dragonfly theme park, our residences look exactly like human houses—better in most cases because our engineering is superior—but inside the parks, this facade sells tickets. Some of these homes are rented to humans, which is why my parents can live here inexpensively. It's convenient for them because they own a store here, and it's lucrative to play into the fantasy."

"Oh," she says. "So some fairies do live here."

"Well, yes. Quite a few actually."

"Then some fairies *do* live in mushrooms." She giggles.

I bristle. "Not naturally. Only for show."

She shrugs. "Humans didn't naturally live in two-bedroom condominiums either, but the cave got old after a while."

"Arden! You know very well what I mean."

She starts walking again, seeming to take in every detail of the street. "Yeah... it's still cool."

While she's distracted, Seven drifts to my side. "How did FIRE finally catch up to you?"

"None of your business."

"Just wondering how the feds found you after all this time. Once Arden called your parents, my people looked into your case. You supported yourself playing poker. Did you get greedy? Use too much luck?"

"The agent never said how he caught me," I mumble with a shrug. Why am I even explaining myself to him? "I still don't know."

The shallow smile he offers says it all. He suspects I made a stupid mistake. He's probably surprised a mere pixie survived outside the wards.

"I didn't think you'd *ever* get caught," he says, and the admission surprises me enough I have to shuffle to keep from tripping over my own feet. "The FIRE agents have enough fairy prisoners working for them now that he was probably able to use their luck. I doubt he'd have been successful without help from one of us."

The connotation is that it wasn't my fault, a kind thing to say. I'm baffled by it. Why is Seven being kind to me now?

Arden chimes in from ahead of us. "She was trying to win my university tuition. My deposit is due for the fall."

"Arden, shhh."

"Aren't you a little young for college?" Seven asks.

Arden preens. "I'm a year ahead. I was admitted to an accelerated premed program at Chapel Hill."

He slants a look of admiration in her direction. "I could tell you were smart the moment I met you."

"Okay!" I say, intentionally interrupting and wedging myself between them again. We've reached my parents' place. "This is it." I usher Arden away from Seven toward the stone path that leads to the front door, rolling my eyes when he lingers in the street. Why won't he just *leave?*

As I knock on the round wooden door, I flash back to a time when I could walk in without knocking. The door was painted red then. Now it's purple. Minutes pass and no one comes. I knock again. They must know we're here. My parents had to have arranged all this.

When the door finally opens, it takes me a full minute to recognize my mother. She's aged. Her once-brown hair is now peppered with silver. Fairies aren't immortal, but their natural lives are long compared to humans, three hundred years on average. My mother isn't a day over seventy, which means her silver hair is caused by negative emotions, not trips around the sun. A pit forms in my stomach as I wonder if any of that gray hair had to do with me.

"I suppose you expect to stay here," she says by way of greeting.

"Where else would I stay?" When she says nothing, I add, "I wasn't hoping for a warm greeting, but a hello might be nice."

"Hello." She folds her arms over her white nightgown.

"Hello," I echo. A moment yawns between us. "Mom, this is your granddaughter, Arden." I move aside so she can get a better look. As soon as she sees Arden's genuine smile, my mother melts and pulls her into an embrace.

"Welcome, Arden. It's so nice to finally meet you." She

oozes warmth toward her granddaughter. I thank the gods for small mercies. "You did the right thing calling us. Go ahead inside. There's a snack for you on the counter."

Arden slips past her into the warm light of the interior, and my mother turns hard gray eyes on me. She doesn't say a word but looks past me toward Seven.

"Eight o'clock sharp," he says in answer to a question that was never asked.

She nods. "She'll be there."

Seven gives me one last lingering look, then utters a hasty good night and, to my relief, finally leaves.

"What happens at eight o'clock tomorrow?" I ask.

She lifts an eyebrow. "You go to see Godmother."

CHAPTER
SIX

On some level, I expected this. Arden and I can't stay in Devashire permanently without Godmother's permission. She controls everything here. Her word is law. Only I thought we'd have a few days to settle in before she summoned me. I assumed there'd be a honeymoon period. Guess I was wrong.

"What do you think I'll owe her?" I ask my mother, chewing my lip. I follow her into my childhood home. It hasn't changed much since I left, and memories swarm me like angry bees.

She clucks her tongue. "It's not the cost, Sophia. Rescuing you *was* expensive, but thankfully that part has been taken care of."

"What do you mean taken care of?"

She chuckles and shakes her head. "Obviously we didn't have the resources to rescue you. The money is one thing, but the luck was well beyond our means. You got yourself into quite a pickle. We thought we'd have to try to borrow it, perhaps take out a lien on the store, but honestly we don't have that kind of credit."

"Then who's responsible for getting me out?" I spread my hands. She implied the cost was taken care of. "Who else would spend that kind of money?"

She tilts her head. "He didn't tell you?"

"He who?" My stomach turns to lead. *Don't say it. Please don't say it.*

"When Arden called us, we called Godmother. We had no other options. At first she was reluctant. I think she would have left you to fend for yourself if it was her choice, but Seven insisted on leading the rescue effort. He offered to pay for the entire thing. We could hear him throwing a fit on the other end of the line. He wouldn't take no for an answer. Insisted Godmother give him permission to take action."

The punch lands squarely in my gut. "Why was he even there? How did he even know?"

Her brows rise toward her hairline. "He works for Godmother now. He's her head of security."

"Wait, Seven *works* for Godmother?" I'm utterly confused by this. It doesn't make any sense. Seven is the heir to the Delaney dynasty, aka Lucky Enterprises. His billionaire father owns the Dragonfly Casino as well as a dozen or so other businesses. Seven should be running some evil enterprise at his father's side by now, steepling his fingers in a shiny glass cubicle in the sky. While I'm sure Godmother compensates him well, I just can't fathom he'd have the time to devote to municipal service above and beyond his responsibilities to Lucky Enterprises.

My mother nods. "He splits his time. I assume there's enough overlap with what he does for Lucky Enterprises that it made sense for him to do both. He's worked for her for years." She raises a finger. "Started working for her right after you left.

Anyway, Seven paid for it all. Even lent his private jet to the task and I'm sure used a fair amount of luck to make it happen. I still can't believe how quickly he brought you home—I mean, here. I suppose this isn't your home anymore." A torturous expression crosses her face.

Ugh. The guilt worms through me and weighs heavily on my heart. "I know when I left it was hard on you but—"

She holds up a hand. "Not tonight. It's too big of a conversation for the wee hours of the morning." Glancing back at Arden, she says, "Finish up and I'll show you to your rooms."

I close my eyes, dread burying me. "Wait, just tell me this: how much do you think we owe Seven?" Maybe I can pay him back anyway.

"I'm sure it cost more money than we've made in our lifetime. But we owe him nothing. He said it was his gift to us. No bargain. No expectations." She frowns. "I think he feels..."

"Guilty? Like he can make up for what he did to me by... by—"

My mother peaks one eyebrow. "Spending oodles of money and luck to rescue you from a lifetime in a rehabilitation center? Honestly, Sophia, if guilt is what made him do it, thank your lucky stars."

I groan. This is unacceptable. I cannot accept a kindness from Seven. I'm unable to reconcile it with the asshole I know him to be. He must have an angle. I place a hand on my stomach. "I think I'm going to be sick."

"I don't blame you. This is far from over. Godmother will demand a price from you tomorrow for what you did. Seven may have covered the cost of your return, but you left Dragonfly without her permission, pregnant with a human child! Pray that she finds it in her heart to forgive you and that her punishment does not include you and Arden being handed back to FIRE. I doubt the conditions of your imprisonment the second time around will be as accommodating as the first."

I flash back to the torture room and feel the hook sliding into my wing flaps. All the warmth drains from my face.

My mother's hand is on my shoulder, and for the first time she looks legitimately concerned. "Are you ill? You've blanched as white as snow."

I swallow down bile and nod. "Can we sleep now?"

Arden hears me and sets her glass and plate down before picking up her bag and joining us. My mother leads us upstairs where she sets Arden up in the guest room across from where I used to sleep. I say my goodnights, then find my room exactly how I left it. The twin-sized bed is wrapped in the same shiny purple comforter—I still love purple—and a shelf above the desk still houses a half dozen archery trophies with my name on them. When I turn around, I see the full-length mirror is still there, mounted on the wall. It catches my reflection. Haggard is the only word to describe my appearance. I hardly recognize myself.

Fucking great. Just the way a girl wants to appear in front of her stunningly attractive ex. *Sigh.*

Not that I care what he thinks anyway. *Fucker.*

Parking my suitcase at the end of the bed, I flop onto the mattress, my heart still pounding in my chest from the overflow of adrenaline.

A few minutes later, Arden appears in my doorway. "Mom?"

I scoot to the far side of the bed and hold up the comforter. She crawls in beside me. I wrap the blanket and my arms around her, rubbing her shoulder and kissing her forehead. "It's going to be okay, kid."

She presses her forehead to mine. "Do you think Grandma will let us stay? She seemed really mad."

I take a deep breath. "She will. I know what I need to do to make things right with her. I just need time to do it."

"Okay."

"Do you trust me?"

Her green eyes flash to mine. "Yeah."

"Good, because I'm going to take care of it."

She closes her eyes. Time unspools between us, and I think she's fallen asleep when she asks in a groggy voice, "Do you think I'll still be able to go to Chapel Hill in the fall?"

I stare at the ceiling, my mind racing with uncertainty. As a poker player, I'm a master at bluffing, but the line I will not cross is intentionally lying to my daughter.

"I'm not sure yet, but I'll do everything in my power to get you there."

She snuggles in closer. "Okay." Her breathing evens out, and she falls asleep in my arms. It's a long time before my swirling thoughts allow me to do the same.

"You've got to be kidding me!" Arden can't stop laughing as she takes in my sparkly pink gown. We're on our way to Godmother's tearoom at the center of Dragonfly theme park, and I am rocking a dress doing its best imitation of a frothy pink cupcake with glitter sprinkles.

"It's the law here," I whisper. "All pixies and satyrs must be in costume when within the boundaries of the theme park. We're all considered cast members, and it's our duty to entertain human customers."

"You said pixies and satyrs. What about leprechauns like Seven?"

I roll my eyes, bristling at the sound of his name on her lips.

"Leprechauns own everything. They're the bosses, not the cast members. They wear suits."

"Doesn't seem fair," she says, her eyes narrowing. Is it possible her young mind is starting to get it? Humans might have their prejudices, bigotries, and racism, but fairies are just as awful, their stereotypes and discriminations revolving around species rather than race.

"It's not. Nothing about life here is fair. I left for a reason. You can wear your regular clothes because you're human." I crack my neck and flutter my wings. "Me? I'm a cast member. We all are when we're on Dragonfly grounds."

"That's harsh," she says. I can tell I've disappointed her. I'm sure she wants to believe in the fantasy, the veneer. We're standing in a colorful wonderland. But I'd be a terrible mother if I didn't tell her the truth.

"That's Dragonfly. It's not worse than the human world, but it's not better either. It's just different." *Different in a way that isn't beneficial to pixies.*

She nods, then giggles again. "That dress..."

I rub my stomach, not used to the way the waistband cuts into my midsection. I haven't gained weight, but after sixteen years of not using a corset, the bodice of the fairy gown is uncomfortably restricting. I try to take a deep breath to calm my nerves. "I wonder how long it will take to rearrange my internal organs to be comfortable in these styles again."

"I can't believe you can walk in those shoes!" Arden squints at my heels, made to look like gilt vines growing around my feet. They're shiny gold delicate, like everything else I'm wearing.

"They're not that bad. The cobblers here are exceptional. They can make stilettos almost feel like sneakers. Plus pixies are naturally light on their feet."

"I can't even hear them click on the pavement." Arden is truly fascinated now.

"That's a pixie thing," I explain. "It's the wings. You just haven't noticed before because I've always acted human."

"About that, you all have wings, but I haven't seen a single fairy fly anywhere since we got here. You can fly, right?"

"We can." I chuckle.

"Then why don't you fly everywhere?"

"Why don't you run everywhere? You can run, right?"

She snorts. "Because it's easier to walk, and running is exhausting."

"Exactly." I'm about to tell her how much effort is involved in flight, especially if you're out of practice like I am, when a human woman grabs me from behind by the elbow and yanks me to a stop.

"Can we get a selfie?" Although she phrases it like a question, it's actually a demand. She's wearing a Tinker Bell T-shirt that reads *I CLAP FOR FAIRIES*. Two children cling to her sides, a boy who looks about eight and a girl who might be four whose lips are stained red from the sucker in her mouth.

"Of course," I say in a falsetto that's just on the edge of singing. I turn my wrist over and hold my hands gracefully to my sides. My smile is wide enough to hurt, and I use a little luck to make myself sparkle.

"Oooh, you're so pretty," the little girl says before she barrels into my legs, her tiny body completely lost in the layers of tulle that make up my skirt.

"Come out of there, Patty," her mother yells. "We can't see you for the picture." The woman reaches into the nest of fabric and withdraws her child. Patty no longer has her sucker, and I wonder how long it will take me to extract the candy after these people are gone.

"Oh, please hurry," I chime. "I'm afraid I have a meeting with the fairy godmother, and I don't want to be late."

"Cute," the mother says, obviously annoyed. "Frank! I need you to take a picture!"

A man wearing suction-cup satyr horns pops up from a nearby bench and draws his phone. The wife squeezes into my side, pinching my wing between our shoulders. Her children press their backs against the front of my skirt. I lift my chin and beam as if I've never had more fun. Several clicks later, they leave.

As soon as they're out of sight, I reach into my skirt and peel off the sucker. *Fuck.* That's going to leave a stain.

"Oh. My. God." Arden grimaces, joining me again from where she'd waited near the benches. "Those people treated you like you were... a celebrity!"

"Hardly. Like their idea of a fairy." I sigh. "It's like I said before, I'm a character in a theme park. Most humans don't think of us as equals or as people. We are things. Ideas. This is how Dragonfly makes its money."

"I heard what you said, but it's different seeing it." She scratches the back of her head.

I turn her toward the center of Dragonfly Hollow. "That's where we're going. Let's hurry before anyone else sees me."

Godmother's Tearoom is a cottage made of gingerbread at the end of a cobblestone pathway. Brown slabs of cookie form the walls and roof, magically held together by swaths of white frosting and decorated with an assortment of giant candy. Gigantic green-and-white swirling peppermints neighbor mounds of gummy confections while massive bright red imperials infuse the air with hot cinnamon fragrance.

Arden pokes a gigantic gummy bear in the stomach with her finger. "Is this real?" she asks.

"Yes. But don't eat it," I whisper. "Everything in Godmother's tearoom is edible, but eat the wrong thing and you'll pay a terrible price. Humans who partake are instantly addicted. They'll come back again and again until they've spent all their money on the treats inside. If they're strong enough to deny the urge, they'll dream about this place, and the memory of it will haunt them until they die."

Arden backs away from the bear and shoves her hands into her pockets.

"Stop scaring the girl, Sophia!" Godmother appears at the gingerbread entrance, her voice a deep timbre. Physically, she fills the space of the doorway, but her imposing presence extends far beyond her skin and bones.

In the human world, an increased body size is often seen as a negative thing. Human society values thinness, sometimes to the point of celebrating a sickly physique. In my time on the outside, I often wondered if they had some bizarre fetish for vulnerability. But here, body size correlates with power. Godmother is built like the human stereotype of an opera singer, tall, wide, and thick. Every bit of her advanced size is filled with luck and overflowing with power. The stones around her neck thrum with ancient energy. Her purple-and-black feather dress sparkles with magic. Twisted off her neck and pinned elegantly behind her head, her silky black hair creates a striking frame for her ebony complexion.

Godmother is a force of nature. Ageless and frighteningly beautiful. Imposing and aloof.

I curtsy but she ignores me and addresses Arden. "It's not as bad as all that, child. Plenty of humans avoid eating my tearoom, and those who pay up front for what they eat suffer no ill consequences. Tell me, do you lick the walls of the restaurants you go to?"

Arden chuckles. "No, ma'am."

"Exactly. Anyone dumb enough to taste a building deserves

what's coming to them." Godmother's gaze falls on me then, still holding my curtsy. "Oh, for the sake of Aibell! Get up and come inside. We open to the public in an hour, and we have much to discuss."

I rise to follow her, but Arden nudges my elbow and whispers, "Who is Aibell?"

"Ancient fairy goddess," I explain under my breath. "There are lots of them... gods, I mean. Fairy religion is pantheistic, and most individuals believe in multiple gods."

Her eyebrows lift. I internally chastise myself again for not teaching her more about Devashire. In my defense, I'd wanted her to have a human life, free of all this. I'd hoped she'd never need it.

At Godmother's direction, we take a seat at one of the tables inside, directly in front of a glass case filled with delectable pastries. Neither one of us had time to eat much this morning, and I watch Arden gaze at the case longingly as she sits down beside me. I'm too nervous to be hungry and too jaded to risk eating anything voluntarily in this place.

"Join us, Seven," Godmother bellows over her shoulder.

I bristle as Seven appears from the back room and strides to the table, his face locked in that permanent closed-lip smile that always makes him look like he's thinking about some lecherous secret. Gods, he's a work of art. No man has any right to be that attractive. His black T-shirt clings to an insanely etched torso, touchable soft material hugging flesh that must feel hard in all the right places. I'm appreciating his abs when my eyes catch on the gun at his hip. Since when does Seven need a gun? He's a leprechaun! He has enough luck to handle any situation without raising a finger.

"What's he doing here?" I say, my voice thick. He's stolen my breath again, left me with nothing but raspy syllables while I—oh for fuck's sake, I look like a pink meringue!

Godmother raises an eyebrow. "He's sponsoring you. He is the reason *you* are here, Sophia." Her words hold an edge that makes me sit up straighter in my chair. I do not want to piss off Godmother. Seven works for her and paid for my recovery. Of course he's here.

I fold my hands on the table and stare down at my threaded fingers.

"Better," she says. "Now you are here today because you left Devashire without my blessing or permission and have potentially created a political situation between us and the human world. Explain yourself. And I warn you, make it good, because if it wasn't for Seven, I wouldn't have recovered you. If FIRE figures out you're here, I'll have a godsdamn mess on my hands. I have half a mind to spare myself the trouble and hand you back over."

Seven winces at this pronouncement, his eyes settling beseechingly on me. Shit luck if he paid all that money and Godmother kicks me out. It might be worth it to get myself ejected just to sock one to him.

But mine is not the only ass on the line here. I've put Arden in danger, and this is the only place in the world I can make sure she's safe right now. Her eyes are wide with nerves. Even though she has no experience with any of this, it's clear she can feel the tension and understands the danger that fills these sweet walls. The worst part is I've never told her the entire story. She knows her father was human, but not the humiliating circumstances that led to her existence. I wanted to spare her that.

"May I speak with you privately?" I implore Godmother. "I'll tell you everything you want to know about why I left the way I did, but I'd rather just share it with you alone."

"I can see this is difficult for you, Sophia, but your request isn't a private one, is it? Every person at this table has a stake in how this goes. Still, I understand it can be difficult to speak of such traumatic memories. I will help you." Godmother claps her hands and yells over her shoulder. "Bring the tea!"

A pixie whom I don't recognize rushes from the kitchen and places a tea service in front of us. There's only one cup. My skin goose bumps, and my stomach drops. Godmother pours for me. "Drink."

Arden stills and meets my eyes. She's remembering what I told her. Godmother's confections come with magical strings attached. But I have no choice. With a trembling hand, I reach for the cup. Fuck, I'm shaking so hard the tea sloshes and almost spills. Godmother gives me a warning glare, and I use my opposite hand to steady it as I bring it to my lips. I'm terrified, but worse, I feel trapped. There really is no other option. The second I stepped through the moon gate and set foot in Devashire, I made a choice. Arden and I are safer here than being hunted by FIRE. Now I need to trust that instinct.

"Tell me why you ran away." Godmother's command leaves her full, burgundy lips and plows between mine, wriggling over my tongue like a living thing and branching out into my lungs. I try to fight it, but when it slithers up again, along the back of my throat, it expands like a set of clamps that scrape up around my skull and squeeze. The pressure is intense. It's like an industrial vacuum has been hooked up to my mouth and will suck out my brains if I don't plug the hose up with words.

My lips start moving of their own volition, and the truth pours out of me in a forced jumble. "Seven... stood me up at the Yule Ball..." I try to force my lips to stop but each word gives me relief from the pressure. Holding back is agony. My sinuses throb. My ears ring. I have to give her more. "I... rode through Winter Wood... alone. Everyone laughed. I was... humiliated... After, I met a human man." I gasp at this admission, and tears start to flow. My head pounds like it might explode. The truth is pried from me by a magical crowbar. "Later... learned I was pregnant... the human way." So far, nothing I've said surprises Arden, but it's the next bit I wish I could hold back. The spell won't let me. I can't fight the compulsion. "My parents couldn't accept it... I left because... I left because..." Tears course over my cheeks and drip from my jaw. I try to hold back, but it's impossible. My skull is in a vise. Magic crushes my brain, pressure building until sweat drips down my face. I must turn bloodless, because Arden cries out. Godmother warns for her to stay in her chair. Permanent damage is highly possible if I don't relieve the pressure in my head, and in the end, I can't resist feeding the magic what it wants. "I left because... they wanted me to terminate the pregnancy. I wanted... to keep... my baby! I... wanted... Arden to live!"

As soon as the last words are out, the pain ceases. I slump over the table, my brain blissfully free of the skull-crushing suction. I close my eyes and let my thoughts float away, my mind blanking out.

"The Yule Ball, sixteen years ago...," Godmother mumbles. "Yes, I remember that night and the humiliation you sustained. And certainly this young lady was worth your sacrifice to save." I can't see her with my head buried in my arms on the table, but there's a long stretch of silence as if she's contemplating something. "Sit up, Sophia. I have made my decision."

I sit up. Only now do I notice that Arden's face is sheet white. I squeeze her hand. It must have been hard for her to watch me go through that and to learn that her grandparents weren't receptive to my pregnancy with her. I give her a small nod to let her know I'm all right. Across the table, Seven is staring at Arden too, eyes narrowed, a line between his brows. He seems genuinely concerned for her.

Gee, thanks. Not that I don't want him to worry about Arden, but I'm the one who just had a confession magically roto-rooted from my brain. Actually, I do mind. I want him to stop looking at Arden. It's weird.

"Sophia Larkspur, while I can appreciate your motives for leaving Devashire, it does not excuse your actions. You should have come to me with your problem. I hope this lesson has taught you there are no answers in the human world that can't be found in Devashire."

"Yes, Godmother. I see that now." I hope I'm convincing. The truth is, I doubt very much that Godmother would have been any more compassionate about a half-human pregnancy than my parents. "Can we stay?"

"You may stay in Devashire."

I breathe a sigh of relief.

"On one condition."

I look up, holding my breath again.

"You will assist Seven in a security matter important to our realm."

"What?" Assist Seven?

"You will serve at his beck and call until the case is closed and he delivers the answers I seek."

"B-b-but—"

"These are your terms. Do you accept?"

Godmother's magic always comes at a price. It takes me a second to get my mouth to work. Seven watches me from across the table, his expression unreadable. Beck and call. He must love this.

"Sophia?"

"Yes. Yes. Of course, Godmother." If it means keeping Arden safe, I'll do it. I'll do anything.

She hands me a small biscuit from the tea tray. "Then eat."

Hazarding a glance toward Arden, I hesitate for a moment. Once I eat this, there will be no going back until whatever this security issue I've committed to is solved. Freedom will be something I watch in my rearview mirror. I'm about to enter a prison without bars. But Arden will be free. She'll be able to go to college as we planned. I'll find a way... somehow. For her, I steel my resolve and place the biscuit into my mouth. As I chew, voices fill my head in a rush. Invisible vines jut into me, coiling and twisting in my veins. Fae chains. I am bound. I swallow down the last of it, suddenly exhausted.

"Thank you, Godmother."

She reaches across the table, and we shake hands, sealing our bargain. I move to stand.

"Sit down. We're not finished yet," Godmother says. Confused, I glance at Seven, but his expression is entirely unreadable. I sink back into my chair.

Godmother turns toward Arden. "There is still the matter of your daughter. What price shall she pay to stay among us?"

"What?" I can't help but raise my voice, although challenging Godmother isn't a wise choice. "But... but I thought you said if I helped Seven, we could stay in Devashire!"

"I said *you* could stay here."

"Exactly, a collective you." I motion between myself and Arden as Godmother chuckles in that deep rich voice of hers.

"Oh, Sophia, you have been away too long if you make such a rudimentary mistake to assume something like that."

My stomach threatens to turn itself inside out as she refocuses on Arden, and this time I can't help but shoot a pleading glance at Seven, who's gone perfectly still. But his eyes are locked on Arden, and it's clear he won't be coming to our rescue.

"How old are you, girl?"

"Sixteen."

"Old enough to pay your own price, I think. What is your name?"

"Arden."

"Your mother says you are human. We don't usually allow humans to live among us long term."

"I wouldn't be my mother's daughter if I wasn't also pixie. It's true that the pixie part of me hasn't exactly blossomed yet, but it's there." Arden stares directly and fearlessly into Godmother's eyes. Her grace under pressure is awe-inspiring.

I shift restlessly in my seat. Godmother retrieves a tiny plate from the tea tray I hadn't even noticed was there. On it sits a brownie the size of a caramel.

"Eat this, Arden. That is my price."

I shiver and desperately want to beg her not to do it. I have no idea what the brownie does, but it can't be good.

"What's it do?" Arden wisely asks.

"Aren't you a bold one," Godmother muses.

"I take after my mother," Arden says, but truthfully I've never been as brave as she's being now.

"It shows me who you truly are." Godmother studies my daughter's face.

What does that mean? Will the brownie show the balance of fairy and human in her? Or does she mean spiritually, like who she is in her heart? In tense silence, hands fisted at my sides, I watch as Arden places the brownie at the back of her tongue.

Godmother never takes her eyes off her, but what she's staring at, I don't know. Nothing happens. At least nothing I can see on the outside.

"Did you enjoy it?"

Slowly, Arden smiles. "It was delicious."

The corner of Godmother's lips twitches. "I thought you would think so."

"What was in it?" I sound desperate, but anything could have been in that brownie. Godmother once turned a man into a goat with a lemon bar. If she's hurt Arden in any way—

Godmother gives me a sharp look as if she can hear my thoughts. She stands from the table. "Go now. Both of you may stay with my blessing as long as you fulfill the terms I've set forth for you, Sophia." She nods toward Arden and then in Seven's direction before striding toward the kitchen, leaving us sitting at the table.

Seven stares at me with a smug, half smile like he's just won a prize he wasn't expecting. Like he's feeling very, very lucky.

CHAPTER

SEVEN

"Are you sure you're okay?" I stop Arden on the sidewalk outside Godmother's and take her face in my hands. We've just endured the most stressful situation I can imagine, but she's smiling, her eyes bright.

She giggles. "Mom, I'm fine. My God, after watching what happened to you, I was worried, but honestly, I think it was just a brownie."

"A brownie from the Godmother is never just a brownie," I say.

"You know she wouldn't hurt Arden," Seven interjects. "Godmother can be brutal, but she'd never harm an innocent." He's followed us from the tearoom and is lingering in my peripheral vision like a mosquito just out of reach of the swatter. I sneer at him.

"Arden." I take her by the shoulders. "I know this was a lot, but do you think you can go back to Grandma and Grandpa's without me? I need to talk to Seven. I promise you, whatever happened back then, they're not as horrible as you might think."

She places both hands on her stomach. "I know. I get it. I mean, it was a long time ago."

"It would be natural for you to have... feelings about Grandma and Grandpa after learning what you did today. Whatever you're feeling is fine—"

"Mom... Seriously, you were a pregnant teenager, barely older than I am now. It's not that big of a surprise that you or someone in your life considered the alternatives."

A lump forms in my throat thinking about those days. "I never considered it."

She throws her arms around me and squeezes. "I'm okay. Really."

I don't release her until I'm convinced that somehow this hasn't scarred her as much as I was expecting. "I'll meet you there then. We'll get something to eat." Neither one of us has had a proper meal since the night before my last poker game. "This won't take long."

"Take your time. I'll be fine." She gives me a half wave as she turns and strides in the direction of Enchantment. "Bye, Seven."

Seven waves cheerfully and offers her a crooked smile that makes my blood boil. As soon as she rounds the corner, I turn on him with the rage of a thousand feral wolves. "What's your angle? Why would you do this to me?"

His smile fades, his eyes wrinkling at the corners. "Do what to you? I paid to have you rescued. That's something I did *for* you, not *to* you."

"You're... up to something. Convincing Godmother to assign me to this case... thingy? Is this your way of torturing me? It wasn't enough to grind my face into the dirt in front of the entire population of Dragonfly. You have to assert your dominance the moment I return like some sort of... some sort of alpha dog. Is this a game? Is it fun for you?"

"At the moment, nothing about this situation feels fun," he grits out. "And you know as well as I do no one convinces Godmother of anything."

We both freeze and smile brightly when a human enters the square. I barely move my lips as I ask through the smile. "Can we go somewhere private to have this out properly?"

"Love to," he says through his teeth. Before I can protest, he grabs my wrist and yanks me toward a door labeled CHARACTERS ONLY. He doesn't release my hand, even when we are safely on the other side. Once the door is locked behind us, he drags me between two giant fir trees that mark the boundaries of fae territory. Humans can't come here or see or hear anything that happens back here. This isn't the Devashire fairies want them to know about. No, that would be Dragonfly Hollow with its bright colors, cheerful characters, and magical shops and restaurants.

Humans have no idea that at the edge of the woods at the back of Dragonfly Hollow is a lake, and across the lake is a wall that separates us from a dark secret. The wall looms on the horizon in all its marble glory, linking mountain to mountain, its ancient architecture radiant with even more ancient magic. It's been years since I thought of this place. How easy it has been to put it behind me.

I tear my hand from Seven's and turn on him. "How dare you? How dare you, after what you did to me! Baiting me, leading me on for months, then ghosting me in the most humiliating way. All the promises we made to each other. I trusted you, and you hung me out to dry."

"It's not what you think, Sophead."

"Stop calling me that!" I used to find the nickname endearing. Now it just feels condescending.

"Why? It happened right here." He gestures toward the lake. "Right before our first kiss."

"Fuck. You." I point a finger at his chest and charge him, teeth bared. "Fuck you for even bringing that up at a time like this." I gather myself. If this was a poker game, I might as well push my chips across the table right now. I'm an emotional mess, and emotions like this trigger poor, illogical choices. Is it his mere presence that's making me crazy or the fact that I'm exhausted and stressed to the breaking point?

"We were fifteen. I'd been teaching you to play poker. We played a game, and I won."

"Gods, your father owned the casino, and you're a leprechaun. Pretty sad how often you lost, don't you think?"

"Your bet was a dip in the lake."

"Right. Bailiwick's uniform. White blouse. You were an adolescent boy." Annoying as hell I ever let him talk me into that one.

"You weren't even knee-deep when a merman pulled you under. I was going to dive in after you, but you freed yourself before I had a chance."

"Punched him in the nose." I still remember the tug of the water as I cocked my fist.

Seven's expression softens, and he takes a step closer. "I helped you to shore, your hair sopping wet, and I kissed you."

That kiss had branded itself onto my heart. It was a rush, painfully addictive and completely consuming. How I hate to think of it now. I take a deep breath and snap on my poker face. When I speak again, my voice is cool and steady.

"The last time I saw you, Seven, you were tying a red ribbon around my wrist. You said you'd never loved anyone like you loved me and you wanted to show the world by escorting me to the Yule Ball. We would have been the first leprechaun/pixie couple to ever attend. I saved for months for my dress and waited for you in the sleigh *you* rented, smiling while the photographer took my picture, growing more and more suspicious as time trickled by. And then..." My tone hardens, even as I swallow back tears. I will not cry in front of him or give him the satisfaction of knowing how much his betrayal hurt me. "You didn't come. No call. No text. No message at all. Just the knowledge that it had all been a cruel, sick joke. So excuse me if I'd rather not remember the name you called me while you were setting me up for the fall."

"It wasn't like that," Seven says through a tight jaw.

"It was exactly like that." Getting it out like this is good for my soul. Freeing. And I've done it all without screaming or crying. Is that a look of shame on his face?

"It wasn't a joke—"

"No? I assure you everyone laughed. It's no secret that leprechauns consider themselves the superior race. I should have known better back then. I was too open and too trusting. I'm not that girl anymore."

"I liked that girl."

"Just not enough to be seen with her in public."

His face is unreadable. "There were extenuating circumstances."

"Oh, I can't wait to hear this. What extenuating circumstances? Why exactly did you leave me sitting in a sleigh for an hour only to be pulled into a dance where everyone would see you'd stood me up? Where your own father confirmed the ruse and rubbed salt in the wound?"

He hesitates, spreads his hands, and heaves an exasperated sigh. The expression that passes across his face is one I've seen before but can't immediately interpret. "I can't tell you. It's..." He seems to be searching for the right word. "Confidential."

"*Confidential?*" I gape at him. "Let me get this straight. Something happened that kept you from meeting me at the Yule Ball—the one that *you* invited me to and insisted I attend—and these same 'circumstances' meant you were unable to text, call, or send a living soul to tell me you couldn't make it? And the same 'circumstances' must have been why you didn't apologize afterward or even talk to me the next day or the next weeks, or like *ever* in the past sixteen years. That is one hell of a confidential circumstance, buddy."

He folds his arms and his eyes narrow. "I wanted to explain later, but as we established earlier today, you were busy. Very busy."

Oh no, he did not go there! My vision turns red, and my inner warrior reaches for the sharpest spear she can find and aims it right at his vulnerable underbelly. "Yes, I was. And it was *fabulous* by the way. Earth-shattering. Human men are sexual machines. Far better than it would have ever been with *you.*"

He raises an eyebrow, and I can tell the barb stings. He'd wanted me then. We'd wanted to be each other's firsts. Instead, I'd lost my virginity to a human.

I got Arden out of it. What did he have?

I open my mouth to say something about the relative size of leprechaun dick, but I'm silenced when I inexplicably trip. My feet fly out from under me, and I land in his arms, flush against his chest. Our faces are close. I can see every gold fleck in his mossy green eyes.

"How do you know it wouldn't be better with me?" he asks in a voice as smooth as hot caramel. "Maybe you should give me a shot. Then you could make a fair comparison."

I shove him away. "Ew, I'm not having sex with you. If you were expecting me to pay you back for rescuing me with my body, you should have saved your money."

I try to stalk off, but a gust of gale-force wind catches my wings and blows me back into his arms.

"Two things, Sophead," he says through a crooked smile that oozes charm. "First, I paid for your rescue because I couldn't stand the thought of you being locked up in one of those FIRE dungeons they like to call a rehabilitation center. I don't expect any reimbursement."

"Yeah, right. I'm sure it was out of the goodness of your heart—"

"Second, if I wanted to have sex with you, I could." His voice drops into a husky timbre, the type that would bring most women to their knees. His words send a chill through me, and I realize what he's done.

"You made me slip just now." I glare at him and try to shove him away, but he's caged me against him.

"Yes."

"And the wind—"

The corner of his mouth tugs higher.

I plant both palms on his chest, willfully ignoring the hard blocks of muscle there as I push him away. I turn to leave, but a small tree falls behind me and splashes into the water. I have to throw myself into his arms again to keep from being struck.

"You just uprooted a perfectly healthy tree!"

"It's a sapling. I'll replant it." His gaze drifts to my lips. "Kiss me, Sophia. Let me remind you what you missed that night."

Kiss him? *Over my dead body*. Fury heats my cheeks.

His arms are around me again. Luck sparks in his emerald eyes. I can feel it, like a static charge rising in the air, a giant, powerful force, invisible but palpable. It winds around me, a hot purr against my skin. There is no doubt in my mind that if this man wanted it to happen, we would fall over, and I would somehow land on his dick. But I sense this isn't as much sexual as playful. He's trying to take me back to where we were before. The way he uses my childhood nickname. The talk of when we were kids. He's teasing me. Playing with me. Well, I don't exist for his amusement, and there is no way I plan to pick up where we left off.

"Is this what you have to do to get a date, Seven? Force women with luck?" The edge to my words is intentionally sharp.

His smirk fades, replaced by a look of disgust. It's his turn to push me away. "Fuck, Sophia, I was just teasing you back after that barb about humans."

"Teasing? Or reminding that you can take what you want when you want it?"

"I asked you to kiss me, not to fuck me."

"I'll take door number three."

He points a finger toward me. "I bought your freedom because I care about you, no other reason," he grits out, looking positively offended. "I've always cared about you."

My hands are shaking. I'm furious and frustrated. I want answers but also to never speak to him again. Worst of all, I can't deny I'd like to be back in his arms. I'm curiously horny, and the memories of our times here, when things were good, are wedging themselves into my already-confused brain. This place, the way he's looking at me, it feels like going back in time. None of it makes sense.

"Fuck it. I'm going home. Leave me and Arden alone." I start for Dragonfly.

A dark and ominous laugh bursts from him. "I *can't*. You're assigned to me, remember? Godmother's orders."

"Fuck!" I bend over and beat my fists against my thighs. This man is going to be the death of me. "Fine! What exactly is this security matter, and how the hell can I help?"

He sighs and looks out over the murky water. "Murder."

CHAPTER

EIGHT

All my anger drains away, replaced by intense curiosity. "Murder in Dragonfly?"

"Godmother and I found the body in the square, thankfully before any of the guests did. It was brutal."

"Humans are always killing each other. It was only a matter of time before they did it in Dragonfly."

"I'm not sure a human did this."

"Why not?"

"The body was missing all its teeth and a few choice bones."

I flinch and press a hand to my stomach. "The agent at the rehabilitation center showed me a murder scene exactly like that. He wanted help finding the killer. He was convinced the perpetrator was fae."

"Where?" Seven rubs his chin, intensely interested.

"I don't know. He never told me. But there was a massive footprint beside the body. Wait, could he have been showing me pictures from here?"

"No. We found the body in the square. No mud. And no authorities were involved. What did the footprint look like?"

"Huge. Skeletal."

"It fits." He looked toward the wall again.

"You think it's Yissevel?" I hadn't lied to Agent Donovan when I said that the human version of the Tooth Fairy did not exist. It doesn't. But there is a bone fairy, a primeval monster obsessed with the skeletons of his prey. He eats organs, but bones and teeth are his passion. What he doesn't consume, he collects.

Seven's eyes narrow thoughtfully. "I've checked with the guardians. No breach in the wall. I think someone went through a lot of trouble to make it look like it was Yissevel though."

"Why?"

"That is the question you and I have to answer. Something like this gets out, it could hurt Dragonfly's reputation as well as its bottom line."

I heave a sigh. "You mean it could hurt your pocketbook. Scare off the humans and you scare off a major revenue stream."

"Your parents too. All of us. Our entire economy relies on human guests."

"Right. What do you want me to do?"

"Come to my office. I'll show you the file on this case, and we can make a plan."

I shake my head. There's no getting out of this, but I need a break... from him, from the memories, from everything. "I just got back. I haven't even had breakfast. Arden needs me."

His lips thin. "First thing tomorrow then."

"Where's your office?"

He hesitates, just long enough for me to notice. "Dragonfly Casino."

"Dragonfly Casino?" I scoff. "Living the dream then. Following in daddy's footsteps."

"I'm a Delaney, and my father isn't involved in the day-to-day like he used to be. I run the place for all intents and purposes."

"Bully for you. If you're waiting for my impressed face, you'll leave disappointed."

"I wasn't trying to impress you... Gods, Sophia, is this how it's going to be the entire time we work together?"

"Until we solve this murder apparently. How do you manage both running the Delaney empire *and* working for Godmother anyway?"

"We have an arrangement," he says vaguely. "A major part of my role at Lucky Enterprises is heading the security division. There's a lot of overlap."

"Busy man," I say cynically. "With all that experience, I don't see why you need my help."

Seven's smirk is back. He winks at me. "You underestimate yourself. I assure you, I have use for your many talents." He manages to make it sound sexual.

I groan in displeasure and scrub my face with my hands. "Fine. The sooner we find this killer, the sooner I can pay my debt to Godmother and put all this the fuck behind me."

"Do you kiss your grandmother with that mouth?"

"My grandmother is the one who taught me how to curse."

He chuckles.

I turn to leave, eyeing the trees around me tentatively and wondering if he'll allow me to go this time or if some lucky event will knock me back into his arms.

"Sophia," he says gently before I get too far. The softness in his tone surprises me, and I turn to meet his gaze. "One day you'll ask me to kiss you. I won't need luck. And when that day comes, you'll remember there's a big difference between leprechauns and human men."

"Not in this lifetime." I take off toward the gate, a shaky feeling lingering in my gut.

MY BRAIN BUZZES AS I TROMP INTO MY PARENTS' HOUSE, desperate to escape the feelings that Seven dredged up on the beach. I wish I could say I didn't want to kiss him, but I'd be lying to myself. No woman can be in Seven's presence and not feel something. I've tasted that brand of honey before, and I know how sweet it is. Kissing a leprechaun is an experience.

And that's enough of that! I shake my head, clearing it of unwanted thoughts. The punishment Godmother has doled out is one meant to open old wounds and make me feel vulnerable in ways I haven't been in years. Whether it is worse than being strapped to the torture table, I can't say. Would I rather have my wings ripped from my back or my heart ripped from my chest? The jury is still out on that one. The good news though is that this prison sentence has an end. All I have to do is solve a murder.

My mood lifts when I spot my grandmother sitting in my parents' living room, knitting what might be a gigantic Christmas stocking. It's shaped like a sock but much too big. And it's April. Typical Grandma. Sometimes her knitting projects don't make sense. One year she knitted me a pencil cozy—a tiny sweater for my pencil. It matched a sleeve for my stapler and a coat to hold a roll of tape. It's a weird habit, but her projects are always made with love.

The moment she sees me, she lights up like a halogen lamp

and pops out of the recliner, sending her needles and yarn flying.

"I heard you'd come home!" she squeals with delight. Her silver hair is wound around the back of her head, and her wings flutter with her excitement. She's more than two hundred years old, but her hug is just as strong, accepting, and warm as it ever was.

"Grandma!" My heart swells at the sight of her. "I've missed you so much. But you didn't have to come all the way out here. I would have come to see you in Sunnyville." Sunnyville is a community outside the theme park in the suburbs of Devashire's capital city of Elderflame. The development is designed for more mature fairies to spend their remaining years. To come here, she's had to fit herself into a glittery blue gown. It doesn't look comfortable.

"Pish-posh. I had to see you. Godmother might have demanded any number of things from you today. When Aurora told me you'd gone to the tearoom this morning, I came right away. I wasn't going to miss a chance to see my granddaughter and great granddaughter!"

"You mean in case Godmother rejected us and ousted us from Devashire, you wanted to be here to see us on our way out."

Her blue eyes twinkle. "Well, yes." A guilt-laden look crosses her face. "I believe in you, Sophia, but you know how Godmother can be. Why, when I was about your age, I watched her enchant a satyr to strip off his own skin as a punishment for deserting his regiment. That was during the war, mind you, but still, something like that sticks with you. She can be absolutely ruthless."

I do know how Godmother can be. I once saw her tear the wings off a pixie who'd stolen from her. He didn't die, but it was a painful yearlong recovery. That was her shtick—find someone's weak spot, their vulnerability, and jab a wand into it until they did what she wanted.

"Well, considering you're not packing your bags, I take it she didn't oust you." Grandma's brows rise over her glasses.

"Arden and I can stay. I just have to do something... difficult." Grandma is far from frail, but the last thing I want to do is burden her with my problems. She is one of the few people I'd stayed in touch with when I was on the outside. One of the few people I trusted... trust.

Grandma squeals. "Whatever it is, I know you can do it, Sophia. You're the strongest fairy I know, besides me. And the smartest."

"Aside from you of course." We laugh. "Now there's just Mom and Dad to deal with."

"Ah, that will work itself out." Tears fill her eyes, and she rubs my shoulders. "I'm just so relieved you're home in one piece. When I'd heard you'd been caught..."

I squeeze her again. "I'm here now, Grandma, and I'm okay." I take a deep breath. I *am* okay. Who cares if I have to spend a few days with my teen crush? I've handled worse.

"I want to hear all about what's happened to you. Why don't you start with why you're covered in mud?" She takes in my splattered dress, worry flitting across her expression.

"Oh, uh..." I hadn't even realized that between my slip on the beach, the wind, and the falling tree, I'm splattered with dirt, water, and debris. I'm lucky no humans saw me like this. The last thing I need is another reason to face Godmother. "I visited Glaive Lake. I must have gotten dirty."

She grins widely. "Were you speaking with that leprechaun boy again? You two always loved the lake."

"He's not a boy anymore, Grandma. He's an asshole."

"They all are, honey. It's up to us to whip them into shape." She pats my hand between her own.

I cluck my tongue. "Grandpa wasn't an asshole."

"Sure he was!" she says through a laugh. "You just came along after I molded him into submission."

We both giggle, and I wonder how I ever survived without this woman's warmth. "Have you met Arden?"

"Oh yes! Bright young lady. She showed me something on her phone called a TikTok. Do you want to see the dance I learned?" Grandma bends her knees and starts rocking her hips.

"Uh, maybe later, Grandma. I should probably find her. She's got to be starving. We haven't eaten anything all morning. Do you know where she is?"

"Your parents are showing her the garden." Grandma's voice turns soft and reverent.

I lower my chin. "Not the back garden."

She nods. "Afraid so. It's time you all had this out and put it behind you. Best not to let it fester. Better to do it on an empty stomach anyway."

"I suppose." I knew this was coming. If I'm going to stay here with Arden—and we *need* to stay here—I have to make things right with my parents. In pixie world, there's only one way to do that. "Tell my story after I'm gone," I say dramatically, pressing the back of my hand to my forehead.

"Pish-posh. No pixie has ever died planting an emotion. Go, get it over with."

I kiss her on the cheek and stride toward the rear of the house and the door that leads to the pixie garden beyond. I am ready.

CHAPTER

NINE

A pixie garden isn't simply a collection of plants but a scrapbook of memories. For my kind, it is the holy of holies. No pixie would ever invite a stranger into their garden. It would be like handing over a stack of diaries containing your most guarded secrets or opening a closet wide to expose the skeletons inside. Leprechauns and satyrs don't have gardens the way pixies do. It's one of the many ways we're different and a practice that is poorly understood outside our people.

My parents' garden waits beyond a mudroom where watering cans and gardening gloves perch on shelves above a massive utility sink and a wall array of gardening tools. I hesitate and take a deep breath, staring at the bright red door that leads to the garden with apprehension. Unlike most similar doors in human homes, this one has no window to see what waits beyond. For us, it would be like putting a window on your bathroom door. But my parents have taken Arden back there for a reason. They want to put the past behind us, and Grandma is right; it will be easier once we do.

My stomach churns. I haven't taken part in a garden ritual

in almost twenty years, and this one promises to be uniquely painful. I take a deep breath and turn the brass knob, pulling the door open. The crisp, fresh scent of lily of the valley washes over me, and my eyes catch first on the carpet of white bell-shaped flowers. As I close the door behind me, I'm over-whelmed by the breathtaking beauty, exactly as I remember it yet somehow even more brilliant than my mind could repro-duce. Red hibiscus the size of dinner plates bloom beside a pod of purple hydrangeas. Roses, the color of blood, vine above me, their trellis laboring from the weight of fist-sized blooms which intertwine with coral-colored clematis. Rhododendron fill in the gaps, the edges of their honey-colored flowers ending in a deep blush.

The floral fireworks welcome me forward, and I inhale the heady scent of the blooms, mingled now with the slight jasmine of the lily of the valley and a wisp of gardenia from a tree that blooms a few yards down the stone path.

"Mom?" Arden calls from around the bend. Breathless and beside herself, she gapes at me, for once looking younger than her sixteen years. "Grandpa showed me where you were born, and it's super weird."

Once I reach her, I find my father nearby, previously concealed by the lush foliage that lines the curving path. We lock eyes for a moment. I haven't seen him since I arrived, but my mother has offered no explanation for his absence.

The only word I can use to describe my dad is *formidable*. People assume that male pixies are slight, but nothing could be further from the truth. They do have wings, but just like the rest of our kind, they've adapted to look human. Matthias Lark-spur looms over me, six feet tall with a thick head of hair the same color as mine except for a smattering of silver over his ears. His wings are silver too, but more steel mesh than gossamer. Today, there's steel in his blue eyes as well.

"You grew a beard," I say.

"It's a goatee."

Arden waves a hand between us. "Are we going to talk about the fact that you literally formed on a vine?" She points both hands at the plant where I was born.

"Sorry, Arden, I guess I should have explained this when we talked about sex. But honestly, it's not something you'll have to worry about, being human." I shrug.

"Half-human, half-pixie," my father insists. "And old enough to know about the birds and the bees."

Arden's eyes widen. "Are there literal birds and bees involved here? Because I'm having trouble getting my head around this."

I take a deep breath and blow it out slowly. "When a female pixie and a male pixie love each other very much, they spend time together, and when the time is right—"

Arden covers her ears with her hands. "Oh my God—"

"Both of them will cough up a seed."

She lowers her hands. "That is not what I was expecting."

"If they own land and are ready to start a family, they plant both seeds in their garden. There must be two, and if both pixies don't plant their seeds, nothing happens. When the seeds sprout, their roots tangle together and only one plant grows from the two seeds. That plant can bear zero to three children. I was an only child."

Arden's eye twitches. "You grew... in like a pod or something?"

"It's more like a glass ball. You might as well know that genetics works differently here as well. Pixies of multiple colors and shapes can grow on the same vine. Never assume that someone isn't part of a family because their skin color or the bones of their face are different. It doesn't work that way among pixies."

"Holy crap." Arden marvels at my birthplant, her fingers coming to rest on her parted lips.

"The mother and father fairy tend the birthplant, and when their child is the size of a normal human baby, they ritualistically shatter the glass and bring their baby into the world," I explain. "And that's how pixie babies are born. After that, our development mirrors human development."

"*Normally*, that's how babies are born," my father says, staring at Arden. "Except for you. You were born the human way."

"The normal way," Arden says, her eyebrows shooting up with her nervous giggle.

"*Not* the normal way for pixies," he says, and there's an edge to his tone that I don't like him using around Arden.

I place a hand on her shoulder. "Don't listen to Grandpa. Leprechauns and satyrs have children the same as humans. Pixies are the exception, not the other way around. And our bodies... well, obviously I was *capable* of having you the human way, just like I was capable of living the past sixteen years without a pixie garden."

My father purses his lips and gives a reluctant nod, conceding that what I said is true. A muscle jumps in his jaw. This is no longer about educating Arden. It's about me and the tip of an iceberg of pain we've all been hauling around with us for over a decade.

"Arden..." I swallow hard and rub her shoulder supportively. "I bet Great-Grandma Betty would love to get to know you better. Why don't you go inside and sit with her until Grandpa and I are finished here?"

"I thought we were getting lunch?" she asks, but then glances between me and her grandfather and changes her tune. "Um, right, I'd like to talk to Great-Grandma, and I'm sure I can find something in the kitchen."

"We'll get lunch. I just need to talk to Grandpa about something first."

She nods, seeming to understand far more than I expect her to. She strides quickly toward the door and disappears inside the house.

"Dad, I—"

"Your mother's waiting in the back. Let's go." He gestures with his head, and we continue along the garden path.

The deeper we advance into the garden, the more the plants change. While the front is a pristine, blossoming rainbow of flowers and shrubs, the landscape changes to typical green hedges halfway back. Eventually, the path is lined with succulents and cacti, prickly but still beautiful. But it's the very back where we are going, to a place hidden in the deepest recesses of the garden, a place where my parents have relegated their deepest, darkest emotions.

We stop in front of a massive black thornbush that rises like a behemoth against an eight-foot privacy wall it's almost overgrown. Its thorns are as long as my hand, and its branches are a tangled nightmare to behold. This is where my parents have planted their feelings about me, and this is what those seeds have grown into.

My mother joins us, stepping out from a small shed at the back of the property with a trowel and gloves. I glance between my mother and father and then back at the monstrosity in front of me. This thornbush is the physical manifestation of their anger, disappointment, resentment, and worry for me. Placed at the back of their garden, it's shameful to them, a manifestation of their deepest secret and most negative thoughts and feelings. I am daunted by how it's spread, choking out some of the green that used to be here.

"It's too big," I say softly. "I'm not sure anything I can say can undo this."

My mother makes a harsh throaty noise. "Not with that attitude."

I take a deep breath. The thing about fairy gardens is that we plant in them the seeds we care about. Negative emotions can be dealt with. Hate is a villain that can be fought. Disappointment can be weeded out and appeased. The only seed that will not grow in a fairy garden is contempt. Those die, if the pixie coughs them up at all. As foreboding as this thornbush is, it proves my parents don't feel contempt for me. They have loved me enough to foster this tangled monster of thorns all these years, waiting and hoping that one day I'd be here to face it down.

This can be undone.

"I'm willing to try." I take another deep breath and turn to face them.

"Start with why you left." My mother folds her arms and pops out one leg.

"You know why. You wanted me to end my pregnancy." My stomach twists, and my muscles tense with the accusation.

My father shakes his head. "We wanted you to go to Godmother and ask for help."

"Do you think you were the first fairy with an unwanted pregnancy?" my mother rattles off. "Godmother has a tea that could have fixed everything."

"By making me not pregnant anymore," I grit out.

"No. Not like that. It was early in the pregnancy. A simple time-travel spell and she could've given your past self something to undo the damage."

"Arden isn't damage," I say through my teeth. "She's beautiful and exceptional and half-human. Maybe I didn't grow her on a vine, but believe me, the human way isn't any less miraculous. And here she is, the fruit of my labor. I love her as much as I love myself. Would you have Godmother undo her now?"

My mother rolls her eyes. "You know that's not what I meant." She coughs into her hand. "Making something as if it never happened is far different than ending something that's already begun."

"We accept Arden," my father chimes in, his voice lined with grit. "She's a lovely, exceptional young woman. Reminds me of you. How dare you suggest we would hurt her in any way? No one would have forced you to Godmother's back then. Sure, we thought it was best, but it was your decision, and if you would have stayed and trusted us, we would have supported you either way."

"Maybe I should have trusted you. I admit that. But I couldn't stay, not after what happened. Not after the stares, the judgment. How could I have raised Arden in that? You know what? If I had it to do over again, I'd do it exactly the same way." Tears slip down my face and pick up speed. I've been holding them back all day, and I just can't anymore. "You don't know what it was like for me. What Seven and his father did to me, humiliating me in public like that, I was the laughingstock of Devashire."

My mother's voice is almost a scream when she responds, "You'd do it again? Abandon us? The embarrassment you experienced at the ball was a shadow of what we felt after you left. You were abandoned by a leprechaun, Sophia. Everyone knows they think they're better than us. But to be abandoned by your own daughter? One who was pregnant with your grandchild!"

"You didn't want her. I did." The words catch in my throat and come out as a croak. I shake my head.

"We wanted her," my father says. "Maybe we didn't admit it right away, but we would have come around if given a chance. I was just so angry that a human had taken advantage of you. I swear if I'd have found him, I'd have—"

"No! Dad, he was *kind* to me. The kindest person I've ever

met. That human male kept me from slitting my wrists that night. Part of the reason I left was to look for him."

"Oh, Sophia, you can't be serious. A crush on a human over one night?" My father's disappointment is palpable.

"I thought I loved him. I know it's crazy, but I did." I sob openly.

"We loved you," my mother says.

My father's gaze settles on my tears. "We *love* you." His voice is choked. He turns to my mother. "We knew she was hurting, Aurora. We'd heard what the Delaneys did to her, and we didn't defend her. We didn't go to Godmother and demand justice."

"What would she have done, Matthias? The Delaneys are untouchable! Both of us hoped if we stopped talking about it, it would blow over."

I give a pained laugh. "It will never blow over. Everyone in this town knows I was the butt of his joke. I'm older now. I understand he was a bully, and I'm a survivor. But the pain is still there." I touch my chest. "And all I felt from you was a desire to hide it. You wanted to sweep it under the rug, just like my pregnancy. I couldn't do it. I couldn't swallow it down. And I couldn't give up Arden. She was... she felt magical, like a cosmic blessing."

My mother squeaked and sobbed behind her hand. "I'm sorry, but for the love of light, Sophia, if you'd given us a chance, we'd have come around."

A growl comes from my father's direction. His eyes are wild with emotion, and his lips peel back from his teeth as he says, "No, Aurora. That's a lie. I remember what it was like back then. She was seventeen, and you know damn well we would have pressured her until she caved. No, we wouldn't have forced her, but we'd have made it hell for her before we accepted it. She was months from graduation. Would we have cherished the idea of her walking across the stage with a human in her belly? Had we accepted it, we would have been cut off by every small-minded fairy in Devashire. You think it was bad when she ran away? Think of what it would have been like if she stayed. Raising a human child here? Endless scorn."

"So you think she did the right thing by leaving?" My mother spreads her hands, her face drenched with tears. Everyone is crying now, even my father.

"I'm saying we're culpable!" he bellows. "We all should have pulled together. We should have rallied the troops and forced Delaney to admit what he'd done to her. The other pixies would have supported us if we took a stand and went public. But we were cowards. How can we blame Sophia for wanting better for herself?" A deep cough racks his body.

Magic stirs in the air around us, pixie magic, fueled by luck and blending with the heady, close scent of the blossoms that make up our family garden. Every one, every plant in here started as an emotion, and there are far more beautiful ones than thornbushes. The air is shifting. With my father's admissions and understanding comes my own.

"I'm so sorry," I say, my face awash in fresh tears. "I see now what it did to you when I left. You would have loved me through it had I stayed. You would have supported my choices." I sob. "I still feel like I did what I had to do, but I should have written to you. I should have called. I should have..." My voice chokes off in a loud, barking cough before I can admit that I should have told them what I was doing and why. We'd always looked out for each other. My parents are good people, we are a strong family, and disappearing as I did didn't give them a chance to be the best versions of themselves.

"I should have defended you," my mother blurts. "I didn't. I was too scared and too traumatized by what had happened.

The panic... the social isolation... I didn't want to admit it, but part of me was relieved." She doubles over in a fit of coughing.

I know what she means. In the deepest parts of her soul, she was as relieved as I was that I left. My parents would have risen to the occasion, but part of them must have been glad they didn't have to.

"I forgive you," I scream, my hair and wings blowing back in the garden wind.

"I forgive you," my father echoes, his eyes locking on mine and then on my mother's.

"I forgive you," my mother cries out, her red eyes still weeping even as a smile turns her lips.

We double over, coughing. My father is the first to spit out his seed, a prickly, walnut-sized pit that represents all the hurt we caused each other. There's a smear of blood on his palm. There was nothing easy about bringing that one up.

I'm next. Mine is smaller, dark blue, and twisted. It represents my youth, my regret, and the mistakes that were meant to be. My love for my daughter is in there too. It's both a misshapen reminder of the agony I've caused all of us and a beautiful work of nature, infinite potential wrapped in a thin organic shell. It hurt coming out but, seeing it in my hand fills me with warm, healing power.

My mother is the last to produce her seed. She raises her hand to her mouth and ejects a misshapen purple one the size of a pecan. Jagged-edged with a smooth, opaque outer dome, it holds all her shame, regret, and a tinge of betrayal.

Three seeds, each with the kernel of forgiveness inside, the magic of a pixie family bond we will never leave behind. The wind bites into us now, and my mother must bend her knees and throw her back into it to spear the ground with her trowel. She digs out earth at the base of the thornbush. Each of us drops our seed into the hole, watering it with the tears that still drip from our faces. Once she's filled in the hole and smoothed it over, the wind dies down and the sun seems to shine brighter. Panting from exertion, we hug each other, my parents kissing my cheeks and helping me to stand.

A shoot breaks ground, rising out of the place we planted our seeds. Before our eyes, a bright green vine wraps around the base of the thornbush, weaving itself along the central stalk of the plant. Squeezing, choking, ending.

"Do you think it will be enough to kill it?" I ask.

My parents both look at me and smile. "I know it will be," my mother says softly.

On the other side of me, my father laughs. "If it's not, I'll get a backhoe in here and rip it out the human way."

"Daddy!" My eyes flash at the sacrilege.

"It will be enough," he promises. We watch the green shoot spiral around and around, tightening its stranglehold on the thornbush, until my stomach growls loud enough for all to hear.

"You haven't eaten yet?" my mother asks.

I shake my head. "I was going to take Arden to Foxwood's."

"Good idea. We'll all go. But it's not Foxwood's anymore," Mother says.

"No?" I turn to her in surprise.

"No. It's River's." She leads the way back toward the house.

"River's?" my mind flashes to River Foxwood, the satyr who showed me such kindness the night of the Yule Ball. A true friend, I'd often wondered what happened to him over the years.

"Took the restaurant over when his mother died and his father retired," she explains.

"Let's all go," my father suggests. "I'm sure Grandma is hungry too."

CHAPTER

TEN

River's Tavern, previously known as Foxwood's Tavern, isn't anything to look at from the outside. It's built from roughhewn logs and mud with a moss roof and a sign that desperately needs a coat of paint. I used to come here all the time as a kid. It's on the outskirts of Dragonfly Hollow, technically part of the theme park but not a location frequented by humans. That's because the human menu is vegan. The food is delicious, but there just aren't a ton of parkgoers clamoring to the farthest corner of Wonderland for a portabella mushroom burger or bee pollen wrap with sprouts. Which means it's the preferred place for "characters" to hang out—someplace they can be themselves.

The fae menu is far less limited than the human one, and I can't wait to sink my teeth into Foxwood's famous burger. I'm curious if the menu has changed now that River runs the place. I'm drowning in memories as I pull open the heavy wooden door. But my nostalgia is soon tempered by apprehension when I experience a prickly reception.

All conversation stops and dozens of fairy eyes stare in our direction. At first brows lift when they see me, but it's when their gazes lock onto Arden that the whispers start. My parents told me they'd kept my pregnancy a secret. This is the first time most of these people are learning I have a daughter. Well, well, well, back one day and already making an impression.

My father loops his arm into Arden's. "Come help me find a table."

I'm about to follow after them when a voice to my left calls out, "Sophia?"

I glance down at a face I haven't seen in over a decade but that I recognize instantly. "Penelope?"

Penelope Hawthorne has aged well. Her hair is still the color of snow, her skin as smooth and fair as the last time I saw her in the sleigh behind me at the Yule Ball. She's not quite as put together today. She's wearing leggings and a long sweater. There are shadows under her eyes.

She rises and pulls me into a firm hug. It's a strange gesture considering we haven't spoken in sixteen years. We were friends once, and my heart gives a little squeeze thinking about those days. My life outside Dragonfly was necessarily lonely, constantly burdened with the fear of getting caught, and I'm sad our friendship was a victim of that fear. I wouldn't blame her for keeping her distance, but she's hanging on like we saw each other yesterday.

Slowly my arms rise, and I hug her back. In a sea of unfriendly stares, her offered kindness is a lifeline. Only when she releases me do I see Flick and two small pixies at the same table. Both children have her nose and Flick's eyes. My heart warms. They've stayed together all these years. "You have kids!"

"Oh, you remember Flick, and this is Caramel and Witsy." She points at the two kids.

I smile and greet them all, then start to excuse myself to join my family, but she grabs me by the elbow.

"It wasn't because of me, was it?" she blurts guiltily. Behind her, Flick slaps his forehead as if he can't believe she's said what she's said.

"What are we talking about?" I ask, totally confused.

Tears fill her eyes. "Did you leave Dragonfly because of what I said to you before the Yule Ball?"

I balk. "No!" It's clear that this answer isn't as common sense to her as it is to me.

"It's just... It's just..." Her tears are flowing now, and I pat her awkwardly on the back because I have no idea what else to do. "I told you Seven wasn't coming, but I didn't mean for it to happen like it did. And then... And then a few weeks later you were gone!" She clutches her chest. Behind her Flick is rubbing his head like it aches.

I give her another hug, then give a little shake. "Penelope... Penelope, listen to me."

She sniffs, her wings hanging limp from her back.

"My leaving had nothing to do with you. You were right about Seven. I should have listened to you. I left for other reasons."

She wipes under her eyes. Her eyes dart in the direction my father took Arden. "Do you have a daughter?" she whispers.

I shrug. "I do. And I don't think you have to whisper. It's not a secret. If there is anyone left in Dragonfly who hasn't heard I've returned with a daughter, I'm pretty sure they will know by the end of the day." I gesture toward the crowd of patrons openly staring at me.

For the first time, Penelope notices all the gawking faces around us and her jaw drops in outrage. Pivoting in my arms, she flips them all the bird with both hands and in a voice I'd never expect her petite body to be capable of yells, "Oh, fuck all the way off, you nosy bastards. Go back to your meals!"

To my surprise, many of the fairies do. I turn wide eyes toward Flick, who's trying his best to cover the ears of their children. "She's a bit emotional right now," he says to me. "We have a third on the vine." He tips his head toward the kids.

Penelope lowers her fingers and turns a smile back in my direction. "Do you want to have lunch sometime?"

"Um, sure."

"Great! I work at the bank. Stop in whenever you get settled." She hugs me again, almost violently, and sinks back into her chair.

My heart warms at the thought. I didn't expect her to welcome me back with open arms, but I'll take it. I plod past the whispering crowd to the table my father nabbed in the back and sink into an open chair beside Arden.

"What's a raindrop?" she asks me, not looking up from her menu. Apparently, the little drama that just happened behind her wasn't enough to distract her from the promise of food.

"Dessert. It's fruity, like raspberry Jell-O, but more of a foam that dissolves on your tongue," I explain. "You should definitely get one."

"What about the forest barbecue?" she asks next. "Will I like it?"

I giggle. "I do. But it's nothing you'll get in the human world. It's a mixture of meats from local forest creatures, usually whatever the Foxwoods hunted the night before."

"What kind of forest creatures?"

"You know, rabbit, raccoon, squirrel. It's a special blend."

"I love it," my father chimes in. "I'm getting one with a side of fried okra."

Arden places her menu down. "Don't you find it weird that

you guys eat forest creatures when you basically are forest creatures?"

I shrug. "I can get you the human menu if you'd like."

She frowns. "No. I want the squirrel burger."

"Forest barbecue," I correct.

"You won't regret it," Grandma calls across the table.

A throat clears behind me, and I glance over my shoulder. A handsome satyr stares down at me, golden-skinned with caramel-colored waves surrounding two curling ram-like horns that sweep along the sides of his head above his ears. A bright smile spreads across his face when his eyes connect with mine, and he stomps one of his hooves.

I pop out of my chair and throw my arms around him in a hug. "River? Oh my stars, it's so good to see you!"

He gives me a firm squeeze. "You too, Sophia. You're a sight for sore eyes." He kisses the side of my cheek. I pull away, smiling.

"Damn, River. Look at you, all grown up!" I raise my eyebrows. Although it shouldn't be any surprise that the boy who was once a scrawny young faun has bloomed into a strapping adult satyr, I am blown away by the change. By human standards, satyrs are naturally ripped to shreds. Human women who go to the Dragonfly Club all want to meet a satyr. They're built tall and broad, are naturally fit, and have a reputation for being free spirits who make generous lovers. I wouldn't know. River and I were friends, nothing more. I can appreciate that he's physically beautiful, but I've never thought of him in that way.

River greets everyone else at the table, and I introduce him to Arden. He bows at the waist. "As lovely as your mother. Welcome to River's."

I let out a held breath. As stressful as the morning has been, at the moment, I actually feel... welcome.

"How is your father doing?" Grandma asks. My brow furrows as her cheeks pink. Did she just flutter her wings at him?

"Just fine, Betty. I'm sure he'd enjoy seeing you again at his new place." He looks at me. "He's retired out to Mermaid Bay. Sometimes your grandma goes to see him."

Oh, I mouth, brows shooting up. Grandma shrugs.

"As much as I'd love to catch up, let's get your order in. The kitchen is busy, and you must be starving this late in the day." He pulls a pad from his back pocket.

River has servers working at the tavern. I think it's sweet that he thinks so highly of my family that he's taking special care of us, taking the order himself. But then he's always been sweet and caring. It's his nature.

When everyone is done giving their order, I place a hand on his arm. "After, do you have time to talk?"

"Come to my office." He tilts his head toward the back of the tavern.

I owe him an explanation for why I never tried to contact him while I was away. "I'll stop in as soon as I'm finished."

He smiles and heads for the kitchen.

IF A HUNTING CABIN AND A MAN CAVE HAD A BABY, IT would look like River's office. After a meal that's as fabulous as I remember, I send Arden home with my family and find the satyr there, sitting in a leather chair with a rip in the side he's repaired with a piece of camouflage duct tape. The desk itself is covered in an orgy of papers. My fingers itch to form a neat stack out of them, but I don't want to be rude. The walls are equally in disarray, with lists, posters, and flyers tacked over almost every square inch.

I laugh. "No computer? Still a technophobe?"

He grins. "Hate it. Not my thing, Sophia. You know me. My idea of modern refinement is sleeping inside on a summer's night. Although I did finally break down and get a cell phone to appease my employees."

That makes me laugh. He is the outdoorsy type, far happier huddled beside an open fire than inside an office building. *So different from Seven,* I think, and then chastise myself for thinking about Seven.

"So... you're back." River gestures at a chair across the desk from him. I move the pile of papers there to the desk and take a seat. "You look exactly the same. It's almost like we were sitting next to each other in class a few days ago. And your daughter... she's beautiful, Sophia. I can't believe how much I've missed."

Same old River. I leave without a word, and when I come back unexpectedly, he's not angry, just mourns our time apart. "Listen, River, I need to tell you something."

"Start at the Yule Ball and end at today. I want to know all of it." He leans back in his chair.

"Actually, that's why I asked to see you. I feel terrible about what happened. You were so kind to me the night of the Yule Ball. What you did for me was incredibly brave and noble, and if I were a better person, I would have written you to tell you so. I would have found a way to keep in touch. You were my friend, and I disappeared on you. I'm sorry about that."

He scoffs. "All I did was bring you some hot chocolate."

"It was far more than that, and you know it." After Chance Delaney had delivered his "Seven did you a favor" speech, it was River who showed up in his truck to drive me home. I hadn't had the strength to walk or fly, and calling my parents would have added insult to injury.

His brown eyes flare. "Oh, come on, Sophia. You must know I had a crush on you back then. I just wanted time in that sleigh with you and to revel in you finally realizing that Seven was an arrogant fuckstain."

I snort. "Truth." Even as I say it though, a little voice in my head tries to tell me that he can't be that much of an asshole if he arranged to have me rescued. I push the thought aside.

Flashing a grin, I say, "Besides, I seem to recall you had something going with Crimson Everleigh at the time?"

"Crimson Never-laid? Yeah, we dated for a while. It never went anywhere."

We both giggle childishly. "You've never wanted for company, River."

He lowers his voice. "You know satyrs aren't really into the whole monogamy thing, right? We love broadly and with open hearts. And we're always fair and honest about it."

I chuckle darkly. "So I've heard." Satyrs are horny, in every sense of the word, and are notoriously caring and generous lovers. But they don't regularly practice monogamy like pixies and leprechauns do. Affairs and multiple partners are culturally accepted among their kind even after marriage. I've always admired the freedom of it, but also wondered at how no one gets hurt. I've never heard of a jealous satyr.

His face grows serious. "One thing I can say for Seven though, I think he did look for you after you left. He seemed almost remorseful."

"Hmm? Why would you think that?"

"When school started back, we had it out over what happened. I took an imprint of his face with my fist." River waves his hand in the air and smiles.

"You did not."

"I did. Fuck, he had it coming."

I snort. "He did."

"Anyway, I thought that was the end of it, but after you left, he kept coming around to ask if I'd heard from you. Over and over." He narrows his eyes. "And I started thinking... With all that luck, I shouldn't have been able to get a hit in. You know, I get the feeling he let me punch him."

I tuck my chin in and gape at him. "Why would he do that?"

River shrugs. "I'll never understand leprechauns. I just thought you should know."

I squirm in my chair. I don't know what to do with that information. Why would he care where I was? Guilt? Fear that he'd be blamed for my leaving? But then I realize it couldn't be true.

"Whatever he was trying to do, his goal wasn't to find me. With the amount of luck at his disposal, if Seven had actually wanted to find me, he would have. Fuck, he *did* find me when my parents asked Godmother for help."

He nods. "True. So he's well and truly an insufferable asshat then."

"As far as I can tell."

River knocks on the desk twice. "I heard you've already gone to see Godmother."

"Just this morning. Did you know Seven is working for her?"

"Yeah. Has been since right after you left."

"Do you know why? He told me he's practically running the casino. He has more money than the gods. Why would he work for her too?"

River gives me a sideways glance. "You know how Godmother works. It's never about money. He must have either made a deal with her for something he wanted or done something fitting of her punishment. But if you're asking me what it was, I don't know, and neither does anyone else in this town. If they did, I'd have heard it. You know this place is a rumor mill. I knew you were back the moment you left your parents' house this morning."

I fold my arms. "Godmother says I have to work with Seven on a security-related case in order to stay."

The grunt he gives holds more than an ounce of pity. "She does know how to dole out a punishment, doesn't she? Analyzes you to find the open wound and then prescribes the thing that pokes a salted blade into it."

"I guess that's why she's in charge. She knows how to pull people's strings. Knows exactly what they can't resist and what fills them with fear. That particular talent gives her power." I look around his office, trying to think of something to say to change the subject. I don't want to talk about Seven anymore or my sentence.

He studies me, suddenly serious. "Let me guess. You have to solve whatever this is or you remain in her employ, working with Seven for free, indefinitely."

I tuck my hair behind my ears. "Sounds about right."

He taps his chin. "Let me know if there's anything I can do."

I take a deep breath. I was hoping he'd say that. "Thing is, River, I imagine one of the benefits of running this place is that you see and hear everything."

His eyes crinkle at the corners. "Very few things happen in Dragonfly without my hearing about them."

"I don't know enough about this case yet, but when I do, will you help me? Having someone like you keep an ear to the ground could give me the advantage I need to meet Godmother's terms."

"Of course I'll help you. Anything you need."

"Thank you—"

"On one condition..."

There's always a condition with the fae. I should have expected this. I raise my eyebrows. "Don't keep me in suspense."

His dazzling smile is back with an impish tilt. "Come to my firepit on the beach tomorrow night. After everything you've been through, you deserve music, ale, and a warm heart to listen to your woes. You can bring Arden if it suits." He turns over a hand in a gesture of welcome.

Bringing Arden is out of the question. A satyr's fire is an adult situation if ever there was one, and although no one would hurt her, she might see things she could never unsee. She's far too young to attend. Still, I find myself longing to go. I didn't socialize much in the human world. Too risky. Always worried about getting caught. The idea of being myself around good friends with music and laughter sounds like heaven.

"I'd love to," I say. "I mean, if that's your price."

CHAPTER

ELEVEN

The next morning, I leave Wonderland on a crowded character shuttle for Dragonfly After Dark, the adult playground of the Dragonfly theme park world, for my meeting with Seven. Dragonfly Casino is a diamond on the horizon, all glass windows and steel girders plated gold. It's a fishbowl, intentionally designed to invite voyeurism, a playland for the see-and-be-seen crowd. The rich love to be watched doing rich people things. Here, those on the outside can witness the glitz and glamor and dream of one day being part of it.

At least *humans* can dream. Fae gambling is prohibited. Too dangerous, with our propensity to bargain and our competing access to luck.

A heavy weight forms in my gut thinking about that. I may have played my last poker game. Gods, I loved it while it lasted. Poker isn't the only thing I was ever good at, but it's the career I built and loved more than anything. What other career combines psychology, game theory, and the thrill of a big win? I've never found any other work as remotely challenging and exhilarating. Losing my ability to be a poker pro is like experiencing a small death. It's losing a part of who I am.

I shake off the thought and soldier on. This isn't about me. It's about Arden. I need to solve this case and earn my freedom. As long as I'm beholden to Godmother, I have nothing to bargain with, and my job prospects are limited due to my obligation to her. Only by solving this case can I help Arden and give her choices and a path back to the human world.

As I pass through the glass entryway, I notice humans already hugging the craps table at the front of the building. It's eight in the morning. Either they got an early start or more likely they were at it all night. I snort. Just like Vegas, Dragonfly Casino is open twenty-four seven. Humans can play until they drop from exhaustion or run out of money. Most of the time they run out of money. The house is run by leprechauns after all. Leprechauns always come out on top.

"I have a meeting with Seven Delaney," I tell the security guard who stops me at the entrance. The leprechaun is wearing a dark suit and an earpiece and scans me from the tips of my wings to my gold shoes, scowling.

The urge to smack that scowl right off his face is almost overwhelming. Getting here required a thirty-minute ride on a shuttle with subpar ventilation. I'm rumpled and annoyed. It doesn't help that I've had to borrow a dress of my mother's and it hangs on me like a sack, not to mention the pastel color is completely wrong for my complexion. Then again, it wouldn't matter if I was wearing couture. I don't belong, not because of what I'm wearing but because of what I am. I'm a pixie, and along with satyrs, we're not welcome in this casino unless we're working here, and even then, our roles are predetermined by our species. This casino has never hired a satyr for a human-facing position. Pixies can be servers or dealers. Any position above that goes to a leprechaun.

I ignore the man's snub. I'm not here to impress, and I don't care what he thinks of me or my dress. I'm here to do what I have to do to unbind myself from my deal with Godmother.

"I have an appointment," I say again, clutching my bag in front of my hips.

He checks a clipboard on his podium. "I'm not showing any pixie appointments today. Nice try, honey. If you want to apply for a job, I can give you an application, but either way you've got to leave. No pixies at the tables. You want to meet a sugar daddy, try the club."

Utterly irritated now, I enunciate each word as if the man is hard of hearing. "I have a scheduled meeting with Seven Delaney. We're working together."

He chuckles. "Sure you do. I'm sure Mr. Delaney has all sorts of uses for a pixie that would require a private meeting, but he's busy right now."

I scoff and peer at his name tag. "Brandon, could you just call up to Seven's office and tell him Sophia is here to see him?"

Brandon stares down his nose at me and shakes his head dismissively.

"That won't be necessary." Seven appears behind Brandon, eyes dark, mouth bent into a furious grimace.

"My apologies, Mr. Delaney. I was just showing her out," Brandon says.

"Why would you do that when she has an appointment with me? One that we are late to begin because you've delayed her?"

"I... I... It's not on my..." He flips papers on his clipboard.

"Get your things, Brandon. You're fired." Seven has a few inches of height on Brandon, but the energy he's putting off makes him appear much bigger. He's livid. The testosterone-charged, big-boss intensity focused on Brandon would make anyone's stomach clench. I take a step back, and it isn't even directed at me.

"But... I...," Brandon blubbers, pointing at his clipboard as if an excuse might spring off the pages there.

Seven snaps his fingers and a woman in a suit appears by his side. Where did she come from? Her lashes flutter when she looks at him like she's staring into the sun. Gods, the Seven I once knew is gone, replaced by leviathan in a dark suit. Is he always this intimidating at work? "Claire, please escort Brandon to the back room to gather his things and then accompany him off the premises. Find someone else to man the door."

"Yes, sir," she says, taking Brandon's upper arm. He's still gaping at Seven and then at me even as he's ushered away.

The severe edges of Seven's expression soften when he turns to me, morphing into that crooked smirk I know so well. He places a hand in the center of my back and guides me toward the elevators. "Shall we?"

Momentarily stunned, I shuffle into the compartment. His hand fills the space between my hips and my ribs, and for a second, I feel small and insignificant beside him. Only for a second. The sound of the doors closing snaps me out of it.

"I can't believe you just fired that guy!" I step away from him and cross my arms over my chest.

"His actions display a level of incompetence we don't tolerate at Lucky Enterprises."

I laugh. "The fuck you don't. Your family has been treating pixies exactly like that for decades."

He grimaces. "I have a meeting with you. It's on my calendar. He didn't even look. It's blatant ineptitude. We pride ourselves on top-notch service—"

The snort I give is laden with derision. "Right. So you didn't fire him because he was a bigot who accused me of trying to sneak into the casino to find a sugar daddy, just for not double-checking your schedule. Makes sense."

His features tighten, and he shakes his head. "He disrespected you. It was wrong. Gods, Sophia, I fired the man. What more do you expect from me?"

"How long has Brandon worked here?" I tap my foot.

He slants me a sideways glance. "I have no idea."

I shift, putting myself in front of him. "How badly did he need this job? Does he have a wife? A family?"

Seven pinches the bridge of his nose. "What do you want from me, Sophia?"

"I don't know. Your heartlessness just surprises me, that's all. It shouldn't, but it does."

Our eyes lock. "Heartlessness."

"Yeah. Heartlessness," I drawl.

He holds my gaze as he pulls his phone from his pocket. "Claire, retrieve Brandon and offer him his job back, with a warning. Yes. Thank you." He hangs up and stares at me. "Problem solved."

If I roll my eyes any harder, I'm going to see my own brain.

The elevator doors slide open, and his hand is on my back again, ushering me through a shiny marble reception area. I don't shrug it off. I should, but I don't.

A lanky redhead in an elegant black sheath dress reaches us right outside his office door. "The report you asked for," she says, shoving a stack of papers into his hands.

He thanks her with a shallow smile. They exchange pleasantries before Seven specifies we're not to be disturbed. She directs a wink in our direction before clopping off in her stilettos. Seven removes his hand from my back and leads me into his office where he closes the door behind us. He squares the papers on his desk.

"I think she has eyes for you, Seven," I say, loading on

maximum snark. "Did you take her measurements before hiring her as your assistant?"

He grunts in disgust. "That's Eva, Sophia!"

I try to remember who Eva is and it comes to me in a flash. Instantly I feel like a humongous jackass. "Eva as in Evangeline? Your little sister?"

"That's the one."

"She's changed since I last saw her."

He heaves a sigh. "Tell me about it. My dad moved her office up here because she was too much of a distraction downstairs. Eva's in charge of our social media presence and public relations—constantly in the public eye. It's a full-time job trying to protect her from overzealous suitors."

A flood of memories comes back to me of how we used to take Eva for honey and lavender ice cream at Twinkleberries. His family once accepted me, when they thought we were just friends. Well, everyone but his father, Chance. A lead ball forms in the pit of my chest just thinking about the man and how cruel he was to me.

I distract myself by taking in my surroundings. Other than a wall of windows with a bird's-eye view of Dragonfly, Seven's office is a much-needed sanctuary from the fishbowl effect of the rest of the casino. He has walls and a desk of warm mahogany that matches the bookshelves that line one entire wall. A muted blue Persian carpet anchors the decor. It looks expensive and imported, just like the furniture. If I had to describe Seven's interior design style, it would be "things I can't afford."

Seven fits in here in his charcoal-gray suit that skims his body as if it was made for him and most certainly was. Gold clover cuff links glint at his cuffs, and a watch that's probably worth as much as my parents' house ticks on his wrist. He doesn't walk back around the desk as I expect him to but returns to stand in front of me so that we're toe-to-toe. He's taller than me by almost a foot, and when he slants a wolfish smile in my direction, I hate the way my stomach flips.

"This dress is..." He takes the material between his fingers and pulls. Two inches of extra fabric come off my body.

"My mother's," I say. "I haven't had a chance to buy more dresses. I had one that still fit me, but a five-year-old planted a sucker in it yesterday, so it's at the cleaners."

Amusement twinkles in his eyes. "How is Aurora doing? I trust that since you're wearing her dress you've reconciled?" He knows about pixie garden rituals. I shared with him while we were dating, although he's never actually been in my family's garden.

"Yes. All is well. I won't be sleeping in the street."

His expression turns serious. "I'd never leave you to sleep in the street."

"No, just alone in a sleigh surrounded by a pack of ravenous wolves," I mumble. I wasn't sleeping, and the wolves included his father and the rest of town, but he knows what I mean.

He scoffs, then moves around to his side of the desk. He opens his mouth as if he wants to say something else but closes it again and squares his shoulders. A professional persona chases away any remnants of the boy I once knew. "As much as I'd love to once again be berated by you about something that happened sixteen years ago, we have a job to do."

Biting my tongue, I take a seat across from him. He opens a file folder on the desk in front of me. "It happened March 20."

"The spring equinox?" I look down at the picture in the file in front of me. It looks a lot like the one Donovan showed me.

"Yes."

"I can't even tell if this is a man or a woman." The body is a bloody, maimed mess.

"It's a man, although the genitals were ripped out along with the teeth and a selection of bones."

I glance up and meet Seven's emerald eyes, thankful that the grisly picture in front of me is enough to make me temporarily immune to his charms. "I don't understand. You found this in the square the night of the equinox? There's always a huge party there to celebrate the coming spring. There would have been revelers until the wee hours of the morning."

"It happened before the party. Godmother arrived at her tearoom around five a.m. to prepare for the day's festivities. The body was already cold. She cast a concealment charm until we could remove it. Estimated time of death was three a.m."

"Who was the human?" I page through the contents of the file, looking for details.

"Michael Murphy. Just a trucker who enjoyed visiting the Dragonfly Club. Had a thing for pixies. Other than that, nothing special about him."

Included in the photos is one of Michael Murphy smiling at the photographer in front of the dragonfly topiary at the park entrance. He's potbellied and mustached, dressed in a T-shirt that says I Brake For Fairies. I flip to the next photo and have to swallow down bile at the sight of his mangled corpse.

"The similarity of this picture to the one Agent Donovan showed me in the rehabilitation center is uncanny," I say. "I think what you said yesterday on the beach is right. Someone has gone through a lot of trouble to pin this on Yissevel. What I can't figure out is who or why. The fact that one of the murders took place on US soil points to human involvement."

"Humans don't know about Yissevel."

"No, they don't."

Seven studies me. "When you were on the outside, did you meet others like you?"

His question surprises me. "No," I answer honestly. "I'd heard rumors... a friend of a human acquaintance was arrested by FIRE. But in sixteen years, I never met another fae. To be fair, I wasn't looking for them and I avoided anything related to our kind. I was too scared it might draw suspicion." I try not to think of how terribly lonely it was living in Vegas. My human relationships were better than nothing but necessarily shallow.

"Understandable."

"If a human did this, it's not like they could come and go. Everyone who passes through the front gate is screened, and the only other way in is through the moon gate, which is only open to the fae. A fae living in the US like I was might have crossed into Devashire to commit the crime, but in that case, Godmother would have their magical signature in the wards. And neither of the scenarios explains why the murderer would try to blame a human murder on US soil on a creature unknown to humans."

He rolls his pen back and forth under his fingertips. "Godmother doesn't know about the murder Donovan told you about. Are you going to tell her, or should I?"

"You," I say immediately.

He gives a brisk nod.

The office grows quiet. He's staring at me again, and my stomach flutters in response. Stupid stomach. "So who was Michael Murphy last seen with?"

"We don't know. There was a planned power outage in that sector of the park the night of the murder. No security footage."

I blink at him. "Who knew about the outage?"

"No one who isn't accounted for. We've checked."

"Nothing on Michael's social? Facebook, Instagram, TikTok?" Humans tend to post pictures of their pixie dates.

"Michael was disappointingly discreet about his endeavors here in Dragonfly."

I ponder that for a minute while I stare at a sterling silver sculpture on the corner of his desk. It's one of those pieces of art that's both ostentatious and purposeless. He probably paid thousands of dollars for it and it doesn't even hold pencils. What is it even supposed to be? A wing, maybe? A lightbulb goes off in my head. "What about Flutter?"

He stares at me blankly.

The corner of my mouth twitches, and then my smile spreads. "You don't know what Flutter is, do you?"

"Don't be smug, Sophia. It's very unattractive."

"Ha! I bet your sister knows. I bet your company advertises on their website."

He leans back in his chair and threads his fingers across his stomach. "Are you going to explain to me what Flutter is or should I go find Evangeline to ask her?"

I get comfortable in my chair and rub my hands together. "Oh no, I'll tell you. Flutter is a dating site like Grindr or Tinder but specifically for humans who want to be matched with pixies and satyrs."

His eyes narrow. "Do users post pictures?"

"Sometimes, but even if they don't, the site tracks who's matched with whom. I bet Michael had an account." I bound out of my chair and charge behind the desk to Seven's laptop. He rolls his chair out of the way, scowling at me like I've broken some kind of unwritten rule. Scowl away. I'm driving.

Gods, this thing is sleek. It looks like it was manufactured by aliens in some high-tech chamber that uses microscopic beams of light to assemble it. The thing is so thin if I turned it on its side, I could probably floss my teeth with it. "Password?"

He rolls to my side and presses his finger to the fingerprint reader to unlock it. I navigate to Flutter. Illustrated fairies flit across the screen, landing on giant flowers where they arch their backs and spread their knees. Nice. I search for a profile under Michael Murphy. Nothing comes up.

"Damn," Seven says.

I search for Michael. Three hundred profiles come up. I start scrolling. On the second page, Michael Murphy's mustached face stares back at me. I click his photo. "There he is. MichaelLovesWings69." *Ick.*

His profile doesn't give us any answers other than his favorite music—country—and his membership in a gun club in Alabama. There's a picture of Michael on the back of a Harley-Davidson motorcycle and another firing a handgun at a shooting range.

"Nothing here about who he hooked up with," Seven says. "I'll get someone from security to see if he can bypass the login and take a look at his profile." He reaches for the phone.

"Gods, that will take too long." I hang up the phone and navigate to a new window. I set up a new email account. MichaelLovesWings69 is taken but I get MichaelLoves-Wings95. Once I've validated it using Seven's system, I navigate back to Flutter and scroll down to the contact number at the bottom of the page. I start to dial but then realize the flaw in my plan.

"You're going to have to do this. My voice is too high. I could use illusion, but you make a more convincing man than me." I hand him the phone.

He looks at it like I'm handing him a scorpion. "What do you want me to say?"

I grab a pen and a legal pad off his desk and jot down a script. "This."

He scans it, then looks at me skeptically. "No way is this going to work."

Quirking an eyebrow at him, I dial the phone and hand it over. "Trust me."

Seven watches me, phone to his ear. "Hello, yes, my name is Michael Murphy and I need to change the email address on my account, only I can't do it online because my wife found my profile and closed my other email account and phone number. Yes. Uh-huh."

For fuck's sake, he sounds too formal and uppity to be a Flutter regular. I pick up the legal pad again and write in giant letters LIE BETTER!! I underline it three times.

"Yeah, I'm in hot water here," Seven says, this time sounding far more like an American trucker. "Just need you to update the email. Yeah. Sure, I can verify my identity." He glares at me in alarm.

I shift the folder in front of him and point at Michael's home address and social security number. He had to provide them to get into Dragonfly since we are a sovereign government. Seven rattles it off along with the new email. I hear the person on the other end of the line say a few words, and then he simply says, "Thank you."

He hangs up.

I smile wider. "Told ya."

Seven looks absolutely baffled. "No security questions. No two-factor authentication."

I sigh. "Flutter doesn't make its money from keeping people from using its site. They try to make it easy for their customers." I click the link to reset Michael's password, navigate to my new email account for the reset link, change it to something I'll remember, and voilà, we're in.

"Gods, you did it," Seven says, perusing Michael's profile.

Michael is what Flutter calls a *Frequent Flyer*. An icon in the corner of his profile sports an FF inside a silver set of wings. There are dozens of hookups. I grab the mouse from Seven and click on his last match. A picture of a blond, blue-eyed pixie with the handle Wing_Gurl pops up.

"Do you recognize her?" Seven asks.

I glance toward the color printer on Seven's credenza and press print. Laser. Nice. "No, but that doesn't mean anything. A pixie like her would use illusion."

Seven grunts.

"The thing about pixies though is that we often use the same illusions again and again. It's exhausting coming up with new faces. I bet if I ask around town, someone will know who this is."

"Great idea," he says. He blinks at me, and then points a finger in my direction. "And the best place to start is with a visit to the Dragonfly Club. Ask around. See if anyone has anything to say about Michael Murphy."

"I would have thought you'd already tried that," I say incredulously. If he knew Michael Murphy frequented the club, why wouldn't he have accessed the security tapes and interviewed his regulars?

Seven flashes that crooked smile. "We've tried, but you know as well as I do that pixies clam up around leprechauns, and everyone clams up around Godmother. I need someone who can change their appearance and blend in, get the other pixies to trust them."

Many of the pixies that frequent the club work in the sex trade. Prostitution isn't illegal in Devashire, and their ability to look like anyone makes them particularly desirable by humans. But a pixie wouldn't admit to it openly, especially not to someone outside their kind. Even among other pixies, it's considered immoral and reprehensible.

"That's why Godmother assigned me to this case, isn't it?" It finally clicks in my brain. If anyone has a chance of getting the pixies at the club to talk, it's me. I know how they think. My punishment isn't just a punishment. Godmother needs me.

Seven nods his head. "Yup."

I plant my hands on my hips. "Couldn't you just use luck? I mean, walk into the club and flex a little juice, and the person you're looking for will fall into your arms. Be a lot faster than me trying to pry information out of some poor pixie about this guy." I wave the printout of Wing_Gurl's face.

Leaning back in his chair, Seven tries to remain impassive, but I see a hint of frustration twitch a muscle in his jaw. If I didn't know him as well as I do, I might not have noticed.

"Oh my gods!" I grip the arms of my chair. "You've already tried, and it's not working."

He rolls his pen back and forth on the desk again. "Luck has to be directed toward something. There has to be focus and intention. I've tried various things, but nothing has worked. Godmother has tried magic. Whoever did this... they covered their tracks."

"And you're hoping I can uncover them the old-fashioned way."

"Yes. Turn on that friendly charm of yours and see what you can find out." He smirks.

There's nothing friendly or charming about me and never has been. I was born snarky and have fully embraced my sarcastic superpowers as an adult. "Right. I'm a people person."

"We go tonight."

I think for a moment and then shake my head. "Tomorrow night. There will be more people there on a Friday. More pixies. The club culture is tight. If I'm going to do this, I need to look the part of a Dragonfly Club regular. That won't be as hard as it seems considering most of them change their appearance regularly. Only by gaining their trust will I learn anything about this guy."

He nods. "Smart. Tomorrow then. I'll pick you up at eight."

My mouth drops open. "You're going too? I thought the entire point of this was for me to get these pixies to trust me."

"You might need me there for luck or a distraction. Don't worry, I'll stay out of your way."

I consider arguing with him, but I don't have the energy. His jaw is set, and the expression he's sending my way is resolute.

"Fine. Do you have a smaller version of that picture of Michael? It might help if I can show it around." I could print his profile picture, but the guest photo is clearer and more recent.

"Snap a picture with your phone."

My cheeks heat. "Don't have one. FIRE took it. How about a scanner?"

"Unacceptable," he says around a frown. He opens a drawer on his right and pulls out a smartphone, tossing it in my direction. "I'll have my assistant reassign this one to you."

"You keep extra phones in your drawer? Who keeps extra phones?"

"In case of emergencies. I've been known to lose mine a time or two."

What? "I can't afford it!" I wave the phone between us. "Even if you gave me the phone itself, I'm not sure I can pay the bill anymore."

He levels a stare at me, looking totally exasperated. "The phone is yours, and I'll have the bill sent here. It won't cost you a thing." He grabs the phone and sets up facial recognition using my face, then puts it in my hand. "Take a picture of Michael."

Slowly, I shuffle the photos to the one where he's not dead and snap a picture. I guess I have a new cell phone. One more drop in the bucket of debt I owe Seven. No, I tell myself that this is needed for the job I'm doing for Godmother. As soon as we're done, I'll give it back. "Fine," I say. "We done then?"

"No." He stands and rounds to my side of the desk, leaning

his hip against the edge tantalizingly close to my face. Something low within me clenches when our eyes meet. "Have dinner with me."

"Why?"

He pauses, licking his lips in a way that sends my heart racing. "To catch up. Get to know each other again. Talk about old times."

I lean toward him, pulled by some unseen force. I wish I could say it was his luck, but not this time. It's him, the charm, the confidence, the intense way he's looking at me like he wants me more than any of the expensive things in this room. "I don't want to know you," I say, thankful I'm a skilled liar.

He sighs. "It would make things easier if you'd just let me explain."

"Does this dinner have anything to do with the case?" I ask, standing to put more space between us.

"No."

"Then I'm not interested."

"Sophia..." He tips his head like he doesn't believe me.

Suddenly I'm exhausted, and my shoulders sag as I say, "The answer is no, Seven." Before he can use his luck on me or I do something stupid like change my mind, I stride from his office.

I move through Seven's door so quickly I almost slam into Chance Delaney. Seven's father is standing outside Seven's office, looking as pretentious as I remember, an older version of his son with shorter graying hair and sharper features that give his face an almost ratlike appearance. His green eyes are narrower, and his cheeks more sunken as well. He straightens in his perfectly tailored suit as his gaze slides down his nose at me.

"What are *you* doing here?" His tone is laced with revulsion.

For a second, I'm caught in his disapproving gaze. The night of the Yule Ball comes back to me—the physical pain of falling from the carriage followed by the emotional agony of Chance cruelly revealing Seven's intentions. *Now you know your place, pixie. You'd do well to remember it.* How it would have sickened him to know I'd had a secret romantic relationship with his son.

I'm tempted to say nothing and flee, just like I did that night. But then I remember I'm not that little girl anymore. I lift my chin and flash him a wicked grin. "Who, me? I was just meeting your son for a quick fuck."

I take my time striding into the elevator as Chance's face turns red with fury. Just before the doors close, I catch a glimpse of Seven behind him.

To my surprise, he's laughing.

I'm still cursing the Delaneys and mumbling to myself about arrogant leprechauns when I stumble off the shuttle at the Wonderland stop. I'm halfway to my parents' place when the phone Seven issued me rings. I roll my eyes. Gods, he's a pain in the ass. What could he possibly need so soon?

"What now?" I answer, loading my voice with annoyance.

"For one, you could cross the border so that I could punish you as nature intended." Agent Donovan's voice is eerily quiet with an undercurrent of malice.

"How did you get this number?" My words are thready with panic.

He scoffs. "Question is, who's helping you? I have your cell phone. That phone is under your alias, Soho Lane. But the thing about doing what I do, Ms. Larkspur, is I have friends in high places. One of them runs the cellular provider you used in America, one that owns towers all over the world. He was able to link Soho Lane to Sophia Larkspur for me and put a flag on the account. That friend called me moments ago to alert me that a new phone had been set up with your real name and, wouldn't you know it, a Dragonfly address."

Fuck! I take a deep breath. *Think, Sophia.* I picture myself at the poker table. My gambler's brain kicks into gear, and I analyze every word I've said and everything he's said. What cards have already been played? What's in my hand, and what's on the table? *Admit to nothing,* I tell myself. "I think there's been some kind of mistake, sir. You've reached a number in Dragonfly Hollow. I'm a pixie, and I've never left Devashire."

He chuckles darkly. "Hmm. I'm overdue for a visit to Dragonfly. Maybe we'll run into each other and you can tell me about your little secret." The line goes dead.

A fit of coughing overcomes me, and a prickly orange seed scrapes up my throat. Anxiety. I spit it into my hand along with a spatter of blood. It's been a long time since I let an emotion manifest like this. Maybe it's my proximity to my family's garden and the redemptive power of our reunion there that has revived the ability in me. Maybe it's the sheer terror Donovan stirs within me. Or it could just be my return to Devashire and the overwhelming intensity of the emotions I'm experiencing daily. *Damn,* I need a hot bath and a serenity candle.

I stare at the seed, a strong, innate desire to plant it squeezing my gut. Instead, I toss it to the sidewalk and grind it under my heel. I don't intend to foster this emotion. Donovan isn't worth it.

By the time I walk through my parents' front door, I'm exhausted and feeling tremendously sorry for myself again. I'm thirty-four years old and living in my parents' house. I'm being forced to follow the orders of an arrogant, pretentious leprechaun who's responsible for the most humiliating moment of my life. A federal agent has it out for me. Could things get any worse?

"We have to talk about signing Arden up for school," my mother says when I walk in the door.

Yes, yes, it can definitely get worse.

"What brought this up?" I join her in the kitchen where Arden is helping her bake moon-shaped cookies. She greets me with a peck on the cheek.

My mother raises an eyebrow. "Well, *she* did! She hasn't graduated high school yet, Sophia. You're here to stay, and she said she's halfway through her semester. We need to get her enrolled so that she graduates on time. Arden was telling me she's already been accepted at a college in North Carolina."

I brush the hair back from Arden's face. "She has. She's brilliant."

Arden smiles proudly. "I haven't missed much school yet. Just a few days. But I only have six weeks left, and if we have to stay here, well... I don't care about walking in the ceremony, but I have to graduate."

I rub her back. "Right. Absolutely. We do need to figure something out. We will figure something out." Gods, I'm exhausted. "I'll call your old school and see if you can finish online."

My mom and Arden exchange knowing looks.

"You two look like you're conspiring. What's going on?"

Arden gives me an exaggerated, toothy grin. "It's just... I'm going to be here for months, and you're going to be here for... maybe forever. I thought it would be nice to go to school here, maybe make some friends in an actual classroom."

I shake my head, shocked my mother didn't put this to rest immediately. "The schools here have an entirely different curriculum, Arden. It's impossible. Mom, didn't you tell her?"

I look expectantly at my mother but she just shrugs.

"We can always ask, Sophia. Arden has Godmother's blessing to stay. That goes a long way."

Threading her fingers under her chin, Arden smiles wider. She bounces on her toes. I can't tell her no when she's like this.

"I'll talk to the headmistress," I say. "Maybe something can be done."

"Cool! I'm going to text Jayden!" Arden leaves the kitchen and heads for her room. Jayden is her best friend from school. Another pang of guilt hits me that I've taken her from her support system. I am, however, relieved that she has her phone and can continue the relationship. Her *phone*.

Grasping the bridge of my nose, I groan. I hear Donovan's voice in my head *...your little secret.*

"What's wrong? You look like your brain is going to explode." Mom pulls a finished batch of cookies from the oven and slides in another sheet.

"It might. FIRE knows about Arden. Donovan linked me back to the cell phone account under my previous alias."

Mom raises a hand to her mouth. "What?"

I hold up the phone. "Seven gave me this phone and put it in my real name. Donovan called me on it not thirty minutes after. Arden's phone was on that same account under an alias. I have to assume he knows about her, maybe not her real name, but he knows she exists. And if he knows she exists, he's likely already suspended her passport."

"Oh dear."

"If Arden leaves Dragonfly, and Donovan has suspended or flagged her papers, he'll find her. He'll try to use her to get to me. I'm not sure it's even going to be safe for her to go to college unless I can get Godmother to pull some political strings."

Mom wipes her hands aggressively on a kitchen towel. "Let's think about this. Arden is human passing, and she was born there. She's a citizen. They can't do anything to her."

I shake my head. "They can do a lot. She aided and abetted me. They know now that she's part fae."

Mom frowns in my direction. Her gaze darts toward the stairs before she says in a low voice. "Devashire has a highly rated medical school. Maybe she could stay here."

I sigh. "It would break her heart. Honestly, I'm not sure how I'm going to pay for it no matter where she goes. I need to go to the bank. I had a half dozen accounts under aliases in the human world. Maybe there's one Donovan hasn't found yet."

"You know you're welcome to what we have, but I'm afraid it's not much," she offers. "The store is as successful as ever, but Mr. Jinx has raised our rent."

My parents run a gift shop in Dragonfly. Because they live here and are characters, their residence is inexpensive, but they have to rent the space to run their shop from a greedy leprechaun. The margins are thin.

"I couldn't take your money."

She holds her head. "Sophia, I'm so sorry. What a mess. I shouldn't have raised Arden's hopes by talking to her about college without checking with you first. I just assumed she belonged in school."

"It's okay, Mom. You didn't know, and it has to be addressed."

She presses her lips together and plants her hands on her hips. "You know, Bailiwick's Academy might be the answer regardless. The fae curriculum is different, but she's certainly capable of catching up."

"Without luck? She'll be at a disadvantage."

She scoffs. "You know half those kids aren't as smart as her using all the luck in their bodies."

"True."

Mom pulls me into a tight hug. "It's going to be all right. You've survived much worse than this. Kids are resilient. Arden will adapt no matter what happens. Plus, you don't know *for sure* that Donovan knows about her."

. . .

I MELT INTO HER EMBRACE, HOPING WITH EVERYTHING IN me that she's right. We're interrupted when Arden calls down the stairs. "Mom, my phone isn't working!"

Pulling back, I meet my mother's empathetic gaze. "He knows."

"IT'S EMPTY TOO." PENELOPE HAWTHORNE GIVES ME A sympathetic look. I'm at Wingtrust Bank of Dragonfly, and she's painstakingly helped me verify that each and every one of the accounts I'd had in the human world has been seized by FIRE.

"Even the one in the Caymans?"

She nods. "Emptied and closed. There's a note on the account that it was confiscated by the US government."

I shake my head. "Looks like Donovan has left no stone unturned."

"I'm sorry, Sophia. Is there anything else you'd like me to try?" She looks at me hopefully.

The list in my hand grows blurry. "Nope. That was the last one."

"Fuck."

"Yeah."

"I can help you apply for a loan, but they're going to want two weeks of paystubs."

I sigh. "No job yet."

She twirls her hair around her finger. "I can recommend you for a position here," she whispers, "but the boss is a leprechaun, and he hasn't hired anyone new in ages. Rumor is we're on the verge of a restructuring."

"Don't worry about me. I've got something lined up." I have nothing lined up, but the idea of working at a bank for a stingy leprechaun turns my stomach.

"So..." She tips her head from side to side. "You want to grab lunch?"

I laugh. "You've just learned I don't have a dime to my name."

"My treat. Please, Sophia. There's something I want to do, and I need a friend to do it."

I look at my watch. It's noon. All I want to do is go home and sleep until an idea of what to do next pops into my head, but the hopeful look on Pen's face is impossible to deny. I don't have the heart to tell her no. And let's be honest, I need all the friends I can get. "Sure."

Twenty minutes later, I'm sitting on the back of a giant bumblebee, eating a cucumber sandwich at a glass table twenty feet in the air. Penelope is beaming, face turned toward the sunshine. "Interesting choice," I say.

"I never get to come here. Flick is afraid of heights, and the kids are too wiggly. I always worry they'll jump. I mean they both can fly, but I don't trust that they won't get caught up in the gears." Pen is sitting atop a purple butterfly with a golden saddle, sipping champagne.

The place *is* charming. It's called Garden Party and consists of two dozen such tables revolving around a giant mechanical rabbit wearing a top hat. "Glad I could be your excuse to come then." I clink my glass against hers.

"It's just..." She shifts in her saddle. "I love Flick, but life can get so... *dull.* And all the pixies here are the same. If I listen to Swallow Everlane talk about her rosewater cookies one more time, I think my head is going to explode. I mean they're not even good! It's all the same people, Sophia. We're all older, but it's just like high school."

"You mean they're still all talking about me behind my back?" I sip my drink.

"They never stopped talking about you. You're the most exciting thing to ever happen to Bailiwick's." We both laugh at the truth in it.

"What was it like out there anyway?" she asks me. "You must have felt so free! To do anything you wanted, whenever you wanted... It must have been amazing." Her eyes twinkle with excitement.

Crap on a cracker, she's completely romanticized my life journey. I'm tempted to just nod my head and let her go on thinking I'm some sort of adventurer, but in the end, I can't bring myself to do it. What if she does something stupid, like leave Flick and try to follow in my footsteps?

"It wasn't like that," I say. "It wasn't what I wanted. It was what I had to do to survive."

Her smile fades. "In what way? It couldn't have been all bad or you wouldn't have stayed gone."

Gah, here we go. At least we're in the air. It would take effort for her to fly away. "I was pregnant with Arden. Pregnant the human way by a human man."

She inhales sharply. "I'd wondered."

"I knew if I stayed things would be difficult."

Her face falls. "You'd be lucky if Godmother allowed you to carry the pregnancy," she says boldly.

"I find it refreshing to hear someone else acknowledge that out loud."

"I'm sure everyone denies it, but you know if you'd stayed that's how it would be."

I nod, beyond grateful for Penelope's company. She actually looks like she might understand. "I think everyone should make their own choices when it comes to motherhood, and I'm sure that another pixie might have stayed and happily allowed Godmother to undo her pregnancy."

"But?"

"But for me, I knew her. Even before the doctor confirmed I was pregnant the human way, I felt Arden. She was this other presence... *becoming* inside me, like a candle burning in the window of my soul. I couldn't risk that they might blow her out."

Pen places a hand over her mouth, then lowers it slowly. "I think you did the right thing, Soph."

I give her a nod, and she reaches across the table to squeeze my hand. "But it wasn't easy. I was homeless for a while. I had to use illusion to survive."

The space between her brows puckers, but she remains silent.

"I ended up playing poker to support us. I survived sixteen years by pushing my luck. Always running. Changing our names. I tried my best to give Arden a normal American life, but never think it was better than what you have here, Pen. You have love. You have a family. Who wouldn't want that?"

She reaches for the bottle at the end of our table and refills our glasses. "Well then, I'd like to propose a toast." I raise my glass and return her smile. "To being happy with what we have but open to new beginnings."

We both drink.

"Maybe now that you've returned, the promise of love and family is back on the table for you," she says through a smile.

I chuckle. "I think that ship has sailed."

"Bull pucky. There are plenty of single pixies in this town who would sell their best shirt for a chance at a gorgeous woman like you."

"Along with the chance to raise a half-human daughter?"

Her smile fades a little. "If they're worth their salt."

"Meh, I've already found my one true love."

"Oh?" She raises her eyebrows and leans in as if I'm about to share some luscious gossip. "Please don't tell me it's a leprechaun. I've never trusted them, not for a day. The looks, the charm, the wealth? Can you imagine being married to that?"

I laugh. "Not that I disagree, but you're not making a great case against them."

"Oh yes I am. It would be all about them. You'd be a moon in their orbit. Who would ever see *you*, lost in the shadow of their shiny existence?"

"Yeah, I guess it would be like being with a Hollywood celebrity or something."

"So reassure me that the center of your affection isn't a leprechaun." She holds up a finger. "And, fair warning, if you tell me it's Seven, I'm hauling you straight to the psych ward."

I shake my head. "No, not a leprechaun and definitely not Seven." I hate the way I have to look away when I say that. "It's Arden." I smile. "She takes up every inch of space in my heart. I don't think there's room for anyone else."

Penelope sighs. "Makes sense. For now." She grins. "Speaking of Arden, I don't suppose she'd consider babysitting for a pixie mom who badly needs a date night?"

I play with my hair and sip my wine. "I'll ask her. I think she'd like that."

"Sophia?"

"Yeah?"

"I'm glad you're back," Pen says. "You are a breath of fresh air."

I look at her, really look at her atop her butterfly, and I get it. She needs a friend as much as I do. "Me too."

CHAPTER
THIRTEEN

After sunset, I make my way down to the beach where River already has a bonfire blazing. A group of satyrs and pixies have gathered on logs around the fire. I wonder if I'll recognize more of them once I'm closer. It's been a long time. People change. I wonder how much I've changed and if they'll recognize me.

A shirtless satyr with a neatly trimmed rack of antlers and low-slung cargo shorts stands and lifts a ukulele into his arms. Voices call out song requests, and soon cheerful music fills the night. By the time I sit down on a log beside River, I'm already smiling.

"Is that Patrick?" I ask, remembering the class clown who used to keep us all in stitches.

"The one and only." He wraps an arm around my shoulders and pulls me into a one-armed hug. "He's on the Dragonfly building crew now but never lost his talent for music." River gives me a smile that lights up the night, then goes on to introduce me to the others. I remember five of the seven, although I wasn't close to any of them. Still, they smile warmly

—some of them drunkenly—and I feel more accepted than I ever thought possible.

"Thank you for inviting me," I tell him. "I needed this."

His hand lands on my thigh and squeezes. "No one holds any of that crap against you, Sophia. Well, none of us anyway. Just stay away from the fuckhead leprechauns."

River's smile is infectious, and I turn my attention back to Patrick's song. River pops off the log and retrieves a goblet of wine for me from a cart parked near the woods. It's elderberry. Delicious.

"Speaking of fuckheads, how did it go with Seven?" He lowers his voice slightly. I look around the fire. No one else is paying the least bit of attention to us, so I tell him the truth. If anyone can help with this case, it's River. He sees and hears everything.

"Happened March 20. A man was killed," I whisper.

His brows rise, and he turns his full attention on me. "On the equinox? That is big. How did they manage to keep that a secret?"

I shrug. "Godmother spent a fair bit of magic hiding it. Apparently the victim had a thing for pixies and frequented the Dragonfly Club." I pull Wing_Gurl's picture from my back pocket and hand it to him. "Do you know who this is under all that illusion? We think she was the last one to see him alive."

River takes the paper from me and whistles. "Interesting. The plot thickens."

I take another sip of my wine. "What do you know, River?"

He sobers as he stares at the photo. "I've seen that illusion before, on a pixie named Phoebe Willowbark."

"Do you know where I can find her? I just want to ask her a few questions."

The corner of his mouth tugs downward when he looks back at me, and I realize it's one of the few times I've ever seen

River frown. "That's the thing. Phoebe went missing on March 20."

I start, open my mouth, and close it again. "Missing? Like missing as in no one knows where she is at all? No contact with anyone?" He knows what I mean. Sometimes pixies go on trips with their human boyfriends, but in those cases they usually let their families know they are okay.

He shakes his head. "Missing as in dropped off the face of the earth."

I furrow my brow. "Does Godmother know about this? Is someone looking into it?"

He chuckles darkly. "You have been gone a long time if you think the powers that be care about a missing pixie, especially one who was last seen in the Dragonfly Club."

"Was she, uh, in the sex trade?" I ask uncomfortably.

"People assume she left Devashire to be a high-end escort for her human john. It's not unheard of, but I call bullshit. I think it's an excuse for the powers that be not to look into the matter."

"The March 20 timing is suspect. It could be a coincidence, but it's definitely something to look into. What did she look like without her illusion?"

He pulls his phone from his pocket and navigates to a webpage with multiple pictures of the beautiful dark-haired pixie smiling with friends. "Her family set this up to get her face out there, help spread the word that she's missing. Special person. Loved it when she came into the restaurant."

I study Phoebe's face on the screen. I don't recognize her, but she looks younger than me. "Thanks, I'll let you know what I find out."

He groans. "I don't think Phoebe's disappearance is related to the murder you're investigating."

"How come?"

"Phoebe wasn't the first pixie to go missing the way she did."

"Huh?"

"Over the years, I've heard whispers of a predator who targets pixies at that club. There are five others, vanished without a trace, the first going back to before you left. No one has done a thing to try to find them or the one responsible. Their families have tried to pool their resources to hire a private investigator, but no one will take their case."

The idea that crimes against multiple pixies have been reported but no one has taken them seriously makes me sick. Unfortunately though, it doesn't surprise me. "I'm not an investigator, but I'll do what I can to look into Phoebe's disappearance, even if it's not related to Michael's murder. I'm going to the Dragonfly Club tomorrow night to ask around. I'll ask about Phoebe as well."

He gives me a nod of gratitude and polishes off his wine. "Just be careful what you tell fuckstain. He's head of security, and he's not going to take kindly to being called out about this."

I think about that and flash back to Seven firing Brandon for his ineptitude. Seven runs a tight ship. He would definitely take offense at the accusation that his people didn't investigate six missing persons cases due to prejudice. "I'll keep it to myself until I know more."

River's brown eyes twinkle in the moonlight. We watch Patrick sing while we drink our wine. Several minutes pass, and I see a couple of satyrs at the edge of the firelight start to kiss. The man's hand drops between the woman's legs. I snap my attention back to the fire.

"So now that you're back..." River's smile has returned, and he turns it on me. "...would you care to take a lover?"

I almost fall off the log. With widened eyes, I ask, "Why? Are you volunteering for the position?"

He grins. "We were good friends, you and me. It could be fun. Friends with benefits as the humans say."

The proposition isn't exactly surprising. River's never hidden his attraction to me, and he's not the type to be ashamed or uncomfortable about sex. But the feeling isn't reciprocated. I do find River objectively attractive, but I'm not attracted to him. Chemistry is one of those things that's either there for me or it isn't. In this case it isn't. When I'm with River, all I feel is kinship, like he's my brother or something. I try not to compare it to the fireworks that go off in my body when I'm around Seven, but I can't help but think of that now. I don't want Seven either, but I hope to have that type of chemistry with someone who deserves it one day.

Besides, as much as I like to think of myself as a modern woman, I'm not into casual sex. My cheeks grow warm, and it's not from the fire. "I'm afraid we'll have to stay benefit-free. My crazy heart just doesn't work like yours, River. I know myself, and deep down, I want love and monogamy. I care for you too much to ruin our friendship with sex."

He laughs darkly. "Have we met?" he jokes.

"Seriously," I say. "Your heart is much too large for one person, and I'm a one-person girl. It would never work."

"Got it. It's important to be honest with oneself about these things, although I can't say I'm not disappointed." Another satyr comes by with a pitcher and refills our glasses. "Friends then!" He clinks his goblet against mine.

We continue watching Patrick sing and play. I'm amazed how comfortable I feel considering the conversation we just had. The wine flows, and we chat about everything from the moon to my experience working as a poker pro. I'm feeling a little tipsy by the time I remember the other thing I planned to ask him.

"Uh, River, do you have any jobs open at the tavern? I need to find work. It seems that FIRE has confiscated all my assets."

"Aww, I'm sorry Sophia. I'm all staffed up," he says regretfully. "I'll make room on the schedule for you if you need it, but it won't be full time. Seems like a waste of talent though."

"What do you mean?"

"You should apply to be a dealer at the casino. You're more than qualified, and the pay there is stellar, far better than a server at a tavern. I'm sure fuckhead would put in a good word for ya. He owes you as much."

I groan. Everything he suggests is true, but the idea of having to potentially see Seven—or worse, his father—every day turns my stomach. "Ugh, working for leprechauns? I think I'd rather poke myself in the eye repeatedly with broken glass."

His smile tells me he understands. "Ask me again if you want me to take a shoehorn to the schedule."

"Thanks, Riv. I'm going to try to find something else, but I'll be in touch if I'm desperate."

"Nothing I like better than a desperate woman asking for my assistance." He gives a deep chuckle and sips from his wine. We stare toward the fire.

The night unfolds around us until there are so many writhing bodies in the darkness that I start to feel awkward pressure to join in. I hug River good night and slip back into the theme park through the CHARACTER'S ONLY door near River's Tavern. A streetlamp casts an ochre glow over a red cobblestone walkway. I jump when I see Seven standing in the shadows just beyond.

"What are you doing here?" I blurt.

He steps into the brightness, and in my inebriated state, I forget to guard myself against the impact of his presence. It's late, and he's traded his suit for a black T-shirt and distressed jeans. His eyes crinkle at the corners as he takes me in, but his smile is too shallow to have caused them. The smile is a ruse to hide something more. He studies me with intense interest.

"Following up on a noise complaint," he says, but I detect a lie in his voice, and I call him on it.

"Bullshit. You're following me."

He steps in closer, his gaze almost predatory. I sense his luck rise around him. It slithers by me, raw, feral energy, and I can't hold back a shiver. His hand lifts to cradle my jaw and run his thumb across my bottom lip. "Fine. Then let's just say I came because I wanted to make sure you were safe."

"I'm a big girl, Seven. I can take care of myself."

He looks at me through impossibly long lashes. "Yes you can. I've always known that about you, from the day we met."

"I was six when you met me."

"You were a very precocious and wise six-year-old."

I'd heard someone crying in the woods behind our school. Seven was there, alone and miserable. I told him funny stories, and we took him back to my house where Mom fed him cookies and eventually escorted him home. I had no idea at the time that it was odd for a leprechaun to cry or that a pixie with any sense wouldn't befriend a leprechaun. I just saw a sad person and wanted to make him happy. My parents must have approved of that plan because they welcomed him in with open arms.

"What were you crying about that day anyway?" I ask, realizing my child's mind had never thought to ask.

"I don't remember." I sense he's lying. "I was using luck to keep people away. It didn't work on you."

I giggle, the effects of the wine making me sway on my feet. "How *did* I do that?"

"I've always had a blind spot for you, Sophia." A ghost of a smile flits across his face. "Also, I was young and had focused my luck on distracting anyone who wasn't a true friend. I didn't expect a true friend would find me. I definitely didn't expect she'd be a pixie."

A lump forms in my throat. "I *was* your friend, and you were mine. Best friends back then, although I suppose you'd never admit it now."

"I admit it. Even my father would. We were together all the time."

"That's right." An early memory of his house in Elderberry Hills comes back to me. His father was indifferent then, and his mother was cool but friendly enough. "The problem didn't start until later, when we became more than friends, did it? That's when you chickened out and pushed me away." I swallow down the lump.

"He'll never be what you need," Seven murmurs, his gaze drifting toward the door I've just come through. "River is too mundane for you. You've always been a thrill seeker. You want the excitement of the big win. It's why you love poker. You've never wanted anything that came easy."

I sneer at him, angry that his words hit a little too close to home. "You don't know shit about me."

He shakes his head. "Then give me a chance to know you again..." His face is close to mine, and my inner Teenage Sophia, what's left of her, thinks it would be a great idea to kiss him, maybe fool around a little in the shadowy grove of trees behind River's. It would feel so good. All that luck would rush into me, a hot and effervescent jet stream. I remember how addictive it felt, being the center of Seven's attention, the focus of all that power. It would be a heady thing. I step in closer until we are chest to chest and there's a flare of heat in his emerald eyes. Teenage Sophia is reveling in the growing erection pressing into her hip.

Thank the gods Adult Sophia is in control and she knows better. I clutch my proverbial cards to my chest and snap my poker face back into place, shaking off his touch and backing out of reach.

"Go home, Seven. Use all that luck on something more important than following me around, like dealing with that erection." I pantomime him tossing off, turn, and stride for home. He doesn't follow me.

CHAPTER

FOURTEEN

"**M**om? Are you still asleep?"

I prop one eyelid open to see Arden hovering over me. She's grimacing and holding a very large box with a giant black silk bow tied around it. I roll my eyeball in its sandy socket toward the clock.

"Is that right?" I mumble.

"It's *noon*! Are you sick? Why are you still in bed?" Arden sets the box on my desk and reaches for my forehead like she's going to test my temperature. Instead, she stops about a foot from me and sniffs the air. "Oh my God, you're drunk!"

"I'm not drunk." I pop open both eyes and do a self-assessment. Am I still drunk? No. Definitely not. I hold up my hand, my thumb and forefinger a few centimeters apart. "I'm a teensy bit hungover. Totally different."

"Mom!" Arden's eyes widen.

I blink a few times and sit up with a groan. "Honestly, Arden. After all that's happened the past few days and all you've learned, the thing that surprises you the most is that for the first time in sixteen years, I drank a little too much last night?"

She folds her arms and pops her hip out. "You'd never let me get away with this."

"I'll make you a deal. When you're thirty-four like I am now, I will definitely let you get away with it. I'll even watch your little rug rats while you do it, if you have any."

A giggle bursts from her lips. "You are not a normal mom."

"Never." I stand and pull her into an obnoxious hug. "By the way, I'm still working on that school thing. I'm going to call the headmistress Monday, as soon as the school opens. I had to visit the bank yesterday." I stop short of telling her there was nothing left in our accounts. I don't want to worry her. "I doubt I'd catch anyone this afternoon, and there's something I have to do for Godmother."

"I'm not missing anything this weekend anyway," she says, although I can see she's disappointed.

"We're going to get you back in school. I promise." I have no idea how I'll accomplish this promise, but for Arden, I'll find a way. "Now what have you brought me?" I move to the box. My mouth feels lined with cotton, and I desperately need a coffee, but this gift looks important.

"It's not from me!" she says. "A satyr delivered it for you this morning. Cutest guy I've seen since we arrived and my age too. I *definitely* want to go to school here."

Part of me wants to warn her off all fae men, but that's not really fair. Arden's always had a good head on her shoulders. No man will ever be good enough for her, but I hope someday she finds someone who's worth her time, either fairy or human. Someone who thinks the sun rises because of her.

"We'll work on it," I say, then turn my attention to the box and tug at the ends of the ribbon. The bow unravels, the dark strip of silk falling away. Lifting the top off, at first all I see is elaborately patterned tissue paper. Intrigued, I unfold it.

"Wow," Arden says. "Is that a dress?"

Pinching the plum fabric between my fingers, I lift it from the packaging. "Part of one," I mumble. I hold it up to my body and turn toward the mirror. It's off the shoulder and backless with a lace-covered bodice adorned in beads and sequins. Below the waist, plum silk flares out in flirty scallops that hit well above my knee.

"There's jewelry in here too. And shoes!" Arden holds up a delicate necklace of ornately crafted diamonds and amethyst flowers, matching earrings, and a diamond cuff bracelet. In her other hand is a slinky stiletto. "I thought you had to wear Cinderella dresses. Is this allowed?"

"Any gown is allowed as long as it covers the important parts," I say, although in practice there is only one place a pixie would wear a dress like this. I dig in the box and find a card at the bottom. In Seven's even scrawl it reads, *Look the part. I'll pick you up at eight.*

My mother gives a long, low whistle as she assesses my appearance. "Gods above, Sophia. You are a beautiful woman, and that is one fabulous dress."

I smooth my hand over the waist and release a deep breath. "Thanks. I just wish there was a little more of it."

"Seven sent it?" She admires it appreciatively when I nod my head. "He knows what he's doing. This is how the pixies who frequent the Dragonfly Club dress. You'll fit in... have a better chance of getting them to talk. And you won't need as much illusion."

"Right." I tug at the hem, but it's not getting any closer to my knees. I'm just relieved that my father took Arden into town to go shopping and she's not here to heckle me.

"How is Seven?" Mom asks, her fingers tangling in front of her stomach.

"Still an asshole."

She snorts. "I know what he did to you was terrible, but it's hard for my mother's heart not to picture him as that sweet boy who first walked through my door."

I pause, remembering something I'd wanted to ask her. "Do you remember what happened that day to him? Why was he crying?"

She sighs. "I'm not surprised you don't know. You were too young to understand." She smooths her hair. "His parents forgot about him."

"Huh?"

"It was the end of the day, and I was volunteering at Baili-wick's. I'd offered to clean up your grade one classroom, so we were the last ones out of the school. You heard him crying in the woods behind the playground and ran to him as if he were a lost kitten in need of rescue. Maybe he was. The boy was a puddle of tears by the time you brought him to me. His parents simply forgot about him, left him at school. Do you know, when I dropped him off at that fancy house of theirs, his mother didn't even apologize? Just wrangled him inside and shut the door."

I close my eyes for a second, trying to reconcile my adult mind with my child's experience. "Wait... they forgot about him? But they're leprechauns! That doesn't sound very lucky."

Mom runs her hand along the misshapen knitted blanket on the back of our couch. "Luck only works when you focus on something. That woman never focused on Seven or Evangeline. Her eyes... it was like she was dead inside. That family might be made of luck and swim in pools of money, but they've never spent an ounce of it on learning to love each other, Sophia. Frankly, I've always thought the lot of them seemed a bit miserable."

I think back to the early days. Seven and Evangeline were always warm to each other and to me, but their parents were largely absent and always indifferent until the end when Chase Delaney was openly hostile to me. Mom is right. Something was missing in their family.

For some reason, the realization that Seven had a troubled family life weighs heavily on my heart. I tell myself that I don't care, that it's been long over between us and what happened back then doesn't matter, but my heart aches of its own accord. I think what bothers me most is that I never noticed. Even my seventeen-year-old self never thought to ask Seven if he was treated well at home. I'd just assumed that because he was a leprechaun—rich and gorgeous—that he couldn't have any problems as common as a poor home life.

I glance at my watch. "I'm going to be late."

Mom follows me to the foyer. "Better hurry then. Wise if you're out of here before your father sees you anyway." She chuckles. "Good luck tonight."

With a peck to her cheek, I'm out the door.

The thing about living in a theme park is that when someone says they'll pick you up, they don't mean at your front door. Dragonfly Hollow consists of five separate but connected parks. Wonderland, Dragonfly After Dark, Sunrise Kingdom, Thrilldare Island, and a water park called Mermaid Cove. My parents live in Wonderland, which includes the Enchantment subdivision, Godmother's tearoom, Bailiwick's Academy, and River's Tavern, as well as a main street full of shops like my parents', a fae learning center, and a selection of rides and entertainment. It's a family park that is appropriate for all ages.

Where I'm going tonight is not. Dragonfly After Dark is home to a world-class hotel and spa, the Dragonfly Casino, as well as a variety of taverns and adult-entertainment venues—improv comedy clubs, sexy magic acts, and darkly lit and intimate music venues. But the cornerstone of the After Dark theme park is the Dragonfly Club.

The entrance to After Dark is about ten miles from the entrance to Wonderland, which means we have to drive there. Only no cars are allowed inside the theme parks themselves. When I visited Seven at the casino yesterday, I got there by riding a character shuttle that runs during the day from the circle drive outside the front of Wonderland to the one outside After Dark. That's as close as Seven can get to pick me up.

My stilettos click on the sidewalk, and anxiety worms its way into my brain again. I'm going to meet Seven. I'm going to have to ride in his car with all that masculine energy and tightly coiled power. Anticipation zings through me. Damn it, why am I still attracted to this man? It's like he's a sore tooth I can't keep from poking with my tongue. I wish I could take the shuttle, but it's done running for the day.

When I reach the circle drive, it doesn't take any detective work to know which car is his. A sleek black Mercedes roadster is parked by the curb, and the man himself is leaning up against it, looking annoyed. His eyes rake over me, from my hair that I've left down in loose curls to the shoes he bought me and then back up again. His expression is pained.

"What's up your ass?" I ask.

"You're late."

"You try walking a half mile in these things," I say, pointing at my feet.

His eyes catch on the hem of my dress. If anything, it's even shorter on than it looked when I held it up to myself. It barely covers my ass. The corner of his mouth turns down slightly, and it makes me smile. He bought this thing for me and insisted I wear it. If he doesn't like it, there's only one person to blame, and it's not me.

He opens the car door. "Get in."

I do, careful to tuck my skirt beneath me. He rounds the car and climbs in the driver's side, but he doesn't start the engine right away. Instead, he just stares at my bodice.

"Do you have a problem with this dress?" I snap.

His gaze lifts to meet mine, and I see heat there. Desire. In my mind, I'm thrown back to an earlier time when he was mine. Fire rushes to my core, and I can feel myself grow wet. I hate that he does this to me. I hate that he can make my stomach flutter with a single glance.

Slowly, he shakes his head, never breaking eye contact. "I don't have a problem with the dress." His voice is lower, gritty. "I have a problem with why you're wearing it. This was a bad idea. Have dinner with me, and we'll come up with a new strategy."

"Dinner?" I ask quizzically. "You want to completely blow off this plan?" I'm flabbergasted. I don't know what he's playing at, but I'm getting whiplash from his mood swings.

"Yes."

"Why?"

"You're not bait." His eyes flick down my dress again.

I swallow. "Seven?"

"Forget it. We'll find another way."

As flattered as I am that he wants to protect me from exploitation, I can't let him pull the plug on tonight. "No," I say firmly. "This is a good idea and our best bet to find a clue to who killed Michael Murphy. I need this." My voice rises in pitch. "FIRE drained my accounts, Seven. I have a kid who needs her tuition paid. As long as I'm working for Godmother, I can't devote myself to working for anyone else. I need to solve this case, and I need to do it quickly. We're doing this." I lean back in the seat and cross my arms.

He focuses all his attention on me, and I battle against a warm, melty feeling that starts in my torso despite my mounting anger. "If this is about money, I'll give you anything you need."

"I'm not taking any more of your money."

"Why not?"

"Because you're a leprechaun from one of the most powerful families in Devashire. Owing someone like you a debt will most certainly come back to haunt me. Maybe not at first. You might have good intentions at the moment. But someday you'll want something, and you won't hesitate to hold it over me. It's in your nature."

He scowls. "I can't deny that it's in my nature to make deals —I am fae after all—but this would be a gift, Sophia, just like when I rescued you from FIRE."

I scoff. "Yes, we can't forget about that, can we? Fae are so good about giving gifts without strings attached."

He runs a hand down his face, looking utterly frustrated. "You know I wouldn't hold it over you."

"I don't know you at all."

That draws a flinch as if I've hit him. "I *wouldn't* hold it over you."

I close my eyes and take a deep breath, blowing it out slowly. "You bought me this dress, Seven. This is our plan, and it's a good one. Now do your fucking job and drive us to After Dark."

He turns to stare out the windshield, a muscle in his jaw twitching. I think he's grinding his teeth. With a shake of his head, he starts the engine. "You're too smart to be used like this."

"Yeah, and sometimes smart people have to do things they'd rather not do."

A dark look overtakes his features, but he doesn't say anything else.

I lean back against the leather seat and stare out the window as he drives toward After Dark, trying to keep my breathing shallow so that I don't sniff the crisp cedar-and-grapefruit scent that wafts off his skin. It's light, clean, and elegant, and it clings to him like the silky fabric of his black shirt. *Oof.*

"So did you have a good time with River last night?" he says, a hint of displeasure in his voice.

My head whips around. Is now really the time to revisit last night? "Yes."

He growls low in his throat.

"Why were you there last night anyway?"

"We'd had a noise complaint."

I shake my head. "You were waiting for me."

"I told you, I wanted to make sure you were safe."

"But how did you even know I was there?"

"I'm head of security here. There are eyes everywhere, Sophia."

I scoff. "But why would those eyes care what *I* was doing? Do you sit alone in your room at night and watch security videos? Seems depraved even for you."

A muscle in his jaw jerks. "In case you've forgotten, there's a FIRE agent with a major hard-on for you out there. Frankly, I'm afraid you'll get caught in his net or, worse, you might run again. I pulled a lot of strings to get you this arrangement with Godmother. I can't have River screwing it up by exposing you."

The high-pitched sound that comes out of my throat is offense made audible. "You can fuck the hell off, Seven. I don't recall Godmother charging you with being my babysitter. Find someone else to toss off to while you sit home alone watching surveillance videos."

His face remains impassive, but a tiny muscle in his eye twitches. He drives faster. After a minute or so, I say, "If you must know, I had the best time until I ran into you on the street. Elderberry wine flowed. The fire raged. Music filled the star-scattered sky…"

"And what about River?" he asks through his teeth.

I smooth my skirt. "River was a perfect gentleman."

Seven pulls into After Dark and parks in a spot near the front reserved for security vehicles. Must be nice.

"You're honestly telling me that the satyr didn't try to get up your skirt?" All this time, he's been focused on the road. Now his clover-colored eyes flash as he turns his head to face me.

I snort. I can't help it. It's just so ridiculous. Is Seven actually jealous? After the way he and his father treated me? "No," I say simply. "I didn't say that at all. I just said he was a *perfect* gentleman." I open the door and stagger out of the car before he can ruin the moment with his own barb.

He's out and after me in a heartbeat. "Did he take you right there on the beach with the others watching? Is that how you like it now?"

Poker face. That's all he gets from me. "I thought your security cameras saw everything?"

"Not the beach," he mumbles.

I stop short, and something clicks. Growing up, Seven would often take me to that beach. I always thought it was to get away from the human guests. Now I realize he was hiding. No one could see us there, maybe especially not leprechaun-run security. The revelation doesn't sit well. "Too bad for you. You'll just have to use your imagination."

He makes a very un-leprechaun-like sound. There's

nothing smooth or elegant about it. It's all male and completely feral.

"What do you care anyway, Seven? It's none of your business who's been up my skirt."

I'm a little ahead of him when suddenly his arm shoots around my waist and scoops me behind the hedgerow near the front gates. My breath leaves my lungs as I'm smashed against his chest. With the added height of my stilettos, we're face-to-face, and a flock of butterflies takes flight within me, their wings fluttering against the walls of my stomach and stirring up fizzy bubbles in my blood.

"What if I want it to be my business?" he says, his warm hand pressing into the arch of my back.

"You gave up that right when you abandoned and humiliated me." I have to say this aloud and repeat it in my head to counteract my body's exuberance at being in his arms again. Stupid body. I thought it had been the alcohol last night, but I'm completely sober now and it's all I can do not to be drawn in.

"I didn't—" He cuts himself off with a shake of his head. "What happened to you was wrong... awful and unforgivable. But I hope you will forgive me one day."

He releases me, leaving me standing before him, completely speechless. Did Seven Delaney just apologize to me? I'm gaping, trying to decide how to respond, when he straightens, filling every corner of his suit with confidence.

"Change your appearance," he commands. His shift from apologetic to alpha boss man gives me whiplash. "You're going to walk in on my arm, and you need to look like my escort. For this to work, no one can recognize you."

I balk at his bossiness but am too flustered to argue about it. He's probably right. The rumors traveled far and wide about what happened between us. If people remember, they may avoid me. My goal tonight is to be one of them, to put them at ease.

I use a little luck and make my skin and hair lighter, my eyes and lips larger, and change the shape of my face from an oval to a heart shape. I don't need a mirror to know I look completely different.

He frowns but holds out his arm. "Let's go."

As we walk into the park and head for the club, I realize that not a single human in the dozens entering seemed to notice Seven pulling me behind the bushes or the two of us bounding out of them now. Then I remember I'm with a leprechaun. No one noticed because he's lucky. One flex of his power and every mind within range was distracted with something else at the precise time he needed them to be. Damn. It's a reminder of the position I'm in.

Seven is even more powerful now than I remember. He can have anything he wants. He's a deadly, fire-breathing beast of a man with almost unlimited resources, and I'm over here poking him with a stick and reminding him of that time he hurt my feelings when I was a kid. I seriously need to learn to keep my mouth shut.

At the door to the club, we walk right past the long line of humans waiting to get inside. Seven's hand rests in the small of my back again in that possessive way that's becoming an annoying habit. My dress is backless, and his fingers are warm against my bare skin, his thumb dusting over my spine. He escorts me past a man in a black suit at the VIP entrance. The bouncer's gaze passes right over me as he nods at Seven and opens the door for him.

The thump of the bass reverberates in my chest, and I'm transported back to the last time I was here, the night of the Yule Ball.

CHAPTER

FIFTEEN

16 YEARS AGO

Cruel. The word echoed in my mind as I lay in bed the night of the Yule Ball. Chance Delaney confirmed that Seven had stood me up, that the ribbon, the invitation, everything was a painful, humiliating joke. "Seven did you a favor..."

Hurt and mortification seeped like rot to my bones, flooding my face with new tears. Images of people laughing at me flashed through my head. Was I any better than a worm caught under a shoe? I was a joke, the laughingstock of Devashire. And the most humiliating part was realizing how naive I'd been. Why had I assumed the social order wouldn't apply to me? I was a pixie. He was a leprechaun. Any relationship we'd had was destined to fail.

How many people had warned me? No leprechaun would be caught in public with a pixie on his arm. Oh, leprechaun men might enjoy a tryst with a pixie. They might do things in private for their own pleasure, but they did not date, and they did not marry, anyone but other leprechauns. It had always been this way. Why would I think we'd be different?

The problem was I'd taken to heart all the lectures in school about ending bigotry between species. I'd thought modern fae society was ready for change. I dreamed Seven and I would be the first leprechaun/pixie couple to publicly marry. The first but not the last. We'd be boundary breakers. After all, it wasn't so long ago that pixies and satyrs didn't share inter-species relationships, but now mixed couples were common. No one thought anything of it.

But leprechauns were different. Everyone had tried to tell me as much, and I'd ignored them. And the worst part was I'd *saved* myself for him. Almost every girl in my class had lost their virginity. But there I was, still a child at almost eighteen years old.

Miserable, I stared up at the ceiling. I couldn't sleep. There was too much pain. Everything hurt. My humiliation seemed to fill the room from floor to ceiling, pressing against the walls. All at once, I couldn't catch my breath. I ran to the window and threw it open, gasping at the cool night as if I'd been drowning.

I had to get out of that room. I had to blow off steam, or I'd never survive this. It would break me. Either I walked down to the kitchen and found a knife to slit my wrists, or I crawled out that window and found a way to numb the pain. There was really no other option.

Before I could chicken out, I got up, got dressed, and snuck out my window. The shuttle didn't run that late, and it was too far to fly, but I hitched a ride with some human tourists. The bouncer let me in the moment he saw me. I was cute and young, the type of pixie human men loved, plus I'd enhanced my features to make the most of my best attributes. And I must have looked vulnerable. Vulnerability made me catnip to human men, a limping gazelle through a savannah of hungry lions.

I hadn't even made it to the bar before men started buying me drinks. There's no drinking age in Dragonfly, but my parents had one. Had my mother known I was in a club, drinking alcohol with humans, she would have grounded me for the next decade. But I drank every fruity cocktail those men bought for me, and I flirted with every man who would pay me any bit of attention.

Anything to soothe the ache in my heart and the humiliation Seven and his father had doled out. They'd made me feel like nothing. Less than nothing. Worthless. The compliments and flirtation temporarily filled a gaping hole in my heart. I was smart enough to know their words weren't genuine, but I didn't care. Bathing in their attentiveness was the balm I needed that night.

And then *he* walked in. I'd always had a thing for American movie stars, and this man could have passed for one. Dark-haired and blue-eyed, he was tall and unbelievably broad shouldered, with a torso that tapered to a narrow waist. Women—human, pixie, and satyr alike—watched him cross the room. I couldn't tear my eyes away, and when he walked straight up to me, my breath caught in my throat.

"You look like a woman in need of some fun," Dark Stranger said, loud enough to be heard over the throb of the music. "Hard day?"

I loved that he called me a woman and not a pixie, although my wings were out. Humans often made the delineation. "The worst," I said. "My date stood me up. Just ghosted me."

He stepped in closer and leaned one elbow against the bar beside me. Gods, he smelled good, like expensive cologne but with a whiff of the outdoors, like he'd just chopped wood or something. I became temporarily speechless as I fantasized about the man wielding an axe, shirtless. I took a deep breath through my nose.

"Couldn't have been an intelligent man if he stood you up," he said.

"I thought he was," I said truthfully.

"You knew him well then."

"I thought I did."

"Now you're not sure."

I shook my head. When I met his gaze, there were tears blurring mine. "I think... maybe I was a game to him. We were playing a game I didn't even know we were playing, and so I lost."

He wiped a tear from under my eye with his thumb. "How could you ever think that? You're not a game. This man, I have a feeling he'll come crawling back to you with his tail between his legs."

The bartender slid a drink into his hand, the dark amber liquid sloshing as he raised it to his lips. The faint tinge of liquor reached my nose as I leaned forward and said, "Maybe I don't want him to. Sometimes it's just all too hard, you know?" I rested a hand on his forearm.

Those fathomless blue eyes stared right into me. "Tell me something, what did you like about this guy who ghosted you— I mean... before?"

I sipped my drink. All I wanted to do was trash Seven. I didn't want to think about why I'd loved him. I'd rather think about how I was going to wreak vengeance on him. But I found the question impossible to resist.

I stirred my drink with my straw. "I guess it was how he saw me."

"How he looked at you. So it was the attention."

"No, it was how he *saw* me. He's from a different world than I am. It would be easy for him to look down his nose at me.

You probably don't realize this as a human, but pixies aren't always taken seriously."

"I've heard." Dark Stranger smiled at me, but there was nothing condescending in his tone. He seemed legitimately empathetic with my situation.

"When he looked at me, it was like he saw me, beyond the wings, beyond the labels. Like straight into my soul."

He scratched the side of his jaw and chewed on his straw. "I bet I can guess what he saw."

I giggled. He'd known me less than fifteen minutes. This should be good. "Okay. Let's hear it." I straightened and squared my shoulders.

"You are... someone who doesn't settle for what's handed to them. You're a fighter. I bet you'd rather try something ten times and fail over and over, rather than not try at all."

Snorting, I turned on my barstool so that my knees were facing him. "How could you possibly guess that?"

His eyes flicked up to the ceiling. "Well, you've just had your heart torn to shreds, and you're here in this meat market offering it up again. Either you're a glutton for punishment or you truly believe only those who take risks reap the rewards."

"Ah, but that's where you're wrong. I'm not offering up my heart. After tonight, I'm not even sure I have one."

"Then why are you here?" He had to lean toward me as another song started and the music seemed to grow louder.

"To forget. I want to lose myself. I don't want to care anymore. I'm tired of it. I'm tired of it all."

"You say you want to lose yourself, but you're beautiful and young. There's a lot about you worth keeping."

"You don't know what it's like here."

He ran his pinky along my arm from my wrist toward my elbow. "I know something special when I see it. You pixies, you're known for your illusions, but you, you're as genuine as they come. Whatever happened tonight, you'll survive. You'll come out on top."

"You're surprisingly deep for a human," I said, *and achingly attractive.* For the first time that night, I didn't feel like something scraped from the bottom of Seven's shoe. The way Dark Stranger was looking at me, I felt beautiful and *wanted.*

"Take me somewhere and make me forget," I said, loading my eyes with heat and desire. I was a virgin, but Seven and I had done other things. Everything but sex. I was ready for more. I wanted more, wanted to wipe Seven and our pact from my mind.

He licked his lips and swirled the ice in his empty glass. "What exactly do you have in mind?"

The alcohol and rhythm of the music mingled, turning me brazen. Before I could lose my nerve, I wrapped a hand around the back of his neck and met the stranger's mouth with my own in a wicked, shameless kiss. His mouth was as dark as the rest of him, lusciously warm and soft. But it was a human kiss. There was no rush of luck to curl my toes. Still, a delicious weight formed low within me.

When I pulled back, he looked crestfallen. "No," he said.

I jolted as if the word hit me on the chin. First Seven rejected me, and now this stranger in a hookup bar was turning me down? It was too much. "No? After that kiss?"

"You've been hurt. You've had a few drinks. I'm not the type of guy who takes advantage of women." He swiveled away from me and leaned his back against the bar.

I huffed my frustration. "I'm not drunk. All I want is to have some fun and make this night not so... hellish. But listen, if you're not interested, I'm sure I can find someone else." I hopped off the barstool and turned toward the crowded dance floor, sweeping the scene for anyone who looked interested. My gaze locked with another human's, this one in a flannel and a ball cap.

Dark Stranger's hand landed on my elbow.

"What's your name?" he asked.

"No names," I said. "It will just complicate things."

He nodded his agreement. "Come upstairs with me. We can... talk."

He took my hand and led me to the adjacent hotel. I'd never been there before and had to stop myself from gaping as we rode the shiny mirror-and-brass elevator to the top floor. I wanted him to kiss me again, like before, but he just stared at the doors. Was he truly planning to bring me back to his room just to talk? Honorable *and* achingly sexy. There was something about him I just *wanted*.

We reached the penthouse and he placed a hand in the center of my back to usher me inside. I paused in the foyer to take in the shiny surfaces, the fireplace, the sitting area. He left my side and moved to a wet bar against the far wall.

"Now tell me more about yourself. What's your favorite book?" He grabbed two glasses and a decanter of amber liquid.

"You took me back to your room to ask me about my favorite book?"

His back was to me as he poured. "I bet it's something like *Jane Eyre*. Some down-on-her-luck heroine makes her way through a vicious world against all odds to find exactly where she belongs."

In fact it was *Jane Eyre*, but I didn't want to talk about books. My brain swam with thoughts of Seven, of the humiliation I'd endured, of my small pixie life and how this might be the only time I'd ever be in the penthouse of this hotel. I didn't say another word. I simply stripped out of my dress and stood naked in front of the fire.

He turned from the cart, drinks in hand, and froze at the

sight of me. For a second, I wondered if I'd be rejected for the second time in less than a day. But then his eyes grew dark and a muscle in his jaw twitched. I watched his resolve melt under blazing heat and desire. He set the drinks down.

When he approached me again, we collided. His mouth on mine was a brand. It took no time at all for his clothes to hit the floor, some of them stripped off by his hands, some of them by mine. He lowered me to the floor and slid into me on the rug in front of the fire. He was a generous lover who made me feel cherished, alive, and wanted. And he delivered more pleasure than I ever expected for my first time. In his arms, I pushed all thoughts of that lying, cheating Seven from my mind.

I didn't regret a moment of it. I'd wanted my first time to be with Seven, but now, after everything, losing myself to the feeling of this man's touch was... a relief.

When I woke, Dark Stranger had gone but Kiko rested on the nightstand. A note under her read, *I want you to have her. She's supposed to bring luck. Worked for me. Luckiest night of my life.*

No signature. No name. Just how I'd wanted it.

I gave that human stranger my virginity, and in return he gave me Arden.

CHAPTER

SIXTEEN

"Hey." Seven nudges me from my reverie, and I shake off the memory, mentally brushing away spiderwebs. "You okay?"

We've reached the VIP lounge, a quiet corner of the second level overlooking the dance floor. I nod. "Just remembering the last time I was here."

He sneers. "That's right, your human *tryst*."

I lift my chin a little and raise an eyebrow. I'm not ashamed of what happened. Honestly, everything about it felt right at the time, and even now the memory of Dark Stranger comes to me in a rosy hue. "I have no regrets. Not only was it a night to remember, I got Arden out of it. One of the best nights of my life actually."

"I bet you're tempted to search the crowd for his face," Seven snips.

In answer, I lift up on my toes to get a better view of the dance floor.

"Gods, will you just..." He hooks a hand through my elbow and tugs me toward the blue velvet sofa behind us. I sit. He sinks onto the cushion beside me, managing to convey both grace and displeasure in the descent. The way he looks at me, I sense he's going to say more about his disapproval of my personal choices, but we're interrupted when a server pops out of nowhere.

"Your usual, Seven?" she asks, her smile directed only at him.

His eyes flick over her. Clearly he has no idea who she is, and his expression remains serious as he rattles off, "Yes, and she'll have a blackberry martini." Without a glance in my direction, the server prances off to retrieve our drinks.

"I'm capable of ordering for myself," I snap. Just like Seven to take it upon himself to order for me.

He narrows his gaze on me. "You don't want a blackberry martini?"

Actually I do, but he doesn't need to know that. "No."

He tilts his head. "Yes, you do."

I scoff. "Now you think you know what I want better than I do?"

"I don't have to know. I'm lucky, and the luck says that's what you want." He flips a hand in the air derisively.

"Well, you're wrong. Next time ask me."

"Fine. I'll call her back and order something else." He raises his hand, searching the floor for our server.

I pull his arm down between us. "Never mind. I'll drink it. We're here to work anyway."

The withering look he gives me relays that he knows I've lied about not wanting it. Luck is rarely wrong, especially when someone like Seven is wielding it.

"That's right," he says. "We have work to do." He throws one arm around my shoulder and runs his opposite hand up my leg to squeeze my inner thigh. His firm grip on my skin, the scent of his cologne filling my nose—honestly, what is that magic?—and the closeness of his body are all so overwhelming. Something low within me clenches. I try to shift away, but between his hold on me and the dip of the couch, I'm not going anywhere.

"What are you doing?" I rasp breathlessly.

"Playing the part." His lips brush the shell of my ear as he says, "You're a pixie on a leprechaun's arm. My date."

I cross and uncross my legs as blood rushes to my core. I'm suddenly very aware just how long it's been since I've had sex, and despite myself, I melt into his side. "Did you just use luck on me?" I whisper.

His smile goes all the way to his eyes with his laugh. "Not even a little bit. Why?"

"No reason," I squeak. With all the strength I can muster, I push myself up off the sofa. "I'm going to use the restroom." I need to put distance between us before I burst into flames.

He grabs my hand as I pass him and gets a faraway look in his eyes. "Do you have that phone I gave you?"

"Yeah, it's in my purse." I glance at the small beaded bag hanging over my shoulder.

"Good. I have a feeling you're going to need it." Our eyes meet and hold. He releases my hand.

Seven's got a gut feeling about the case. I don't trust Seven, but I trust his lucky-ass gut.

Striding away from him, I suck in a shaky breath and reach into my bag, allowing my fingers to graze Kiko. Holding this illusion requires plenty of luck, and I need an extra hit. Luck flows into me in a rush as my mind focuses on finding a clue to Michael Murphy's murder. Not two seconds later a pixie cuts me off and darts into the bathroom ahead of me. *Bingo.*

Instead of heading for a stall, I wait at the mirror, fixing my lipstick. The toilet flushes, and then the pixie appears beside me and starts washing her hands. I'm about to ask her about

Michael Murphy when she blurts, "You're the one who came in with Seven. Damn. I don't think I've ever seen him with a pixie before."

My brow furrows. How did this become about Seven, again? "Thanks, but I'm sure he has a different woman on his arm every night."

"We all look like different women." She laughs pointing at her face which is obviously masked in illusion. "Don't worry, I won't ask you who you are. Any pixie on that man's arm needs to hide her identity if she values her life and reputation. The jealousy must be real."

"Yeah. It's important to be discreet."

"But to answer your question, no, I've never seen him with anyone." She shakes her head. "Believe me, many have tried; many have failed. I assumed he was like his father."

"What about his father?"

"You know, a pixaphobe." The pixie raises her eyebrows like I must be from another world if I don't know this. "Before Seven took over, his father tried several times to impose the casino rules on the club. Wanted pixies and satyrs banned from this place unless we were working. Thinks we're fae garbage."

I snort. "That couldn't have been a popular opinion. The humans come here for the pixies."

She laughs. "Right? Anyway, things are better now that Seven's in charge. Took it over from his father a few years ago. Before that he was a major reason his father didn't get his way. He even got Godmother involved. Everyone knows it would be terrible for business if pixies didn't frequent this club."

"Leprechauns." I groan.

She laughs.

"Hey, I wonder if you might help me with something." I pull my phone from my purse and show her the picture of Michael Murphy. "Have you seen this guy around?"

"Why do you ask?"

"I met him a while ago. Lost his number. Just wondering if he's been in recently."

"He's not Seven, but he pays well. I'll give you that." She leans toward the mirror to fix her makeup. "Haven't seen him in weeks though. Sorry. He sort of dropped off the face of the earth recently, but you know how humans are. They party until they run out of money, and then you never see them again."

I nod. "Right."

She tosses her lipstick into her purse and turns to leave. "What about Phoebe Willowbark?" I blurt. "Do you know her?"

She stops and turns around to face me again, a deep vee wrinkling her forehead. "How did you know Phoebe?"

I shrug. "Around. Haven't seen her in a while."

"That's because she's missing," the pixie says through tight lips. "It's been weeks. Her family has been worried sick."

"Maybe she ran off with Michael," I say lightly.

The other pixie doesn't laugh. "You must not have known Phoebe well if you think so."

"No?" I try to keep my voice light, but my luck is sending a chill through me.

She shakes her head. "No. She hated humans. Wouldn't have been seen dead with one. Just wasn't her thing. She came here for the other fae."

"Oh." My mind races trying to process that information as the other pixie tells me to stay safe and hurries from the restroom.

Phoebe didn't care for humans, and now she's missing, but she arranged a date with Michael Murphy. She went missing around the same time as Michael's murder. I see three possible scenarios here. One, the two aren't related at all. Two, Phoebe tried something new, but when Michael came on too strong, she killed him, then tried to frame an unseelie for it and vamoosed before she could get caught. Or three, someone Phoebe was with committed the murder. Perhaps another fae that didn't appreciate the attention Michael was showing her.

Hmm. I need to talk to Seven. Phoebe hated humans, was the last to be seen with Michael, and Michael is dead. That's officially enough to be suspect in my mind. He needs to know.

I finish in the bathroom before heading back to the lounge to tell him what I've learned. I stop short when I almost collide with a dark figure coming from Seven's direction. "Excuse me," I say, automatically. Then I lift my gaze and stop breathing.

Agent Donovan! My heart pounds, and panic pumps through my veins until I realize he doesn't recognize me. I reinforce my illusion. What the fuck is he doing here? Then I remember his call and that he said he'd come. Is he looking for me?

His dark perusal skims over me. "You're new."

I give a curt nod. I try to walk around him but he steps in front of me. "How about a ride?" He reaches out and strokes my wing. I tug it from his grasp before the blue iron in his system can threaten my illusion. My stomach wants to turn inside out at his touch. The way he's looking at me makes my skin want to crawl off my body.

"I'm taken," I say in a voice that is not my own. I point my chin in Seven's direction. Donovan turns to the side and glances that way too. I'm surprised to see Seven's not alone. He's standing in front of the couch with his back to us, and his father of all people is ripping into him. For a second, I worry about catching Chance's eye—the last thing I want is to run into that man again—then I remember I don't look like me. Fuck, they're really going at it. Chance has Seven by the collar, and he's shaking him. I can't hear what he's saying, but it looks like it's escalating.

Donovan takes a step away from me when he spots the two men, seemingly put off by the idea that I'm with the leprechauns. *Good.*

"Maybe next time," he says, raking me over with a lecherous gaze. I press a hand into my churning stomach. He strides past me toward the back stairs and descends to the dance floor where humans and fairies alike gyrate to the music below, and I breathe a sigh of relief. Over the railing, I watch him disappear into the sea of bodies. Everywhere patrons grind against each other, or do their best to pick up fae at the bar. Pixies, wrapped in illusion, attempt to make themselves more desirable to lure in the best humans.

None of them realize there's a FIRE agent in their midst who dreams about making them scream.

I jump when a hand wraps around my upper arm. Seven. He plants his hand on my waist and starts guiding me toward the back of the club, moving fast. "Where are we going?"

"I need to talk to you, *now.*" He looks furious. He moves faster toward the exit.

"Seven, I can't run in this dress!"

Luck bubbles in my veins. Suddenly the skirt of the dress gives, and I increase my stride to match his. We're down the back stairway and out an emergency exit before I can say another word. He opens the car door for me.

"What's going on?" I stop short of getting in and fold my arms.

But Seven isn't paying any attention to me. His expression is dark, menacing. I've never seen him so angry. "Can't do this to me. Not a kid anymore," he mumbles.

"Seven, what the hell is going on!"

Emerald eyes flash, and the intensity almost makes me stumble. "Get in the car. There's something I have to tell you."

SEVENTEEN

Reluctantly, I slide into the leather seat, feeling painfully uncomfortable about everything that's happened. All I want to do is go home and have a hot cup of tea, but as soon as I close the door Seven starts the engine and races in the opposite direction of Wonderland.

"I thought you had something to tell me," I say, buckling my seat belt. It would be highly unlikely that a leprechaun would get into a car accident, but call it a habit from living among humans.

"I do. But first we need to get somewhere safe. Somewhere he doesn't have people watching."

"Who? Your father?"

"Who else, Sophia?" He glances toward me, and his lip curls in displeasure. "Drop your illusion. It's unsettling."

I shake off the disguise. "It was your idea!"

He glances back at me, and it might be my imagination, but his eyes seem to spark when he sees me this time. "Better. You're a work of art in that dress."

"I'm a..." Did he just call me a work of art? I hold on to the door as he takes a sharp corner. "Where are you taking me?"

"Home."

"Wonderland is that way." I point over my shoulder.

"My home. It's the only place he doesn't have access to the security footage. He owns fucking everything else."

The night grows thicker as we break from Dragonfly and enter Elderflame, the capital city of Devashire. Before I can even process that Seven is actually taking me to his inner sanctum, we're parking in a private garage under a skyscraper.

"Seven, I don't think—"

He's out and around the car, opening my door and pulling me from my seat. Still intensely angry about whatever he fought about with his dad, his steps are quick and I almost have to jog to keep up. With his fingers entwined with mine, he ushers me toward the elevator, the heat from his hand making me oddly flustered. Why does his touch do this to me after everything?

There are a dozen reasons why I should protest going home with him, not the least of which is that I'll be completely vulnerable there. Seven can overpower me in a heartbeat. Even if I use Kiko, he has more luck than I'll ever have. I shouldn't trust him.

But I can't bring myself to say anything, and despite myself, I can't move away when he clings to my hand in the elevator. I feel his touch deep within me. There's so much sexual tension in the small, enclosed space I can feel it pressing against my skin like moisture on a humid day. It ricochets off the walls. I'm carnally aware of every square inch of him beside me. It's so quiet, I can hear myself swallow.

And then he moves. His hand slides from mine as the doors open and he walks into a sparsely decorated but elegant foyer.

"This is a bad idea," I mumble as I follow after him. He ignores me.

Another leprechaun in a dark suit waits at a desk beside a beautifully crafted door. Seven nods to him. "If anyone asks, I'm not here. No one goes in or out. Understood?"

The man nods. Before I know it, Seven has unlocked the door and swept me inside.

What have I gotten myself into? This is a far more intimate scenario than what I wanted to experience with this man tonight. I'm not sure that I'm strong enough for this. His presence ignites too many memories. Too many feelings. They're all tangled up in me in a confusing knot that weighs heavily at the pit of my stomach and has the blood rushing lower. It's a thrill, and Seven was telling the truth when he said I was a thrill seeker. My desire to self-protect wars with my need to dive headfirst into the excitement of the moment.

I fold my arms, a barrier between us. "What the hell is going on, Seven?"

He doesn't answer right away. Instead, he moves through the foyer—oh my gods, this apartment has a massive foyer—and into a main room with a wall of windows overlooking the city. *Fuck*, who lives like this? If I thought Seven's office was decorated in a style called things-I-can't-afford, this condo is things-so-out-of-my-price-range-I-didn't-know-they-existed!

I glance down to watch three koi fish swim through the center of his living room. A custom fish tank winds like a river through the pale marble floor under a thick pane of glass. I've never seen anything like it.

"Nice fish."

He glances at me. "The river ends at a pool on the balcony. You can feed them if you'd like."

Is he really asking if I want to feed his penthouse fish? Now? "Maybe later."

He nods, then crosses to a bar in the corner of the room. Across the glass river with the fish is a seating area anchored by an ecru carpet with a subtle geometric pattern of interlocking rings. Atop it a stone coffee table that's big enough to accommodate a human sacrifice is neighbored by a sofa the color of fresh whipped cream and two chairs that belong in a museum. Everything faces the windows and the balcony beyond. There's no TV or magazines or clutter of any kind. If there is a single grain of dust anywhere in this room, it's well hidden. There is, however, a shiny black baby grand piano in the corner.

Does he even play?

"Would you like something to drink?" Seven pours himself a glass of amber liquid from a decanter.

"Who even fills that thing? Why can't rich people pour from the bottle like everyone else?" I ask.

The corner of his mouth twitches. "My housekeeper, and it oxygenates the whiskey. Any other questions?"

"Yes," I say immediately. "Why the fuck am I here? And why the clash-of-the-titans action in the Dragonfly Club? I thought the glasses were going to shatter from the luck coming off you two."

He snorts and walks to the windows, taking his glass with him. He leans an arm against the pane and rests his forehead against it.

"This thing between us, Sophia, it's a mess. A big, fucking mess."

I bristle. "There is no *thing* between us, Seven. There hasn't been for a long time."

He just keeps staring out across the city.

"Tell me what you remember about that night. Hit me with it."

"You know what happened. We talked about this on the beach."

"I want to hear it again, from your perspective."

"My perspective?" I stiffen. What the hell is his game? But then something inside me decides it might be fun to lash out. He's asking, and I have a lot of rage to air. "Fine. Here's what happened. I arrived at the staging point exactly on time. My dress was the same color plum as this one. You probably didn't know that considering you never saw it. It was strapless and full, and my mother had rented a tiara. I looked and felt like a princess. But the only thing that really mattered to me was the red ribbon tied around my wrist. As excited as I was for the ball, I was more excited about you. We'd dated in secret for two years and had been friends since first grade. That night we were going to make everything public."

"We were going to do more than that," he mutters.

"I thought I was telling this story."

He tips his head. "Please."

"None of my friends believed I was actually dating you. A pixie dating a leprechaun was unheard of in Devashire. Dating a Delaney was impossible. But I was sure you loved me. We'd spent so much time together. For fuck's sake, we'd made a pact to lose our virginity to each other."

I study his reaction as he shifts uncomfortably and takes another drink. When he doesn't turn from the window, I continue. It's easier, talking to his back.

"The sleigh was blood red, and a thick blanket of gray fur was draped across the seat. My shoulders were cold, and I wanted to wrap that blanket around me. But since you were late, Mrs. Harper—do you remember Mrs. Harper?—told me I'd have to sit in the driver's seat and hold the reins because it was too late to get out of line by the time I admitted to myself you weren't coming. So I lifted my massive skirt and somehow situated myself on the bench to drive the sleigh. That put me up high enough that all the other couples could easily see me.

Giggles and whispers exploded around me. Everyone knew you'd set me up."

He closes his eyes and gives his head a shake. His voice is gritty as he says, "Go on."

"I didn't believe them of course. I thought you loved me." I curse my voice for cracking. "You'd never do that to me, I told myself. But you *had* done it to me, and for the entire journey through the Winter Wood, every fairy we knew, and plenty of humans we didn't, pointed and laughed. Why was that girl driving her own sleigh? Who was that? Was she going to the ball *alone*? Was that even allowed? I heard it all, Seven. Can you imagine the humiliation? No, I don't suppose you can. How can I paint you a picture? Every word was a paper cut, and by the time I reached the square, I was hemorrhaging."

"Sophia..."

"Not done." My voice is stronger now, my emotions tilting toward anger. I cough into my hand but force down the prickly emotion that threatens to come up. "As soon as we were given the okay to leave our sleighs, I attempted to disembark, but with no one there to help me down, I tripped. I landed face-first in the snow."

Seven makes a sound deep in his throat and takes another drink. I'm glad he's still not looking at me because a stupid, fucking tear has squeezed out of the corner of my eye. I wipe it away quickly and continue. I need to get this out. It's cathartic.

"So I'm on the ground, my heels hopelessly tangled in my skirt, tears streaming down my face, and suddenly *your father* appears in front of me. I think he's going to help me up and explain what's happened to you. I mean, I was over at your house a lot as a kid. He'd known me since I was six. But he doesn't reach out his hand. Instead, he looks down his nose at me and says, 'Pity it came to this, but Seven did you a favor tonight. Now you know your place. You'd do well to remember it.'"

I cough harder into my hand, feeling that seed of resentment and mortification climb my esophagus. I swallow it down again.

"Then what?" Seven asks.

"Then he walked away, leaving me inside a ring of staring, pointing, whispering people," I say incredulously. "I couldn't get my feet under me. Not until River appeared, unhooked my skirt from my heel, and helped me stand. He walked me to his truck, where he used his hunting knife to cut that fucking ribbon from my wrist. And then he drove me home."

Seven winces. Gods, he looks like he might be sick. He walks to the bar and pours himself another. "But you didn't stay home, did you?"

"No."

"And then there was Arden, and you were gone."

"Yes."

"A matter of weeks."

"I left at the end of winter break. I'd done a fabulous job avoiding people until then. I couldn't face going back to school, given the circumstances."

He turns to me. Only then do I see that his eyes are rimmed red and the look he gives me is dark, murderous. It's so unsettling I have to take a step back.

"Have you ever wondered where I was when this was going on?"

I jolt. "Of course I have! But based on your father's comments, I had a pretty good idea you were home, having a good laugh at my expense." I scratch my jaw.

"Oh, I was home." He shakes his head as the words open a wound in my heart I thought had healed long ago. "That afternoon, my mother told my father that I was taking you to the ball as a date, not as a friend. He pitched a fit. See, up until then, he'd tolerated the fact we were friends because he never thought his son would dare slum it with a pixie romantically. The very idea was beyond his comprehension."

My breath flows out of me as if he's punched me in the gut.

"I stood up to him. Told him that not only was I going to the Yule Ball as your date but that I loved you."

Now my breath catches, and I'm just confused. If that's true, then—

"He poisoned me with blue iron, Sophia. I didn't come to the ball because I couldn't. I was locked in a room, completely drained of luck."

CHAPTER

EIGHTEEN

Icy tendrils crawl along my skin and make the tiny hairs at the base of my scalp stand on end. "W-what?" I ask, unable to keep my voice from trembling. Blue iron is prohibited inside Devashire. If anyone knew about the small amount inside Kiko, I could get in big trouble. Poisoning another fae with it is grounds for imprisonment.

His jaw works and his eyes meet mine. "My father poisoned me and locked me up. In his words, he was keeping me from tarnishing the Delaney family name. I was so fucking sick. He drained me of so much luck I went negative and puked for hours. It was so bad, my mother couldn't take it. Eventually, she packed her bags and left. Ended up divorcing him over it. That and other reasons."

"Your parents are divorced?" I had no idea. All the luck in the world and they couldn't fix their family or their marriage. I shake my head. "Wait, this doesn't add up. I didn't leave immediately. It was... weeks. Why didn't you come tell me? Why didn't you try to explain?"

His jaw is so tight, I think he might snap a muscle. A shadow moves behind his eyes. "Several reasons. First, we were out of school, on winter break. I had no excuse to leave the house and my father forbade it—forbade it in the sense I was watched twenty-four hours a day. He wouldn't let me speak to anyone, so I couldn't get a message to you. He took my phone. When I finally got it back, you wouldn't answer my texts. You wouldn't take my calls."

"I left without my phone. Too easy to track."

"Your mom eventually told me as much. Soon after, my mother moved out and left me behind ... left me with him. My home life was in tatters."

"Wait... your mom left without you? Knowing he'd poisoned you?" After what I learned about how she purposefully forgot him as a child, this doesn't surprise me as much as it should, but still seems exceptionally cruel.

He brushes a hand over the sleeve of his suit, a disgusted expression twisting his lips. "She didn't have a choice. My father is the most powerful leprechaun in Devashire. I don't blame her, not really. She was trying to make it out alive. And that's the second reason, Sophia. He's too strong. What do you think would have happened if I'd found a way to get to you? What do you think he might have done to you if I'd tried to make things right back then? He'd poisoned his own son. He's above the law. Even if I could have found my way out of his grasp, I couldn't put you at risk by being seen with you again."

For a second, I'm tempted to doubt what he's saying to me. For years I've convinced myself that Seven was the villain of my life. Except I can see the pain etched into his face, and it's real. He's many things, but unlike me, he's a horrible liar. Besides, what he says about Chance being above the law rings true. Chance isn't just lucky, he's rich and well-connected politically. A sick feeling swells inside me, and I cough again.

His gaze narrows on me. "After you left, I looked for you. I was barely eighteen when I got involved with the security division of Lucky Enterprises to have access to the systems I needed to search for you. When I became an adult, I amped up the search. I've got to hand it to you Sophia. You vanished. I started to think you'd died."

"I was careful. I changed my appearance and used luck to secure a passport. Still, with all the luck at your disposal, I don't know why you didn't find me. I was good, but not that good." It's so weird. Donovan was able to find me, after all, and he's human. "What does this have to do with what happened with your father tonight?"

"He saw me at the club with a pixie. You, but not you. He doesn't usually come in, but he said he was there to meet a colleague. He laid into me. Threatened to cut me out of the Delaney Empire and leave everything to Evangeline if I didn't check myself."

I can't curb my sharp intake of breath. I knew Chance was an asshole, but hearing it from Seven's lips is still shocking. "Can he do that?"

"Unfortunately, yes. He owns a controlling interest in everything under the Lucky Enterprises brand. I might be CEO of the club and COO of the casino and hotel, but he can still have me ousted. My father is a greedy son of a bitch, Sophia. My mother got precious little in the divorce. Enough to keep her comfortable for the rest of her life, but nowhere near what she deserved. But it's not the money that worries me. I don't care about the money. I never did. What worries me is the man himself. If he wanted to hurt you..."

"He's not going to hurt me." I shake my head. "You said yourself he didn't even know it was me there today."

He rubs a hand over his face. "He saw you at the casino yesterday... Tonight, he blamed you being back for reviving my interest in pixies. He said he was disappointed that he hadn't gotten rid of you back then for good."

"Gods, he's a dick." I want to vomit. Never did I realize how deep Chance's hatred ran for me and my kind. "Don't worry about it, Seven. When we meet about the case, we'll just be careful to meet where it won't be an issue. I'll stay on my side of Dragonfly, and he can stay on his."

Seven closes his eyes and gives his head a hard shake. My words seem to have enraged him rather than comforted him. He strides toward me, sending the koi darting off as he stomps over their river to reach me. "What if I don't want to stay away from you?"

I take a step back. "What do you mean?"

"Please say you forgive me, Sophia." His voice cracks. "You have no idea what this has done to me over the years. Once I heard what happened to you, what he said to you, I tortured myself thinking about it. I couldn't apologize then, but I can now. I'm sorry. I'm so sorry."

"So you knew... before this. You knew what he'd said to me?"

He grunts. "River told me. Popped me one too." He rubs his stubbled jaw as if he can still feel it. "I couldn't explain to him what my dad had done. I was too embarrassed and afraid of what would happen next. This can't get out. You know that, right? Not ever."

I scoff. "You were a kid, and he was abusive. You should have been removed from his care. Your mother should have protected you. She should have taken you with her. People need to know what kind of awful man he is."

He waves a hand dismissively. "My mother didn't stand a chance against him. I admire her for saving herself."

I swallow and try to look at the situation objectively. He's right. There is no version of reality where Seven would have been removed from his father's home.

"Even now, this can't get out," he says firmly. "You can't tell anyone. I brought you here because it's the only place I know he doesn't have eyes or ears. He's too powerful, and if he feels threatened, he'll strike in ways you can only imagine. You understand that, right? It's why I couldn't tell you at the lake. I've been trying to get you back here for days."

All those invitations for dinner. He wanted to bring me here. He wanted to tell me.

I'd say that no one would care about a leprechaun poisoning his own son with blue iron, but it would be a lie. No matter how many years had passed, the *Daily Hatter* would lap it up. Poisoning another fairy with a prohibited substance, especially a child, is scandalous. The patriarch of the Delaney family doing it is media fodder. And he's right that Chance would likely not suffer any consequences. Seven wouldn't have any proof of what his father had done back then, and the fallout from a story like that would be devastating for Seven. His father would cut him off, and the tabloids would rake him across the coals. He'd be disgraced. He could lose everything.

And so could I.

If my name were dragged into the mix, my future and that of my family would be in jeopardy. My parents run a store they rent from a leprechaun. One word from Chance Delaney and that leprechaun could choose to raise their rent or force them out some other way.

"Please," Seven begs. His tortured expression is incongruent with the demanding and arrogant man I know him to be. The man is made of suits, ties, and expensive scotch. I never thought I'd see the day he had a conscience. "Say you forgive me."

There it is. The demand. His eyes hold me in their intense embrace, and his mouth forms a straight line, his jaw tight. I expect to feel his luck like I did on the beach, but my skin doesn't tingle, and I don't feel compelled in any way. Which means he's left it up to me. He wants my uncoerced forgiveness.

Maybe that's what does it. Suddenly my mental construct of him cracks, and all I see is the boy I knew, the one I liked and then later loved. I believe him. And I am floored by the vulnerability he's showing. The pain his father caused might as well be an exposed wound over his heart. The entire situation is messed up.

I can't carry my hatred for him anymore. Not now, knowing what I know. It's too heavy. But my brain is reeling trying to process everything, and I can't put into words what I'm feeling, so I simply blurt, "Yes, I forgive you."

It's as if I've dropped an invisible shield. He reaches out to cup my jaw, his fingers wrapping around the base of my head in an astonishingly possessive fashion. I barely get a breath in before his lips crash down on mine and my back and wings bump the wall behind me. Gods, the kiss takes me by surprise. It hits me like a force of nature, fierce and wild as a hurricane. If there's any part of me that questions if this is a good idea, it sails away before I can examine it closely.

I tip my head and let him in, his tongue stroking mine in a dance that stirs up long-forgotten memories. Inside, that flock of butterflies takes flight, and then the warm rush of his luck stirs my blood.

Here's the thing about kissing a leprechaun. When he wants to, when his focus is on me, all that power that saturates his body becomes a firebrand of pleasure. It feels like someone has popped the cork on a bottle of champagne inside my torso. My insides turn light and bubbly. My body feels effervescent. Everything comes alive. If kissing a man is like being lowered into a warm bath, kissing a leprechaun is like a warm bath full of Pop Rocks. This kiss is an *event*.

It's fireworks.

Among fairies, luck isn't something we can see, but we can feel it. We can sense it. It's as unique for each of us as a fingerprint. I've encountered Seven's luck before but it never registered what exactly I was dealing with. Now, an image pops into my mind, formed from the size, the power, the temperature of the *beast* in the room with me. Seven's luck rises like a giant, hot-blooded dragon whose purr vibrates against my skin where it brushes me. Heat rushes to my core. I'm throbbing between my legs instantly as his fingers work themselves into my hair. His kisses trail to my ear, down my neck. Gods, his thumb feathering across my jaw almost makes me moan.

Seven tastes of forbidden fruit and interrupted destiny. I *want* him. I crave him like a drug.

Luck purrs around the back of my neck and sinks, warm and intoxicating between my shoulder blades. It travels lower, tingling along each vertebra with firm but achingly effervescent pressure. I'm breathless as that hum shifts over my hip and down my lower abdomen to tease the tangle of nerves at the apex of my thighs. I moan into his mouth.

I'm playing with fire. This feels too good. I could lose myself in this kiss and then lose myself in him. What happened tonight is confusing enough. I forgave Seven. That's a play I wasn't expecting to make. Anything more is risking too much.

His fingers trace along the top of my bodice, a soft caress over the mound of my breast as his hips grind against mine, the hard length of him enticingly close to the ache between my legs.

Before I can lose my nerve, I plant both hands on his chest and push. "Seven, stop."

He pulls back, panting. "What's wrong?"

"We need to stop."

"Why? You want me, I can feel it." He moves closer again, and I push harder to keep space between us.

I close my eyes and try to put it into words, even as my blood sings in my veins and my core throbs with need for him. "I forgive you, okay, but that doesn't mean we can go back to the way it was."

He backs up a step. "No, but we sure as hell can create something new."

I shake my head. "It's been sixteen years. We don't know each other anymore. Not really. When you kiss me, you're kissing a memory."

"Then let's get to know each other."

I'm speechless. It's too much to take in. I hated the man only days ago, and I can't sort out my emotions in the moment to respond. I want him, undeniably, but I haven't had time to digest what a new relationship with him would mean for me. So I say nothing.

Silence stretches between us.

I'm saved from his intense scrutiny when his phone rings. "This better be important," he barks, and I can picture the person on the other end of the call cringing. No one would interrupt him now if it wasn't important. That security guard in the hall could barely make eye contact. "Fine. Yeah... Mmm-hmm."

Seven's jaw hardens. "We'll be right there. Yeah, she's here with me."

He slides his phone back into his pocket. "That was Godmother. There's been another murder."

CHAPTER
NINETEEN

There was a time in my life when Seven was the center of my world. I loved him in a way that's only possible when one's heart is new, unbroken, and unjaded. The pedestal I put him on was tall, and I would have changed anything and everything about myself to make him mine forever. All that has changed now. My heart isn't new. It's been broken before... by him. And although I realize it wasn't exactly his fault, a cracked vase pasted back together never holds water the way it did before it was damaged.

So why am I tempted to allow myself back into his arms?

It's clear he wants me, and hell, I want him. I'd be lying to myself if I said I didn't. But the difference between teenage me and thirty-four-year-old me, is that now I know my worth. I deserve better than to be treated like a pet, a lesser being meant to be happy with clandestine moments behind closed doors. I've survived things Seven couldn't imagine. I'm perfectly fine alone; I'm resourceful and smart. More importantly, I'm a mother, and I know Arden is always watching. I'm not ever going to exist for the pleasure of a man, any man, no matter how lucky or rich. No way. Not even for a little while.

It's just after ten when Seven and I arrive at the scene of the crime, tension still painfully thick between us. "I thought you said it was supposed to be right here." I scan the cobblestone near the back of the park, not far from River's Tavern.

"It is." Godmother's voice comes from in front of me. There's a snap, and I see her standing beyond a shimmering wave of purple. I step forward, through the concealment spell, and she snaps her fingers again. The murder scene appears where before there was nothing.

When I see the body, I can't help but gag and turn away. The victim isn't human—she's a pixie—and the state of her corpse turns my stomach. There's so much blood. The stench of death hangs thick in the air around us.

Everything about the scene repels me. Unlike Arden, I never wanted to be a doctor or an investigator or any other career that involved bodies, blood, or bodily fluids. My dreams were of running my own business, far away from anything like this. I never had the stomach for horror movies or hospitals. I cover my mouth with my hand and try to think happy thoughts.

Seven appears in front of me. His voice is low and soft as he asks, "You okay? If this is too much, you can go. I can show you pictures later. It might be easier."

I open my mouth to tell him I'm okay, but I never get the chance.

"She's staying," Godmother says in her deep, resonating voice.

"I guess I'm staying." I flash him a half smile, then take a deep breath before turning around again.

It's not like I'm some delicate flower. I left Dragonfly at only seventeen and lived on the street, pregnant, until I could luck my way into a job and then a closet that called itself an apartment. I saw things out there, drug users who fell asleep under the same underpass as I did and never woke up, prostitutes beaten by their pimps and left for dead. This brutality seems harsher here though. Blood seeps into cobblestone under a flickering gas lamp crafted to look like a mason jar filled with fireflies. The dichotomy catches me off guard. Gods, just behind us is a neighborhood of pastel mushrooms.

Whoever did this has shattered some last vestige of my childhood I didn't even know I was clinging to. There should be no safer place than Dragonfly Hollow. But evil is here, death is real, and no one is safe.

"Her teeth are gone," Seven says. "And half her rib cage."

I swallow down bile and really look at the victim. It's the left side that's missing and something else. "Her heart's gone too."

Godmother grunts and reaches for a red box that looks like it should hold an assortment of chocolates. She selects a brightly colored paper tube that reminds me of the sugar candy humans call Pixie Stix, tears off one end, and scatters the contents in the air. The yellow powder swells like a cloud and then settles over the scene. Footprints appear on the concrete that were not there before. Gigantic footprints. Both Seven and I inhale sharply. They're weirdly shaped, skeletal, and they end at the eight-foot privacy fence that forms the boundary of Wonderland. On the other side of that wall is forest, beach, the lake, and the wall.

"Yissevel," Godmother says through her teeth, her fists clenching.

"It can't be." My gaze darts between them. "Can it?" The unseelie have been locked away for centuries. If they'd found a way through the wall, there would be a hell of a lot more death and destruction than just one human and one pixie. Yissevel isn't just any unseelie. No one could miss this monster.

Seven tips his head back and looks from streetlight to streetlight. He points toward one with a black glass dome embedded in the design. I wouldn't have noticed it if he wasn't pointing at it. "There's a camera. I'll have to go to the security office to see what it captured."

Godmother waves a hand dismissively. "Go. I'll determine time of death and try to identify the victim." She pulls a vial of silver liquid from her box.

At Godmother's words, I realize that I've been avoiding the victim's face. I'd taken in the scene, but a part of me hadn't wanted to see this pixie as a once living, breathing person. I might be able to identify her. Her head is rolled to the side, and I step around the body to get a straight look at her face. I grab my stomach, instantly chilled through. I know who this is.

"That's Phoebe Willowbark." I feel breathless as I look between Seven and Godmother. "She went missing the same day Michael Murphy was murdered."

No one says anything for what feels like a full minute. "How do you know this?" Godmother's normally large dark eyes become slits.

"A pixie I met at the Dragonfly tonight told me about her when I asked her about Michael." No need to get River involved in this mess. I pull up the family's page on my phone and show it to them.

Godmother darts a glance toward Seven. "Why did I not know that a pixie went missing on the same day Michael Murphy was murdered?"

Seven straightens, looking livid. "This is the first I'm hearing of it."

"Let me know what you find out." The tone of her voice has the hair on my arms standing at attention. Something ancient has crept in. Ancient and deadly.

The nod Seven gives her is the most deferential I've ever

seen him give anyone. He extends his hand and gestures for me to come. I do, relieved when we are through the concealment spell and I can no longer smell the blood. "That was intense," I say.

He says nothing, doesn't even look at me. His entire demeanor has turned icy.

"What the hell is wrong with you?" I ask in my usual irreverent way. I'm not going to bend to this man's moods.

He continues to ignore me, until we're around the corner and out of sight of the crime scene. When he finally does turn, his expression is hard, his spine stiff, and his lip is curled in disapproval. "Is there any other information about this case you'd like to share with me? Now would be a good time. Now rather than later, when we're with Godmother."

I recoil. Fuck. His poker face is gone, and the full force of his anger plows into me. I force myself to stand a little straighter. "I just found out myself! It was important information."

"So you thought it would be a good idea to make a fool of me in front of Godmother? I'm head of security, Sophia, and a Delaney leprechaun. How exactly did you think your reveal was going to go over?"

The turn of events shakes me. Not an hour ago, this man had his tongue down my throat, and now my skin buzzes with his anger. His luck coils around him like a defensive, pissed-off dragon.

I try to take a step toward him and find that my heel is caught in the cobblestones. I glance down at my shoe, but it refuses to give. My nostrils flare. "Real mature."

He scowls like someone kicked his kitten.

Stepping out of my shoes, I flex my own luck and she rises like a tiger at my side. It's all bravado. His dragon could eat my tiger in one bite.

"My reveal? I didn't *reveal* anything. I recognized the victim and told both of you in the moment. It's not my fault no one had informed Godmother about Phoebe. How was I even supposed to know that?"

"Bullshit, Sophia. You kept this to yourself. You said the pixie at Dragonfly Club told you about her. You've known for hours and didn't share it?"

I raise a hand. "I didn't have a chance! I was too busy being whisked away to your apartment to revisit the past. Besides, since when do you care what anyone else thinks?" My poker face snaps into place to conceal how shaken I am by the emotional whiplash of the night. "Gods, Seven, you just finished telling me that you didn't care what your father thought about pixies, but suddenly you're swelling with some hypermasculine need to know everything first and be in total control?"

Emerald eyes blazing, he juts a finger in my direction. "Wanting to appear competent in front of the most powerful creature in both our lives isn't hypermasculine, Sophia, but thanks for letting me know exactly how you feel about me."

He turns to continue toward his car. I bend over and use both hands to pry my shoe from the sidewalk, then follow after him.

Whirling on me, he makes a sound like a laugh. "Go home, Sophia."

"What? Why? I thought we were going to go look at the security recording."

His eyes turn cold as ice. "Oh, I see. You don't get it because you've never managed anything but yourself." That barb slides between my ribs and almost breaks the impassive expression I've been holding in place. "Here's what happens now. I have to go back to the office and start the process of figuring out why my people didn't flag Phoebe Willowbark as a missing person. If there's some sort of bias involved, I'll have to fire the people responsible on the spot, people with families, who need their jobs."

He slams me with a disdainful look, and I realize he's echoing what I asked him when he fired Brandon. Ouch. "While that's all happening, I'll have to spend a gods-awful amount of luck to gain access to the recording of Phoebe's murder without drawing attention to it. No one else can see it. No one else can know what happened here tonight. If any of my guys have already seen it, I'll need to make damn sure they don't say a word, one way or another, because if this got out to the human population, Dragonfly could lose millions in lost park revenue until PR got things under control."

"Don't forget the Delaney empire," I say flatly. "Your bank account might shrink from the size of Jupiter to the size of Uranus, and that's also exactly where you can shove this guilt trip." Beside me, my luck tiger growls. "I know these murders are high stakes for us, but don't act like I don't have just as much on the line. My freedom hangs in the balance—my life if Godmother kicks me out of here. There's a reason she put me on this case, and it's not just to feed you information so that you can play the hero and take credit for every chip of progress that comes our way."

He recoils at that, a scowl marring his face.

"But since we're on the topic, six pixies who frequented the Dragonfly Club have gone missing over the past decade, and none of them have been investigated as potential victims. Phoebe was just the most recent one. Your people always assume they left for the human world like I did, but their families disagree. I sent word to my family. Most people would if they weren't in trouble. When an otherwise normal person vanishes without a trace, there's probably foul play involved. So maybe it's time you talked to that team of yours, and maybe it's right that a few of them are fired. I'm not going to apologize for telling the truth or for doing exactly what you brought me on this case to do."

He grunts. "Fine. But I'm still leading this investigation, and you're officially off duty." He slashes a hand through the air dismissively and turns coolly away from me. I watch him stride toward the parking lot, the press of his luck going with him. The tingle of his power slides from my skin and then vanishes.

I head for home feeling oddly cold.

CHAPTER

TWENTY

"Mom, what do you think of my new uniform?" Arden rushes into my room the following morning wearing the plaid skirt, emblemed blazer, blouse, and tights that I recognize as the uniform for Bailiwick's Academy. I blink at the clock, wondering if I've overslept again, even though I was home at a reasonable hour and I hadn't had anything to drink. It's only seven fifteen. My alarm was set for seven thirty.

"Where'd you get that?" I ask her. "I promise I'll call the school on Monday. I just haven't had a chance."

She grins and starts jumping up and down. "I'm already in!"

I stare at her until it's clear she's not joking. "Explain."

"I went down there yesterday with Grandpa while you were getting ready for your mission and asked to speak to Headmistress Sullivan."

I shake my head. "It was late Friday afternoon. Wasn't the school already closed?"

"Yes, but I took a chance, and she was still there! I explained everything that happened, and we had a conference call with my old high school's principal. Everything just fell into place! I start Monday." Her voice is a little breathless, and excitement is rolling off her in waves.

"But... what about the tuition deposit?" I have no idea how I'm going to pay it, but Bailiwick's is expensive. Usually, they'd hold off on admission until the financing was nailed down, but if they gave her a uniform, she must have already been admitted.

She squeals. "That's the best part. It turns out you overpaid my tuition in Nevada and they've agreed to send the balance to Bailiwick's. We won't owe anything!"

My stomach clenches. I'm happy for Arden, but warning bells are going off in my head. This is one positive coincidence too many to give credit to fate. I sense luck was involved, and a serious amount of it. Overpaid tuition? That's never happened before. Instantly, I think of Seven. Last night, before things went sour, he'd tipped his hand that he still had feelings for me. He'd apologized and kissed me. Is it possible that he is behind this?

If he is behind it, I hope to hell he doesn't renege after last night. I've never seen him so angry, and I guess I can understand why, now that there's some distance between me and the situation. Yes, it would be important to anyone in his position to be perceived as competent. I get that he wants the best for his employees, and this puts him in a tight spot where he might be forced to let someone go. But I was right too. Had I withheld that information from Godmother and she found out, I might be in more trouble than I already am. And Seven did need to do something about the bias against pixies in his shop. I don't regret what I said, but I also understand where Seven was coming from last night. It's unsettling. Between knowing the truth about his abusive family life and understanding his point of view, I can practically feel my heart making room for him, maybe even expecting the best from him. It was so much easier to just hate him.

"Congratulations," I say to Arden. "I'm glad you got what you wanted, and I'm proud of you for going after it on your own."

"This is going to be amazing!" She claps her hands and bounces out of the room.

Gods, I hope she's right. It scares me to think that she might be bullied for being human or that this might all come apart. I need to talk to Seven, see if he's behind this. If so, I'll eat crow if I have to. Arden has been through too much for me not to do everything I can to make this better for her.

I dress and descend to the smell of toast and eggs. My mother is waiting in a silver ball gown that would be at home in a Cinderella movie. My dad sports dark breeches, boots, and a flowing white shirt reminiscent of a fairy-tale prince. They both give me an exaggerated smile when they see me.

"You didn't have to make me breakfast," I say, plugging my mouth with a piece of toast.

"Yes, I did," my mother says, her smile widening. "We just got a shipment in at the store, and we could really use an extra set of hands today."

Dad clears his throat. "What do you think, sweetheart? Want to take a trip down memory lane and contribute to the family business?"

When he puts it that way, how can I say no?

AN HOUR LATER, I'M DRESSED IN MY DRY-CLEANED PINK ball gown and designing a display of Dragonfly snow globes at my parents' gift shop, the Silver Ember. Each glass ball depicts a different street in Wonderland with a pixie stretching her arms toward the sun. When you shake them, purple and silver glitter swirls around her and her wings flap. All of them are inscribed with the Dragonfly Hollow logo and the tagline WHERE MAGIC LIVES AND DREAMS COME TRUE.

Humans buy the weirdest shit.

"Are acorns really lucky?" a man in shorts and a Dragonfly Casino polo asks me. I stop what I'm doing to give him my full attention. The polo he's wearing isn't for sale. It's a gift for VIPs. This guy has money burning up his pockets.

"Very lucky," I say. I pick one up and hold it between my thumb and forefinger. "This one acorn has all the potential to become a mighty oak tree. It's concentrated luck. Very powerful."

"Good. I'm registered for the poker tournament tonight and need all the luck I can get." He rubs his hands together.

My chest constricts. How I wish I had a poker game to look forward to.

He lifts one of the acorns and turns it in his fingers. "It's so... common. Do you have them in gold?"

I repress a laugh and flutter my lashes at him. "Sir, there is nothing common about these acorns. Each one is hand selected from our Winter Wood, the luckiest forest in all America. And we at the Silver Ember are very careful to limit the amount that they are handled to preserve the greatest concentration of luck the acorn can hold. Why, the only thing luckier in this entire store is the goldfish, and if you are interested in one of those, I'd be happy to show you. They're in the back."

Shifting uneasily, he says, "No, no. They always die on me."

I hold my smile while inside I judge the man harshly for his inability to keep a goldfish alive.

"How much are they?"

"$25.99 each," I say. Right now they are. We don't label the bin for a reason.

"All right, I'll take four." He reaches for his wallet.

"Very good, sir. Would you like me to throw in a four-leaf clover preserved in resin? They're 10 percent off since you've spent over a hundred dollars." I flash him my most charming smile and hit him with a bit of luck.

"Oh, why the hell not? Can't be too lucky, can you?" He chuckles, his eyes dropping to my boobs.

"Never," I say with a wink. I gather his goods and deliver them all to the counter where my mother starts ringing him up.

I've turned back to the snow globes when he taps me on the shoulder, bag in hand. "Are you free later for a drink?"

I shake my head and point to a sign above the cash register: Employees are Prohibited from Fraternizing with Guests. "Thank you for visiting Silver Ember."

He stumbles out the door mumbling something about stupid theme park policies. Once he's gone, my mother rounds the counter and hugs me. "$25.99? Last week I sold a dozen for five dollars!"

I huff dramatically. "For these gorgeous hand-selected specimens?"

She peers at me over her glasses. "Your father literally rakes them off the forest floor."

We share a good laugh, and she returns to the back room and the inventory. When the front bell chimes again, I don't even look up. "Welcome to the Silver Ember."

"Is that you in those snow globes or another pixie who can't hold her liquor?"

"River!" I embrace the satyr. His brown eyes are dancing with mirth, and he's actually wearing a shirt for a change. This is as dressed up as River gets. "What are you doing here?"

"I have a date on this side of the park and thought I'd bring you a sandwich and some chips for lunch."

"A date, huh? What's your date think about you bringing me lunch?"

He chuckles. "Presumably that you must be hungry. What else would she think?"

I laugh. Must be a satyr. I'll never understand the lack of jealousy. "Who's the lucky lady, gentleman or gentleperson?"

"Lady. Katy from the education center."

"Ah." I try to remember if Katy is the redheaded satyr or the one who never smiles. I decide it must be the redhead. River's too friendly to be dating a downer.

I take the bag from his hand and set it on the counter. "Thank you. I'll put this to good use."

He rocks back on his heels, staring at me.

"Is there something else?"

He sighs. "As your friend, I feel you should see this." He reaches behind his back and pulls something from his waistband to hand to me. It's a newspaper. The Daily Hatter, Spilling the tea in Dragonfly Hollow since 1845.

"What exactly am I supposed to be looking at here?"

River's shoulders droop. "Page six."

My eyes flick to him and back to the paper as I flip to the location of the gossip section and zero in on Fairly Goodweather's neighborhood news column. "Prodigal daughter Sophia Larkspur returned to Dragonfly Hollow this week after her life of crime was thwarted by the Fairy Immigration and Rehabilitation Enforcement agency. Although her inappropriate and illegal actions brought pain and suffering on this community (her poor parents!), it appears she will suffer no punishment or penalty. I have it on good authority that she visited Godmother the day after arrival and left with skin and wallet intact!

"Although this reporter was as disappointed as you that justice wasn't served, she is more concerned with the company

Ms. Larkspur keeps. A sixteen-year-old daughter, seemingly half-human, enrolled in Bailiwick's Academy just yesterday. Lock up your sons, Dragonfly families! If this acorn didn't roll far enough from the tree, we are surely in store for more heartbreak and drama from the youngest Larkspur descendant."

My mouth falls open, and I stare at River in disbelief. "Did she? Was that? Pain and suffering! Life of crime! Acorn and tree!" My throat squeezes until my voice is high and tight.

"It's going to be okay," River says, holding up his hands. I just thought you should know.

"No! It's not okay. Where does Fairly Goodweather live, River? You know everyone in this town. Tell me. I'm going to *kill* her."

River chuckles and turns over one hand. "While you and I know the best way for you to win over the love and support of Dragonfly Hollow is to commit murder, perhaps that particular action will be confusing to others."

"Pfft!"

He places a hand on my shoulder. "It will blow over, Sophia. Six months from now, no one will even be talking about you anymore."

"People are talking about me? What are they saying? What have you heard?"

River sighs and scratches behind one of his horns. "Do you want to come by River's for a free beer later?"

I offer a tight grin. "I'll take that to mean 'yes, people are talking about you, Sophia.'"

"Drink more beer and it won't bother you."

I laugh. "Got it." I hand him back the copy of the *Hatter*. "Thanks for lunch, River. You're a good friend."

He pulls me into a hug and kisses me on the cheek, just as the bell above the door chimes and Seven walks into the Silver Ember.

CHAPTER

TWENTY-ONE

"This is cozy." Seven wears the same face he wore when he fired Brandon at the casino, like he owns the world and gods help anyone who gets in his way. Damn, he's larger than life. His suit hangs like it's in love with him, hugging muscle and draping elegantly in all the right places. He's broad shouldered and narrow waisted with just enough ass to make things interesting. Plus he's obviously jealous which makes my heart do a happy tap dance in my chest. Damn stupid heart. After the way he dismissed me last night, I should be making some excuse to leave the room right now.

Focusing all my attention on River, I release him with a warm smile. "Thanks again for stopping by... and for the sandwich."

"Anytime." He turns to leave. As he passes by Seven to get to the door, the two men lock stares. I feel luck rise in the air like static electricity. Seven's is a fiery dragon, an energy that's become so familiar the past few days. River's has the presence of a great horned stag. River towers over Seven physically, taller by four inches at least and with the broader shoulders and defined muscles satyrs are known for. But Seven's power dwarfs what River is putting off. It's so big it steals the air from the room.

I watch River's hand ball into a fist before he slips out the door. Absently, Seven rubs his cheek as the door chimes and closes behind the satyr.

"That was fun," I say. "For a second there I thought one of you might get piss on my shoes."

"Is he why you won't be with me?" Seven's gaze drills into me.

My mother chooses that moment to poke her head out from the back room. "Oh, Seven! I thought I felt..." She furrows her brow. "Well, I thought I felt something. What brings you in today?"

"Always a pleasure to see you Aurora." All anger has drained from Seven's expression, replaced by good-natured charm. He reaches her in three long strides, takes the heavy box she's carrying from her hands and sets it on the counter.

"Oh, thank you." She smooths her dress.

"Would it be all right if I borrowed Sophia for a few moments? It's Godmother business. I'm afraid it's important."

My mother smiles warmly. "Of course."

What? She looks like if he stayed she'd offer him coffee. Gods!

Seven holds open the front door, and I follow him out onto Main Street where we begin to stroll toward Godmother's. "Why are you here, Seven? I thought you said I was off duty."

"I owe you an apology."

My breath catches. Seven Delaney is apologizing to me... again? That's twice in twenty-four hours. Someone send heaters to hell; it's officially frozen over.

He rolls his eyes. "Don't look so surprised. I can admit when I'm wrong."

"Leprechauns aren't well known for admitting wrongdoing or apologizing for that matter."

He shrugs. "When are you going to learn, Sophia? I'm a different sort of leprechaun."

"Hmm." Up close now, I see shadows under his eyes as if he hasn't slept well. He's still sexy as hell, but clearly something is bothering him.

"It would have been risky for you to hold back Phoebe's identity last night. I realize that now."

I release a heavy sigh. Hell if I'm going to allow him to be the bigger person about this. "I'm sorry too. I didn't mean to embarrass you. I'd meant to tell you earlier, but we were... distracted."

"Did Sophia Larkspur just admit she was wrong?" His lip quirks and eyes flash.

"When are you going to learn, I'm a different sort of pixie?"

Our eyes meet. Now there's something else in his expression, the same wolfish, masculine heat I'd seen last night. The tug of his luck slides over my skin, and I picture that dragon wrapping around me again.

I turn away and walk on. "You may wish to mark this day on your calendar and commemorate it annually in the future, preferably with cake and sparklers. I doubt it will happen often."

He chuckles and moves closer to my side. "It's not your job to preserve my reputation. Besides, you were right. I'm embarrassed to admit that the cases of those six pixies were completely mishandled by my team. In every instance, their files were closed as assumed runaways despite evidence to the contrary from their families. We have six missing pixies and one dead human, all with links back to *my* club."

The stress in his voice is obvious now, and he's lost some of his charming demeanor. I'm surprised he's admitting this in public. Until I notice we are very much alone. The nearest guests are across the street. I take in the emptiness of the usually busy street and clear my throat. "Um, are you doing this? Because if so, we should walk faster. My parents really need the midday business."

He grunts. "Sorry."

The tingle of his luck shifts like a rush of bubbles against my skin, and then a flock of families seem to see the Silver Ember for the first time and flood into the store.

"Thanks."

"Don't mention it."

I walk faster until we put additional space between us and the crowd again. Lowering my voice, I ask, "Was there anything on the security footage?"

"Yup." He heaves a sigh. "But you'll never believe it unless you see it with your own eyes."

The Wonderland security office is a single-story circular building intentionally designed to blend into the background. Its indistinct white brick walls give no clues to what goes on under the ordinary shingled roof. The only indication of the purpose the building serves is silver lettering on the glass front door that reads SECURITY.

Seven keys us in and tells a blue-uniformed satyr behind the reception desk that he's going to be in the monitoring room for a few minutes and is not to be disturbed. He leads me into an office filled with screens showing every aspect of public life in Wonderland. There's no one in here, although there's a steaming cup of coffee on the counter and a Dragonfly security jacket on the back of one of the chairs.

Seven locks the door behind us.

"Someone's going to miss their coffee," I say.

Seven types feverishly on the keyboard. "Ye of little faith.

Ravi is in the restroom, and we are going to get very lucky and be out of here before he's finished."

"Of course we are," I say flatly.

A few more keystrokes and the location of the murder pops up on-screen. It's dark, but I can make out the patch of sidewalk at the back of the park in the circle from the streetlight. The time ticks along the bottom of the screen. Seconds roll by. And then the body appears in the arms of a monster.

"Yissevel," I say. "Oh my gods! He's out."

Seven nods. "Keep watching."

The monster is at least eight feet tall and looks like a skeleton aside from a thin layer of stretched pale skin that seems to barely hold bone, tendon, and muscle together. He drops the mutilated body, then takes off, bounding back over the security fence in the direction of the wall.

"That's weird," I say. "It's almost as if he's sneaking back into Shadowvale."

Seven laughs. "What else is weird, Sophia?" He rewinds the recording again. I watch.

I press my fingers against my lips. "The teeth and bones were missing before he ditched the body. She was already dead!"

"Exactly."

"This just gets weirder and weirder. Did Yissevel kill her in the unseelie realm and then dump the body here? Why? How would she even get to Shadowvale? And if she was killed here, why would he move her body?"

"All great questions. What we know for sure is that Phoebe was already dead. Did Yissevel kill her or just scavenge her bones and dump her? And if he didn't kill her, who did?"

"Who else would though? Just because he dumped and ran doesn't mean he didn't do it. But I understand what you're saying. It's so odd. How did he even run into Phoebe? And if she went missing the same day as Michael showed up dead, did he somehow lure her back to Shadowvale, kill her, and then return to dump her? Why?"

Seven shakes his head. "That's what we have to find out. None of this makes sense."

"But how do we find out? Yissevel had to have returned to Shadowvale. He's... giant. Someone would have noticed him. You would have caught him on camera."

"Yep."

"And how is he getting past the wall? We need to talk to the guardians about this."

"They will never admit that a creature made it through without their knowledge."

"We can show them this." I gesture toward the footage.

He steps in closer and looks me in the eye. "I have a better idea."

I cross my arms and wait expectantly. "Why are you hesitating?"

"Because you're not going to like it." At the impatient look I give him he says, "You and I are going to go through the wall and pay Yissevel a visit. We're going to ask the beast himself what happened."

"Go into Shadowvale?" My voice rises around a nervous laugh. The idea is senseless. Shadowvale is brimming with unseelie monsters, things without a conscience that would eat our throats out as readily as talk to us. "Are you insane? It's suicide."

He pinches my chin. "It's not suicide because you'll be with me and we will get very, very lucky. Between my luck and your illusion, we'll be fine."

I stare at him incredulously. "Are you sure about that? I have a daughter, Seven. I can't take unnecessary risks with myself."

He chuckles and slants me a crooked smile. "Nothing will happen to you, Sophia, and from what I hear, Arden is doing just fine on her own."

My breath hitches. "What have you heard about Arden?"

He narrows his eyes on the screens as he logs out and returns everything to the way Ravi left it. "Heard she made it into Bailiwick's, our old alma mater. Betsy Sullivan said she was quite charming in her interview."

"Seven... Did you have something to do with her admission?"

He gently guides me toward the door and keys us out. "I'm on the school board. I'm involved with all admissions." He winks at me.

I follow him past the front desk and out the doors just as a young leprechaun in uniform comes out of the bathroom and strides toward the room we were in. So Seven *is* to thank for Arden's admission to Bailiwick's. I knew luck was involved. It was the only explanation.

"Thank you," I say.

"For what?" He leads me down the street a few yards and then pauses on the sidewalk.

"For helping Arden get into Bailiwick's."

He scoffs. "I didn't need to help her. Everyone who meets her *loves* her, Sophia. She's just like you."

His words knock the air out of me. I had friends, sure, but I wasn't universally popular. "No one here ever loved me like that."

His green eyes flash. "I did."

I shake my head, my cheeks warming at his admission.

"You seriously don't remember? You were the darling of every teacher, a sweet pixie girl from a salt-of-the-earth pixie family."

I scoff. "If that were ever true, they don't think that now.

According to the *Hatter* and Fairly Goodweather's social column, I'm a criminal who needs to be punished, and my daughter is a half-human temptress whom people should hide their children from."

Seven scowls. "This is why I never read those columns. Fairly Goodweather is an idiot."

"Yeah."

"Would you like a coffee?" He gestures to a cart nearby with an espresso machine and a selection of pastries.

I shake my head. "I have to get back to the store."

"What are you doing there anyway? You always hated working at your parents' store. You once told me working retail was a torture that would be illegal if forced on animals."

"It isn't my favorite thing to do, but I need the money."

He swaggers closer to me. "Why haven't you applied at the casino? You'd make an excellent dealer. I assure you the compensation package is the best in Dragonfly."

I heave a sigh of frustration. "I'll think about it."

"What's there to think about?"

I circle my gaze toward the sky. "Um, working for and with your abusive, dickhead father, for one. Two, watching other people play my favorite game in the world and not being able to join in. That's its own torture."

His smile fades slightly. "You can play me."

"Not the same." My brain fills with images of playing poker with him. I miss it more than I'll ever admit.

"If I could change the rules for you, I would. Even if I wanted to make an exception, I couldn't. The law comes straight from Godmother. Poker with fae isn't fair to the humans, and the last fae-only tournament we tried ended badly. There was so much luck swirling in that room, a satyr's chair broke, and he fell into the player next to him, sending the pixie crashing through the second-floor window. Thank gods he could fly."

Even as a kid I remember what a disaster those yearly tournaments were. All fae have varying levels of control over their luck, just like humans have varying levels of control over their emotions. The difference is, in a gambling situation, a typical fae combats more than just their need to control the cards. Fairies in general find it difficult to turn down a direct invitation to wager. We learn early on not to say things to each other like, "I'll bet you five dollars you can't climb the flagpole." It's not that we can't deny the urge to take those bets. It is possible, and more emotionally mature fairies will have no problem saying no to such a wager. But it creates a hunger in us, an impulse.

If you're at the poker table and someone goads you with words like, "You can't fold! Can't you see he's bluffing? You're not going to let him get away with that, are you? I'll bet you a chip he doesn't have the hand he says he does." It's difficult for us to resist. And while I've learned to suppress this impulse playing among goading humans, most fae would give in to the temptation, especially if they were tired after long hours of play. It would be an absolute mess.

"I'll think about the dealer job." I need work. There's no getting around it. The Delaney family owns half the businesses in Dragonfly, so it would be hard for me to avoid working for them in some capacity anyway, and he's right about the pay and benefits being the best I could get.

We stand there staring at each other for a moment, Seven taking me in like I'm a painting hanging in an art gallery. He's studying me.

"About Shadowvale...," he starts.

I groan. "Fine. When do we leave?"

"Tomorrow. You'll need something more appropriate for

the terrain." He eyes my gown with distaste. "I'll send over some hiking gear."

The last thing I want to do is to take anything else from him, but there's no way I can afford proper clothing and equipment for a trip like this. "Fine, but seriously Seven, you've been far too generous. You know I can't repay you, right? Like ever."

"It's necessary for the job Godmother charged us to do. It's covered."

I nod, still feeling awkward about not paying my own way. "I should get back to the Silver Ember. My parents need the help today."

He cups my elbow and steps in closer. "About last night. I meant every word of what I said in my apartment."

"So did I. I forgive you."

"About what happened afterward too." His gaze settles on my lips. "We'd be good together. We *belong* together."

I look him in the eye and shake my head. After hours going over everything last night, I finally know my feelings on the subject and I boil them down into one word. "Why?"

The corner of his mouth pulls back in confusion. "What do you mean why?"

"Why do you think we belong together?" I ask. "Why not find someone more suitable? Someone of your own kind."

He gets a faraway look in his eye. "I tried that. It hasn't worked out."

Hmmm. I'm going to have to ask my grandmother who Seven was seeing while I was gone. Internally, I slap my own face. Why do I care who Seven was seeing? Ugh.

"You want me. You kissed me last night. I didn't imagine that."

I glance away toward the safety of a bird soaring across the sky. "I did kiss you, and if I'm being honest, I do want you. But we're not kids anymore. Sexual attraction isn't enough."

"It's not just about sex."

"Isn't it? It's like I said before, we don't know each other anymore, not like we used to."

"I know you, better than you think." He brushes invisible lint from the sleeve of his suit jacket.

"Right now, I'm the fish who got away. You're intrigued. But once you had me and got me out of your system, what would be left? You'd move on to the next woman who caught your attention. A woman who most likely would fit better into your lifestyle."

He shakes his head. "That's not how it would be."

"It wouldn't? What's changed, Seven. Are you telling me you'd risk your father's wrath and fae society's scorn to have a real relationship with me? You still work for your father. You're an adult now. You have more wealth, power, and influence than anyone I know, but as far as I can tell you haven't done a thing to break his hold over you. You're still that little boy under his thumb, drinking his poison. And if I was with you, it would be back to hiding and secrets, like two horny teenagers."

He runs both hands through his hair, leaving it uncharacteristically in disarray. "I can't change the way the world works."

"So then, I ask you again, why?"

"Because I can't stop thinking about you," he says, fisting his hands. "Because there's no one else I'd rather spend time with."

"I have Arden to think about now. I can't be your dirty little secret. I don't want to lie to her or model unhealthy behaviors. If I'm going to date again, I want a real relationship. A public relationship."

"It could turn into something more, Sophia. My father won't be around forever."

"No, he won't." I heave a sigh. "But you won't do anything

to upset the applecart. Even after he's gone, you have to steer the ship, right?"

His gaze drops to the sidewalk, and I know I'm right.

"You would never risk going public with our relationship because it would threaten your position in Lucky Enterprises. You have to live up to the family name. A relationship with a pixie would be scandalous, and your father would likely find a way to have you ousted from the company. Even after he's gone, going public with our relationship would be a PR nightmare. You'll never do that...."

"You're wrong." He looks at me through his lashes.

"I'm not. There's something between us, Seven. There always has been since the day I was drawn to you in the woods as a child. But we're bad for each other. The only thing that can come out of pursuing this relationship is pain. Right now, we've been apart long enough we can both move on without falling to pieces. But if we date, if we fall in love? What then?" I back up a step. "I could be wrong about this, but if I am, I'm prepared to live with the consequences. They're safer than starting something with nowhere to go."

"You done?"

"Yeah."

"This thing between us, Sophia, it's not something that comes along every day, and it promises a lot more than pain. Give me a chance and I'll prove it to you."

There's nothing else I can say. Lifting onto my toes, I kiss his cheek. "See you tomorrow, Seven."

I stride back to the store. At the door, I glance behind me to find him staring, unmoving, in the same place I left him. Slipping inside, I let the door close between us.

CHAPTER
TWENTY-TWO

That night I sleep fitfully. I tell myself it's because we'll be crossing into Shadowvale in the morning and it's the likelihood of imminent death keeping me awake. But a tiny niggle at the back of my brain replays my conversation with Seven over and over again until I drift into dreams in the wee hours of the morning.

Seven and I sit on the beach—our beach—cross-legged in the sand before a flat stone that's serving as a table. He's shirtless, his skin glinting in the sun as if he was knitted by the gods from flesh and gold. Hard muscle cords his arms, his torso a terrain of peaks and valleys I desperately want to map with my fingers. The corners of his lips, almost too full for a man, turn up when he notices me watching him, framed within a square jaw under a direct, unyielding nose. He's a luscious specimen of a man, fueled by an intimidating, tightly coiled, almost-regal strength. I picture him with a crown on his head and a scepter in his hands, sparkling from his gods-anointed throne. Seven would be a powerful ruler, but not one who exercised brute force with an iron fist. No, he'd be the type of king defended by nature itself, a tsunami that wore down his enemies, unlimited in his persistence as any mountain.

"It's your move," he says.

Only then do I notice the cards in his hand, the art on the back a picture of Kiko nestled in a field of clover. I glance down to find I'm fully dressed. There are five cards in my hands. Five-card draw. We must be playing strip poker, and I'm winning.

Power brushes past my ribs, his luck coiling around us, the purr of a contented dragon. The energy licks my skin, threatens to consume me. His eyes glow a brilliant emerald green—keen, insightful eyes that hold the promise of pleasure and something I want far more. My breath comes in pants as my body heats, the desire to strip off my dress almost unbearable.

I force myself to concentrate on my cards. Two kings, two queens, and a ten. I toss the ten into the discard pile and draw. But the card I select isn't from a poker deck at all. It's a tarot card. A picture of a man and a woman in a garden, the Lovers. My brow furrows. Confused, I drop the card in the center of the stone table.

Seven's smile fades. "You win again."

He stands, and I realize he's already completely naked. A dark storm moves in overhead. He thrusts his hand into his chest, pulls out his heart, and drops it, still beating, into my hands.

BUZZZZZZZ. My alarm screams at me from the side table. I sit bolt upright and slap the Off button, then stare at my palms. There's no blood.

Of course there's no blood. What the hell is wrong with me? I massage my temples. All the talk of playing poker with Seven yesterday must have worked its way into my subconscious. Weird.

I shake the memory of the dream from my head and go in search of coffee.

"I don't like this, Sophia," my father says in that deep, commanding voice dads everywhere use on their daughters when their safety is at risk. "Going into Shadowvale? It's foolish. When was the last time you heard of any seelie going through the wall? If anyone has done it in the past century, I haven't heard. And what about Godmother? It seems as though she would be the best candidate for this task given her relative power."

It's before sunrise, and I stand in front of my father decked out in the equipment Seven had delivered to our address the afternoon before. I'm wearing high-tech clothing made from insect-repellant fabric, specially designed to work with my wings, and boots that make me feel like I'm walking on clouds. The pack on my back is filled with more wing-friendly clothing, designed for any weather, as well as a hat and other sun-protective gear. A plastic bladder in the lining holds plenty of water, strategically positioned to fit between dual compartments containing dried food and a survival kit. Kiko's back there too. I've filled her jade belly with as much siphoned luck as she can hold.

"Seven is one of the most powerful seelie fae in existence, and he's working with Godmother. He won't let anything happen to me. It will be a short trip, in and out. Everything will be okay." It's a good thing I can bluff with the best of them because I have no idea if what I just shared is true. Will Seven be lucky enough to avoid hostile unseelie? Who knows? Will it be an in-and-out mission? No idea. It certainly isn't safe.

"I think Seven just wants to have you to himself in the mountains for a day or two," Grandma says slyly. She came by again to see me off and holds a purple mass of knitted yarn in her hands. She thrusts it at me. "I made you a hat, dear."

I hold up the purple bowl-shaped project. It's a hat for a giant. If I poked my head through a hole in the center, it would easily cover my shoulders like a stole.

"Thanks, Grandma."

I kiss my dad on the cheek and tell him to try not to worry, then hug my mother. I save Arden for last.

"I'll miss you," she says.

"Are you sure you'll be okay?"

She rolls her eyes. "I'll be fine, Mom. More than fine. Everyone here has been incredibly nice to me, and I have Grandma and Grandpa. Don't worry about me."

I squeeze her tight and kiss the side of her head unnecessarily hard, hoping it will stick. "You're the best kid, Arden. I'm not sure any other teenager would have survived being completely uprooted as well as you."

She shrugs. "Honestly, it's a dream come true."

My brows shoot up in surprise. "Really?"

She smiles sheepishly, her green gaze darting away from mine. "I'd been thinking a lot about this, actually, before everything went down. All my school friends had another year and planned to apply to different colleges. Everyone seemed distant once I told them I was graduating early. And I'd always wanted to meet Grandma and Grandpa and see what this place was like. Plus it bothered me how you never connected with anyone because you always had to hide who you were. I just wanted us to be a family before I had to go away and everything changed. A real family without secret identities. I'm sorry you got caught by FIRE, but to be honest, I'm happy how things turned out. I wished for this. Does that make me a terrible person?" Arden blinks at me as I realize that what started out as a lighthearted confession has taken on a note of heavy guilt.

"No, it doesn't make you a bad person. I'm glad you're focusing on the positives and making the best of the situation." I hug her again. "Now I told Seven I'd meet him at Godmother's in fifteen minutes. I better get a move on before the park opens and I have to explain to some human family why I'm dressed like this.

"Wait," my father says. "You're forgetting something." He hands me my old bow and quiver from when I was on the archery team at Bailiwick's.

"Oh my gods! I can't believe you kept this all this time!" I graze a hand over the items like they're long-lost friends. "And you made me living arrows!"

"Just three to get you started. We used wood from our new birch tree out back."

A tear forms in my eye. The birch is the plant that crowded out the thornbush at the back of their garden, the one born of the three seeds we planted the day we forgave each other and became a family again. Living arrows are a pixie thing. We are the only creatures who can carve the wood in such a way that the branch remains alive. Bright green leaves form the arrow's fletching. They can last days if watered properly and fly as if they are guided by the wind itself.

"We?" My voice cracks.

"Mom, Grandma, and me. One from each of us." I look toward Grandma, who's smiling lovingly, then at Mom, who steals another hug, and then to Dad, who gives me one last peck on the cheek.

"I'll be home soon." My eyes blur with unshed tears. I stroke a hand over Arden's hair. My heart swells with love for each of them. And then I really do have to go because I'm definitely going to be late. To a chorus of goodbyes, I charge out the door and hope to the gods that I'm doing the right thing.

We are not the only fae on this planet.

On the other side of the wall, the unseelie rule.

The seelie are the only thing keeping the unseelie from devastating the human population.

Humans don't know about the unseelie. While pixies, satyrs, and leprechauns evolved to live with and among humans, the unseelie evolved to have a taste for human flesh. Unseelie don't blend in. They're monsters, ancient and dark. The unseelie are to us what sharks and alligators are to humans, if the sharks and alligators had human minds and could tell you they planned to suck out your eyeballs before they chomped on your head like it was a cheese ball. They are a leftover race from a barbaric time now relegated to the annals of our history.

Tens of thousands of years ago, a war broke out between the seelie and unseelie fae in the Americas. The seelie fae had evolved to look, sound, and act like the early indigenous humans who lived on these lands. The unseelie had evolved to think of humans as either food or slaves. Evolution turned them into monsters with sharp teeth and claws and a taste for blood. When the seelie conquered the unseelie, the ancient rulers of our kind erected a wall to contain the unseelie in Shadowvale, a massive fairy realm where they live freely in the wilds, safely separate from the rest of us.

The seelie though were not solely responsible for winning the war against the unseelie. The god Odin sent his *light ones*, elves with an ancient magic foreign to us, to help our people. To this day, a religious order of elves called Guardians maintains the wall. They fortify the magic that keeps the unseelie where they belong and keep watch over the border. In over ten thousand years, there has never been a breach, or at least that's what we're taught in school. As far as I know, Yissevel is the first.

Seven and I arrive at the wall just after sunrise, and an elf dressed in a dark blue hood greets us at the door.

"Godmother told us you were coming," he says in a deep melodious voice that sets me on edge. Like Godmother's, his voice seems to be too big for his body. I've never met an elf before—they never leave their priory, and I've never had a reason to come here. I try to glimpse under the hood. All I can catch is jet-black hair and light blue eyes that seem too big for his head. I've read that elves have pointed ears, but his are covered. He's a bit shorter than Seven and is built slight, more like a pixie, but I know better than to think his narrower stature means he's powerless. Just like Godmother, elves have old magic, true magic not limited to luck. It's the same magic that fuels the wards surrounding Devashire.

"I'm Sophia, and this is Seven," I say, because it seems like the polite thing to do and I'm too nervous to remain silent.

The elf bows at the waist. "I am Elred."

While I'm wondering if I should bow back or maybe curtsy, Seven draws a box from his pack about as long as his hand and half as deep. It looks like it's made of solid gold. "A gift in appreciation for your help today." He bows and holds it out to the elf who accepts it with his own obeisance. He opens the lid. I can't see what's inside, but golden light reflects onto the elf's face.

He closes the top. "By Odin, your offering is found worthy. Welcome to Heimdall's Priory. Come with me."

The elf leads us through a door and down a long, narrow corridor. The structure might be better described as a dam. Now that I'm inside it, I realize our entire house could fit within its width and height. In school they'd made us memorize that the wall was around 600 feet tall, but it's different seeing it up close. From the outside, it's massive and awe-inspiring, carved with symbols that reveal it for the ancient relic it is. Being inside it is something else altogether. The inner world of the wall is bustling with modern activity. Elred explains that Heimdall's Priory is a subsection of the wall, where the guardians live and work. Their living quarters are on the second floor. The first floor is where they monitor the barrier between us and Shadowvale. We pass a glass room, and I notice elves with security equipment similar to what Seven showed me in Dragonfly.

"You have electronic surveillance?" I sputter, flabbergasted.

The elf flashes me an amused grin. "You didn't think it was all prayers and rituals, did you? Even Odin needs a little help these days."

My jaw drops, and I exchange looks with Seven.

The elf keys us into a secured room, and my sense of amazement ratchets up a few more notches. We are standing in front of a mirror—a massive, gilt-framed mirror—that ripples occasionally as if it's formed of liquid silver. My eyes snap to the corner when I think I see the shadow of a fishlike creature swim beneath the surface. The silver swells after the thing and then settles smooth again.

"What is this?" I say under my breath because the sound in here reminds me of a library or a funeral home. Every instinct I have tells me to whisper.

"This is how we go through," Seven whispers against my ear. He's behind me, watching me. I'd been so distracted with the mirror, I hadn't noticed him move in close.

The elf approaches a rack on the wall and selects a gold staff with a bulbous hook on the end. "There's a reason that

Seven can't fly you in his helicopter to take you to Shadowvale."

I clear my throat. "I assumed the magic prevented that."

The elf chuckles. "Oh, you can fly over this wall, but you will never reach Shadowvale. You'll pass right into US airspace. The only way to the unseelie kingdom is through this mirror."

"It's a portal?" I narrow my eyes. How in the hell did Yissevel get through this without anyone noticing?

"Yes." Elred approaches the mirror.

"Is this the only one of its kind?" I ask quickly.

"No," Elred says, "but they are rare, and each is heavily guarded."

I open my mouth to ask how many elves work here, but Seven's hand clamps over it. Elred raises his staff, uttering some words in ancient elvish. "Once I stir the silver, you must go through before it settles. Do not stop until you reach the meadow on the other side. I cannot help you if you become trapped."

That sounds ominous.

Seven slides his hand into mine and a fine shiver travels through me. I'm really doing this. I'm going to see a world no one I know has ever seen. Anticipation drives my pulse. Adrenaline floods my system. I should be scared, but I'm not. I'm... excited.

The elf plunges the staff into the silver and grunts as he stirs in giant strokes. His muscles bulge beneath his robes from the effort. A swirl, like a whirlpool, starts at the center of the mirror and then opens into a tunnel.

He draws out the staff. "Now!"

CHAPTER

TWENTY-THREE

Seven leaps into the swirling silver, dragging me by the hand behind him. I rush after him, my feet landing on a squishy, wet floor of questionable constitution. I almost stumble. I find my footing but lose my breath at the sheer magnificent beauty that surrounds us.

This tunnel isn't the molten silver I expected it to be from the anteroom. The reflection is fragmented, composed of swirling night. Stars twinkle and jet across the sky above me. They cascade along the sides of the tunnel, sparkle, fizzle, and darken at my feet. I'm inside a galaxy spiraling on fast forward. I feel small but connected, like a very important barnacle clinging to the side of a whale.

I'm tempted, oh so tempted, to dive into that sea of stars. If Seven's hand wasn't gripping mine, I'm not sure I could avoid sticking a finger into the whirl of twinkling energy that pulses around us. It beckons, a universe to be discovered. I can imagine what it would feel like against my skin, the cool hands of a lover, the lap of gentle waves. The velvet darkness between the silver promises the sweet oblivion of deep sleep. Oh, how I long for it. I deserve a rest after all I've been through.

Shadows shift in the beyond. Silhouettes dancing just out of sight, causing ripples in the silver stars. Ghosts reach for me. I lift my hand to reach back.

Seven's warm grasp tugs me forward harder, and I see the field beyond. It looks dull in comparison to the glittering world we are part of. I want to stay here! I want to touch and taste what lies within. I pause, but Seven isn't having it. Luck rushes through the connection of our touch, and then with one last tug, I'm flying out of the mirror and landing on my stomach in a field of bright green clover.

"Breathe, Sophia!" Seven removes my pack, then rolls me over.

I try to pull air into my lungs but can't. Have I forgotten how to? Black spots circle in my vision.

"Sophia! Come on, breathe!" Seven commands, slapping my cheek. Both his hands land on my chest. He works them under the collar of my shirt until his palms are skin to skin against me. A bubbly rush of luck flows into me, seeming to inflate my lungs from within. A loud, eye-popping gasp breaks my lips. Seven removes his hands from my bare skin, leaving two cold spots in their wake.

"That's it," he says, softly brushing the hair from my face. "Deep breaths." He stretches out beside me. I'm seized with chills and shiver hard, my teeth clacking together. Seven pulls me against him, wrapping me in warm limbs and blasting me with another bubbly rush of luck that feels like direct sun on an eighty-degree day.

"Ahhh." I moan at the feel of it.

I feel his lips press into the side of my hair.

"I'm okay. I'm okay." I rotate in his arms to face him. I'm

shocked at the level of concern I see on his face. A tear escapes the corner of my eye. I wipe it away with a trembling hand.

"I don't know why I'm crying," I admit, although he never asked me. He strokes my hair, and the feel of his touch and his silence are like a truth serum. "Being in that tunnel, I felt... full. And now I just feel alone." I rub my chest.

"You're not alone," he says softly. "I'm here. I won't leave you."

Warmth returns to my bones, along with an acute awareness of how close he is. The clover under us is soft as a feather bed. It matches his eyes. Sun bakes my skin, its light drawing out the copper and blond highlights in his toffee-colored hair. Gods, he's beautiful. Beautiful and powerful and at the moment entirely focused on me.

"Did you feel it?" I ask. "The draw of it?"

He nods. "But it was different for me."

"What did you feel?"

His brow furrows, his expression going serious. "I felt entirely in control, as if I could command my own fate."

I snort. "So like always then."

He gives a low laugh but doesn't respond to that. Some part of me acknowledges that I should get up, but his fingers are still in my hair, the palm of his hand is now cupping my face. I can't bring myself to move.

"What was that anyway? I saw figures beyond the stars."

"Niflheim. It's the Norse version of the afterlife."

"Would have been nice if someone warned me that the tunnel would try to tempt me to my doom."

"Elred did. He told you not to stop until you reached the meadow."

I groan. "Oh yes, that fully encompasses the danger of walking through eternity," I say sarcastically.

He tucks hair behind my ear. "They say it draws you in with the promise of delivering you from your greatest fear."

I recall the feelings inside the tunnel, like I was surrounded by people who knew me. People I could trust who would never betray me. "So my greatest fear is being alone, and yours is losing control."

"More or less."

"Thank the gods you were strong enough to pull us through."

He gives a roguish grin. "Just lucky I guess."

I lay there, staring into his face for an embarrassingly long time, the smell of the clover beneath my cheek bringing back long-ago memories. The sun shimmers across half our faces, filling me with warmth and contentment. His fingers stroke my hair. My heart remembers this. My heart wants to live here again in this place of intimacy, of sweet words and casual touches.

My heart is stupid.

I climb to my feet and swing my pack onto my shoulders, checking that my bow and quiver are secured to the sides. With a sigh, he dons his own. For a moment, we simply take in our surroundings.

We stand in a field of clover that stretches for miles in every direction. Heimdall's Priory and the symbol-etched marble wall it's a part of stretches behind us, to the east. To the north is the lightly forested base of a rolling mountain range. To the west, a dark, twisted forest, mist curling over knobby roots of densely growing trees. To the south, a river with an ancient looking stone castle beyond. Rumor has it that King Kieran, our former monarch, moved there after Godmother rose to power following the Civil War and cast him out of Devashire, but no one has seen him in decades.

"Thistlebend Castle. Do you think Kieran actually lives there?"

"Where else would he be?"

I shrug. "Maybe she killed him and only says he lives there to keep the people from electing another—someone stronger who might threaten her power."

He laughs. "Seems like something she would do."

I widen my eyes at him, not because I'm surprised—I've heard stories about Godmother—but because he admits it. "Why do you work for her if you know how brutal she can be?"

He cuts off my train of thought with a raised hand, his luck brushing by me as it serpentines around us. "Mountains," he says with certainty.

"What about them?"

"I have a strong feeling Yissevel lives in the valley between the two peaks." He points toward the mountains to the north and the squiggle of green between them.

"Should I even ask how you know that?" It's not as if there exists a celebrity map of unseelie residences. Yissevel is ancient and well known in the lore of fairies, but as far as I know, no one's actually visited his lair.

He winks in my direction. "I don't know for sure, but that's where my luck is telling me to go."

"Great. Here's hoping your luck knows what it's doing."

He laughs. "It hasn't failed me yet."

We start for the mountains. Halfway across the field, a black horse darts out of the dark, twisting forest to the west and races across the clover toward the mountains. The animal turns its head to look at us, and its horn glints in the sunlight. I blink and blink again, but yes, I'm watching a unicorn gallop no more than a hundred yards in front of me. It races off into the trees at the base of the mountains, and I lose sight of it.

I turn toward Seven, my mouth dropping open. For once he looks as awestruck as me. "I've never seen one in the wild before. I mean there was that crippled one they had in the petting zoo at Sunshine Kingdom for a while, but this is entirely different."

He shakes his head, his eyes sparkling with amazement. "I guess we're not in Devashire anymore, Sophead."

"Will you stop calling me that! I'm a grown woman. It sounds like a nickname for a child or a little sister. I doubt you want to think of me as either."

He snorts. "I disagree. I think it's the nickname earned by a woman who was formidable enough at the tender age of fourteen to punch a merman in the nose before her leprechaun boyfriend could even gather enough luck and focus to rescue her from his clutches." His laugh seems to vibrate in the air around me. "It was the first time I realized how different you were. Indomitable."

Warmth blooms in the general region of my heart, and I deny an urge to rub away the ache in my chest. It takes all my willpower to keep my mouth shut. If I say a word, I'm afraid he'll see right through me, right down to that tiny sliver of hope that lingers at my gooey center. I snap my poker face into place.

"I think you should reconsider a relationship with me." He doesn't look at me, just keeps walking toward the mountains.

The problem is that the tiny sliver of hope I cling to when it comes to Seven is locked behind a wall and guarded by a warrior forged in the urban wilds of America where I survived by protecting my heart with a ruthlessness that wasn't there before the Yule Ball. He doesn't know what I resorted to in the early days. He doesn't know the person I've become.

"Why? Because you ripped me a new asshole when I told Godmother I knew who the victim was? Was that meant to sweep me off my feet?"

"No."

"Oh, then I'm supposed to swoon into your arms because you dressed me up like a doll and treated me like an accessory at the club the other night."

"No!" He huffs in exasperation. "I didn't even want you to go! We were on a mission."

"Right, right. Gee, Seven, I'm having trouble making a case for why I should reconsider turning my life into a pretzel to have sex with you on the sly. Am I supposed to be impressed by how you somehow roped Godmother into putting me on this case—"

He stops walking and whirls to face me, grabbing my arm so that I can't ignore him. "How about because of the chemistry? The kiss we shared. The kiss you returned after you said you forgave me. How about because I can't stop thinking about you?"

I bark a laugh. "Teenage me. The me you think you remember."

"No, woman." He gives me a little shake, his eyes sparking with flecks of gold in the sunlight. "You, *now*, the pixie who was clever enough to survive and raise a daughter on her own. The one who has no problem mouthing off to my father even though he's kicked her in the teeth. I can't stop thinking about the woman who's half my size and even less lucky but won't take an ounce of shit from me or anyone else, who's brave enough to stir up answers about a murder that I wasn't able to find even though I run the godsdamned security office! The one who never backs down from a fight and would do anything for her kid. I'm talking about the woman I kissed and the one who kissed me back."

Gods, the fire I've ignited in his soul is such a turn-on, I almost let my feelings slip. But my warrior raises her spear and strokes the head of the tiger that waits by her side, all my luck, all my power, defending what's left of my heart.

"Oh that," I say with a breathy laugh. "I thought we said everything that needed to be said on the subject."

He studies me for a moment, his eyes narrowing, and then the corner of his mouth lifts. He drops my arm, and we begin walking again. "Right. You told me all about it. The world we live in, leprechauns and pixies, dirty little secrets, yada, yada, yada... Thing is, I think that's all talk. I think you want to give this thing a go as much as I do. As I recall, you held *something* against me Friday night, and it wasn't a grudge."

My mind immediately sends me a brilliant memory of my body flush against his. "I guess I let the music and the liquor get the best of me," I blurt.

"You hadn't been drinking. You never had a chance, and we'd left the music behind in the Dragonfly."

"I was tired. Thinking about the past made me nostalgic," I toss out.

"You were wet for me, and your tongue promised things your body longed to deliver."

My cheeks burn at his words, and I can't help but inhale sharply at the truth in them. I can't think of a witty comeback, so I go for the low hanging fruit. "Maybe you just got lucky. There was a lot of it flowing that night."

A deep growl rumbles in his throat, and he scowls at me. "I did not use luck to get you to kiss me. That was all you, Sophia, and you know it."

"I definitely felt your luck in that room."

"After. After you kissed me back and only for your pleasure."

I scoff mercilessly, my warrior pounding the end of her spear against the floor of my inner cave. "I guess we remember it differently," I say coldly.

"That's it," he says under his breath. Before I can react, he's taken me in his arms and his lips crash against mine.

I try to maintain my cool, try to tamp down my emotions and keep the warrior front and center, but my blood heats. It isn't luck that makes me return the kiss. There's no rush or tingle against my skin. Pure, old-fashioned passion rolls through me. I open for him and welcome a deeper kiss. His hands are in my hair. Mine are on his stomach, pressed flat and skimming the hard planes of his torso. He's hard and lean. I can't get enough. Without breaking the kiss, he finds my hips and tugs me against him. The feel of his cock, long and thick between us, is unmistakable. Gods, he really was born lucky. As I lean in, I feel light, and my left foot lifts behind me, my wings fluttering.

I've all but melted into him when he suddenly pushes me away with both hands. I'm adhered to him so thoroughly, I can almost hear a pop as the kiss breaks and I'm left cold and wanting, the weight of my backpack perceptible again.

I make a noise that sounds like "MMMhuhwah?"

He tips his head and slants me a purely masculine smile. "It's settled. It wasn't luck." He turns and starts strolling toward the mountain again.

TWENTY-FOUR

I catch up to him once my legs agree to obey. I'm livid. He's toyed with me one too many times. "Are you saying that kiss was some kind of experiment?"

Now a self-satisfied grin has taken over his face. "You claimed I used luck to get you to kiss me. I simply proved that no luck was required. You *wanted* to kiss me. You enthusiastically kissed me back."

My mouth drops open. "You asshole!"

"An asshole you enjoy kissing." He bounces a little on his toes. Did he just skip? Oh my gods!

I grumble, but I can't deny it. Instead, I just lower my head and shuffle after him, keeping space between us. "Didn't enjoy it," I mumble, but it's so obvious I'm lying that my cheeks burn hotter.

"Don't worry, Sophead, I'll do it again soon. I have every intention of making up for lost time with you and proving to you that we belong together."

Still a little dizzy, I murmur, "This again. Are you kidding me?"

Now he looks in my direction. "No. Not kidding." After a few more steps, his gaze locks on the horizon and he says, "You asked me why I thought we belonged together."

"Yeah, and I think your answer was something like I'd be a good bang."

If looks could burn, I'd be crispy. "You told me you thought I was living in the past, that my attraction to you wasn't real, but based on how I remembered you as a kid."

"It has to be. We haven't spent enough time together as adults."

"Thing is, it's both."

I glance in his direction, but his eyes are pinned to the horizon. "The day you met me, when we were both six, I was crying. I told you before that I didn't remember why, but I do."

I knew it!

"My mother forgot me."

I wince at the undercurrent of emotion in his voice, even though I'd suspected this piece of information based on what Mom had remembered.

"My father worked constantly, and my mother stayed home. She didn't have anywhere to be or anything to do. We had a housekeeper, a butler, a cook..." He scratched the back of his head. "The only thing she had to do was care for my sister and pick me up from school. She forgot. I stood outside Bailiwick's and watched all our classmates meet their parents and walk away, one after another, until I was alone. That's when I'd gone into the woods."

"That's horrible, Seven. But how could she forget you? Wouldn't your luck make sure she remembered?"

He snorted. "It should have. But the thing about a leprechaun's luck is it's directed based on our will, and another leprechaun's will and luck can counteract it."

I feel breathless as understanding bridges the space

between us. A heavy weight forms in my chest. "Your mom didn't want to remember. She left you on purpose."

He gives a solid nod. "When I was older, I realized that she'd wanted me to have to ask the headmistress to call my father. She abandoned me to get my father's attention. That never happened because you came. Your family was warm and kind to me. She always hated that. Cursed about it after your mom dropped me home."

I catch myself grinding my teeth. Seven's family situation is seriously fucked up. What type of mother tries to use their six-year-old as a pawn? A vision of Seven as a child fills my mind, and tears prick my eyes. All that luck, all that wealth, and his family situation was a steaming pile of bear dung.

"I'm so sorry, Seven. You were a child, and you deserved better."

He grins and focuses that brilliant green gaze on me. "I want to be with you, Sophia, because when I look at you, I not only see the little girl who was there for me that day, but I see a woman who uprooted her entire life for the sake of her daughter. You would never forget Arden. And more, you don't give a fuck about fae society. You are your own person. Being with you is a total escape from the constant pressure to be on all the time. You can't imagine how appealing that is to me."

I open my mouth to respond, but I'm completely speechless. My inner warrior is gone, and in her place is a warm, gooey heart-shaped pat of butter that slides over my rib cage and drops, sizzling, into my lower abdomen. I trudge toward the mountains, my memories and emotions forming a huge knot that I can't untangle.

In some ways, I wish Seven was a pixie and that I'd planted the seeds of humiliation, grief, and betrayal I'd coughed up the night of the ball. The physical manifestation of my emotions would have been a brutal thing, a dark tangle of thorns to rival my parents' feelings about me. But had I planted them, and had they grown in my parents' garden, I could have managed them now. The seeds of Seven's apology and explanation, if he were able to produce them, would choke it out. And I would know—definitively know—exactly how he felt and how strongly. I'd be able to *see* it.

But he's not a pixie, and his feelings will never take physical form like mine. Which means I have to trust what he says is true. I have to trust him. And that's a tall order for a poker player like me who's always prepared for a bluff. A woman like me who knows the sting of betrayal. It's all made more complicated by the societal pressures, including his father's control, that keep us from being together publicly. A secret relationship means no stakes and no accountability to anyone but each other. There's so much that bothers me about that.

The benefit of all this rumination is that it's distracted me from the walking we're doing. By the time I think about how far we've traveled, we are closing in on the sunny wood at the base of the mountain. I haven't felt the distance at all. It's as if my agitation has its own wings.

"You're awfully quiet over there," he finally says. "Have you sworn off speaking to me now?"

"I'm not sure what to say. You're right, I'd never forget my child. But I don't think you should romanticize what I did. There were days I regretted it. In some ways, I think, had I known what I was in for, I would have found another way."

His shoulders sag. "Tell me what it was like for you after you left... out there."

"You've been beyond Devashire. You know what it's like."

"For business. That was temporary and sanctioned. Not like what you did."

I don't want to tell him. It's not pretty. I hook my thumbs in the straps of my backpack and heave a sigh. "I don't think you really want to know."

"Try me."

I haven't told anyone this story, not even Arden. By the time she was old enough to understand our surroundings, I'd done what I'd had to do to make us a home.

"I'll start you off. When I went looking for you, I learned that you disguised yourself as a Ms. Effie Conrad. You used your luck to temporarily trap the real Effie in her hotel room by making the bathroom door handle break off in her hand. Then you used illusion to make yourself look like her, stole her passport, and boarded a bus to Tennessee. That's when you dropped off the face of the earth as far as I could tell."

Wow, he really did look into my disappearance. "I did in a way." I laugh darkly. "If you count sleeping beneath an underpass falling off the face of the earth."

His smile dissolves, but I'm relieved that the nuance in his turn of lip doesn't seem to hold disapproval. Instead, there's pity there, delayed as it may be, and I'm okay with that. It was a pitiful time in my life.

"I couldn't continue to impersonate Effie because she'd be let out of that room as soon as the cleaning crew found her. I shed her illusion in the restroom at the first stop outside the border and abandoned her identification there. Tossed it in the back of a truck."

"We wondered how it ended up in Pennsylvania."

I chew my lip. "Only problem was I couldn't be myself, obviously. So I took on the identity of a woman who was cleaning the bathrooms. Once I looked like her, I was able to take her purse from the employee area. I used her identity to get as far as Nashville, but after paying cash for the bus ticket, I only had enough for one very meager meal. I didn't dare use her credit cards. When we stopped in Lexington, I knew I had to change again and find some food quickly. Between the morning sickness and starvation, I was in danger of running out of luck. The only thing saving me was Kiko."

"Who's Kiko?"

I clam up. I don't want to tell Seven about Dark Stranger. What if he judges me? On some level, he knows what I did, but knowing something in the abstract is different from visualizing the details. I strip the memory down to its most basic components and say, "She's a Japanese lucky cat statue. She's made of jade with a blue-iron arm. I siphon off extra luck into her to store for later. She helped me a lot in the early days when I couldn't produce enough luck at one time to get by."

"Hmm." Something unreadable passes through his expression. Curiosity about the lucky charm?

I glance toward the woods. Almost there. "She was a gift from a friend," I say vaguely.

He grunts.

"Anyway, I used what luck was left in her to pose as a human undocumented worker and take a job as a maid. No one I worked with had papers, and the hotel owner was kind to me. But the pay wasn't enough to cover a place to live, so I bought a sleeping bag and slept along the underpass with other homeless people. Slowly I saved money, and with time and regular meals, I recharged my luck."

I stop speaking when Seven's finger goes to his lips. We've reached the woods, but he's hesitating to step onto the trail in front of us. Luck swirls around him like an anxious dragon. He darts a glance in my direction. "I have a feeling we shouldn't step on the path."

"What sort of feeling?" My bow is in my hand and I've nocked an arrow before I take my next breath.

He swipes a stone from the ground near our feet and throws it as far as he can down the path. As soon as it drops to the trail, a dozen six-inch tall creatures swarm it, teeth and claws flashing. Pebbles fly. The stone is reduced to gravel in seconds.

"Brutal little suckers," I whisper, backing behind Seven and returning my arrow to its quiver. My bow is useless in this situation. There are too many of them.

Seven grabs my elbow and yanks me into the thick of the trees. He holds a finger to his lips, clasping my hand in his. We begin silently picking our way through the woods until the ground ramps up and the walk becomes a climb. Hours later, we break from the trees and find ourselves on an outcropping of stone at the mouth of a cave. Seven motions for me to wait and searches within. When he comes out again, he's smiling.

"Our lucky day," he says with a wink. "It's vacant. We can spend the night here. It should be safe."

"Spend the night? I didn't know we were spending the night," I say, my voice rising in pitch.

Seven looks confused. "You thought we would cross into Shadowvale, find Yissevel's lair, and get him to answer our questions, all before popping back home in time for dinner and bed?"

I shrug. "Honestly, I was too focused on coming here at all to think about that. It sounds obvious now. Hey, there's no tent or bedroll in my pack!"

He chuckles. "That's because your old friend Seven is carrying it for you. There's only the two of us after all. More efficient to share."

He doffs his pack at the mouth of the cave and starts digging inside it.

Realization dawns. "Wait, is that your way of telling me there's only one tent?"

"It's only one night, Sophia, and I promise to keep my luck

to myself, unless you don't want me to." He casts me a crooked smile and then wanders off toward the trees.

"But... but... Where are you going?"

"To collect some firewood. Do us both a favor and find some meals in that pack of yours. I'm starving."

TWENTY-FIVE

I'm going to have to sleep next to Seven tonight, on the same mat, under the same covers, inside the same tent. Anticipation and anxiety war in my gut, flip-flopping my stomach until I can barely taste the reconstituted stew I'm eating or feel the warmth of the fire glowing in front of me. All I can think about is the kiss we shared earlier. I squirm on my log, thinking about the sleeping arrangements. Seven must sense my discomfort because we haven't said anything to each other in over an hour.

"You never finished your story." He breaks the silence, crumpling the remains of his stew bag and stowing it back in his pack to carry out. "You said you'd been... living on the streets, regaining your luck." He swallows heavily and stares down at his feet.

"Right." I'm thankful for the distraction and pick up where I left off. "I was working as a maid and posing as a human undocumented worker when the unthinkable happened." Seven is staring at me now, unblinking, as if I'm the most important person in his world. That unwavering, focused attention is intoxicating. I wonder how many women would kill to be in my position at the moment. I savor the feeling and keep on talking. "My boss figured out I was a fairy. I was so young and incredibly stupid. One day when I thought I was alone in the hotel, I spread my wings. I just needed to stretch. I'd never had them tucked away for so long before. I should have known that he'd have hidden cameras."

Seven pulls two tin cups from his pack and fills them both with boiling water from the kettle. He drops a tea bag in each and offers me a cup. "Let me guess, he threatened to turn you in."

I dunk the tea bag, watching the liquid darken within the mug. "Actually, he made me an offer. Turns out he also owned a strip club, and he was willing to pay handsomely if I could impersonate popular celebrities and show up to strip."

Seven glares at me over his tea, his expression humorless. "You worked as a stripper?"

I can't tell if the sudden tension his body is putting off is from disbelief, judgment, or plain old-fashioned male interest. "I did. It was good money, and it wasn't like I was exposing my own skin. I wasn't even naked under my illusion. All the audience saw was what I wanted them to see. But apparently that illusion was enough to attract the attention of a local pimp. He followed me back to my camp under the bridge. Of course I ditched my illusion right after the show, but this guy had figured out that one woman walked into the locker room and a different woman came out. He suspected what I was."

I've never seen Seven go so still. He isn't drinking. He isn't fidgeting. He's not even blinking. He looks like a statue across the fire, his face carefully impassive, his attention completely fixated on me.

"I'd seen this guy around. There was a prostitute who used to sleep near the spot I did. She died a few weeks after I arrived. Drug overdose. This guy was her pimp, and I guess he figured a pixie would be a stellar replacement for his dead girl. He grabbed me and tried to force me into his truck. Clocked me right in the eye. I drained all the luck I had left in Kiko and landed a knee squarely in his balls. I left him lying in the street, grabbed everything I had that could fit in my pack, and raced directly to the bus stop. I changed my appearance and bought a ticket to Las Vegas."

I look down at my tea. My hands are trembling, sending tiny ripples through the liquid. Seven stands and rounds the fire to take a seat next to me and pull me into his arms. For a long time, he doesn't say anything, just tucks my head under his chin and stares at the fire.

"Why Vegas?" he finally asks.

I sigh. "You. You'd taught me how to play poker, and it dawned on me that playing cards was safer than stripping. I had a plan. If I used luck irregularly and sparingly, I knew I could win. I was four months pregnant by that time. I needed better living arrangements, but I couldn't go to a homeless shelter because I didn't have papers."

"Smart. FIRE monitors those regularly."

"I had enough to make it to Vegas. Started playing in back rooms of bars, cash games, under the table. Sometimes I posed as a white man. Sometimes as a sweet old lady. People fell for it. And after all those games we played together, Seven, I was more than good. I was great. I hardly had to use my luck at all. I won, and I kept winning. Soon, I had enough to pay a man for a fake ID. Then I rented a tiny apartment and used the utility bills to establish a new identity. As my due date grew closer, I purchased better papers. My passport was indistinguishable from a real one. I used it to get an actual driver's license. I even obtained a social security number.

"By the time I went into labor, I had enough cash saved to pay for the delivery. A few more wins, and I'd rented my first house. And then Arden and I, we just lived. I played a half dozen big games each year and tried to avoid as much human interaction beyond the table as possible. Arden enjoyed an almost normal childhood. Oh, I told her what I was when she was old enough to keep our secret, and I eventually showed her my wings, but otherwise, she was a normal, happy little girl who attended public school and who everyone seemed to love the moment they met her."

Seven draws back and looks at me, and there's so much pain in his eyes. It's more than regret. He's tortured. I see guilt and more in his expression, though I can't fully interpret the emotions there, but I sense he blames himself for what happened to me. "It never should have been like this," he says in a voice laden with self-loathing. "You shouldn't have had to be this strong. I looked for you, Sophia. I swear I tried."

"Seven, it wasn't your fault. Your dad poisoned you." Saying the words aloud brings the horror of it to the forefront for me, and I grimace. I wonder at the damage it caused him, the scars inside that no one else can see. I wonder how he gets out of bed every morning and faces a man who cost him... I can't define what I meant to him back then, but if what he tells me is true, his father's cruelty changed everything. "Gods, how do you continue working with him after that kind of abuse?"

Seven sits up straighter and gives a maniacal laugh. "Why do you think I ended up head of security for all Dragonfly? How do you think I came to work for Godmother, Sophia?"

"I don't know. I assumed she asked for your help at some point."

He scoffs and looks away from me, shaking his head. When he speaks again, it's through his teeth. "No one will ever punish my father for what he did. He's too rich and too lucky. But I see everything now. I've made it my mission to cultivate a network that's beyond his control. Yes, he's chairman of Lucky Enterprises and has ultimate control over the Delaney family fortune. But by becoming head of security I'm in the only role in Lucky Enterprises that reports to no one but the board of directors. That position gives me the resources to stay two steps ahead of him. It gives me a feasible reason to keep secrets from him, like when I searched for you. And even his influence can't reach me when it comes to the work I do for Godmother. How do I face him every day? By knowing I've created safe zones where he can't always see me. He can't always reach me. He can't always control me. It's not total freedom, but it's a start." He takes a sip of his tea.

Everything becomes clear in that moment. Seven's path had everything to do with me and everything to do with breaking free of his father's hold. My mother said he started working for Godmother right after I left. He was trying to use his position to find me. He was trying to gain enough power to stand up to his abusive father. I don't know why with all Seven's luck and resources he didn't find me over the years, but I suspect his father had something to do with it. His bigoted, abusive, and vindictive father probably used his own luck and resources to keep me from his son. Maybe that's why I was finally caught. Maybe dear old Dad lost focus on me after all these years.

I end my internal speculation when Seven's hand cups my cheek and his touch interrupts my higher-level thinking. His face is close, our breath mingling. All my concentration is diverted to the heat rushing to my core and the need pulsing in my veins. Seven didn't mean to hurt me. He wanted me. He still wants me.

"Is it too late for us?" he asks, his lips hovering close to mine. "A relationship with me is risky. More risky for you than for me. But I know you, Sophia. You've never said no to a challenge."

"No," I admit.

"There's something here between us, a spark that refuses to go out. And it's not just from before. It's now. It's here."

"There is." Where is my inner warrior? I can't find her, and if I could I'd probably throw a bag over her head and send her packing anyway. I'm breathless from desire, my skin tingling, not from his luck but from mine. All of me wants to reach for him. I know it's a bad idea.

Despite our tangled pasts, we are nothing alike. He's a privileged, filthy-rich leprechaun who's used to getting exactly what he wants when he wants it. A relationship with him would be a constant battle to hold my own with less luck, fewer resources. It's true what he said, I'd be assuming most of the risk. If his father found out about us, the man who poisoned his own son to keep him from me, I don't even want to consider what type of hell he'd make my life to pressure me away from Seven. That possibility aside, there's the social risk. Other women would hate me and try to bring me down for stealing Dragonfly's most eligible bachelor. The social columns would be all atwitter about the scandalous relationship between a pixie and a leprechaun. Arden might be teased about it at school. My parents' shop might suffer.

For all those reasons, I know that Seven will never truly be mine. Any relationship we might have will exist in the shadows, impermanent and secret. I know this, and I am having trouble remembering why I should care. Whatever the future might bring, this thing between Seven and me has been fated for a long time. Our connection is written in the stars. What would it be like to take Seven as my secret lover?

"Maybe we should leave it up to fate," he says suddenly, standing and crossing to his bag. "Care to make a wager?" He reaches inside and pulls out a deck of cards. "Five-card draw. If I win, we give this thing between us a chance."

"And if I win?"

"You tell me."

"If I win, you owe me a favor to be named later." A favor from a leprechaun is worth far more than any amount of money.

A smile warms his expression. "Deal." He spreads a blanket from his pack on the ground beside the fire and sits cross-legged. He shuffles the cards.

"The use of luck is strictly prohibited," I clarify.

He hands me the cards. "Agreed. You deal."

His gaze holds an edge as I shuffle the cards a few more times and then deal. I place the deck in the space between us.

Everything about this situation reminds me of the poker lessons Seven used to give me. They started when I was around eleven, I think, with him showing me the different poker hands and their rankings. Over the years, our lessons turned into games, and those games turned into dates.

I look at my cards. I'm one short of a straight flush, queen through nine of clubs. He tosses two cards and draws. I toss one and grin when the king of clubs fills my hand. Our eyes lock and I tip my hand. He whistles and shows me his full house.

I've won.

His smile fades as he stares at my winning hand. "All my luck is worthless when it comes to you," he mumbles.

"What?" I heard him well enough, but my mind replays my dream. Hadn't he said something similar? A chill runs along my spine.

"Nothing." He pulls his knees into his chest and turns toward the fire. "You win. I owe you a favor. Joke's on you, I would have given one to you anyway."

He looks vulnerable, so vulnerable I can picture his heart on the ground between us. Was that what my dream was about? On some level, did my subconscious see what's been in front of me all along, since the moment I returned to Dragon-fly? The boy who once was my best friend and then my first love, the man with all the luck in the world, was still unable to win against his circumstances.

I stack the cards between us but can't stop looking at him. What happens in Shadowvale stays in Shadowvale. There are no cameras here. No prying eyes. If there's one place I can safely explore my feelings for Seven, it's here and now.

I'm probably going to regret this.

Crawling forward on my hands and knees, I press my lips to his.

TWENTY-SIX

Seven kisses me back without question, and he drags me onto his lap, supporting my back with a firm hand. My eyes close. This feels right. His kiss is soft and warm, a thorough worshipping of my lips within the fire's crackling glow.

My hands move to his face, the prickle of his stubble fascinating me. I trace my fingers behind his ears, drag my nails through the short hair at the back of his neck. The touch seems to ignite something within him. His fingers wrap around my neck, his thumb stroking the front of my throat. I open wider for him, welcoming him in. He growls his pleasure into my mouth.

That's when I feel that dragon he carries within him come to life. Luck rises in the air around us, a hot coiling purr that makes me tremble as it brushes my skin.

"Is this okay?" he asks softly.

"Yes." I can't deny this any longer. His kiss holds the promise of intense pleasure. It's been so long since I've been with anyone. So long since I've been touched. It's time we had the night we were supposed to have all those years ago. "I need you, Seven, please."

When his lips meet mine again, they bring a current of luck like I've never felt before. My blood bubbles in my veins, hot and light. Tingles slide between my breasts and out to the tips of my nipples, tightening the sensitive flesh. Effervescent heat rushes between my legs, teasing the bundle of nerves there until I ache with need for more. I gasp and he moves his kiss to my neck. I can't catch my breath. His hands work under my shirt and find my breasts, rolling their tips between his thumb and forefinger, even as his luck fizzes electric under the skin there.

"Breathe, Sophia," he says, and I realize I'm holding my breath. I blow out a shaky sigh and meld into his chest.

"This won't do." His hands circle my waist, and then I'm being lifted. My legs wrap around his waist of their own accord. Gods, in this position, his hard cock rubs against my center in a way that draws that hot tingle south, eliciting a moan that he captures in his mouth. With a grace no human man could accomplish, he gets to his feet, carries me into the cave and through the mouth of our tent, where he kneels on the pallet he's made there. A small lantern he's hung from the ceiling of the tent casts the space in a dim light.

"Up." I lift my arms. His hands are under my shirt again, and he tugs it over my head and off me. I arch into the heat of his mouth as it finds where his hands left off, teasing my nipple through the lace of my bra. Anticipation shoots through me, the tight grip of his fingers stoking my internal fire. Any attempt my thoughts make to surface are forced down by a primal instinct to give myself over to him.

A firm touch traces along the center of my back, and he unhooks my bra, casting it aside. His eyes are a hot, molten green, as if someone had melted down emeralds and mixed them with moonlight. Luck sizzles against my skin, that invisible, purring dragon winding around my neck, around my arms, between my thighs.

"Show them to me," he commands in a deep voice, all grit, that reverberates at my core, leaving me breathless. My wings unfurl. Ah, the feeling is heavenly, like letting go, like falling. He strokes each wing appreciatively, gentle and teasing at the tips, adjusting to a deep massage when he reaches the sensitive area of my back where they join the rest of my body. I lean into his touch and he sucks one of my nipples hard. Oh gods, my body hums for him like a musical instrument.

He draws back and places a hand between my breasts, pushing gently. I lean back onto my elbows so he can see me, and his fingers trace slowly over my stomach. His luck follows his gaze as he takes me in, luck, like effervescent velvet, teasing my flesh lower and lower until the ache between my legs is an exquisite torture. I tip my head back and pant. If he keeps this up, I'm going to come before he even touches me below the waist.

"Not yet. Not before I taste you." It's a command, and his luck draws back. I desperately want to chase after the feeling, but he casts a wicked grin in my direction. "Have a little patience, Sophia."

He pulls my boots off one by one, then makes short work of my zipper. My pants and everything underneath come off next. He's still fully dressed, and I reach for his fly, but he dodges my touch. "Not yet. Lean back."

"You're not the boss of me." I reach for his fly again, and his luck plows into me like a hot fizzy wave. It fills me from within, pressing against my inner walls. I gasp and fall back on my elbows, arching into the hot purr.

"That's better," he says. His hands land on my knees, stroke down to grip my inner thighs tight enough that it's just on the edge of pain, and he spreads my legs, baring me to him. I'm so exposed in every way. Completely naked, my body thrumming under the influence of his power. He's kneeling between my thighs, fully clothed and watching me hungrily. What must I look like? Mouth swollen from his rough kisses, nipples hard, core slick with need.

"Gods, I've waited a long time for this." His voice is lower, gritty. Luck pounds into me again. I arch and spread my knees wider. I'm beyond words.

"Mmm. Good girl." He presses a kiss at the apex of my thighs. I moan, tension coiling deep within me. His hands find my hips and he pulls back, blowing cool air over my clit. I've only just processed the sensation when he flattens his tongue and licks up my slit from back to front. I almost buck off the mat. I feel his dark laugh rumble against me as his tongue toys with my most sensitive flesh and the rush of his luck fills me from the inside again.

This is what it's like with a leprechaun. When he gets lucky, he gets lucky. He knows exactly where to touch me. Exactly what I need. His tongue is fluttering in just the right spot as his fingers follow the vibration of his luck to massage inside me.

I lose all control. I arch and cry out as an orgasm rips through me. It's intense, all-consuming, but he doesn't let up. He sucks me into his hot mouth as his fingers work deep inside, thrusting in just the right place.

"Seven, it's too much," I say breathlessly.

"Again," he commands, and that hot purr fills me once more.

I haven't even come down completely from my first orgasm when the second one plows into me, more intense than the first. I turn boneless, riding out the aftershocks flat on my back. "Seven!"

This time, he stretches out beside me, a decidedly male and self-satisfied grin on his face, and watches me recover. His hand is splayed across my belly, warm, firm fingers bridging from hip to ribs.

"I've waited a long time to do that," he says. "I wanted it to be memorable."

Memorable? More like life altering. I shudder in his arms as an aftershock of pleasure rocks through me. I stare at him through my lashes, tipping up the corner of my mouth. "Goal achieved. But the game isn't over." I reach for his fly and hear his breath hiss between his teeth.

Things are just getting interesting when a feral growl splits the night. Seven grabs my wrist and tips his ear toward the tent flap. He frowns and leaps to his feet, zipping and buttoning his pants again. "Stay here. This won't take long."

Bullshit. I'm not letting him face whatever unseelie might be out there alone.

He slips out the tent and into the night. I dress, pull on my boots and grab my bow and quiver, following him into the darkness. Light on my feet, I move silently toward the edge of the plateau. I can't see Seven, but I'm so hopped up on his luck, I can sense him. My eyes adjust to the dark and I meld into the woods.

Almost immediately, I spot the beast facing off against Seven. It's cerulean blue with lime green spots that might be beautiful if the creature wasn't obviously deadly. With a mouth lined with three rows of teeth and six sets of nostrils that run from the upper lip to its ridged brow, I'm sure its bite is every bit as deadly as its roar.

Seven stands in its line of sight, about a hundred feet from it, sweat blooming on his brow. His eyes flare that brilliant emerald green. I can feel the brush of his luck but can't see what he's trying to do. The night sky is clear. None of the trees look as if they might fall. The ground doesn't quake. He might be trying to stop the beast's heart, but if he is, it isn't working.

The beast prowls slowly toward Seven. I raise my bow and nock an arrow. A bird lands on a heavy branch that stretches far up and across the pathway between the beast and Seven. Another bird lands and then another and another. The creature prowls forward. Luck surges off Seven, and the fattest raccoon-like creature I've ever seen bounds out on the same branch.

Crack. The branch drops, smashing onto the beast's head. The birds scatter and the raccoon creature leaps to the tree with a shriek. It's a huge branch and a long drop. The beast's chin slams into the ground and blood dribbles from its nostrils. Seven dusts off his hands and turns back toward camp.

Shit, he's a sweaty mess. He looks... empty. There are dark circles under his eyes, and he's limping a little. His appearance doesn't make sense. That tree branch couldn't have drained a leprechaun's luck. Then it dawns on me that he's drained because of *me*, because of what we did. He was thrumming my body with luck only minutes ago, and damn, he must have pulled out all the stops.

He hasn't seen me yet. I've used my luck to camouflage myself. I'm dark as night and the texture of tree bark. Still, if he had any luck left at all, he'd have noticed me. He must be bone dry.

The branch moves. I look back at the beast and it's rising, shaking its head and snorting angrily. Seven's eyes widen when he sees it. He pulls something from his pocket that flashes gold in the moonlight.

The beast pounces.

My arrow flies, and I focus all my luck on making my aim true. The living arrow enters the creature's ear and slices through the thickest part of its head. Its body seizes in the air, but Seven has to throw himself out of the way to avoid its claws as it crumples to the earth, dead. Now Seven's eyes find me, and I drop my illusion.

"Thanks," he says.

"Don't mention it." I wink. "But I might. I might mention it a lot to as many people as possible. I think the story of how Sophie the pixie saved the ass of Seven the leprechaun would make a great bar ballad." I sling a slow cheeky smile in his direction.

"Sophia Larkspur, was that a joke? Gods, she still has a sense of humor." He swaggers toward me, his confidence outweighing the luck he has left in his arsenal.

"No," I say flatly. "I'm not being funny. I plan to tell everyone who will listen that I saved your life with my badass archery skills."

His eyes narrow. "Will you also tell them what we were doing that caused me to almost drain myself dry?" His gaze rakes lasciviously down my body, and I quell the desire to squirm.

"Eating by the fire?"

"No. After the eating but before the monster. In the tent." He's standing right in front of me. Close. Temptingly close.

I rub my chin. "I'm not sure I remember exactly how you got yourself into this mess, Seven."

He grabs me around the waist and sweeps me against him, leaving me breathless. "Perhaps I should show you again."

We're both panting now, and all I can think is that Seven is in my arms. He's mine again. It's like something out of a dream.

"I'd like that," I say breathlessly.

He sighs. "Unfortunately, we both need to sleep and recharge in case any of his friends come back." He points his chin at the dead beast.

As a pixie, I can't propel luck into him like he's done to me.

It crosses my mind to give him Kiko, but it takes time to siphon off enough luck to fill her. She's for emergencies, and having hot leprechaun sex with Seven hardly fits that description as much as it might seem so at the moment. "You can't have hot leprechaun sex without luck?"

Taking my hand, Seven tugs me toward the tent. He arches a brow and shoots me a look that makes my stomach do a little backflip. "Patience, Sophia. For what I plan to do to you, I need a full tank."

TWENTY-SEVEN

Lucky me, I wake with a leprechaun curled around me. We're both fully dressed, but his arm holds me firmly against his chest and his breath skates along the base of my neck. The corners of my lips curl upward, as a warm, contented feeling fills me.

Warning bells draw me fully awake. It's dangerous to feel this way. This emotion is too close to the blind adoration I felt as a teenager, the same feeling that came before the worst experience of my life. Allowing myself to think Seven is mine, to flirt with loving him again, makes me vulnerable. It's foolish. It's fantasy.

Then I remember that fooling around in Shadowvale means nothing. No one can see us here. Seven doesn't have to face his father's wrath here. It's the ultimate place to keep a secret. Since I've returned to Devashire, our relationship has been all about secrets. He has a professional reason to be near me thanks to Godmother. He's been careful not to show public displays of affection. At the club, he made me change my appearance. He's always kept his distance or used luck to keep anyone from noticing us together.

I'd be an idiot to think this is anything more than exactly what it was, one night of pleasure. Isn't that why I allowed myself to indulge in it in the first place? It was supposed to be a safe way to get this thing with Seven out of my system.

A bone-deep sadness weighs me down at the thought. Last night, I'd convinced myself I'd be okay with becoming Seven's secret lover, at least for one night. This morning, in the light of day, it's oh so clear that my heart—my crazy, vulnerable, traitorous heart—wants more. I know this feeling. I've been here before. I'm falling in love with Seven.

A tear streams down my cheek and I wipe it away.

"Hey, what's going on inside that pretty little head?" He shifts to press a kiss to my temple, and frowns as he wipes away another tear.

"I think... last night was a mistake," I say softly.

He pushes himself up to a seated position, his expression turning stone-cold serious. "No, it wasn't."

I sit up too, pressing both hands to my chest. "Last night was incredible, but we both know that once we leave here, it will be like this never happened. Sure, we could carry on in secret for a while, but at some point, you'd be expected to marry some equally powerful and successful leprechaun to carry on your family's dynasty. Sooner or later, what happened here will be a distant memory. It will be better, less painful for both of us if it's sooner."

"You seem to think you know my future better than I do." He folds his arms in reproach.

"We both know it's inevitable." *And I feel too much for you to taste what it's like to have you, knowing I'll have to give you up.* I wipe another round of tears.

"Because you think I would never take this relationship public."

I tip my head. "You have your father, your company, and your reputation to think about Seven. I don't judge you; I just need... more."

He snorts and points at his chest. "You don't judge me? I don't care about any of that, Sophia. If this were just about me, I'd do it in a heartbeat to have you. I might be able to keep you safe from my father, but the minute people found out about us, they'd gossip and harass you. The things they would say would make your and Arden's life hell. The secrecy is as much for your sake as mine."

"I know," I say, my heart clenching painfully.

He shakes his head. "You don't. Not all of it. Standing up to my father means being prepared to break from Lucky Enterprises. He holds a controlling interest. Honestly, I'd consider it if not for what it would mean for people with fewer choices than me. I wouldn't be there anymore to buffer Evangeline from his bullshit. I've done it since we were small, and she's not ready to handle him herself. And then there are the employees. You know, before I took control, there were no benefits for pixies and satyrs, and the pay hadn't kept up with inflation in twenty years. Oh, and under Dad's control, pixies wouldn't be allowed as customers in the club anymore. He doesn't think they belong."

"More of a reason we should end this here, before it gets more... complicated." *Before I fall in love with you.*

He considers that for a moment. All at once, his eyes go wild, feral, like an animal backed into a corner. "No," he says firmly.

"No?" I wait for him to elaborate.

His jaw clenches and his lips twitch. But he just looks at me and repeats, "No!"

I gape at him, unsure what to say to that. It's just as well, he slips out of the tent before I have a chance to say anything.

For the time it takes to pack up my things and roll up the blankets and the mat, I consider his "no" and my blood starts to heat. Since when does he get to decide? I haven't made any commitments. I'm a grown woman and I know what's best for me. I burst from the tent in a full huff, throwing the roll at him with an unnecessary amount of force.

"I'm sensing you have something to say." He starts strapping the rolls onto his pack.

I lift my chin. "You don't get to tell me no, Seven."

He slams a cup into his pack. "I've waited too long to get you back. I'm not giving you up that easily. We should have never been apart in the first place. If it wasn't for my father's interference—"

"You know, I thought about that. I asked myself just now, if we'd kept our relationship secret sixteen years ago, would we still be together?"

"Of course we would," he says. "You wouldn't have left Devashire if the Yule Ball never happened."

I shake my head. "I don't think so. Because even if I never left, I would have grown up, Seven, and I would have wanted more. I am *worth* more than being someone's dirty little secret."

"I never suggested you become my *dirty little secret*. I'd never treat you that way."

"You didn't have to suggest it. It's the only option left once going public and staying apart are off the table." Tears blur my vision as I step into him and fist his shirt, bringing our faces close. My voice cracks as I say, "I am a pixie, and I am a woman, and I deserve love and happiness. I've been through too much to settle for less. Arden has been through too much. The fact is, I have lived a lie for the last sixteen years, and I was good at it Seven." I shake my head. "I've perfected the bluff. But I realize now, facing another life of lies, that I just don't want to do it anymore. It's time for me to cut my losses, fold, and leave the table. Last night, I thought I could settle, I thought stolen moments with you would be enough, but I was wrong. I want it all or I want nothing, and in our world, all just isn't possible. I'm sorry." I'm trembling as I release him.

Pain travels through Seven's expression before his face turns impassive and cold. His voice is flat and emotionless as he says, "You're right. You deserve more."

He turns from me and we dismantle the tent in silence.

An hour later, I find myself hiking along a path between two mountains. It's cold, and I've donned every layer of clothing in my pack and tucked my wings inside for warmth. We haven't said a word to each other since we left the campsite. But we're going to have to get over what happened and move beyond our feelings because I see a flash of bone white through the trees up ahead and I think we've reached our destination.

"What's the plan, Seven?" I whisper. The hair on my arms is standing on end, and I find myself touching my bow to reassure myself it's still there.

He grunts. "We walk into Yissevel's lair and ask him what he was doing in Dragonfly. See what he says."

I laugh. "Do you expect him to answer us before or after he tears our teeth and bones from our bodies?"

"Hoping for before," he says a little too seriously. He's scanning our surroundings, likely analyzing how he can leverage luck in this situation.

"Hope isn't a strategy."

He snorts.

"What happened to that gun I saw you wearing the other day?"

"The guardians won't let it through. We're in unseelie territory. It's considered a human weapon and isn't allowed."

"But my bow is?"

He kicks up an eyebrow. "Invented by a pixie."

Hmm. I had no idea. I blow out a deep breath. "Yissevel can't fly," I say. "I'll ask the questions, and you pummel him with luck. If we get into trouble, I'll take off. You'll be okay, right?" He knows what I mean. I want to know if he's recharged the luck he spent on me last night.

A corner of his mouth tips up. "At full power. I'll survive. Don't worry about me."

"It's a plan." Not a very good one but the best I can think of.

I take my bow off my shoulder and nock an arrow. We're close enough now that I start to worry. Yissevel's home is bone white for a reason. Up close, I can make out pyramids of skulls, bleached white from the sun, wedged together to form a foundation for a network of femur bones, some human, some not, that create the entrance. The path to his front door is pebbled with teeth.

I wonder again how this creature could have spawned the human folklore of the Tooth Fairy. It was like people couldn't tolerate the horror, so their minds created a more palatable fiction, a creature who took sacrificial teeth in exchange for money and looked more like a pixie than a monster. What would they do if they knew the truth?

We approach the eight-foot-tall doors made of polished ivory. Seven grabs on to the bone handle and pulls. I guess we're not knocking then. The door swings open.

I have a bad feeling about this.

The crunch of our boots on the millions of teeth lining the entryway sends chills along my skin as I follow Seven inside. It's quiet here. Too quiet. Only now do I miss the strange sounds of birdlike creatures that accompanied us on our journey here. This place is as silent as a tomb and smells like one as well. Not a rotting smell—no fresh dead here—but the scent of ancient things, bleached bone, leather, and dust. I make the mistake of looking up and realize we are in a catacomb of sorts. The room is shaped like a church, the bones narrowing to a point, the gaps between letting in enough daylight to see by.

The teeth in front of my toes rattle although I haven't moved. They settle, then rattle again. "Seven?"

I draw a shaky breath as I whirl toward the hall at the end of the large room we're in. Seven is already turned in that direction. Luck coils around him, and something gold glints in his hand. It distracts me for a second before my eyes snap back to the hall.

Yissevel is there, the floor vibrating with every heavy footstep.

The creature is more horrific than I'd imagined. Seeing him on camera and in sketches hasn't prepared me for this. He's at least eight feet tall and composed entirely of bones held together by sinew and what must be magic. His head is a flesh-less skull with tufts of hair growing from the bones, rheumy eyes, a hole where a nose should be, and a lipless smile of narrow teeth. Within his rib cage, a heart must beat because I see the leathery connective tissue pulse beneath his left arm. He stares down in our general direction, wearing nothing but a loose and filthy cloth that circles his waist and ties over one shoulder. Yissevel is a walking, breathing skeleton from my deepest, darkest nightmares, and he's staring at Seven as if he's his next meal.

"Back so soon?" Yissevel sniffs the air.

What? I look between Yissevel and Seven, who is visibly shaken. Yissevel's eyes swivel in his skull and I realize he's not focusing on either of us. His eyesight must not be very good. He tips his head back and sniffs the air again. He can't see us; he smells us.

"What have you brought me this time, leprechaun?" Yissevel takes another step forward. "More meat? More *bones*?"

"We've come to ask for your help," I say in a loud clear voice. My arrow is still anchored between my fingers, the bowstring drawn taut.

Yissevel stops, pivots toward me and sniffs. "A pixie? Not expecting you. You need help? First, you bring Yissevel teeth!" he booms.

"Was a leprechaun here before?" My hands are shaking, and I try in vain to steady my arrow. Beside me, Seven's eyes glow. He's completely focused on the bone fairy.

The creature's head turns right, then left, sniffing the air. "A leprechaun brings me a pixie, and now a pixie brings me a leprechaun? What treachery there is among the seelie."

A leprechaun *was* here before. I glance at Seven, but he doesn't look my way. His luck slithers around the room. Out of the corner of my eye, I see him squat and pick something up from among the carpet of teeth.

"What did the leprechaun who was here before want you to do?" I ask. "You said he brought you a pixie. Was she dead or alive when he gave her to you?"

"Just dead. Yissevel prefers dead. He will not do it again."

"Do what again?"

"Yissevel does not care for the smell in that place. Too sweet." The creature sniffs again. Takes another step toward me. "Pixie hearts are sweet but small. Barely a meal. Not enough payment to cross the silver. Yissevel will only leave for human meat, human bones. He likes them best."

"Who was here before? Who offered you pixie flesh in exchange for your help?"

"You would know, little one. Tell him Yissevel will not go

again for only pixie. Man flesh is what I crave." The creature whirls faster than anything that big should move. He sniffs the air in front of Seven. "Although Yissevel wouldn't mind sampling leprechaun. You are different. Younger. Sweeter."

"Was it an *older* leprechaun who visited you before?" I ask.

He snorts and sniffs closer to Seven.

"There's been a mistake," Seven says. He backs for the door, waving a hand at me to do the same. "Sorry to have bothered you."

What's he doing? We can't leave now! We still don't know who killed Phoebe or how Yissevel made it through the silver.

"No bother." The creature takes a step toward us. "Come closer. Let Yissevel look at you."

Seven starts moving in earnest toward the door, motioning for me to go too.

"First taste of leprechaun." Yissevel lunges, faster than I expect. His hand sweeps toward Seven... and misses! The boney fingertips of the creature's fingers brush against his shirt as Seven leans out of reach.

My arrow flies. *Fuck!* I didn't consciously release it, but seeing that thing dive for Seven, my fingers acted of their own accord. I was aiming for that pulse under its left arm, but he's already shifted and the arrow bounces harmlessly off Yissevel's rib cage. The only thing I've accomplished with that shot is to turn its attention from Seven back on me.

Yissevel growls and charges. "Come here pixie treat!"

I jump and lift straight up as his fist closes around the space where I just was. "I thought you liked your meat dead!"

"Hungry," Yissevel bellows. "Exceptions must be made."

I flutter my wings faster but I can only fly so high. The ceilings in this bone dwelling aren't tall enough for me to rise out of his reach.

"Get the fuck out of here!" Seven yells, motioning for me to fly toward the door. True anger rattles his voice.

I try to flee, but Yissevel is on me, sniffing the air and reaching for me. As I drop to fly through the open door, a boney hand closes around me, crushing my wings.

"Let me go!" I scream.

"Pretty teeth. Pretty bones," it says, its rank breath blowing back my hair as it brings me toward its mouth.

"Put her down, Yissevel," Seven warns. His voice is charged with luck, and it rattles the bones over our heads.

Yissevel's milky gray eyes shift, but he doesn't even pause. He holds me as the claws of his opposite hand reach toward my chest. "Heart first. Then spleen. Then the bones in between," he singsongs.

Just like he did to the others, only I'm alive to experience it. *Fuck!* I turn my face away.

Gold flashes through the air and plunks against the bones of the roof. Yissevel has just enough time to swivel his eyes up before the ceiling collapses on his head. I scream as he drops me, my crushed wings unable to recover fast enough to carry my falling weight.

Seven catches me in his arms with an oomph, barely an inch outside the collapse of bones. He sets me on my feet, then holds out his hand. A gold coin falls from the sky into it. I've never seen a coin like this. I watch him flip it over his knuckles and between his fingers. There's a woman on one side, a dragonfly on the other, and it looks positively ancient.

He pushes me toward the exit before I have time to ask him about it, and I don't hesitate to move. He's right behind me... until suddenly he's not. Seven's being dragged across the carpet of teeth. Behind him the pile of bones rattles and falls away from Yissevel who rises, pissed off but otherwise unhurt. Seven dangles by one leg over Yissevel's mouth. The coin flies from his hand, hitting the creature in one eye. Yissevel roars and drops Seven but catches him in his opposite hand. The gold rolls under the pile of bones.

I nock my last arrow and aim it at Yissevel's heart. I don't let it fly, however, because the ground has started to quake. Seven. He's sweating buckets, luck coiling off him and between us like the massive invisible dragon I picture it to be. He has limited options; there's nothing around us but fallen bones. My skin tingles with the intensity of the power flowing off him.

Yissevel sways on his feet. He snaps at Seven with his teeth, but he can't steady himself enough to get the leprechaun into his mouth.

The ground cracks to my left, bringing down one wall of Yissevel's lair. It only serves to enrage him more.

Leprechaun or not, there's no way Seven can keep this up. I take a deep breath and stretch my wings. They're sore, but when I flap them, I lift off the ground. Once in the air, the earthquake can't shake my bones and I level my arrow, aiming at Yissevel's heart.

"Make it count, Sophead. I'm almost out of juice!" Seven yells, his eyes two emerald green spotlights in the dim interior.

I close one eye and release my held breath. The arrow flies. It slips between Yissevel's ribs and pierces the throbbing sinew there. Seven drops like a stone from the creature's hand and crumples into the piles of bones, but my aim was true. Yissevel topples, blows out a breath, and moves no more.

Only after I'm sure the unseelie monster is dead do I land and pull my arrow from his side. I wipe it on the creature's garb before sliding it back into my quiver. I might need it for the journey home. The earth has stopped quaking. *Seven.* I run to him. His shirt is soaked with sweat, and he's lying perfectly still, face pallid.

"Are you hurt?" I ask.

He nods. "Ankle." A shard of bone from the collapsed wall protrudes from the flesh just below his calf. I reach for it, but he stops me, "No!" He swallows hard. "I used too much luck. I'm negative. If you remove that now, I'll bleed out."

"You let yourself go negative?" I say disbelievingly.

"Gods, Sophia. It wasn't intentional. I was trying to save our hides and heal your wings at the same time."

I remember my crushed wings, incapable of flight when Yissevel had dropped me. I was able to carry my weight at just the right time. Not my doing. "Hold still."

He gives me a wary look.

I reach into my bag for Kiko and press her jade belly into his hand. He takes a deep breath. Slowly, color returns to his cheeks. I dig out the first aid kit and find the bandages. He sits up and yanks the bone from his leg. Lucky him, it wasn't in as deep as I'd feared. I press a piece of gauze to the wound to stymie the blood and then start to wrap it.

"Who do you think was using Yissevel? It sounded like it was a leprechaun."

Seven frowns. "I'm not sure, but I intend to find out." His voice sounds funny. I glance in his direction, my mind fighting my heart on what to do next.

"Yissevel thought you were him at first."

"Because a leprechaun was behind this."

"A leprechaun who smells like you."

"It wasn't me, Sophia."

"No." I want to look away from him as I say it, but I force myself to hold his gaze. "But maybe it was someone in your family."

He shakes his head, but I sense it's not in denial but disappointment. "Why would he do this? He already has everything."

"Why would he poison you?" My voice rises in volume.

"Why would he say what he said to me? Why does he hate pixies so damn much?"

"Think about what you're accusing him of. This is more than bigotry. This is murder. Murder of humans, inside and outside Devashire."

"But he has a special pass from the US government, doesn't he? He has to as the chairman of Lucky Enterprises. All those slot machines your company sells to US casinos and the Dragonfly merchandise... He has to meet with buyers. That can't all take place in Devashire."

"No," Seven says through his teeth.

"He hates pixies." I frown. "I don't know why he used Yissevel or why he killed those two humans, but he is the most likely to have the means. He must be working with one of the elves or somehow have a mirror."

As soon as I've tied off the bandage, he hands Kiko back to me, clambers to his feet and limps toward the exit. I put her away before hoisting the pack onto my shoulders and following after him.

"I'm not trying to upset you, Seven. I just think we have to consider the most obvious explanation for what just happened. Chance Delaney is our most likely suspect."

"Shut up, Sophia."

I balk, a weight forming in my chest at the harshness in his tone. I'm exhausted. I don't have the energy to fight him on this or to carry the burden of the truth alone.

His eyes spark emerald when he turns back toward me. "I'm not saying you're wrong." His expression softens. "But please, for five minutes, just let me think."

All righty then. I drop back a few feet. I won't let Seven deny this, but I understand why the trauma he's lived through might cause him to avoid the hard truth. I can't be part of that denial. When we get back to Devashire, I'll tell Godmother everything, whether or not Seven is on board with that plan. I don't know why Chance Delaney committed these murders, and I don't care. He's going to finally pay—for this, for what he did to Seven, and for what he did to me. I will take him down with my own boot on his neck if I have to. I'd rather have Seven on board though, so I back off and remain silent.

The journey is thankfully uneventful, and we set up camp on the same plateau we did before. Once the tent is erected and the fire blazes between us, Seven finally looks at me and breaks the silence with four little words.

"I lied to you."

TWENTY-EIGHT

I lower the cup of tea I'm holding and glare at him. "You lied to me? About what?"

"The night my father poisoned me, he didn't lock me in my room."

My blood turns to ice at the admission. There's something about the way he says it that unsettles me, like he's sharing a dark secret, like he's peeling back the curtain on a deep shame. I give him my full attention.

"So you *were* free to leave, but still didn't find help or a way to tell me what happened?" I say the words without judgment. The thought will be hard to live with, but I can forgive him for it. He was just a kid, in a horrible situation. I think of him back then, barely older than Arden. The memory hurts, but I can move beyond it.

He rubs his palms together slowly. "What I mean is, my father didn't hold me in my bedroom. He has... cells under his hunting cabin in the mountains outside Elderflame. He took me there when I was unconscious and locked me up. I'd never been there before. I didn't know how depraved he was until then."

The horror of the revelation makes my skin crawl. "Seven, are you saying that your father has actual prison cells under his hunting cabin where he locked you up?" I lower my voice although there is no one here to overhear us. "Was it like a sex dungeon or something?"

He shakes his head. "I don't know for sure what it is or why it's there, but there was nothing pleasurable in that room." He's silent for a moment, staring down into his tea. "And I wasn't alone."

My hand trembles, and I almost spill my drink. "Seven..."

"There was a woman in the cell next to mine. I never saw her face, but she spoke to me through the wall. She comforted me." He closes his eyes, and I can see the burden this secret has placed on him. Then it dawns on me, this conversation isn't just about then. It's about now.

"Oh my gods, Seven! Do you think he was keeping the woman prisoner there? Was she a pixie?"

A muscle in his jaw twitches, and he rubs it absently. He hasn't shaved since we left Devashire, and I can hear his stubble grate against his fingers. Seven, the leprechaun who always looks fresh and acts smooth, suddenly appears old and worn. I've reached the great and powerful Oz and pulled back the curtain to find the heart of an emotionally exhausted boy.

"Anything is possible." He rubs his eyes. "And then there's this." He holds a button up between his thumb and forefinger.

"What is that?"

"It's a button. A custom-made button with the initials VS on the back."

"Who's VS?"

"Valentine Sullivan. He's a satyr who makes custom

buttons. These things are hundreds of dollars a pop. Whoever was using Yissevel was extremely rich."

I set my tea on the ground beside my feet and round the fire to sit next to him. "Your father has always outwardly hated pixies. What if he abducted those women?"

Seven stares into the fire. "Maybe he didn't have to. Maybe they were there willingly."

"What?"

"The woman who comforted me didn't seem unhappy, Sophia. She didn't ask me to send help once I was freed."

"Oh my gods."

"He's the luckiest creature in Devashire, and every one of them was in that club, looking for... something."

"But... but... if they were his mistresses, why would he use Yissevel to have one of them killed?"

"I don't know that he did. I've been thinking about this, and Yissevel said it was someone who smelled like me. Not necessarily my father. Maybe it was another leprechaun. A jealous rival who wants to embarrass my father by creating enough havoc that his pixie fetish is made public."

I wince. Pixie fetish. *Fuck.* It makes sense. Chance was always extreme in his outward hatred toward me and other pixies. It's like those human homophobes who finally come out as gay. If pixies were his secret passion, it explains why he worked so hard to insulate himself from suspicion.

"It's possible a rival is trying to frame him or perhaps blackmail him." I place my hand on Seven's leg supportively.

He exhales a shaky breath. "If my father was involved, we have to have proof before we go to Godmother. He's too powerful. If he finds out we're on to him, he'll have all his t's crossed and i's dotted before Godmother can even question him or I can call in enough officers to contain him."

"We have to go there," I say. "If you can get us into that

cabin, there might still be women there. We can question them, find out what they know. We have two dead humans and one dead pixie. It's possible that your father has no connection at all to Phoebe, but there's only one way to find out for sure."

He nods his head. "Tomorrow is Wednesday. Dad will be meeting with the accountants at the casino to review their weekly breakdown of revenue and expenses. We can go while he's distracted."

WE WAKE EARLY AND ARRIVE AT THE WALL BEFORE midday. One of the elves spots us from the watchtower, and minutes later the mirror liquefies to allow us to pass. Either I've become resistant to the pull of the swirling stars or it's easier to pass into Devashire from Shadowvale than the other way around. Whatever it is, this time I'm not tempted to dive to my doom.

I lean back against the leather seat of Seven's Mercedes as we zoom through the streets of Elderflame and up into the mountains where only the wealthiest of his kind maintain homes. Ancient forest surrounds us. We gain elevation, and the road becomes narrower until eventually blacktop gives way to stone and Seven has to slow his vehicle to keep from kicking up rubble.

I've never been to this area. To say it is remote would be an understatement. We are over two hours from Dragonfly, and that's with Seven driving at top speed. There is no one out here. I haven't seen a home or driveway in twenty minutes.

No one to hear you scream.

This entire mess is creeping me out. I'd suspected Seven's family was dysfunctional after what I'd learned the past few days, but "dungeon under the hunting cabin" is a step beyond what I ever imagined, even on those nights sleeping under that bridge when Chance became every devil in my nightmares. I comfort myself with the thought that we might be minutes away from the clue that connects us to the killer and solves this murder. If we take Chance down in the process, more reason to celebrate.

Seven pulls into a winding drive and stops before a log cabin that is far bigger than my parents' home. It's grander than any home I've ever lived in. Luxury cabin would be a better descriptor than hunting cabin. It's perfectly landscaped with eastern bluestar, butterfly weed, and cardinal flower, edged in partridgeberry. A walkway of bluestone leads to the door.

"Leave your bow," Seven says.

"What? Why?"

"In case we run into the housekeeper. It'll be hard to explain. I promise I'll protect you from anything we find down there."

Housekeeper or houseguest, if we do find someone in Chance's dungeon who wants to be there, I can see how sticking an arrow in her face would be a poor way to say hello. I leave my bow and quiver with my pack.

Once the car is parked, I open the door and start for the cabin but Seven stops me with a wave of his hand. "Careful."

I look where he's pointing. A circle of red-capped toadstools lines the property. "A fairy ring. He's warded the place." Not a particularly strong ward but the best he could do with luck alone. He'd need old magic like Godmother's to create something stronger.

"I've got it." Seven focuses his energy, and I feel his power swirl between us. He leans down and digs up one of the mushrooms with his bare hands, breaking the ring. He carries it to the fountain and places the bottom in the water. "I'll replace it on our way out."

We walk together toward the front door, but then he takes my hand and leads me around to the back of the cabin. He stops in front of a subterranean window with a deep well lined in stone. It's dark, dank, and home to one too many spiders.

"You can't be serious." I flash him an incredulous look.

"This is how I got out last time."

I feel my eyes bulge. "Wait, you had to break out? I thought your father let you out!"

He reaches down and jostles the narrow window. The lock gives way, and it slides open. Without another word, he slips through the dark opening.

I can't believe I'm doing this. My skin turns clammy and my heart flutters at the sight of that dark hole. *Sure, drop into my father's dungeon where pixies are being held and maybe tortured and killed.* Pixies like me. Held by a leprechaun who outwardly hates *me.* Why am I doing this?

"Crazy," I mumble to myself. But I know why. There's no other way. If the worst is happening, Seven and I are in a unique position to take Chance down, but only if we can stay ahead of him. If I don't do this, his next victim could be someone I love, someone like Penelope or gods-forbid, Arden. That last thought drives me on. I blow out a breath and drop through the window.

My eyes adjust, and I see Seven at the end of a long stone hallway. It's too dim for me to read his expression but his body language is grim, his shoulders slumped, his head bowed. I walk toward him but pull up short when I pass the first room. These aren't cells with bars but chambers with glass-paneled doors. I can see inside, but if the pixie caged there can see me, she doesn't show it. She's filthy, dressed in rags and thinner than any pixie should be, sitting cross-legged on a narrow bed.

A primal urge to run sends a tremor through me. I force myself to try the doorknob, but of course it's locked.

"Seven, get her out of there," I say. It will take more luck than I have to find the key or crack the lock.

"There are five of them, Sophia. The other five."

I rush down the hall, counting the women behind the windows. My voice shakes as I say, "I see that. Let's get them out of here and call Godmother for backup. Your father did this. He has to be stopped."

Seven turns to me, and I realize why he isn't moving. A lump forms in my throat at the defeated look in his eyes. He's broken. Damaged. Burning up from the inside. I can see him turning to ash right in front of me.

I take his face in my trembling hands. "This is not your fault. Your father did this. Not you. He's a very sick man. But right now it's up to us to make this right. Help me get these people out of here."

The words are barely out of my mouth when the door that must lead to the rest of the house flies open and Chance Delaney strides in.

CHAPTER

TWENTY-NINE

"What are *you* doing here?" Chance growls. He straightens his tie, looking as if he came directly from the boardroom in his carefully tailored suit. Not a hair out of place. No one would suspect the horror show he created here just by looking at him.

My skin crawls thinking about what he's done. Slowly, I inch toward the window. If I can slip out, I can call Godmother for help.

"Why? Why did you do this?" Seven gestures toward the locked rooms, toward the vacant eyes of the women inside them.

"This is where they belong, son," Chance says seriously. "They're a lesser species. They're ours to own. Don't tell me you haven't wanted one for yourself. Dammit, the truth is standing right there." He points at me.

"I want her but not to own. As a partner... to love." He glares bravely at his father.

I stop moving, frozen by the revelation. Seven wants me *to love*. Warmth spreads through my torso, even as the horror around me leaves me cold.

"Don't be a fool. No one will accept it. It just isn't done. Besides, they *want* to be owned."

"Then why kill her? Phoebe?" Seven asks through his teeth.

"That... was an accident. That little bird swore she'd never sullied herself with a human. I caught her with her hands on him. I thought it would be enough to kill the human scum in front of her, but she wasn't content like my other birds. She wanted out. And of course I couldn't allow that to happen. Once something is mine, it's mine. She said she wanted a relationship, then changed her mind. Flighty little bitch. I *had* to punish her. Sadly, she broke under pressure."

My blood turns to ice at his evil grin, and I take another slow step back. Almost there. I can feel a breeze drift through the open window and my heart races, desperately wanting out of this room.

"So you killed her and fed her to Yissevel."

He chuckles. "Brilliant plan on my part. Convenient way to dispose of the body."

"But why leave the remains in the square? You must know how bad it would be for business if humans saw that." Seven's face is distorted in disgust. He steps slowly to his left, drawing Chance's attention away from me.

Chance scoffs. "So much to learn..." He shakes his head. "Dragonfly isn't everything, Seven. Lucky Enterprises is on the verge of something big, far bigger than you could ever imagine. Did you think fae would act as jesters forever? This failed experiment of Godmother's is almost over, and the sooner the humans know their place, the better."

"You're a madman." Seven looks like he might be sick.

It hits me like a ton of bricks then. Seven is doing the thing I thought he'd never do. He's standing up to his father, and he's not backing down. And he's doing it for me, so that I can escape. I take another step back as tears well in my eyes. I know this hurts him, and as proud as I am of him, I'm anxious to call Godmother and relieve him of this torment.

"You only think that because you don't know the truth. Not yet. But I'll teach you. We'll manage this together." Chance's eyes drift to me, and I realize I'm the thing to be managed in this scenario.

I take another step back. The window is right behind and above me. But before I can take off through it, Chance raises his hand. Instantly, my feet slip on a patch of slick flooring, and my legs fly out from under me. All the air is knocked from my lungs when my back slaps the floor. For a moment, I can't draw a breath.

"Leave her alone!" Seven places himself between us, and I feel his luck fill the room, that invisible dragon of energy coiling, fueled by fire and ready to do battle.

Chance laughs, and another kind of energy forces its way into the room. His is also serpentine but cold as ice. I picture it pale blue and slick as a viper's belly. All the oxygen in the space is crowded out by the monsters who've filled it, and I struggle to take tiny sips of air. My ribs ache.

"They're tougher than they look, you know," Chance says through a sneer, pointing his chin at me. "Those delicate bones and gossamer wings are camouflage. They're wildcats underneath." His face spreads into a lecherous grin, and my stomach turns over at the connotation. What did he do to these women? I scuffle to my feet, my ribs aching.

"Stay down!" Chance orders me. "Or I'll take you down. We're not done with you."

Seven's expression turns deadly. "Don't talk to her like that! Don't look at her. You overbearing, psycho, perverted freak!" His fist shoots out, but it never makes contact. Chance bends backward, body rotating at an unnatural speed and angle, and Seven's strike misses his face by a quarter inch. The older man retaliates, fists jabbing toward Seven's center in rapid succession. Seven easily dodges them, his body contorting just out of reach. His feet barely move, but it's enough. Seven ducks and kicks, his foot skimming past Chance's knee.

Luck matches luck. The fight speeds up. Jab, hook, kick. Nothing lands. Power wraps and tangles as the dragon and the viper clash, becoming too big for the room and rattling the walls.

These two men are not expert fighters. I've seen enough fights firsthand to know that on skill alone, neither would last long in hand-to-hand combat. Both are desk jockeys, not UFC fighters. There's nothing inspired about the moves they use or their athletic ability. This isn't a competition of speed or strength. It's luck vs. luck. Neither will land a punch or kick until their power starts to wane. The one who runs out of luck first will be at the mercy of the other.

Crap, this is bad. Chance is stronger. It's a simple matter of age and experience. He's older and heavier. In the fae world that coincides with a greater ability to store and use luck. This is a fight Seven can't win. Not without my help.

I push through the ache in my ribs and rush for the window, flapping my wings to lift me through the small opening.

"Stop!" I hear Chance yell. I duck as a piece of the ceiling above me collapses, and then the lights go out.

I COME AWAKE TO PAIN AND THE SOUND OF GRUNTS AND falling stones. I couldn't have been out long, because the dust hasn't settled, but I'm trapped under pieces of the ceiling and wall. Ironically, the opening above me is bigger now, the window having caved in, but it doesn't matter. I can't move. My ribs ache, and I think my leg might be broken. My left arm is numb and caught under the rubble.

Power twists in the air around me. I tip my head and get a glimpse of Seven. There's a red welt on his face. Chance must have gotten a punch in. We're running out of time.

A gaunt face with two haunting blue eyes appears above me. I almost gasp but she places a finger over her thin lips. I dart a glance to the room beside me and see that when Chance caused the collapse that trapped me, he destroyed part of the wall of the closest cell and freed one of his captives. I don't know her name, only that she's a pixie like me.

Help me, I mouth, my eyes moving to the stones pinning me down.

She glances over her shoulder at the men. They've moved out of my field of vision, and I can't see what she sees, but I can feel it. Seven's power is barely detectable in the room, and the cold viper of Chance's luck slithers against my skin. I sense it going in for the kill, and flash the pixie a panicked look. Together, we're able to shift enough stones to free me.

Silently, I stand. I know Seven sees me, but he doesn't make eye contact. Instead, he pivots and strikes, intentionally distracting his father. I help the other pixie through the window and then fly out after her where I grab her hand and sprint for the car.

"Can you speak?" I ask.

"Y-yes," she says.

Quickly, I open the car door, grab my cell phone, and dial Godmother's emergency number. She answers on the second ring. I rattle off the address of the cabin and then shove the phone into the pixie's hands.

"Explain to her," I say. "She'll have questions."

The pixie nods.

I retrieve my bow and quiver, slinging them over my shoulder. I have one arrow, the one I pulled from Yissevel's side. I grab Kiko, then realize she's empty. We used her to recharge Seven yesterday when he went negative, and I never refilled her. *Fuck!* The lucky cat has been my salvation time and time again. What am I going to do? Seven is doomed if I don't go back in there.

This is crazy. I need a plan. I'm injured, and I'm low on luck. Think, Sophia. What do you do at the poker table when you're short on chips and don't have the cards? Think. Think. Think. I stare at Kiko again, and an idea sparks.

I'm an excellent liar. There's only one thing to do in a situation like this—bluff.

I grab what I need from my pack and move toward the window. The pixie lowers the phone and whispers, "What are you doing? He'll kill you!"

For a split second I consider that I could stay out of it. I could wait, safely outside the fray, for Godmother to save us. But Seven was right when he'd said I never shied away from a challenge. Seven promised he'd protect me, and he sacrificed himself to live up to that promise. I'm not leaving him. I can't.

"That's a gamble I'm willing to take. I won't let Chance get away with this." I limp back to the window and drop into the dungeon again.

My ribs throb when I land. I can't put weight on my left ankle. It hurts when I breathe, and there's a trickle of something warm and wet running near the corner of my eye. I steady myself, nock my only arrow, and point it at Chance.

"Welcome back, little bird," Chance says through an evil smile. He's straddling Seven's bloody body. My breath quivers in my throat. Seven looks dead, and I can no longer sense even a hint of his luck in the room.

"Back away from him or I'll put an arrow through your heart," I threaten.

He laughs and turns, spreading his arms. "Try it, honey. It won't hurt me. I've still got enough in the tank to take you down and show you what I do to little girls who don't know their place."

Chance is tired, drained, and critically arrogant, but he's the oldest and strongest leprechaun in Devashire. *All in.* I close one eye, aim, and release a deep breath. Every ounce of luck I have left, I pour into my arrow. Will it be enough?

He swaggers another step toward me. My arrow flies and lands in his right pec, under his collarbone. It's a shot that might be painful but certainly isn't deadly.

I school my features into a carefully impassive mask.

Chance scoffs. "You missed."

"Maybe I did, but at least I tried. At least I had the guts to stand up to you. How many people know about what you've done to Seven, what you've done to these women? How many people have done nothing?"

He laughs at me. "Stupid girl. Who do you think you're talking to? I make the rules."

Another step toward me. "Fine. You win. Are you going to kill me now like you did Phoebe?"

Another step and he grabs the end of the arrow and yanks it from his flesh. There's a spurt of blood that blooms like a rose on his white dress shirt. "I'll let you in on a little secret, Sophia." His face contorts into something from my nightmares. He's the devil come to tear off my wings. "I was jealous of Seven the night I poisoned him. The thought of him having you when I couldn't drove me insane."

Eww. I back away, all the way to the wall under the

window, but he keeps coming. He reaches me, grabs my throat and squeezes. I'm trembling and in so much pain I can barely remain standing. I don't try to hide it. I notice the remaining four pixies are at their doors. I don't know if they can see or hear anything through that strange glass, but they know something is going on.

"I'll have you now," Chance says darkly. "A little luck and a lot of money and I'll have you in that empty cell. They'll all assume you ran away again. You'll be mine."

"Before you do, can I ask you something?" I wheeze out through his choking grip, meeting his gaze straight on. His expression changes and I know I've surprised him. He expected me to crumble and I'm still standing. "When you poisoned Seven, how long did it take for the blue iron to take effect?"

"Minutes," he says. "Why? Morbid curiosity, little bird?"

"No. I just want to know how long to wait before you fall." My eyes drift to my arrow on the floor and the glint of blue— the remains of Kiko's blue-iron arm—tied to the tip. I'd pulled a string off the hat Grandma knitted for me and used it to tie the arm to the tip of my living arrow. Then I funneled what remained of my luck into my arrow, to make sure the tip shattered when it entered his body. I was never aiming for his heart. I was aiming for center mass. I knew Chance would use his luck to knock my arrow off course, but also that in his weakness, there was a limit to how much. My shot hit him in a place that would be harmless to him normally. But I didn't care. All I had to do was hit him. Anywhere would do. Several pieces of blue iron are currently lodged within him, poisoning his blood, festering.

He looks down and seems surprised by the amount of blood staining his shirt. His wound isn't healing. He snorts as if he can't quite believe what he's seeing and then sways on his feet.

I have no luck left, but that never stopped me before. I cock my arm back and deliver a very human jab to his nose with the heel of my palm. He staggers, confused by the blood dribbling from his face. It drips onto his palms. His eyes are wild.

I hobble after him.

My voice comes out loud and strong, rage inflating my lungs. "You think you're better than me because you have more money and power. When I was in America, I met guys like you at the poker table, Chance. You have a lucky streak, and you think it means you're superior. You think because you were born with a silver spoon in your mouth that it will always be there. But the problem with relying on luck is eventually it runs out, and then all you have left is your skill to play the game. You've never had to play on empty, and it shows."

I clock him again, and he stumbles away from me, swaying on his feet.

"You're not better than me," I hiss. "You were *never* better than me. You were just luckier and wealthier. And now that's over. I've. Outplayed. You."

The daggers he shoots at me would turn me to swiss cheese if they were real. He swings a bloody paw at me, but I easily move out of the way. No luck necessary.

"No one loves you," I continue, a smile in my voice. "They might fear you, but they don't love you. No one is in your corner. When your luck runs out, people like me who've actually paid our dues move in. People with skill and patience. Good people. Today is not your lucky day."

I raise my bow, wind up, and swing it like a bat, throwing my weight behind it. It smacks into his temple. His head snaps to the side, and then he crumples. He doesn't get up. With everything I have left, I kick him in the ribs. No response. I squat down and take his pulse. Alive but definitely out. *Fucker.*

"Seven." I leave Chance and rush to his side. I'm so tired,

but somehow I flip him over. He's beat up bad. One eye is swollen shut, and his T-shirt is soaked in blood.

"Gods, Sophia, run!" he mumbles when his good eye flutters open and he recognizes me.

"Chance is knocked out. I'm okay." I brush back the hair from his face. A gash in his forehead bloodies my hand.

"Tried to distract 'im so you could get away."

"It worked. I got out. I got help. Godmother is on her way."

He takes my hand, and a corner of his mouth twitches. I think it's the only part of his face he can still move. "So sorry..."

"Shhh."

A drop hits our coupled hands, and I realize it came from my face. I wipe away the next tear, and then lean down to press a kiss to that unbruised corner of his mouth. All my adrenaline is gone, and I stretch out beside him on the floor, closing my eyes and pressing my forehead to his temple. "It's over."

I'm not sure when I pass out, but when I wake, I'm no longer touching Seven. He's still there, a few feet away from me but appears to be unconscious.

I hear a snap like a thick branch breaking over a knee and reposition myself so I can see the source. Godmother is there, power swirling around her and filling the room with the scent of violets. Chance hovers in the air in front of her, held within bonds of light that tether him to the walls like he's trapped in a massive spiderweb.

"You stupid fuck," Godmother says, her voice reverberating in the space. "Now you will finally pay for your crimes." There's another snap, and his calf bends at a painful angle, the foot kicking toward her while the rest of the leg remains stationary. My eyes widen as I take in his mangled fingers, his dangling arm. Chase screams, his voice already going hoarse.

Oh my gods. She's breaking his bones one by one!

Godmother's gaze drifts to me. Our eyes lock. I haven't

made a sound, and my poker face is firmly in place. I convey no judgment or approval. I make no attempt to move.

Two satyrs arrive with a stretcher through the main door that must lead to the rest of the cabin. They move toward Seven.

"No, not that one." She points at me with her chin.

The satyrs lower the stretcher beside me and lift me onto it. While one straps me in, the other slips a needle into my arm.

"Oww," I say. The pain fades, and a warm, floaty feeling overcomes me. I blink, and Godmother and the dungeon are gone. We're halfway up the stairs I assume lead to the main floor. A moment later, we reach the top. I glimpse a well-appointed living room with a large mirror that covers most of one wall. My head spins. There's something familiar about it. I need to ask Seven...

I blink again, and this time my eyes remain closed.

CHAPTER

THIRTY

I wake in a hospital bed. There's only one hospital in Devashire, and I know I'm in it by the buzz happening in my blood. I'm as light as air, and bubbles brush the underside of my skin. They've been feeding me luck along with the fluids dripping into my arm. My chest, arm, and ankle are wrapped, but the pain is gone. I don't know what kind of painkillers are involved, but I'm feeling remarkably better.

Until I meet a pair of reptilian eyes in the face of a dark man in an even darker suit. He hovers over me, too close. I cringe, pushing myself deeper into the bed and wishing the mattress would swallow me.

"Well, well, well, it appears you've slipped through my fingers once more," Agent Donovan says. He's as terrifying as ever, a psychopath in law-enforcement clothing.

"Touch me and I'll scream," I warn.

"Relax." He rolls his eyes. "I'm not here to hurt you."

"What do you want?"

He folds himself into a seat beside the bed. "I came to say goodbye. It seems you have friends in high places, Sophia.

Godmother traded access to Chance Delaney for expunging your record. As far as we're concerned at FIRE, you and that human daughter of yours are free and clear of all wrongdoing."

I breathe a heavy sigh of relief.

He shakes his head. "Sad. You and I could have had so much fun. I doubt Chance will be as... amusing."

I shudder at his tone.

"If you feel the same way, by all means, leave Devashire again. I'd love to bring you back into the fold." He flashes that psycho smile that makes bile rise in my throat.

I'm relieved when Godmother appears in my doorway, her commanding presence reaching into the room. It's the first and only time I've ever been relieved to see Godmother.

"Ah, you're awake." She gives my tormentor a once-over. "Donovan, what the hell are you doing here? I thought we had an understanding."

He smiles his weirdly blue smile. "Just checking in on the woman of the hour. I'm on my way out. I've filled Sophia in on our agreement. She's officially off our roster... unless she decides to cross the border again, and as a law-abiding citizen, her daughter's passport has been reinstated." With one last glance at me, he scurries out the door and hopefully out of my life for good.

"That man is damaged in ways I never knew humans could be," Godmother says with a low grunt. She sits down in the chair Donovan vacated. It's then that I notice a flower arrangement in her hands. She sets the small vase on the end table beside me, and I breathe in the scent of red roses and purple daisies.

"Thank you for visiting," I say, although after watching her torture Chance, I'm ready for her to go. "Is Seven okay?"

"He's fine. Although for security reasons he's opted to recover at home with a private nurse. With the news of his father's arrest going public, Seven is now chairman of Lucky Enterprises and head of the Delaney empire. A lot of responsibility comes with the role and plenty of risk. There are many who would like to disrupt that dynasty."

I can only imagine. I knew Chance's imprisonment would change Seven's life, but I've never lived that lifestyle. I'm sure there's much I don't understand about what he's going through. "So Chance is finally behind bars."

"Our prisons don't have bars." Godmother's dark eyes twinkle.

"That's right." Ashgate, the fairy prison, is a mountain with cells carved into its depths. Criminals are magically sealed inside. "Behind stone."

She gives a dark chuckle. "I owe my thanks to you for taking him down. Brilliant to use his own blue iron against him. I assume you obtained it from his stores. It would be illegal to bring it into Devashire."

"Of course," I say immediately. She doesn't need to know about Kiko. Besides, a human gave her to me at the Dragonfly Club. I simply brought her back again. That's different than bringing something in that originated on the outside. "Did you know Chance once poisoned Seven with blue iron?"

"I am aware," she says, lifting her chin. "Although back then we lacked enough proof to hold him accountable. Now we have five pixies willing to give details of their horrific abduction, not to mention testimony by you and Seven. It's enough to put him away for a very long time. He won't be able to buy his way out of this one."

"He admitted to us what he did," I say. "Yissevel was a convenient way to dispose of the bodies. But he also said there was more, some big plans Seven didn't know about. Do you know what he was talking about?"

Godmother smooths the front of her gown. "Unfortunately,

no. But when I interrogated Chance, it was clear to me that he's lost his mind. He's been drunk with power for so long he thinks of himself as a god. Whatever he was up to, you can be sure it stops here. We confiscated the silver he was using to travel to Shadowvale. It's safely with the guardians now."

I remember the mirror I saw when they were hauling me out of the hunting cabin. So it was a portal. I heave a relieved sigh that it's in good hands, although a little voice in the back of my head would love to know how he got it in the first place.

"What he said... It was so disturbing. He made it sound like Lucky Enterprises wanted to destroy Dragonfly. Like he had plans to subjugate humans."

The knowing smile that turns Godmother's full lips creates a dimple in her dark cheek, as if she finds the concept wholly amusing. "Do you know why we named the park Dragonfly Hollow when we established it in 1864?"

I shake my head.

"Dragonflies sparkle, Sophia. Humans are fascinated by their colors and their beauty. But they are also the deadliest predator in existence. In fact, they catch over 95 percent of their prey thanks to their almost supernatural agility and focus. They ambush their quarry, hovering just out of sight, then attacking from below or behind. Their game is torn apart and consumed immediately, and their appetite is insatiable.

"Humans... all they see is a shiny insect, bright with fragile wings. They assume it is a creature created for their pleasure, when in reality the dragonfly owns their world and their space. Dragonflies have been the apex predator of their environment since before humans existed.

"We are the dragonflies, Sophia. There are fewer of us than there are humans, just as there are fewer dragonflies than mosquitos. But we are the more powerful beings. They think they are in control. They think we are a beautiful dalliance. But we take from them exactly what we want and need, and they bring it to us willingly. We help them, and they help us. Just as the gods intended.

"After the Civil War, there were those who felt we should abandon the old ways, eschew peace, and free the unseelie to conquer our human attackers and take control of the Americas. I was of the mind that no blood need be shed to conquer. The secret to subjugation is finding a person's weakness. That's how you bring them to their knees. We've done that with humans. They worship us with their dollars.

"Thankfully the Guardians agreed, and so together we created this place and the peace we enjoy. Chance is not the first to suggest that the fae could and should have more: more power, more money, more glory. None of them have ever understood the value of peace. Power doesn't always come by the sword. It isn't bought with the shedding of blood. That is a human fallacy us fae have no time for. It comes with the adoration of hearts and minds. It comes with control. What we have now is as good as it gets, Sophia. And as long as I'm in charge, it will remain this way."

I stare at her for a good long moment, her power looming thick in the room. The only thing I can think to say is, "I'm glad it's you in charge."

She smiles and tips her head in my direction. "I'm glad you think so because we have business to discuss."

I blink nervously.

"You solved this case. Dragonfly couldn't have done it without you."

"Then am I right in assuming that I'm officially free of our bargain?" I hold my breath hopefully.

She waves a graceful hand between us, and the air grows thick with her power. Bright white vines appear around me. They snap and recede. I feel light and free.

"It is done. As of now, you are unbound. Although I must say, given the position I found you and Seven in, it seems you rather enjoyed your time together. You have a talent for this kind of work. I hope you'll consider helping me again in the future of your own volition."

Not likely. I glance down at my tangled fingers.

"Regardless, I'm happy things worked out and you've returned to Devashire. It seems your young Arden has already endeared herself to the staff at Bailiwick's. I understand that her passport has been reinstated, and she is once again a US citizen, but we'd all like to see her call Devashire home. She belongs here, surrounded by family."

My stomach clenches, and my eyes flick to the wall where the date is scrawled across a white board with my nurse's name and my care itinerary. I've missed Arden's first day of school. Holding back tears, I say, "Well, at least until she leaves for college."

Godmother spreads her hands. "There are fine universities in Devashire too. Who knows, her talents might change our world. There's never been anyone like her." She stands to leave just as Arden and my parents appear in the doorway, over-flowing with flowers and gifts.

I open my arms wide, and Arden rushes into them. I kiss the side of her head, anxious for her to tell me everything.

Over Arden's shoulder, Godmother meets my eyes. "Good-bye, Sophia."

I watch Godmother slip away, the realization that Arden and I are truly free settling over me with the warm, comforting hugs of the people I love.

THIRTY-ONE

Three days later, I'm discharged from the hospital. My rib is still healing, but the rest of me is back to normal again thanks to plenty of luck and fae attention. The most bothersome part is the ache unrelated to my injuries. Seven didn't come to the hospital. River came, as did Penelope. My family visited daily. But no Seven. He hasn't called or texted. He hasn't sent flowers.

Undeniably, he's healing too, and as Godmother mentioned, he's got a lot on his plate taking over the family business. I could make excuses for him. But I'm not doing that anymore. The truth is that Seven hasn't carved out five minutes to check on my well-being. I wish that didn't hurt, but it does.

Once I'm home, I shower and change into my most comfortable clothes and make myself a giant mug of tea. My parents can see I need rest and alone time, and so they take Arden shopping while Grandma stays with me. But even wrapped in one of Grandma's knitted blankets in front of a roaring fire, I can't seem to take any comfort. All I want to do is cry, but that warrior inside me refuses to let the tears fall. I'm not going to let him do this to me.

"I always knew you would take that bastard down one day," Grandma says. She's come from the kitchen and slides a plate of cookies onto the table beside me.

"Thanks, Grandma. I get it from you, you know."

"Of course you do, honey. Kick-assery runs in our blood." She sits down in the big chair next to the fire and picks up her knitting needles.

"What are you making?" The oddly shaped rectangle she's knitting is bright purple and as wide as her arm.

"Isn't it obvious? A scarf, dear, for Arden. I thought she could use one for school."

I can't hold back a laugh. "Grandma, that thing is wide enough for her to wear it as a cape."

She holds the massive square up to the light and flutters her silver wings. "You're right. I'm making a cape! I've never made a cape before. It's *lovely*."

My new goal is to be as confident as Grandma when I grow up.

"Are we ever going to talk about Seven?" she says, her needles working again. "I'm an old woman, Sophia. I can't wait forever."

"What's there to say? He hasn't called or come to visit. Our job for Godmother is over, so..."

"Oh, but he did! He came to see you at the hospital."

I almost spill my tea. I throw off my covers and scooch to her end of the sofa. "When? I don't ever remember Seven coming to see me." Did he come when I was knocked out on painkillers? Did I forget?

"That's because he never made it to your room." Grandma blinks at me over her knitting and flashes me a gossipy grin.

I grab a cookie from the plate and plug it into my mouth to

keep from raising my voice at her. "Please explain," I say around a mouthful.

"Well, he hobbled in the same day Godmother came to see you. We were all waiting in the hall, but I had to go to the restroom. You know when you're my age, you always have to pee. So I went to that restroom by the nurse's station. Did I tell you I knitted a cover for their phone?"

My fingers curl in frustration, and I hold my hands out to her, palms up, eyes to the heavens. "Grandma, when did you see Seven?"

She clears her throat. "My, a person might think you had feelings for the boy considering how excited you've become, Sophia. Should I start knitting something in white?"

I heave a sigh toward her. "Grandma, please!"

"All right. Godmother left your room, and Arden and your parents went in. I'd just come out of the bathroom. Seven stepped off the elevator, looking like he might fall over at any moment. The man wasn't well, honey. Bruises everywhere. Swollen eye. And Godmother was in his face. She told him that if he loved you, he would leave it alone. She said you were free, and he should let you be happy. I thought the poor boy was going to pull his hair out. He took one last look at your room and then turned and left."

My mouth drops open. "Why didn't you tell me this before?"

She raises her shoulders to her ears. "You know me, honey. I don't like to get involved in other people's drama."

I huff incredulously. "Grandma, you literally live for other people's drama! Your nose prints are all over your front window from watching the neighbors so closely!"

"Hmm, well, maybe I was worried you'd try to go after him, and you were in no shape to leave your bed. *Now*, however, you are in fine shape, and if I were to speculate, he is likely feeling much better as well."

My throat makes a little squeak as I try to respond and find my brain has turned into a jumble of nonsensical impulses. I can't believe my grandmother kept this from me! Then I narrow in on her crooked little smile, and think I can definitely believe it.

"You've been sitting on this for days!"

She slants me a mischievous grin. "It took a righteous amount of stamina, I'll tell you that." She nods her gray head. Our conversation is interrupted by the doorbell. Grandma and I exchange curious looks.

"Who could that be?" I ask.

"Maybe he's feeling better." Grandma bobs her gray brows.

She's insufferable. I hoist myself off the couch and hobble to the door. When I open it, a runway model is standing on the other side, shiny red hair falling over one eye in a wave, svelte body poured into a violet dress with a satin belt above tall black boots with stiletto heels. Radiant emerald eyes find mine, and she smiles. It's like the lights come on.

"Hi Sophia! Just who I came to see." She brushes her hair back behind her shoulder.

"Evangeline? What are you doing here?"

"I came to drop off your key. My assistant was supposed to do it, but we've been so swamped redistributing job responsibilities after what happened with our father that all of us are overwhelmed. I had an appointment in the neighborhood and thought, *What the hell?*" She pulls a large envelope from her purse and hands it to me. I tear it open to see a key and a short stack of papers inside.

"Seven told me to tell you not to go to the room yet because the work crew is still in there. Something with the flooring." She waves a hand. "I don't know. Anyway, it will be a few more days until we can get tables set up. Then I'll want to bring in a photographer for some pictures and video for social media. You should be ready for your first class by the end of the month." Her teeth are so white. What the hell sort of toothpaste does she even use?

I shake my head. "I'm sorry, but I don't know what you're talking about. What room? What class?"

She juts her chin out incredulously. "You're going to give poker lessons to humans at the casino! Why do you look like this is the first time you're hearing about this?"

"Because it's the first time I'm hearing about this!"

"Huh." She looks confused. "Seven's been selling it to the board since the second you two got back from your mission. I'm sure if you tell him you don't want to do it—"

"Oh, I *want* to do it." The thought of playing my favorite game again, legitimately, in Dragonfly, is too good to be true. There has to be a catch. I can't believe Seven pulled this off.

"Good," Evangeline says with a sigh. "All the details are in there. Salary, benefits, hours of operation. It's all negotiable. Let Seven know if something isn't to your satisfaction; he's heading this project. Someone from my team will be in touch about the advertising blitz." She brushes her hands off. "Great to see you again, Sophia. Welcome aboard!" She turns and strides gracefully toward the parking lot.

I slowly close the door, the manila envelope heavy in my hand. Grandma appears by my side. "What in carnations was that all about?"

"Tarnation," I correct.

"Huh?"

"The expression is what in tarnation, not what in carnations."

She rolls her eyes. "You say it your way; I'll say it mine."

She tears the envelope from my hands and pulls out the letter inside. She starts to giggle.

"Why are you laughing?"

"You're going to be making more than your mother and father combined!"

I snatch the letter from her hands. Two hundred thousand per year. Full benefits for myself and my dependents. Tuition reimbursement for self and dependents. All in exchange for me teaching two classes a day, five days a week and for my permission to be used as a spokesperson for Dragonfly Casino's upcoming ad campaign.

"There has to be a catch. Don't you think there has to be a catch?"

My grandmother shrugs. "I can't think of one." I stare at her for a moment, and then we both start jumping up and down, squealing. "What are you waiting for? Don't you have somewhere to be?" Grandma asks. "This sort of thing deserves a thank-you, in person."

I stop jumping. A heavy weight descends onto my shoulders. "But if he wanted to see me, wouldn't he have come to me?"

Grandma frowns. "Not if Godmother convinced him that he could only make your life more difficult. Oh, if he cared for you less, he might, but I think we both know how he feels." She touches the letter in my hand.

I think about that for a moment. The last time Seven and I spoke about us, I'd told him that I deserved more and he'd agreed. Was staying away and doing this for me his way of giving me what I wanted?

Every impulse tells me to go to him. The desire is so strong, I know a younger me wouldn't be able to deny it. But I force myself to pause and think. "Godmother is never wrong about these things. He *will* make my life more difficult."

"As if it's been so easy up till now," Grandma says softly. Her blue eyes twinkle above a sad smile. "Life is short, Sophia, and when you're my age, you'll know that regret follows things you did and things you didn't do equally. The real question is, which will you find easier to live with?"

I stuff the letter back into the envelope with the key. "Will you tell Arden, Mom, and Dad where I've gone?"

She grins a conspiratorial grin. "Of course I will."

I take two steps toward the door, then realize what I'm wearing. "I should get changed... and do my hair and makeup."

"He's not going to care about any of that, and you know it."

I kick off my slippers and shove my feet into my sneakers. My hand is on the doorknob before a much bigger problem comes to mind. "I don't have a car, and I can't ride the bus like this. The rules say I have to be in a gown."

Grandma reaches into her giant knitted purse and retrieves her keys. She jingles them. "Maribelle is parked in lot A with a full tank of gas. Use a little illusion to get to her and you're home free."

I swipe the keys from her hand and spend a little luck to transform my appearance into something more appropriate, a purple gown, heels, full makeup and an updo. Then I swoop down to deliver a kiss to Grandma's cheek. "Thank you."

She waves a hand dismissively. "I don't need that car back tonight, Sophia. I think I'll stay here. I'll see you in the morning."

"Grandma! Just because I go over there doesn't mean I'm going to spend the night!"

The look she gives me over her glasses is full of mirth. She shrugs again. "What do I know? I'm an old woman. I go to bed early." She waves at me, and I'm out the door.

THIRTY-TWO

Seven's building is locked down tighter than Fort Knox, and I don't have the benefit of parking in his private garage. Worse, I had to drop my illusion because it was costing me too much luck and I'm still recovering. It's not strictly necessary here in Elderflame, so it didn't make sense to keep it up. But as I stand in front of the security desk in full view of dozens of passersby through the wall of windows on the ground floor, I'm ashamed of my messy bun, sweats, and T-shirt. I do not fit in here.

"You say you have an appointment with Mr. Delaney?" the security guard behind the desk asks, eyeing me skeptically and clicking his mouse. He's a satyr, big, burly, and perfectly capable of throwing me out on my ass if he so chooses. "I don't have any record of that."

"No, I don't have an appointment. We're friends, and I stopped by to... to... listen, just call up there and tell him I'm here."

His lips draw into a flat line. "Mr. Delaney is in a very

important meeting this afternoon. If you'd like to leave a message, I can give it to him tonight and ask him to call you."

I cross my arms and tap my foot, glaring at his nametag. "Eric, is it? Do you know that the last person who kept me from seeing Seven got fired?" A deep groove forms in his brow. "It's true. Seven and I are friends. Very *good* friends. And if he finds out you didn't even tell him I was here, he will be extremely displeased."

I have no idea if this is true or a bald-faced lie. What exactly did my grandmother hear? Could she have been mistaken about Seven wanting to see me? What if he *is* in an important meeting and I disturb him? I don't relish the thought of making him angry at me. Oh, this was a bad idea. Am I really here in my sweats threatening this guy?

Eric reaches for the phone and brings it to his ear. He presses a button and relays that I'm there to someone whom I can only assume is another security guard by the exchange. There's a pause, and then all the color drains from Eric's face. Slowly, he hangs up the phone. Our eyes lock.

"Mr. Delaney is on his way down. He'd like to show you up himself," he says softly.

I can't help the knowing little smile I give him that has "I told you so" written all over it. "Thank you."

A few minutes later, elevator doors to my left open, and Seven, in all his dark-suited glory, walks into the hall along with three other leprechauns in professional attire. He shakes hands with each of them, exchanging pleasantries and apologizing for ending the meeting early. The others are on their way out the door when he turns a focused laser beam of attention on me.

He approaches until we're toe-to-toe. The footsteps of the men stop, and I glance over my shoulder. They're staring, open-mouthed, as are a crowd of onlookers who are gathering on the other side of the window. My wings are out. I'm not using illusion. Every one of those people know exactly who I am and exactly who he is, and he's looking at me with the kind of focus that only comes from a lover. My heart rate quickens.

"It's good to see you," he says softly.

"Good to see you too." I shift from foot to foot. "Evangeline brought me a key and an offer today. I thought I'd come by personally to tell you I accept."

Seven beams. "You deserve it. You'll be brilliant. Humans are going to swarm to learn how to play from Soho Lane herself."

"Thank you for this. You have no idea what it means to me."

His eyes crinkle at the corners. "I think I do."

Silence unspools between us. The security guard is staring. Behind me, the other leprechauns are still staring. Outside the window, there is now a crowd of all manner of fae all staring. A flash goes off. Someone just took our picture.

"Um, aren't you going to invite me up?"

"I'd hoped you'd come." He places his hands on my shoulders, his intense focus ratcheting up my pulse another notch.

"I just..." I glance around me again. "Everyone is watching."

He drops his hands, his face falling. "You only came to say thank you."

I stare at him for three long heartbeats. "No. I also came to tell you to forget what I said before about deserving better. There's no one better than you for me, Seven."

"What about the part about wanting it all," he whispers.

"I still do. I probably always will. But I'm willing to take what I can get."

"But you'd prefer no secrets."

I glance over my shoulder at the crowd gathering on the other side of the window. "Yes."

He inhales, looking down at me through his lashes. "You sure about that?"

"Positive."

In the next second, his hands are cradling my face and his lips are on mine in a kiss that could never be mistaken as simply friendly. It's head-spinning, oxygen-depriving madness. I feel that kiss down to my soul. Luck fizzes through me, and I rise up on my toes, meeting the kiss with deliberate passion.

Lights pop. People snap our picture through the window, their murmurs rising. I pull back, panting. "As much as I appreciate this, can we go upstairs?" I allow my eyes to flood with heat. "There are still some things that belong behind closed doors."

Warming me with a dazzling smile, he leads me to the elevator. There's a bob in my step as I enter. I catch a glimpse of Eric's baffled expression as the doors close behind us. As soon as they do, I'm hyperaware of the exact position of Seven's body in the enclosed space, of the bright, citrusy fragrance of his cologne, the way his suit drapes perfectly off his shoulders, the way his eyes haven't left me since they landed on me moments ago.

His face is healed. I can't even tell he was beaten almost to death only days ago. Tension builds between us, a deliciously weighty feeling in my torso turning over as he takes me in, his stare palpable. "You look like you have something to say to me."

"My grandmother told me you stopped by the hospital to see me but that Godmother sent you away."

He nods.

"What were you going to tell me?"

He blinks rapidly, his tongue darting across his lower lip. "I think you know what I came to tell you." He reaches out and hits the red button on the panel. The elevator stops. "What happened downstairs, I might be able to manage the fallout if you change your mind right now, but if you come home with me and we do this, Sophia, there's no going back for me. You said you wanted it all. I do too, and there's no one standing in our way anymore. I want you to be mine. Entirely mine. Do you understand? I can't settle for halfway with you. I can't wait any longer."

"Who says you have to?" The words come out a croak, strangled by the intensity. He moves in until my back hits the far wall and his arms are bracketing my head. His face is close, and it's like someone released a thousand dragonflies in my lower belly. The butterflies have been replaced by something far more thrilling and aggressive. Hot, fluttering, bubbly luck rises in me. My breath hitches.

"This is just the beginning. I will take us public, and it will be the most selfish thing I ever do. You won't have a moment of peace. The press will be all over you, and the gossip pages will enjoy a heyday like you've never experienced. The *Daily Hatter* will have you on the front page, not just the gossip column."

My mind fills with streams of color, and I have to take a deep breath to steady myself. "Let them talk."

He winces. "I can't promise there won't be fallout for your family or Arden. I can help with some of that but...."

"I don't care," I say breathlessly. "We'll manage it. Arden's passport has been restored. She'll be gone in a matter of months. I want you, Seven. Nothing you tell me will change that."

He drops his forehead to mine and releases a shaky breath that skates across my face. "You have no idea how happy it makes me that you feel that way."

"I think I do."

Slowly, his face moves in closer, but just as his lips softly brush mine, a bell chimes. Seven doesn't move, but he reaches an arm out to lift the red phone off the hook. "Hmm? Yes. Fine. Bumped it," he says. He hits the button without breaking eye contact and the elevator starts up again.

When the doors open, he sweeps me into his foyer and kisses me right in front of the security guard waiting outside his door. It is not a chaste kiss. This is a claiming, deep, bend-you-over-backward kiss that instantly turns my knees to water and my blood effervescent. I want to live inside this kiss. When he draws back to unlock his door, I catch a glimpse of the security guard's face, and it almost unsettles me. There's surprise but also something darker, something I might describe as disgust if I wasn't so high on luck and blissfully drawn into the moment. Fuck him. If he wants to be a bigot, he better keep his thoughts to himself, or I imagine he won't be around for long.

I giggle as Seven pulls me inside and closes the door behind us. He tugs the elastic from my hair. "Oh. Sorry about my appearance. I should have cleaned up before I came."

"Why?" he says breathlessly. "I'm just going to mess you up again."

Zing. Holy crap, I've never been this turned on. His mouth is on mine again, and his hands are hot under my shirt, coursing along my ribs, thumbs grazing the underside of my breasts as he backs me through the large entryway deeper into the apartment. I gasp for breath when he pulls my shirt over my head and giggle as my bra clasp conveniently breaks and the garment all but falls off me.

"I liked that bra," I say.

"I'll buy you another one. I'll buy you the whole fucking store." His hands are on my waist again, and I wrap my arms around his neck and climb up his body, my legs riding his hips. He growls, clutching my ass and driving the kiss deeper.

His knees bump something behind us, and we tip over, my back bouncing on a velvety black comforter. He reaches for my waistband, but I catch his wrists. "Oh, we've already done the thing where I'm the only one naked in the room." I bite my lip. "This time you're coming along with me."

He doesn't miss how I stress the word *coming*. I push him back and reach for his fly. His belt buckle jingles as I unbuckle, unzip, and free his erection. I have him in my mouth before I've pushed his pants and everything else down his legs.

"Gods, Sophia. *Fuck!*" His fingers grip my shoulders as I bask in the taste of him, licking and swirling my tongue before taking him deep into my throat. The closer he gets, the more I feel his excitement fizzing at my core. He's pounding luck into me. It vibrates between my legs, filling me. It dances across my skin, slopes along my breasts, tightening the tips.

Seven moans, and hot liquid jets down my throat at the same moment my own orgasm grips me in its clutches, wringing pleasure from me with both hands.

I swallow him down and turn boneless, flopping onto the big black bed and closing my eyes.

"Look at me, Sophia," he orders and I obey. Fuck, the intensity in his gaze is preternatural. "We're not done."

My eyes widen as he tosses off his jacket and dress shirt, then steps out of his pants. My shoes are next and then my sweats and panties. He's already hard again. *Lucky me.* Gods, the man is a work of art, thick and long, his body a canvas of lean muscle with broad shoulders and a tapered waist that begs to be licked. I open my mouth to do so, but he hoists me back into the center of the velvet spread and stretches out over me, running the head of his cock along my slit.

His eyes meet mine. "No going back," he says. "After this, we leave the past behind and we build something new, together, come what may."

"Come what may," I repeat. I can't form any more complex thoughts than that. I need him in me so bad I can hardly breathe.

I get my wish.

His hands thread into mine on either side of my head as he slides into me, forcing a gasp from my throat. My vision blurs with unshed tears. I try to blink them away, but one falls.

Seven stops immediately. "What's wrong? Am I hurting you? When I said there was no going back, I meant emotionally. If you want me to stop, I will."

I laugh a little. "I don't want you to stop."

"Then what is it?"

With a nudge of my hip, I roll him onto his back and rise above him, spreading my wings. More tears fall against his chest. My throat feels thick as I admit, "This is the first time I've ever had sex truly as myself."

He grimaces as if I've hit him in the stomach, then reaches up to stroke along my upper right wing. His fingers trace along the side of my face, between my breasts. "I'm honored it's me." He lifts his hips and fills me until I moan.

I flutter my wings, sending a vibration down my body that makes him arch under me. "Keep doing that," he growls. His fingers dig into my hips. I ride his thrusts until that delicious, coiled tension builds deep within my core again, deeper than before, bigger.

It unravels all at once, like I've sliced open a ball of elastic bands. I lose myself entirely in the bubbles, snaps, and flares of pleasure. My head tilts back, and I grind myself against Seven in the most brazen way. I feel him come apart beneath me, hear him yell my name. Luck swirls around us, brushing me with its fiery energy and drawing out my pleasure.

When I've finally flopped forward and rolled on my side,

Seven reaches for me and tucks me into his chest, his lips brushing the top of my head. "You make me feel lucky, Sophia. Truly lucky."

"Me too."

THIRTY-THREE

Waking in Seven's arms is like a dream. He's warm and beautiful, even with his hair mussed from our love-making. I've lost count of how many times he made me come. We've been sleeping and fucking off and on all night long. His arms reach for me again, and I push them away.

"I need water, Seven, and maybe a snack. Sustenance!"

He blinks at me sleepily. "Help yourself to anything in the kitchen. Hurry back." He presses a sleepy kiss to my temple.

I slide out of bed and snatch his shirt from the floor. It's as long as a dress on me, and I roll the sleeves and button the front. There's no one here but us, but the last thing I want is to see my naked reflection in all the polished gold and ebony in this place. I slip out of the room, closing the door quietly behind me.

This penthouse is huge. I stroll down the hall in the direction of the kitchen only to realize that I've gone the wrong way. Where I expect the living room to be with its koi river and floor-to-ceiling windows, I find a library with floor-to-ceiling books. I must be at the back of the building. A short investigation confirms my hypothesis as the windows in this room have a southern view of the city. Wow. His home takes up the entire top floor.

I whirl, forgetting about my hunger and thirst when I see the books and artifacts lining the shelves. At the very center of the room is a desk with an ink blotter and a reading lamp. Surrounding it are leather volumes and the occasional piece of art. I start walking the first row. Interesting. Most of these are anthropology books. The next row is biology. The next chemistry. Gods, what I would give for a good romance. I had no idea Seven was into such heavy courses of study. If anything, I'd think he'd have business books.

As I turn down the center row, I spot a door in the side of the room. It stands out because it's made of glass and there's a pad to the right with a digital display of the temperature and humidity inside. Interesting. I've seen this before. A friend at the Bellagio once took me on a tour of the museum archives. Seven must have a special collection of rare artifacts to require such a room.

Curiosity fills me, and I attempt to enter. It's locked but there's a keypad. I think for a minute and then spend some luck to come up with my best guess. I type in the date we met. It doesn't work. I try the day I came back. Locked. My mouth twitches. Gods, I could just ask the man. An hour ago, I had my finger in his ass; I'm sure he'd show me around his special collection. But the gambler in me is obsessed now. I want to break the code. Using a bit more luck, I concentrate, and another date pops into my head, one that holds far less enjoyable connotations. It's the date of the Yule Ball. The date Seven ghosted me and I took out my sorrows in the arms of a human man I never saw again.

The door clicks. Lights turn on automatically with my movement, and what I see on the shelves inside *confuses* me.

Seven isn't preserving archaeology or artwork. I'm surrounded by... charms. For a moment, I feel like I'm back in my parents' store, only the items here are preserved like butterflies under glass. Stacks of wide and thin display drawers are stored inside three large shelves. I slide a drawer out. Acorns composed of all different materials and in a variety of sizes are displayed on blue velvet behind the protective panel. I slide it back into the shelf. The next one exhibits evil eyes and hamsas. I return it to its place. My mouth drops open when I inspect the next display. Horseshoes, and one of them is blue. That is definitely blue iron.

Frost fills my veins, and I all but shove the drawer into place and then back away from it. My ass bumps another shelf, and I whirl. Something gold catches my eye, and I pull out the second drawer down. Rows of maneki-nekos stare up at me through the window of their box. None of them is exactly like Kiko, but they're all similar. I make out the familiar hint of blue on one of the arms.

What the hell is this? Blue iron is forbidden in Devashire, and these objects thrum with their own power. Seven is collecting good luck charms, some of them ancient, some of them newly minted. I glance down to see a display of gold coins on the bottom shelf similar to the one he'd used in Shadowvale.

This is a strange hobby at best. At worst, it's the sign of a man obsessed with amplifying his power. I stare and stare. Something about all this is bothering me, but I can't quite put it together.

And then the door behind me opens, and Seven is standing there in a pair of black silk pajama bottoms and nothing else. "This isn't the kitchen." His eyes wrinkle at the corners.

"I got lost." I swallow. "What is this, Seven? There's blue iron in here." I shake my head.

He leans a shoulder against the inside of the door. "My

mother collected lucky artifacts. Some of these were hers. She got me started when I was young. Leprechauns are born with more luck than any creature on the planet, but luck requires focus and experience. After my father drove you away and my mother left him, I started researching magical objects in earnest. Have you ever wondered how Godmother went from lucky to inherently magical? Some say objects like these amplified her power and then changed it altogether. My mother used objects like these to free herself from my father. I thought I might need to use them one day as well."

What? I knew Seven's mother had divorced his father, but I didn't realize she had escaped his clutches using ancient luck magic. "Where is your mother now, Seven?"

He chuckles. "No one knows. Not even me."

A chill courses through me.

"Oh, she's alive. She sent me a letter a few years back to say she was safe but couldn't risk telling me where she lived. She's using luck to protect herself from discovery." He rubs the back of his neck. "Maybe if she hears that Dad's in Ashgate, she'll come out of hiding."

I turn back toward the case. "The coin you used against the beast in Shadowvale and Yissevel..."

"Protects its bearer from harm. Unfortunately, it doesn't protect anyone else. I had to throw it at Yissevel's eye to distract him from you."

I run my fingers along the maneki-nekos and stare at them longingly. "I had to destroy Kiko to take Chance down."

"Take one."

"Where did you find them? I've never seen them in any of the shops. It's always been a mystery to me where Dark Stranger got Kiko."

"Dark Stranger?" He squeezes his eyes shut for a long blink and laughs. "They don't exist anywhere in Devashire but here, not with the properties you want. I obtained these from Koyasan."

I start to reach for one but stop when his words hit home. "If these lucky cats aren't available in Dragonfly, where did Arden's father get the one he gave me?"

Even though I've never told Seven that Kiko came from Arden's father, he doesn't react to the news, and I stiffen when I see the look on his face. He's suddenly distant, like his mind is somewhere else.

"I looked for you, Sophia. I used every bit of extra luck I had to try to find you. I thought you must be dead or under the protection of another leprechaun because nothing I tried worked. I was amplifying myself with every type of charm I could get my hands on. I searched hours of security footage. I hired investigators."

I'm so confused. If that were true, he should have found me. I'm good but not hide-from-a-leprechaun-who-understands-technology good. "That doesn't make sense."

"I didn't understand it until you came home and Godmother helped me put things together."

"What are you talking about?"

"The night of the Yule Ball, my father poisoned me and locked me in that dungeon under the cabin."

"What has that got to do with—"

"My father made a mistake. I recovered from the blue iron faster than he expected and escaped through the window well. Once free, I went directly to Godmother, hoping she'd protect me. When I told her what happened and how much I loved you, she said she'd give me what I wanted in exchange for my promise to work for her. I agreed."

"You struck a bargain with Godmother? Over me?"

"I thought she'd make everything right. I ate what she gave me without another thought."

"Seven?" I wasn't sure where he was going with this story, but I didn't like it.

"I saw you sitting at the bar in Dragonfly. You didn't look like you, but I knew it was you. I could always tell. It's the way you hold your shoulders. There were so many men around you that night. All I wanted to do was explain. But when I spoke to you, I couldn't bring myself to—"

"When did you ever speak to me?"

"You didn't know it was me that night because Godmother had changed my appearance."

"What?" None of this makes sense. I want to say more but all breath has left my lungs.

"She also told me exactly where to find you. Once I spoke to you, I knew I couldn't tell you who I really was. You were so angry with me. So I gave you what you asked for. I comforted you. And I planned to tell you. I planned to explain everything, but I didn't even have school as an excuse to crawl out from under his thumb. My mother left, and my father, angered at the circumstances of my escape and hers, locked everything down to keep me from following her. He assigned a security contingent to me twenty-four seven. I was a prisoner in my own home for weeks. By the time I had any way to see you or get a message to you, you were already gone."

A sob seeps out my tight throat. My heart is pounding.

"I didn't know Arden existed until she called your parents and you returned to Dragonfly. Godmother fed her that brownie with the intention of visualizing what part of her heritage was dominant. Was she more human or more pixie? The magic revealed her origins. I couldn't see it, you couldn't see it, but Godmother did. And when she did, she instantly welcomed Arden into the fold.

"I didn't understand why until the hospital. Oh, I suspected. Anyone would have suspected. The timing seemed to prove what my instincts were telling me, but I hadn't thought it was possible, you understand. There's no history of it. You need proof before you allow yourself to believe something like this, and Godmother was the only one who could give it to me."

He scrubs his face with his hands and runs his fingers through his hair.

"And she waited. She held it over my head like she always does. Godmother waited until the hospital to confirm what I already knew. Deep inside I knew."

"Seven?" my voice comes out as a raspy whisper.

"She warned me to stay away. Everything will be harder, especially now." He paces the small space. "I think she knew I wouldn't keep it from you, and once you knew, Arden would know. And there are expectations, Sophia. There are things I won't be able to control. That's why I tried to stay away, but then *you* came to *me*, and I couldn't turn you away. Not after everything. I won't ever turn you away again."

"Just say it! I need to hear the words." I can't breathe. It's like I've been pulled under water, and I can't get to the surface.

"Don't you see? Everything makes sense when you put it together. I couldn't find you all those years because another leprechaun was protecting you. Her luck made you invisible to me until recently when she changed her mind and wished for something else. A tiny leprechaun with ten fingers and ten toes."

"Seven... Oh gods..."

He looks me in the eye, spine straight, jaw hard as steel, and says the thing that changes everything.

"I'm the man who left you Kiko, Sophia. Arden is mine."

CHAPTER
THIRTY-FOUR

A steady throb begins between my temples, and for a long moment I can't speak. All the words lodge in my throat. At first I want to deny it. I shake my head and try to think of some way it isn't true. But that thought dissolves as fast as I think of Kiko and what I saw in that room. I don't doubt his story. It all makes sense. The little things about Dark Stranger I was drawn to. The way the night unfolded. If I had been older back then, more experienced, I might have detected the signature of magic on his skin, but I was young. I didn't want to see it that night, even if I could have. Now, looking back, it all fits. Oh gods, bargaining with Seven at his most vulnerable fits Godmother's MO to a tee.

But believing him doesn't do a thing to help ease the overwhelming sense I've been deceived. Seven slept with me under false pretenses and kept it a secret all this time! It's a betrayal that stings. A violation. I can't resist the temptation to lash out.

"Arden is not *yours*," I snap, my face hot with rage.

"She is, Sophia. Godmother confirmed it. She's half leprechaun."

I glare at him, and everything I am feeling must come through as clear as day because he takes a large step back. "You might be her father, but she isn't *yours*. Was it you who fed her in the middle of the night and rocked her back to sleep? Picked her up when she fell and kissed her boo-boos? Did you teach her how to ride a bike and how to stand up to the bullies at school?" I hold up a finger between us. "You might be her father, but she is not *yours*."

His throat bobs on a swallow. "You're right. It was a poor choice of words." Tension thickens the air between us. "I'm sorry this is how you found out. I wish there was an easier way. I should have told you... before. Even before Godmother confirmed it. I just... *couldn't*."

I bury my face in my trembling hands, all my cherished memories of Dark Stranger rushing back to me. Those memories and Kiko—oh gods, she came from Seven!— kept me alive the years I was living on the streets. I try to reconcile everything that happened that night with the man standing in front of me and all that's happened over the last weeks. I have to swallow down the emotion rising in my throat and I sob openly from the effort.

I want to kill him. I want to run into his arms.

"Please forgive me," he rasps. "I was so young. I couldn't say no to you." He rubs my shoulders. "What can I do? How can I make this better?"

"Godmother told you not to tell me, didn't she?" I say through my teeth, lowering my hands to look at him. I know it's true, and I know why.

He takes a deep breath. "She refused to confirm Arden was mine until we solved the case and threatened to keep the truth from me forever if I confessed to you that I was the stranger you'd been with that night. She didn't want the distraction from our work. Once we solved the case and she finally revealed that Arden was my daughter, I came to the hospital to explain, but she convinced me it would ruin your life and Arden's. She told me if I loved you, I'd stay away from you."

My conversation with her in the hospital comes back to me—the way her eyes twinkled when she'd said there had never been anyone like Arden. She knew. She *knew!* And not only did she not tell me, she used her influence to convince Seven not to. "Godmother never does anything out of the goodness of her heart. There's a reason she didn't want you to tell me, and it isn't to save me or Arden from pain."

"Godmother stores up secrets like currency." He runs a hand down his face. "And this is a powerful secret."

My mood darkens further the more I think about it. Exhaustion and hunger combine to stir my stomach, and I brace myself against the wall.

Seven reaches out slowly, cautiously, his eyes meeting mine in silent question. I give him a barely perceptible nod. "Come to the kitchen. I'll make tea."

I allow him to wrap an arm around my shoulders and usher me out the door. He leads me to a surprisingly cozy kitchen in the otherwise modern penthouse and starts a kettle. The sound of the steam building fills the space. All of what he's told me swirls in my brain, and I feel the seed of an intense and prickly emotion forming deep within me. I repress the urge to cough. "Everything changes now. It has to."

He spoons loose tea into a pot and pours in the boiling water. Reaching above his head, he retrieves two mugs from the cupboard and sets them on the counter. When he speaks again, it's with the confidence and authority of a man who fills out every inch of the suits he wears daily.

"In all likelihood, my father will spend the rest of his life in prison. Evangeline has no children. My mother has cut all ties with the family. As my daughter, Arden is the sole heir to my half of the Delaney fortune. It won't matter that she's part pixie, Sophia. The leprechaun elite will want to meet her. She'll become the most eligible bachelorette in Devashire overnight."

I can't keep my face from betraying my feelings. "You say it like it's a good thing, but they won't want her for her. Those elites are a pack of wolves desperate to bite a piece off of her. She can't even wield luck! They'll eat her alive!"

He presses his lips into a thin line. "She can wield luck. That's what I've been trying to tell you. She's been using her luck all along."

I think back to what he said in his secured room. "You think she protected me when I was living in the US?"

"I *know* she did. And when she called your parents and they needed help getting you back, I just happened to be standing right next to Godmother when she got the call."

I can't believe I didn't see the signs. "But if Arden's fae, why couldn't she pass through the moon gate?"

"The ward keeps out anyone foreign to Devashire. Any fairy born outside the boundaries might have had the same problem until Godmother welcomed them in and they became a citizen of Devashire."

Lifting the mug, I take a sip of tea. It's too hot, and it burns my tongue. I stare at the mug as if it's betrayed me. "She got herself into Bailiwick's, didn't she?"

"She did. I was prepared to help her, but I didn't need to." Seven said something like this before but I discounted it. "She doesn't know she's doing it, Sophia. It's as natural to her as breathing."

I bury my face in my hands. "Oh my gods, Seven! What are we going to do? All she knows is the human world. She's wanted to be a doctor since she was twelve. Her entire life, we've made decisions based on the assumption she was a US citizen, human, and born on US soil. This means she's not. She's one hundred percent fae. If this comes out, she won't be able to leave Devashire. They'll suspend her passport again."

"She seems happy enough here." His expression is controlled, but I glimpse a spark of hope.

"Because she thinks her stay is temporary. This will crush her."

"Maybe not. I hear she's thriving at Bailiwick's."

I stare down into my tea, my thoughts racing. "Who knows about this, other than us?"

"No one. You, me, and Godmother. That's it."

I take a deep breath and brace myself. "She's still human-passing. That gives her options. We need time to break this to her gently and give her a chance to decide for herself without any pressure from the outside. We can't draw any extra attention to her. No one can suspect the truth until we know for sure what she wants."

He cocks his head. "Unlikely we can avoid scrutiny. We're together now. We kissed in front of a dozen cameras. Tomorrow, our pictures are going to be all over the *Daily Hatter*. Arden's life is about to change no matter what she chooses."

My brows squeeze together and I can't meet his eyes as I say, "Can you stop it? What would it take to undo what we did tonight?"

The sharp rasp of his inhale fills the space between us and he braces himself on the counter. His stare turns cold as ice, but there's something more behind the mask he's slid into place. I see it then, *fear*. The dragon rises, his luck flailing as if he's not exactly in control of it. Pure, concentrated power blows back my hair and all the cabinet doors fall off their hinges at once, rattling as they slam into the floor.

What had he said to me before? *You'd never abandon your daughter.* But what he meant when it came to us is I'd never abandon someone I loved. He showed me his vulnerable under-belly and I just slid a dagger into it.

I leap off my stool and round the counter, reaching for him. The tornado of energy in the room is a force to reckon with. It beats against me like a storm, deafening in its inten-sity. I try my best to push through it, to get to him. "No, Seven, I didn't mean that! I'm here. I'm here! I'm not going anywhere."

The dragon settles, slithering around me and I rush into him, taking his face in my hands. His gaze softens as he looks at me. "What happened tonight with you, I meant it. I'm yours, okay?"

He releases a shaky breath. "You forgive me?"

I hesitate, searching my heart. This is one thing I won't bluff about. Am I angry? Yes. At him, at me, and at Godmother. Shocked? Undeniably. But sad or disappointed? *No.* I check my emotions again, just to be sure. "Yes," I say. "I forgive you, Seven."

He releases a sigh of relief.

"And there's something else." I meet his eyes and touch my forehead to his, tears coming again. "I'm glad it was you. I'm glad you were my first, and I can't think of a better father for Arden."

"Oh Sophia..." He kisses me desperately. I give him what he needs but then put space between us. "Seven... about what I said before... We need to talk about this."

He pulls me harder against him. "It can wait."

"It can't. I need you to cover up what happened tonight."

He stares down at me, jaw clenching.

"I'm just asking for time before we go public," I say quickly, swallowing the lump in my throat. "To see if this is right for Arden, without... complications. If there's a way she can still have the life she wants, I want to give that to her. If we tell no one and get her into college in the US, she can live a normal human life."

Seven tips his head back and stares at the ceiling. "Until people notice she's not aging."

"We can worry about that fifty years from now." I place my hands flat on his chest. "You don't know what it's like being a pixie here. We are second-class citizens, only eligible to work certain jobs, always struggling to make ends meet, used for our bodies because we've got nothing else to sell."

A growl of frustration rips from his throat. "It won't be like that for her or for you. I'll make sure of it."

I shake my head. "You only say that because you've always had privilege. Everyone knows she's mine, Seven, and the things people say and think about pixies will be hurled at her from day one. Her fellow pixies will distrust her because of her leprechaun blood, and your fellow leprechauns will keep her at arm's length because of her pixie blood. It will be a lonely, bitter life."

"You don't know that."

Everything becomes as clear as day in my mind. "If you act right now, you can use your luck to make sure those pictures of us don't turn out. You can have Evangeline spin this as a PR stunt for the casino. If you stay away from me, people will buy it. And most importantly, Arden will have the time and space she needs to decide. You can teach her about what she is in secret, without interference, without risking her options."

"I just got you back." His voice cracks. "I'm so tired of secrets."

I feel a hot, wet tear roll down my cheek. "I know. I am too. But she leaves for school in the fall. Things will be different then. You know I'm right. The publicity we'll draw as a couple if those pictures are published will put too much scrutiny on her."

"So then we manage that, together."

"Seven, you deceived me—"

"I didn't mean—"

"I know you didn't mean to. I remember how you tried to do the right thing that night. I know how Godmother works, and I can only imagine how she tricked you into that situation."

His gaze shifts away from mine but he doesn't say anything.

"The fact of the matter is that because of how things went down, in the eyes of the law, Arden is human, and it's to her advantage to stay human. Unless and until she chooses something different for herself, I feel we have a responsibility to protect her." I sigh. "If there's one thing playing poker has taught me, it's that there are things you can control and things you can't. Some moves are skill. Others are probability. With luck, we can skew the odds in our favor, but we can never focus on everything. We can never know for sure what power the other players bring to the table. Right now, we have a chance to control this. We have a chance to protect what remains of Arden's childhood and give her choices we never had."

He releases me and rubs his head as if it hurts.

"Help me do this. It's only a matter of months before she leaves for college. After she's safely outside Devashire, we can go public, see where this goes." I regret the choice of words the moment they are out of my mouth.

"See where this goes?" Profound disappointment clouds his eyes, and he holds out his hands to me. "I'm already there, Sophia. I love you. I have always loved you."

"I love you too." The words almost shatter me. I want to give him what he wants, but I can't do it at Arden's expense.

"Then let's not waste any more time," he whispers.

Gods, I never thought it would be me begging Seven to keep our relationship hidden. My entire life has been turned on its head.

"It's four months. Please give her this," I beg. "Give her a choice." When he shakes his head, I add, "You owe me a favor."

He freezes, eyes narrowing.

"I won it fair and square."

"The poker game." He scoffs and runs his fingers through his hair, backing away from me.

"Yes."

Hesitating, he stares at me as if he's pondering every other option. "Fine. But for the record, I hate this. If you think it's right for Arden, I'll do it. I'll do it for you, and I'll do it for her."

"I promise, this is temporary."

He pinches the bridge of his nose, looking as tired as I've ever seen him. "I'll take care of the pictures. Anything I can't do with luck, Evangeline will manage with lawyers and spin."

I nod. "I'll get dressed. You should have your driver take me home. Say I was here to discuss my new position with your company."

Reluctantly, he agrees and I move for the bedroom and my clothes. A strong hand lands on my arm and whirls me into his chest. I don't fight it when his lips crash down on mine. The room spins. Heat claims my mouth as luck rushes over my skin, brushes along my collarbones, tightens the tips of my breasts. His hand presses into the space between my wings, and I arch into him, fluttering, aching with need in a heartbeat. The rush of his luck inside me is a delicious, bubbly purr. I moan and grind against him, needing him in me.

He breaks away and looks at me through his lashes. Cool air rushes between us. Seven closes his eyes, his throat bobbing on a swallow. When he opens them again, the unguarded Seven I've glimpsed is gone, replaced by the public façade he shows everyone else—Mr. Delaney, now chairman of the board of Lucky Enterprises, cool and totally professional. He reaches for his phone. "Ready the car," he says to whoever answers. "I'll text you the address."

Our eyes meet one last time. After a long beat, we both turn and walk in opposite directions.

I'm halfway to the bedroom when a fit of coughing overcomes me and a seed pops out of my mouth and into my waiting hand. It's smooth, red, and heart-shaped. Tears form in my eyes as I stare down at *love* in physical form resting in my palm. I picture it again, that fantasy of mine. A house for Seven and me with a fairy garden, the first one ever planted with a leprechaun. This seed has all the potential to become something beautiful and unique. Something as special as our love.

I find my purse and drop it into the zippered compartment before reaching for my clothes.

Not today, but someday.

Part II
His Dark Wish

Bombshell Kiss Gives Less Bang Than Expected

Devashire is once again abuzz with rumors about most eligible bachelor, Seven Delaney. In what is being called the bombshell of all kisses, no less than a dozen fairies have come forward to attest that they saw Seven kissing prodigal daughter Sophia Larkspur through the window of the Victory Building in Elderflame on Tuesday. This reporter has it on good authority the two engaged in a bout of tongue wrestling worthy of an Olympic medal.

Despite the purported heat of this public encounter and the enthusiasm their audience had for capturing it, oddly none of the pictures or videos taken are intelligible. If you are equally puzzled at the plausibility that a glare from the glass should occur at every angle in conjunction with simultaneous equipment malfunctions, then you will understand why I sought out Seven for a statement. Clearly luck was at play.

Although yours truly did not score an audience with the leprechaun, PR spokesperson and sister to the man himself, Evangeline Delaney, offered this:

"Do we have your attention, Devashire? The Dragonfly Casino is pleased to announce that for the first time ever, we will be offering poker lessons to human guests with the potential to expand the program to interested fairies in the future. Beginning later this month, Sophia Larkspur, aka Soho Lane, who made a name for herself as a poker pro while living in the United States, will bring her personal expertise to the table for a fee. Specific session dates and times to be announced. And yes, this partnership was sealed with a kiss!"

There you have it, Hatters! We should have suspected, given the circumstances, that this was a publicity stunt. A public relationship between a leprechaun and a pixie would be shocking, but the unconquerable Seven Delaney choosing a pixie is truly preposterous. Far more logical that the Lucky Enterprises mogul knows how to get your attention!

What do you think about opening poker lessons to fae despite the ban on regular play? Your favorite columnist wants to know. Leave me your comments at DailyHatter.com.

Fairly Goodweather
Columnist

CHAPTER
ONE

Everyone thinks they want a fairy-tale life, but those stories always focus on the wrong things. Cinderella rises above her circumstances when she enchants the prince. No one stops to consider that everything the prince knew about her was a deception. None of it was hers. Not the dress, not the shoes, not the pumpkin carriage. She pulled fictional history's greatest bluff. What happened next? After the wedding in the castle, did she rise to the demands of being a princess? Did the townspeople magically set aside their envy and spite and accept her as a regent? Or did happily ever after come with a dark and dangerous edge? It's possible Cinderella found herself in an equally difficult predicament, simply serving a new master.

I think about that story a lot when I ponder my own situation. Seven and I have known each other since we were children and our love is built on more than just a single night's dancing, but the divide between who he is and who I am couldn't be more complete. And I wonder if we will ever close that gap. Will there ever be a time I don't have to bluff? Will my relationship with Seven ever be accepted as real? I don't know. At the moment, I'm still riding in the pumpkin.

"Tip your head back and to the right, Sophia." Evangeline motions for me to adjust my position and I do, arching over the poker table at an angle that I'm sure makes the best of my figure but is terribly uncomfortable. The elbow I'm braced on prickles as if it's fallen asleep, and I'm starving. I missed lunch because the photographer is in a time crunch. My stomach growls a threat that it might start eating me from the inside.

Still, I smile as the camera shutter releases a series of fast clicks and the photographer, an artsy-looking leprechaun with long silver hair, moves around me. At least my outfit is flattering. With me leaning back like this, the floor-length dress splits midthigh, revealing one gold stiletto and the majority of my right leg. The sparkly red number hugs my waist and gives my breasts a marvelous, strapless boost. There's no room for a bra of any kind. The thing is backless—convenient, considering my wings have to be out for this shoot—but that means my upper half is precariously tucked into a stiff panel of fabric that runs from my sacrum to just above my nipples. Honestly, the fact I'm not spilling out of it is a feat of fashion genius. I'd thank luck or magic, but being fae, I'd feel it if there was any involved. We can sense both even if we can't always see them at work. Alas, my skin does not tingle and my own luck is nestled deep within me, snoring peacefully.

"Okay, darling, turn toward me and look directly at the camera, ankles crossed, both hands on the table on either side of your hips." The photographer squats down, adjusting his lens.

I do as he asks, beaming down at him, but he doesn't take the picture.

"Drop the smile. Look at me like I'm a competitor. I'm the player standing between you and a big win." He makes a few more adjustments while I try to dredge up the right look.

I spent the majority of my sixteen years in the United States supporting myself by playing poker. One of the skills that came with the territory was the ability to hide my actual emotions behind a poker face, the ability to either be unreadable or to telegraph an emotion that is inconsistent with what I'm feeling. The look I give the photographer now is one of supreme confidence and determination. It's an expression meant to intimidate. I'm projecting intensity, telling my opponent that I'm holding cards so good they might as well push their chips into the middle of the table right now. My smile dissolves, but not entirely. I close my lips but keep them slightly upturned at one corner, preserving the tightness in my eyes. When I lower my chin, my dark hair falls over one eye.

"Gods, Sophia," Evangeline says in a low voice. "You look like you're holding the secret to the universe behind your back."

"Maybe I am," I say, sending her a wink.

The photographer stands, studying his screen. "That's it. I think we got it. Thanks, darling. You were a wonderful model." He takes a step forward and kisses me on the cheek, his breath skating over my skin. He's a leprechaun, but up until this point, he's kept his luck to himself. Now I feel it beside me like a large, predatory bird. I give him a nod, and he hurriedly collects his things before kissing Evangeline on both cheeks. "You'll have the comps tomorrow by end of day."

"Thanks, Mac." She brushes her shiny red hair over one shoulder as she watches him leave.

Only a few short weeks ago, I thought the Delaneys hated me, especially Evangeline's brother, Seven. He stood me up at the Yule ball when we were teenagers and humiliated me in front of everyone in Dragonfly Hollow. Turns out Seven didn't want to hurt me at all. He was a victim of his psycho father, Chance, who'd poisoned him with blue iron—the only substance in the world capable of draining a fairy's luck—and kept him locked in a dungeon beneath his hunting cabin.

Weirder still, it turns out Seven is Arden's father. That little revelation is thanks to some serious magical interference by Godmother. I still don't completely understand her motives, but I do know this: Seven and I deserve to make up for lost time. Unfortunately, until we have a chance to tell Arden about her unlikely origins, we've decided to keep our relationship a secret. We want to give her choices. We want to give her a chance to control the narrative about her own life.

Seven's responsible for getting me this job teaching poker, and his sister, Evangeline, the head of public relations for Lucky Enterprises, is leaning into the moment. This photo shoot is just the start. I have interviews with all the major news outlets in Devashire scheduled over the next two weeks, at the end of which I'll be teaching my very first class.

"You did a great job today." Evangeline hits me with one of her ten-thousand-watt smiles. Just like her brother, she's supermodel attractive, the kind of person who walks into the room and turns every head. She's tall, thin, and radiates confidence. But then that's what being a leprechaun does for you. Leprechauns are always beautiful. Their luck seeps out of their pores.

"Thanks. I'm not used to being photographed. I hope Mac can get what he needs from what we did today."

She laughs. "Are you kidding me? Sophia, I don't think you realize how lovely you are."

"For a pixie," I add in for her.

"For anyone. If it weren't for the wings, I'd swear you were a leprechaun. I think living among humans was good for you." She shakes her head. "That look in your eyes. I've never seen a pixie look like that. You're a badass. And if people knew what you really did for Devashire, they'd treat you like one."

What I did was help take down her father and prove he was imprisoning pixies in his rural sex dungeon. He also murdered a few people for reasons that only he and maybe Godmother fully understand. Together, Seven and I proved Chance was guilty of murder. He's now serving a life sentence in Ashgate Prison.

I try not to think too much about the night we took him down. It still shakes me. I'm not sure if what Eva says is true—if Devashire society knew, would they respect me more? It's a moot point. Godmother took credit for solving the case, and the only people who know my part in it are Seven, Eva, and my friends River and Penelope, all of whom have been sworn to secrecy. One does not challenge Godmother's narrative of events. Not unless one wants to have one's wings broken.

I glance down at my toes. My stomach growls loud enough that I'm sure Eva hears it. "Uh, thanks. Are we done for the day?"

She laughs. "No, I want to introduce you to some high rollers. But go ahead and take a break. It sounds like you need one. Eat and get changed into something more comfortable, then meet me in my office."

I open my mouth to say okay, but the word never leaves my lips. My breath hitches when the buzz of Seven's luck skates across the back of my neck, over my shoulder, and between my breasts. My nipples tighten at the feel of it, and I have to draw a breath to steady myself. The tingle of it causes the tiny hairs on my arms to stand on end, and everything inside me takes on an electrical charge.

Evangeline's lips quirk into an impish grin. There is no way she can't sense that. "In my office by four, Sophia," she singsongs before striding out the door without looking back.

I adjust my dress and smooth my hair, suddenly filled with a different type of hunger. My heels click on the hardwood floors of the new poker room as I push my way through the gold-plated doors and into the foyer of the Dragonfly Casino. My steps falter when I see Seven standing in front of a poster advertising the latest Cirque du Soleil production going on in the theater.

My very own personal Prince Charming.

His back is to me, which means I have a moment to observe him as my inner world goes topsy-turvy with attraction. The soft shine of his toffee-colored hair picks up the gold reflected off the shiny surfaces in the room and contrasts perfectly with his dark suit, specially tailored to make the most of his broad shoulders. His jacket skims down to his hips in a perfect taper, both professional and somehow sensual, as if the material loves to touch him as much as I do. His long legs end in polished Italian-leather loafers.

As quietly as I can, I sidle up to him, leaving a few feet of space between us. Nothing to see here. Just two people who happen to be reading the same poster at the same time.

"That dress should be illegal," he whispers, his head still tilted as if he's studying the picture of the aerial act in front of him. "I take that back. It should be perfectly legal in the privacy of my bedroom. Outside of it, I'd prefer you wrapped in a hooded cloak."

I lick my bottom lip. "So sad. This dress, with me in it, is about to be plastered all over social media to promote the new poker classes. Evangeline picked it out."

A growl rumbles from his chest. "Is there no justice in this world? If she must flaunt you for all to see, shouldn't I, at least, be the first to enjoy you in it, to touch you beneath the material, to... help you out of it?"

My lips twitch. "Who are you to claim first dibs?"

Only his eyes move, but I see him glance in my direction,

his emerald gaze twinkling with his regard. "The one who loves you."

He's said it to me before, but hearing it now still sends a thrill through me and makes my heart thump in my chest. I know what he wants to hear. There is one thing that Seven needs from me more than anything else, the thing I've learned holds his pieces together.

"Be the first then. I'm *yours*, after all. Do with me as you wish." Aside from his sister, I am the one person in his life who knows him, his true heart, and knowing that I accept him, that I want to be his and want him to be mine is a balm to the wounds his neglectful parents left behind.

His throat bobs on a hard swallow, and his chest rises and falls at a faster rate. "Come."

His luck coils around me, nudging me to follow him as he turns and strides through an unmarked door near the banquet hall. I check over both shoulders. No one is watching. Of course not. Not with him concentrating his luck to make sure we're alone.

I duck inside.

Seven's arm circles my waist, and he pulls me against his chest in the darkness. I hear the lock slide into place, and then the light clicks on. We're in some kind of utility room, surrounded by shelves of tablecloths, aprons, and cloth napkins. At the back is a stack of folding tables.

I pivot in his arms to face him. "Classy digs, Seven, but I was hoping for a gas station bathroom."

He gives one breathy laugh, but the heat in his eyes shows me he isn't in a comedic mood. His expression is ravenous, predatory, *feral*.

"Are you done modeling for photos today?" he asks, deep and low.

"Yes." My voice comes out in a squeak, my throat tight from the intensity he's putting off.

The smile he gives me is positively wolfish. "Good."

Luck slams into me like an ocean wave I didn't see coming. Someone has popped the cork on a bottle of champagne and bubbles rush between my legs, through my torso, and to the tips of my breasts. Electric fizz tingles in my blood. My knees wobble but he has me, one hand between my wings and the other in my hair.

When his lips crash down on mine, it isn't gentle. He's claiming me with a desperation that tells me exactly how Seven feels about our clandestine circumstances. Leprechauns aren't used to being denied what they want, and he wants me. All of me.

I melt into him, opening wider for him, his tongue stroking expertly against mine. His thumb braces under my jaw, his fingers wrapped firmly around the base of my skull. The way he's gripping me is almost painful. Almost. Instead, it makes me feel secure. Safe. And completely turned on.

He shifts me back to the tables and lifts me as if I weigh nothing, perching my bottom on the top of the stack. My dress shifts. Despite hours of staying in place no matter which way I moved, my breasts spill out of the top. He catches one in his mouth, sucking hard. I have to flutter my wings to stay balanced in this position, and I dig my fingers into his hair to steady myself.

"You are so beautiful." Emerald-green eyes flash in the dim room, and he smiles wickedly at me, breath skating across my nipple. "I saw that photographer kiss you."

"You were watching me?" Not surprising really. Security cameras record every corner of the casino.

"Only at the end. I wanted to check if you were done."

"Did it bother you when he kissed me on the cheek?"

He laughs darkly. "Only because I have no way of marking you as mine. I wanted to throw open the doors to that room and make it clear as day that you're spoken for. Instead, I'll have to settle for reminding you of the same."

"How do you plan to do that?" I ask breathlessly.

His hands work under the skirt of my dress, bunching the shiny material around my hips. Adroit fingers hook into the sides of my panties and slide them down my legs. Once they're off, he brings them to his nose and inhales. My blood heats at the sight, and my breath comes in pants. He slips them into his pocket, then plants his hands on my inner thighs and shoves them apart, exposing me.

"Seven," I gasp.

He lowers himself to his knees in front of me and licks up my center with the flat of his tongue.

My cheeks heat. I arch against his mouth, and he flicks and circles my clit before plunging his tongue inside me. His luck follows, filling me with a rush of effervescence that presses against my inner walls even as he worships every inch of pleasure-inducing skin between my thighs. I can't form words.

It takes an embarrassingly short amount of time for my head to tip back in a silent scream of overwhelming pleasure. I'm still blinded by the light of the first orgasm when he rises, hooking one of my legs over his shoulder, and enters me fast and hard, sending me over the edge again.

"Oh. Gods. Sev. En." He's thrusting so hard it feels like my teeth might clack together. The only thing I want is for him to thrust harder, to hold me tighter. I want him so close I can smell him on my skin days from now when we have to be apart.

He grips my hips, his face buried in my neck as he pounds into me until he finds his release, tremors of ecstasy rippling through him in my arms. We're as close as two people can get, all my limbs wrapped tight around him, and I hold him to me.

He runs his nose from my jaw to my ear. "I love you, Sophia."

"I love you too."

Drawing back, he returns my panties and helps me fix my dress, which thanks to his luck hasn't ripped or sustained a single wrinkle, then zips his pants and takes a seat next to me on the tables. Leaning against the wall, he pulls me against his side. I make myself comfortable.

"So tonight's the night," he says.

"Yeah. It took some doing, but my grandmother is playing bridge in Sunnyville, my parents have a date planned, and Arden isn't babysitting for Penelope. We'll have the house and her all to ourselves for at least two hours."

It's taken a few days for me to arrange everything, but it's important to both of us that Arden be the first to know that Seven is her father and that she is the only pixie/leprechaun hybrid in existence. What a heavy hammer to be dropped on her. She's lived her entire life believing she's half-human. She believes it because I believed it, thanks to Godmother's trickery. But it's time she knows the truth. She deserves to know.

"When should I come?"

"Six should be safe."

He nods.

I tip my head back until it clunks against the wall behind me. "I hope she doesn't hate me."

"If she hates anyone, it will be me. You couldn't tell Arden what you didn't know, and I'm going to make sure she understands that."

"You're putting a lot of trust in a teenager to have a logical response to this situation."

He frowns. "Admittedly, I don't have much experience with teenagers. When Evangeline was her age, I was just two years older and still a teenager myself."

I groan. "Let me fill you in on raising teenagers. Arden is an exceptionally responsible, levelheaded, and remarkable young woman with the potential to turn into a hormonal, irrational beast when pushed beyond her limits. It doesn't happen often, but it does happen."

He strokes the back of my head. "Whatever happens, however she reacts, it will be okay." His voice is soft. "We're in this together. I'll do whatever it takes to protect both of you. I promise."

Is that my heart or a warm pat of butter sliding down my ribs? "I know you will."

A shadow passes through his expression, and he glances away from me. "You know it's a lie though. If I was willing to do anything, I'd stay away from both of you. You'd be safer and happier."

I grab his chin and turn his face toward me. "Safe is over-rated, and I couldn't be any happier than this."

He sighs and kisses me before glancing at his watch. "I'm fifteen minutes late for a meeting."

"You'd better get going then." I scamper off the stack of tables.

"Before I do, there's something I want you to have."

"Hmm?" I straighten my dress.

He reaches into his pocket and pulls out a necklace with a coin dangling from the end. I recognize it as one from his collection of charms, the magical objects he keeps in a hermetically sealed room in his office. He once brought a coin just like this with us to Shadowvale and used it to distract Yissevel the bone fairy so that I could escape the unseelie's clutches. It's gold with the imprint of a goddess on one side and a dragonfly on the other, and he's mounted it on a matching chain.

"I want you to wear this."

"Why?" I ask hesitantly.

"Because it protects its wearer from harm and because it will make the man who loves you happy you're wearing his gift," he says around a half smile.

"Who could say no to that?" I pivot, moving my hair aside so he can fasten the chain around my neck. The coin rests just below the hollow of my throat. "Thank you."

In response, he kisses me just below my ear. "One day this will all be easier."

I smooth my hair and check my makeup in the bottom of a silver tray, but like everything else, it's fine. Seven's luck has kept every one of my hairs in place.

I replace the tray and turn in his arms. "I'm not sure it will ever be easier exactly." He frowns, and I continue. "But it will be worth it. I know it will be worth it."

His usual lopsided grin comes back in full force. "See you tonight."

CHAPTER

TWO

When I was living in the United States, I read somewhere that children come *through* their mothers not *from* their mothers. The idea the author was trying to convey was that although our children share our genetics and are influenced by how we raise them, they come into the world their own person. Back then I laughed at this notion, chalking it up to silly human religiosity. The idea that some greater power had sent Arden through me, as if I were a portal between worlds, was something I couldn't take seriously back then. But as I look at my beautiful daughter now with her auburn hair and those emerald eyes that remind me so much of Seven's, those words return to me and they finally make sense.

I have no idea how she's going to take the news that Seven is her father. Arden and I have never been apart more than a few days. I know she likes avocado toast for breakfast and her bacon must be extra crispy. I know her favorite book is *Little Women*. I know she can't sleep with her closet door open. Before today, I would have sworn that no one knew her better than me, that I could predict exactly how she would react to almost anything. But not this. She's no longer my little girl. She's a woman. A whip-smart, stunningly beautiful young woman.

And I can't protect her from this. I have no idea what the truth will do to her, only that she deserves to know it.

"What was it you wanted to talk to me about?" Arden's voice is a low whisper. We wave goodbye to my parents as they slip out the door dressed in their date-night clothes. Both of them look great, younger than when I first arrived. I despise the thought that the years I spent raising Arden in the US prematurely aged them, but our current situation seems to be undoing some of the damage.

I clear my throat. "I'll tell you in a minute." I haven't seen Seven since our rendezvous in the banquet closet this afternoon. Afterward, we both went our separate ways. But he said he'd be here by six, which means I need to keep Arden busy for another fifteen minutes.

"Why can't you tell me now? We're alone." She shifts from foot to foot.

"I'm just, uh... We have a guest coming."

Her brows crowd together. "Oh my god, is it Godmother? Is there something wrong with my passport again?"

I hold up my hands. "No. Nothing like that." *Fuck.* That's not exactly true. It might be like that depending on what she chooses. I don't want to lie to her, but nothing I say will make sense until she knows everything. Only, I can't tell her the truth until Seven gets here.

She places both hands on her stomach. "Please just rip the Band-Aid off, Mom. You're giving me anxiety."

Should I tell her? Break the ice before Seven arrives? Make her wait? I'm still contemplating my options when a knock comes on the door.

"Hold that thought," I tell her, then move to answer it.

"I'm early, but I took a chance," Seven says from the stoop. Of course he did. He's lucky and he's been thinking about this all day. I breathe a sigh of relief and invite him in.

"Hi, Seven." Arden's gaze darts between us. If anything, she's even more nervous now. "What are you doing here?"

He gestures toward the dining room. "Sit. We'll talk."

"Am I in trouble with Godmother?" Arden blurts. She looks like she might bolt for the door.

It doesn't surprise me that she might think that—Seven works for Godmother after all. I have to calm her down before she passes out or does something stupid.

"Arden, you're not in trouble. It's nothing bad. Just please sit down." I gesture toward a chair across the table from us.

She sighs heavily but plops herself down, although her expression is nothing short of exasperated.

Seven pulls a coin from his pocket, an ordinary quarter, and slides it across the table toward her. "Has Bailiwick's ever tested your luck?"

Arden looks at him and snorts. "Um, no. I told them I'm human, so..." She licks her lips. "I'm given accommodations. I don't need it for lessons."

Seven taps a finger on the table. "Usually children in Devashire are given a test before they enter grade one. On average, leprechauns are born with more luck than pixies, who are born with more luck than satyrs. But there are exceptions. A few satyrs have tested at the top of the pixie range. More than a few leprechauns have disappointing results and test in the pixie range. Our natural ability to store and wield luck varies greatly by the individual, even among the normal species ranges."

She nods, her brows bunching as if she's confused.

I lean my elbows on the table. "The reason they test children is that luck is like a muscle. Use it regularly and your capacity to use it grows. Don't use it and it atrophies. You're my daughter, and it's possible you have more luck than you realize, it's just you've never tried to use it."

Arden lifts the coin from the table and raises her eyebrows. "Do you want to test me?"

Seven and I nod in unison.

"What do you want me to do?"

"Flip it," Seven explains. "Concentrate. Picture tails in your mind."

Arden places the coin on her thumb and flicks it into the air. When it lands, it's heads up.

I frown. "Did you concentrate on tails?"

Arden laughs. "Not really. I mean, it's not like I can change how it lands. That's ridiculous."

Seven plucks the quarter from her fingers and awakens his power. His luck rises to fill the room, a hot-blooded, long-bodied dragon of energy that slithers and coils around the table. Arden shifts, glancing over her shoulder.

"Do you feel that, Arden?" I ask her.

She nods. "What is it?"

"That's Seven's luck. What does it look like to you?"

Glancing around the room, she frowns. "It doesn't look like anything. It's invisible."

"Is it? You have a picture in your mind, don't you? Based on what you're sensing."

The beast brushes by her again, blowing the hair off her shoulder.

"It's a... It's like a... dragon!" Her eyes widen. "Long and red. Fire-breathing."

I laugh. "Good job. Can you tell mine?"

I concentrate, and my luck rises in the room beside Seven's and pounces across the table.

She giggles. "Tiger. Oh my god, Mom, yours is so much smaller than Seven's."

Teenagers! "Well, I'm a pixie, so..." I frown and pull my luck back inside myself.

To his credit, Seven doesn't laugh at Arden's jab. He holds up the quarter. "Observe." He launches the silver disc straight up off the tip of his thumb, where it flips over and over again in the air. He locks eyes with Arden as it drops, landing perfectly on its edge. Seconds pass, but it does not fall over.

"Holy shit!" Arden gapes.

"Language!" I can't really blame her. It's fucking incredible.

Seven knocks the coin over and pushes it across the table toward her. "Try again, and this time concentrate."

With Seven's luck still circling Arden, she places the quarter on her thumb. My lips twitch into a smile as I realize what he's doing. He's using his luck to draw hers out, focusing his power on her. If there's any luck in her, he'll coax it out.

She tries again, her face tightening with concentration. There! Another presence pops into the room with a small, bouncy energy. Raccoon, I realize. Its ringed tail waves as it holds its tiny hands out to catch the coin. I want to squeal in delight, but I can't break her concentration. The quarter lands.

"Tails!" I clap my hands together.

Arden chews her lip. "Holy crap. I think I did that!" She rubs her chest. "I... I felt it."

I nod vigorously. "What did you picture in your mind when you felt your luck working?"

A blush colors her cheeks. "Well, it wasn't a dragon."

Seven chuckles. "I once knew an old woman with luck that manifested as a mouse, and she was ten times as strong as me."

That seems to encourage Arden because she blurts out, "It was a raccoon."

I straighten. "That's what I sensed too."

"Try again," Seven says. "We can measure the strength of your luck by how many times in a row you can flip tails."

Arden eagerly picks up the coin and flings it into the air. This time Seven's dragonish luck disappears from the room and only the sweet and bright energy of Arden's raccoon remains. She squeals when it lands on tails.

"You're doing it, sweetheart. Keep going!" I clap my hands.

Seven holds up two fingers. "That's two. Go for three."

An hour later, Arden is visibly fatigued and I can barely feel the raccoon in the room anymore. She's flipped tails successfully 175 times, but this time it's heads. She slumps in her chair, forehead hitting the table. "That's all I got."

Seven and I beam at each other.

"What? How did I do?"

I rest my chin on my threaded fingers. "Do you want to tell her, Seven, or should I?"

"Oh, I'd love to," Seven says. "The probability of a human being flipping tails one hundred and seventy-five times in a row is almost zero. It's possible but so unlikely we might as well consider it impossible. The average satyr can reach twenty-five flips regularly, although it's not unusual for exceptional satyrs to near the one hundred mark later in life."

Arden's fingers go to her lips. "Mom, I did inherit your pixie luck!"

"The average pixie can manage sixty-five flips, but an exceptional pixie might hit 145 on a good day," I say. "My test was 105 as a child."

The grin fades from her face. "That doesn't make sense. It's genetically impossible," she says. "I can't be luckier than you. Not with a human father."

Seven rubs his jaw. "The average leprechaun can reliably make 150 flips as a child. I've managed five hundred myself as an adult, and the only reason I stopped was because I didn't have time to continue. The test was taking too long."

She stares at him as if he's not making sense. "So then how did I do 175 if I'm half-human?"

This time Seven turns to me and waits. I made him promise to allow me to be the one to say the words. Here we go. Please, gods, help her take this well.

"Because, Arden," I begin slowly. "You're not half-human after all. It turns out I made a mistake in assuming that. You're half-pixie from me." I press a hand into my chest and take a deep breath. "And half-leprechaun... from Seven."

Arden stops breathing, and the smile fades from her face. She tips her head, her eyes swimming with unshed tears. Confusion and betrayal war in her expression, and I want to explain but I can't find the words around the lump that's formed in my throat. Thankfully Seven rises to the occasion.

"Your mother never lied to you," Seven adds quickly. "She didn't know. Neither of us did until recently."

I hadn't thought it possible, but Arden seems even more confused. "I think she'd know who my father was!"

I shake my head. "Godmother changed his appearance and there were circumstances..." I sigh and look away. "I didn't know until very recently, but it's true. Godmother changed Seven into the form of a human man, and I didn't know who he really was the night we conceived you. I thought he truly was a human man."

"The three of us and Godmother are the only ones who know," Seven adds.

The moment Arden realizes the ramifications, I watch fear chase the other emotions from her expression. "Wait... I'm not human. Not at all?" She stands, sending her chair tumbling backward across the wood floor.

I shake my head, eyes locked on hers. "No one has to know,

Arden. You have the choice. You can either keep this a secret, and so will we, or—"

"Or you can take your rightful place in leprechaun society." Seven's body language tells me exactly what he feels about keeping this a secret. He wants to shout that Arden is his daughter from the rooftops.

Arden snorts. "My rightful place? You make it sound like I'm in one of those movies about a teenager who finds out she's a secret princess." Her eyes rove between me and him and she snorts.

Seven brushes invisible lint from the sleeve of his jacket. "We have no royal title, although you do have a family crest and are currently the sole heir of my portion of the Delaney family fortune, currently estimated at approximately thirty-five billion dollars."

All humor drains from Arden's expression, followed by all color as she looks to me and realizes that this isn't a joke. That what Seven says is true.

"Mom?" she squeaks. "What does this mean?"

As I suspected, there's no immediate joy in learning she's extremely wealthy. Arden isn't like that. The money won't in and of itself mean much to her. Like she always has in the past, she's waiting for me to frame this up, to help her make sense of it.

"It means you have options. You can pretend to be human and go to medical school as planned. Once you graduate, you can work in America. As far as the US government is concerned, you are human and a natural-born citizen. But you'll have to be careful. You should probably come here for medical care, and you can't overuse your luck no matter how badly you want to. If anyone determined that you were fae, the Fairy Immigration and Rehabilitation Enforcement agency would come knocking on your door. Also, you won't age like other humans, which means that at some point you'll have to return here."

Seven clears his throat. "Or we can take this public. Every year on the summer solstice, leprechauns throw a ball called the Gilded Gala. It's basically a coming-out party where all the young leprechauns of marriageable age are introduced to society. If you decide before then, I will introduce you to Devashire's elite. Everyone will know you're my daughter. You could attend university and medical school here, and of course you'd have plenty of resources to start your own practice."

I almost gape at his mention of the Gilded Gala. It's more than just a ball—it's an exclusive, televised event. All the attendees dress in gold, although how much gold and to what shiny degree is open to interpretation. The *Daily Hatter* puts out a special edition each year covering the best dressed, and designers clamor to outfit the wealthiest families. Although pixies and satyrs rarely attend the ball unless they're working at it, humans and fae alike line up to watch the procession of leprechauns down the rainbow-colored carpet that leads into the Dragonfly After Dark hotel where the ball is held each year.

Seven must really want Arden to stay to pull out the Gilded Gala, but it's important she understand the cons as well.

"But Arden, once it's announced that you're not human, it will invalidate your passport." I shoot Seven an apologetic look for popping his gold-plated balloon. "If you go public with this, there's no going back. Devashire will be your home... forever."

She blinks at me. "I can never leave."

Seven shifts uncomfortably. *Back to you, good cop.* "Lucky Enterprises' employees are sometimes granted special temporary visas in order to conduct business in the United States. I've been there twice this year. But no, I can't stay without permission, and if they know you're my daughter, you won't be able to stay either."

Arden rubs her face with both hands. "But if I go, I'll have to be careful not to get caught. I'll have to live like we lived before. No one can ever know who I am."

"It wasn't so bad before," I say defensively.

"Mom, you never had a real relationship my entire life. Anytime someone got close, you'd push them away."

"To keep you safe."

"And I'll have to do the same to keep myself safe."

I nod. "I liked our little life before I was arrested, Arden, but what you say is true. Now that I'm back here, I realize there is nothing more valuable than the freedom to be who you truly are."

Seven locks eyes with me, what I leave unsaid passing between us. One day *we* will be *us*. If all goes as planned, the two of us will live here, in our truth, come what may. We've agreed to spare Arden the burden of knowing about our relationship for the time being. Whatever she decides, I want it to be for her, not for me, and telling her would feel too much like pleading our case for her to stay.

My heart breaks when I turn back to her and she buries her face in her hands and slumps in her chair. No one wants to hurt their child like this. For a second I question whether we should have told her at all.

Seven reaches over and places a reassuring hand on my arm. Bright emerald eyes flash with his intense emotion. How could I miss how similar they are to Arden's for all these years? His expression isn't happy exactly, but he seems resolved.

"Arden." Seven's voice is low but certain. "You don't have to decide now. You have time to think about this. While you're thinking over your options, we can meet and I can help you learn to use your luck. I can answer your questions."

She lowers her hands. Here face is wet with tears, and I give her my most reassuring smile.

"Seven mentioned the Gilded Gala. That's June twenty-first. That's also right around the time we have to confirm with Chapel Hill. Why don't you take until then to decide?" Releasing a deep sigh, I reach across the table and grasp her hand. "In the meantime, you can put graduation behind you, enjoy some of the summer here in Dragonfly, and practice controlling your luck with Seven. You have time to process everything."

I glance at Seven and see weariness return to his expression. His fingers slip from my arm where I realize he's been resting his hand the entire time. Arden doesn't miss it. She darts a questioning gaze between us but doesn't say a word.

She takes a deep breath before wiping under her eyes. "Okay. Before the Gilded Gala is fair. And I'd like to meet with you, Seven, for practice."

"How does Saturday afternoons sound? Down by the lake."

She nods. "I can do that. I also want to visit the university here. I'll need to apply... make sure I actually have an option."

Seven's smile turns smug. He probably knows the admissions people. She'll have no trouble getting in. I have to hand it to him for not saying anything. Knowing Arden, she might insist on doing it without help. By not offering, he has more freedom to do as he pleases.

She leans back in her chair, looking exhausted. "Thanks for telling me," she mutters. "Thanks for giving me the choice."

"You deserve it. The truth is something Godmother never gave us a choice about."

Arden's eyes narrow. "Godmother knew, and she kept it a secret my whole life."

My hand curls into a loose fist. "She did. It's a fact of life here, unfortunately, and something you'll have to accept if you stay. Godmother doesn't play fair, and you can't trust her to do what's best for anyone but herself. Not ever."

She stands and crosses her arms over her chest. "I'm going to go lie down."

Before I can think of anything to say, she flees the dining room, leaving two possible futures in her wake. In one future she stays, and along with Seven and me, we become a family. In the other she goes, and we make do with stolen moments and vacation memories. I squeeze Seven's hand, reminding myself that I'll be fine either way so long as Arden's happy.

CHAPTER

THREE

Five weeks later...

"**W**hy did you raise on that hand, Mr. Tannenbaum?" I squint at the elderly human sitting to my right. I've been teaching this class for three weeks now, and he still doesn't seem to be getting it, although he's a pleasant enough pupil. He's got to be at least eighty years old, and I suspect the only reason he's here is to spend time with his wife, who's an absolute shark.

"Just mixing up the play. Gotta keep these suckers on their toes." He gestures vaguely at the rest of the table.

Mrs. Tannenbaum bursts out laughing. "Harold, they won't need to be on their toes. They'll just need to lean forward in their chairs a little to rake in your chips. You have a seven and a two, nonsuited, for cripes' sake!"

Harold shrugs and holds up both hands. "I was bluffing. That's part of poker."

I hold up a finger to get everyone's attention. "This is a great opportunity to enforce a point I've made before but perhaps you didn't catch. It's important to understand not only the cards you're holding but..."

"Your position at the table," they say in unison.

I nod reassuringly. "Exactly. Harold has the big blind, which means..."

A young woman named Margaret lifts her hand, and I call on her to answer. "He had to ante up in full before he saw his first two cards."

"Exactly. So as the last to bet before the flop, bluffing isn't a bad idea. He's already put his money in after all, and he has the advantage of the most information anyone at the table can have this round. But because he has very bad odds of actually winning with a seven and a two, his only strategy has to be to get the other players to fold. The best way to do that would be to signal a strong hand. In other words, to raise before the flop. There's a good chance that if he does that, other players with weak hands may fold rather than meet his bet. Winning small pots like that by bluffing can be a great way for a poker player to increase their bankroll."

"See, Janice? I know what I'm doing!" Harold harrumphs.

I can't help but chuckle. "Where you went wrong though, Mr. Tannenbaum, is to keep up the charade once Margaret raised significantly post flop. She's played conservatively the entire time we've been together. Chances are she has something with that sort of a bet. So at that point, knowing you've got nothing, folding would have been the more prudent option."

Janice crosses her arms over her chest and looks at him smugly. Harold isn't happy.

I check the clock. Saved by the bell. Clapping my hands together twice, I say, "Great job, everyone. I'll see you Tuesday for more tips and practice!"

"What about Monday?" Margaret asks.

"I'm sorry, I have the day off. My daughter is graduating from Bailiwick's Academy on Sunday, and we're taking Monday to recover from the festivities."

Margaret laughs. "It's so weird to think you have graduations here."

I grit my teeth. I get that a lot, little comments that show how humans really see us, as if our lives exist for their pleasure. As if we don't have lives of our own and an existence that doesn't involve them. Sometimes it's hard to swallow.

"Thank you for understanding," I force out.

Thankfully all eight of them get up from their seats and filter out into the casino without any more questions. I lock up the poker training room and head for the door, anxious to get back to the Wonderland theme park. There are a million things I need to do before tomorrow, and the character shuttle takes a long time.

"Ms. Larkspur?" Saul, Seven's head of security, is waiting for me near the front entrance. I've gotten to know him fairly well over the past few weeks. He often drives me to and from Seven's place after our many private meetings, and although we've never shown affection toward each other in front of him, I imagine he must suspect our relationship. That said, I've never felt a hint of judgment from Saul, and he's always been discreet. Plus Seven trusts him, which is saying a lot.

A woman passes us, and she turns her head to give Saul another look. The security guard makes an immediate impression. Unlike Seven, who has the build of a man who works out but spends most of his time in an office, Saul clearly spends a lot of time at the gym. He's a leprechaun but is as broad-shouldered as a satyr with a gun peeking from under his dark suit jacket and a gleam of alertness in his eyes that telegraphs "don't mess with me." I immediately feel safer in his presence.

"Hi, Saul. What's up?"

"Mr. Delaney would like me to drive you back to Wonderland. He told me to tell you he'll meet you there."

Sweet of him. It's Saturday, which means Seven is in Wonderland at the beach, giving Arden her luck lesson like he has every week for the past five weeks. "Lead the way."

Saul ushers me toward the elevators. I found out about the garage under the casino a few weeks ago. Only a select, privileged few have spaces there, which includes the officers of Lucky Enterprises. The existence of the garage is top secret, likely for security reasons. All the other employees have to park in the front lot and walk in each day with the guests.

Seven introduced me to the garage once we resumed our relationship and he decided he hated the thought of me riding the character shuttle. The revelation was eye opening. Secret passages exist between theme parks. It's how Godmother moves from place to place securely and quickly and how Seven and Eva and their personal security team travel as well.

The fact that Saul is taking me this way today makes it impossible to forget just how big the chasm between Seven's life and the regular existence of most fae in Devashire actually is. Because he loves me, I get a glimpse of this world, but I can't shake that this is not real life, at least not my life.

I climb into the back of Seven's Mercedes Maybach, the car he prefers when he requires a chauffeur. Saul slides behind the wheel and starts to drive. The concrete blocks that make up the tunnel create the illusion of collapse as he picks up speed, and I close my eyes to stop the overwhelming claustrophobia that sets in.

"You're the only one Seven has ever allowed down here," Saul says.

I open my eyes, and he's watching me in the rearview mirror. Why do I sense this conversation is to distract me? I like Saul. "I guess I'm lucky then."

He smiles. "The first time I learned these passages existed, I found it upsetting."

I can't hide my look of surprise, and he doesn't miss it. "You didn't know either?"

"You think because I'm a leprechaun that I have a life like Seven's?"

"Sorry if that's offensive. I know all leprechauns don't have the same upbringing as Seven, but I thought you had more exposure to this type of lifestyle than I did as a pixie."

Saul grins. "I can understand why you'd think that way, but I was born to a more humble family than the Delaneys. My dad was a security officer before he retired. My mom is a property manager. A good life for sure, but even we didn't know this existed until I got this job. This belongs in a Batman movie."

I laugh at that. "Well, Seven is a brooding billionaire."

We travel in silence for a few minutes, until the tunnel widens and we ascend, circling another parking garage.

"If you don't mind my saying so, Ms. Larkspur—"

"Call me Sophia."

"—he's not done as much brooding as before you came to work for the casino, and I don't think it's the poker lessons."

Uh-oh. My relationship with Seven is a strict secret. It has to be for now. The only person who knows about us is Eva, and that was necessary for her to help us.

"I don't know what you mean," I say breathlessly.

He pulls to a stop in front of a set of elevators and looks over his shoulder at me. "He told me you were friends as children. I think Mr. Delaney needed a friend. Someone who likes him for him and not all this, you know?"

"Since we were six." I nod. "And you're right. I don't care about any of this."

"Everyone should be so lucky to have that sort of friend."

He exits the vehicle and opens the door for me. "You want the fourth floor. It exits into the Wonderland Security building."

"Thanks, Saul." I tap him gently on the shoulder with my fist.

"Anytime, Ms. Larkspur."

"Sophia."

He gives me a wave goodbye and climbs behind the wheel again.

I follow his directions and make my way quickly to Glaive Beach where I find Seven and Arden playing poker at the same flat-topped rock where he taught me all those years ago. Arden lights up. "Mom, you've got to see this."

I pad to her side and take a look at her cards. "A royal flush. Very lucky."

She hands her cards to Seven, who is smiling like the Cheshire cat. He shuffles them into the deck. "Show her how it's done, Arden. Remember to shield."

Arden nods.

As Seven raises the deck to deal the cards, his luck rises in the air around me, a red-hot beast. I feel Arden's rise too. Raccoon energy weaves in and out of Seven's, a faster, more playful vibration that blocks the dragon from reaching the cards while also tapping them with its little paw. All of that happens in my mind. How we perceive luck as fairies is hard to explain to anyone who isn't fae. I don't see a dragon and a raccoon; I sense them, and it's as real as anything else around me.

Seven deals the cards.

Arden anxiously swipes them from the rock and then beams up at me. She laughs and fans them out. Royal flush.

"Wow, Arden. I'm impressed." I hug her around the neck.

"She's done it fourteen times in a row." Seven's expression is brimming with parental pride. "I'm not throwing all my power into it, but she's shielding against a significant attack and waging her own counterstrike. She's very clever."

"Of course she is." I press a kiss to her temple. "That's more than I can do, Arden. I can't split my luck that way. You're really talented."

The smile she gives me tells me everything I need to know. Arden loves this. She climbs to her feet. "Thanks, Seven. Will I see you next week?"

He rises and glances toward me. "You'll see me tomorrow. At graduation."

"You're coming?" Arden looks excitedly between us.

"I wouldn't miss it."

She launches herself at him and throws her arms around his neck. "I can't believe this is real."

He pats her back, the craziest look of satisfaction on his face. "It's as real as you want it to be."

Our eyes lock over her shoulder, and understanding passes between us. Something has shifted. For the first time, I feel like Arden might actually choose to stay. A new warmth sparks in my heart. Is it too much to hope we could one day be a family?

"Closer to the front, Sophia! My eyes aren't what they used to be." Grandma shoves me in the middle of my back. Her bony hands are surprisingly strong. I walk faster up the aisle between the rows of white folding chairs, stopping at the third row of seats reserved for guests. We're early but already the first two rows are completely full.

"This is as close as we're going to get without wrestling someone for a seat," I tell her.

Grandma's eyes narrow. "I could take 'em. I'm stronger than I look, Sophia."

"You're going to get us thrown out of here if you keep staring like an axe murderer." I nudge her with my elbow.

She shrugs. "Well-behaved women rarely make history."

"Instead of quoting Laurel Thatcher Ulrich to me, why don't you grab a seat? It's the third row, Grandma. Any closer and you risk a sprained neck." I gesture for her to go in first.

"I want to be on the end."

I love my grams, but I have to put my foot down. "I have to be on the end to take pictures."

"Pictures, schmictures. You just want that seat because it's the best view of the stage." She fists her knobby hands and rests them on her hips.

"Caught me. I'm pulling the mom card."

My mother saves me from Grandma's comeback, tugging her down the row after my father. "Come on. Sophia gets to choose this time."

Reluctantly, she moves into the row and sits in the seat directly next to mine, arms crossed. "Not sure what a shorty like me is supposed to do in this seat. How am I supposed to watch people from here?"

My mom gives Grandma side-eye and spreads her hands. "You'll just have to ask your friends to spill the tea after the event."

"Oh, all right." Grandma's voice quivers. "But I hope you know you're seriously injuring my gossip potential right now."

Mom sighs and takes the chair between her and Dad.

"Is their room for one more?" I look up from my seat to find Seven standing beside me at a respectable distance. He could be anyone just asking about a seat, but his eyes are filled with longing. I see his fingers twitch. He wants to touch me. He wants to experience this with me. I can read him as if he were saying it out loud.

"You want to sit here? With us?" I love that he's here, but this is going to be too obvious. My gaze jumps around the crowd.

He stares down at me. "Yes. We should watch this together. It's important."

As much as I'd love to sit next to Seven to watch our daughter graduate, this isn't the time or place to draw attention ourselves. People are already turning to stare, wondering why a Delaney leprechaun is talking to a pixie.

"If you sit with me, it will be a distraction," I whisper. "These kids deserve undivided attention."

"Back here then." He steps into the fourth row and takes the seat on the end, directly behind me. I give him a nod of thanks, but he doesn't look happy.

I'm about to lower myself into my seat when two burly arms sweep me into the aisle and against a chest that might as well be a concrete wall.

"River!" I smile up at my friend and satyr, trying my best to breathe through the crushing hug.

"Congratulations! Graduation day. You did it!" His smile is bright enough to make my heart leap.

"I think Arden had something to do with her success," I tell him.

"Don't underestimate the importance of a doting parent." River is the type of person who has never met a stranger and has to touch everyone he greets. He keeps his hand on my shoulder as he speaks to me, and I can practically feel Seven's gaze burning into the side of my head as he seethes with jealousy.

"Thanks, River. Do you have a seat yet? There's one open next to Dad." I gesture with my chin down the row. Out of the corner of my eye, I catch the annoyed twitch of a muscle in Seven's jaw.

"Can't. I'm catering the after-party. I just wanted to drop this off for our Arden." He hands me a box about the size of a small book wrapped in brown paper and tied with string. "Tell her congratulations for me. I expect a full play-by-play the next time she comes into the restaurant."

I take the box and slide it into my purse. Lifting on my toes, I place a kiss on River's cheek. "Thank you. Sweet of you to remember her."

He says his goodbyes and then gives Seven a nod before

striding toward the restaurant. I do a double take when I see Seven's face. Shit, he looks like he wants to kill someone. His foot taps.

I lift an eyebrow.

He lifts one right back.

I wave a hand in the air dismissively and take my seat.

Around us, beyond a red velvet rope, humans are lined up to watch the festivities. A family near the front is eating a bowl of green, gray, and white plaid ice cream—Bailiwick's plaid—a Twinkleberries graduation-day exclusive. Magic gives the dessert its characteristic pattern, but the flavors are common enough—a combination of mint, vanilla, and lavender. One of the humans catches me staring and waves. I look away like I didn't see him. This is a ticketed event that makes loads of money for Dragonfly, but damn if it's not like being in a fishbowl.

"Ice cream looks good," Grandma mumbles. "So does Seven."

"Grandma, shhh."

She giggles.

The steady tone of a bow being drawn against the string of a cello meets our ears, and I squeeze Grandma's hand. "They're starting."

A band of satyrs seated on the corner of the stage starts to play. The music is nothing like human music. Although I remember this tune from when I was young, it never fails to move me. Along with the cello, one of them plays a gold violin, another a piccolo, and another something like a xylophone made of bones. The music is bright but somehow haunting, like a child's music box in an empty room.

I dig a Kleenex from my purse and dab at my eyes as everyone stands and turns toward the head of the aisle. A collective gasp rises from the crowd when they see Godmother leading two rows of robe-clad students. The students stop at the head of the aisle, but Godmother proceeds forward.

Everything about her is larger than life. She's tall and curvy, her larger size packed with luck and magic. Today she's wearing a deep purple dress with a black corset and a skirt that looks as if it were built from stringing together thousands of cicada wings. It's dark and delicate and flutters as if it's alive when she walks. Peacock feathers fan behind her head and perfectly complement the rest of the dress and her deep mahogany complexion. Pixies garbed entirely in silver manage the train of her gown.

Once she reaches the top of the dais, she raises a jeweled scepter. "It is my pleasure as Godmother and queen regent of Devashire to give you this year's graduating class!"

Two by two, the students parade toward the stage to the sound of thundering applause. Dressed in deep green robes and crowned with laurel, the pairs diverge at the end of the aisle and ascend staircases at either side of the stage. When I see Arden, I whistle and Grandma whoops like she's a frat boy at a football game. Arden's smile warms me. I worried this event wouldn't mean as much to her what with her having only attended Bailiwick's for a few months, but she seems genuinely happy and proud. She catches my eye and places her hand over her heart.

Once the students have all filed onto the stage and to their assigned seats, the music stops. Godmother nods her head, and they all sit down at once. She steps to the podium. There's no microphone, but her voice projects over us, laced with magic.

"Each year, I stand before the graduating class and am called on to speak about the future, the world these young people are graduating into, and their prospects for a better tomorrow. Each year I say something about opportunity and hard work. I wax poetic about how with the right attitude and enough courage, anything these students want can be theirs."

The crowd has gone silent, and I can't tell if it's because they are riveted by what Godmother is saying or appalled at the lie. A satyr will never run Dragonfly Casino. Most pixies won't own their own home until they are over one hundred years old. She might say it every year, but it's all drivel.

"Each year, I say those things," she continues. "But not this year. This year I want to focus on today. Because every day we wake up in Devashire is a good day."

Grandma coughs into her hand, and I swear it comes out "Bullshit!"

Godmother spreads her hands. "We live in a world of magic and love. We are a community of fae with the honor of sharing our gifts with the world." She gestures toward the humans watching the event. "What you do from today forward isn't half as important as who you are. Being fae means being part of something larger than yourself, whether you're sweeping the streets of Dragonfly Hollow or teaching in the education center. Every position is important and equally valued."

"But rewarded at completely different levels," Grandma murmurs. "Gods, this woman."

"Today, my dear students, as you traverse the river between adolescence and adulthood, worry not about what the future brings. As long as you are here, your future is bright, as it is for all fae. Now I am pleased to honor you, the next generation of fae who have demonstrated through your studies your commitment to upholding the values Devashire holds dear. Today you commit yourselves to keeping the magic alive for all. It's important work. We alone have the power. Without further ado..."

She starts calling names, and one by one the students move across the stage, receiving the scroll that memorializes the day. I mop my face when they call Arden's name. Seven's luck coils around me and then threads between my fingers. It's as close to holding my hand as he can get. I glance back at him. His eyes glint, and he smiles proudly.

Once the last student, Blossom Zolder, is announced, Godmother brings the festivities to a fast close. We stand up as one, and the crowd lumbers toward the reception tent.

"Can you believe that nonsense," Grandma says on the way. "As if we're all living in some utopian paradise."

"I think that was for the human audience's benefit, don't you?"

She shrugs. "I hope so. She can't possibly be that cut off from reality."

"Oh, there's Arden!"

Arden plows into me, spinning me around with the force of her hug. "I did it! I'm a high school graduate!" My parents pat her back and she hugs each of them with equal gusto. When she turns back to me, she asks, "Where's Seven? I saw him sitting with you."

"He's right—" I thought he was behind me but he's not. I turn around and scan the crowd, finding him in close conversation with a gorgeous leprechaun with sleek black hair and oversized hazel eyes.

"Who is that?" Arden asks. I don't say so, but I'm wondering the same thing.

Grandma's head pops up between us. "Oh, that's Alicia Faust of the Armon-Fausts. She was once engaged to Seven."

"Huh?" Surprise and jealousy fight for control of my brain, and I turn toward Grandma, desperate for her to spill the tea.

She raises a finger. "It all started when—"

A loud pop interrupts her, and the crowd turns as one.

"Was that a firecracker?" Arden asks.

Seven appears beside me in a heartbeat. "No, that was a gunshot."

A few seconds later, a scream cuts through the afternoon festivities. The crowd scatters, some moving toward the sound and others seeming to rush to the safety of the nearby buildings.

Godmother appears before us out of thin air and grabs Seven by the arm as if she owns him. "Come with me."

I move fast to keep up, but with Arden, my parents, and my grandmother with me, we lose them in the crowd. By the time we reach the sidewalk in front of River's Tavern, a crowd has already gathered. My stomach lurches at what I see at the center of that circle of onlookers.

River is on his knees, and he's covered in blood. It's with some relief that I realize it's not his. He's pressing on the chest of a stranger, whose blood spurts between his fingers. On the ground beside him lies a gun.

CHAPTER
FIVE

Breathless, as if someone has punched me in the gut, I turn back to Arden and look between her and my family standing behind her. Around us, things have turned to complete pandemonium. Someone shoves my mother, and she huddles into my father's side.

"It's not safe, Sophia," my dad says.

I lock eyes with him. "Take Arden home. I'll meet you there."

"Mom?" Arden clings to my arm.

"It's all right. I'll meet you there. I just need to—" I gesture toward Seven. What do I need to do? I'm not beholden to Godmother anymore. This isn't my job.

Arden studies me for a moment, then says, "Okay. I'll meet you at home."

My father wraps his hands around her shoulders and, together with my mother and grandmother, moves through the crowd in the direction of the house.

Once they're gone, it takes me a second to process what's happened. Although I'm too far from the scene to distinguish every detail, I can tell by his build and manner of dress that it's a human man who's been shot. River is covered in blood, his hands still pressed to the wound. A gun rests next to River's knee—a black handgun. Guns aren't allowed in Dragonfly but from my time in the States, I'd guess it was a Glock or maybe a SIG based on size and shape.

The scene is total chaos. Humans are screaming and gathering up their children. Fairies are rushing in every direction. Godmother looks livid.

With a wave of her hand, a purple shimmer casts through the crowd and two things happen at once. A rope goes up, the fairy equivalent of police tape, and a team of uniformed security personnel arrive in a rush.

Godmother and Seven approach River and the victim, but when I try to join them, a large hand shoots out in front of me.

"Sorry, ma'am. Only authorized personnel."

From behind the rope, I watch River, Seven, and Godmother exchange heated words, and then with a snap of Godmother's fingers, River rises from the cobblestone as if lifted by an invisible force. Two leprechaun security guards rush forward and clamp blue-iron cuffs around his wrists.

I can't read Seven's expression from this angle, but he's not smiling.

"Gods, they're arresting him," Penelope says from beside me.

I hadn't even noticed her arrive. Her kids are young, so she wasn't at the graduation today.

"Pen! When did you get here?"

"Only a second ago. I was having lunch in River's when I heard the shot."

"What the hell is going on?" I press the tips of my fingers into my temples. "Did you see what happened? Was there some sort of altercation?"

Penelope leans in to whisper in my ear behind a curtain of her platinum hair. "I didn't see. No one seemed to. After it happened, everyone went wild talking about it and watching through the windows, but the incident itself... No one saw."

I stare at her for a beat. "That's... odd."

She nods.

"Why did they cuff him? River's not capable of causing someone intentional harm. Not unless he was defending himself or someone else."

An emergency vehicle cuts through the crowd, and a team of paramedics rushes out with a stretcher. In no time, the stranger is wheeled into the back. River, still in handcuffs, is also helped into the back of the vehicle. In literally seconds, the gun and all signs of blood have been wiped from the walkway as if the incident never happened.

"Wow, that was fast," I mutter.

"Shhh. I think Godmother's going to speak." Penelope points her chin toward the center of the crime scene.

"If I could have your attention please," Godmother booms in that larger-than-life voice that reverberates in my bones. Her skin glows with power, as do her eyes, bright amber and intense. "Take heart, my dear guests—no one is in any danger. What happened today was a quarrel between two men that ended in an unfortunate accident. The injured party is being rushed to Elderflame Hospital as we speak, and the shooter, River Foxwood, will be held until this incident can be fully investigated and charges brought. Thank you for your patience and please know that we in Dragonfly Hollow do not tolerate any violence in our theme parks. Crime within our borders is so low as to almost be nonexistent, and guns are strictly prohibited. Please know this was an isolated incident and we will be taking steps to ensure it never happens again."

I bristle at the lie. Only recently, Seven and I helped solve two murders that occurred in the park. But this *is* the first act of violence where Godmother hasn't been able to hide the crime scene from the public. It's broad daylight, and the man responsible for the previous murders is in Ashgate Prison. Whoever did this—and I know it wasn't River—wanted this to be seen. And that's terrifying, because if I'm reading the situation accurately, River just became a very convenient scapegoat.

"Poor River. What can we do?" Penelope presses a hand to her chest.

My gaze drifts to the nearest security camera, and I point up at it. "Everything here is recorded. We'll know soon enough exactly what happened. The faster we can pull the footage, the sooner we can clear River of suspicion and refocus the investigation on the actual perpetrator. I'll ask Seven to do it right away."

She makes a face. "Are you still working with him? I thought that was over?"

"It is, but we're still... on speaking terms. I'll ask him nicely."

Penelope chuckles. "Good luck with that. I'm going to go talk to some people inside again. Maybe someone saw something." She strides off toward the restaurant.

Seven makes eye contact with me and has started walking in my direction when he's swarmed by security officers. He's Godmother's head of security. Has been since the night he bargained with her for a second chance with me. It looks like he might be a while. I'm sure the officers need a debrief, especially when it's clear Godmother is spinning this.

I find myself itching to know exactly what River said before he was hauled away. I'm not a detective or anything like it. I'm a poker pro and I'm a pixie. Does that make me qualified to investigate a crime? Hades, no. But it does make me an expert at reading other people's body language and a damn good liar when I need to be. That and my archery skills were enough to put Seven's father, Chance Delaney, away in Ashgate Prison for murder. So if there's anything I can do to save my friend River from being prosecuted for a crime he didn't commit, you bet I'll do it.

"Gods, Sophia!" Evangeline appears in front of me, her usually composed persona visibly flustered. "This is a complete disaster. Have you seen Seven?"

"He's over there with the other security officers and Godmother. I think they're trying to contain the situation."

"This is a fucking nightmare." She frowns and shakes her head.

"You're a PR genius. I'm sure you'll find a way to spin this just like Godmother did. I'm just worried about River. There's no way he's responsible. Can you get your hands on the surveillance video?" I point toward the dark orb under the streetlight that houses the security camera.

"No." She fists her hands at her sides. "I don't have access. Just Seven." She looks me in the eye and drops her voice. "It would make my job far easier if River didn't do this, Sophia. Unless we can blame this on another human, Dragonfly is going to take a hit."

This is why Evangeline is so good at what she does. She understands how precarious our relationship with the outside world actually is. Humans shoot humans all the time outside the parks. Out there, no one would blink twice over this incident. But in here, our ability to draw people into the park is predicated on them feeling safer within our borders than outside of them—safe among beings they believe are *other*. They don't think of us as people. Some call us creatures or even monsters. They have no idea what a monster truly is.

I glance in Seven's direction. "I'll find a way to get his attention. The video will prove River's innocence and show us who's really responsible. Once the victim recovers, we can ask him to fill in the details. Meanwhile, you can use your luck to smooth things over."

She closes her eyes as if she's truly relieved that I've agreed to help. "Thank you, Sophia. After everything we went through to manage what happened with our father, this is just exhausting. At least in that case, Godmother was able to conceal his crimes. No one outside the family knows exactly what he did, especially not the humans. This... It's too late. People saw. We can't hide it."

I lean in and give her a quick hug. "So we'll roll with it. I have faith in you. It's going to be okay."

Her green eyes lift to meet mine, shiny as if she's trying not to cry, and she tucks her deep red hair behind her ears. "You're a good friend."

She kisses both my cheeks and then strides away from me, looking exquisite in an indigo dress with ruby pumps. Only a leprechaun could be as stressed as Evangeline is right now and still look as fresh as if she'd just walked out of the salon.

As soon as the security team breaks and the rope is lowered, I head straight for Seven, who's now in a heated conversation with Godmother. When he sees me, his lips press into a straight line and his eyes crease at the corners. He isn't happy, but he seems resolved about something. Godmother, on the other hand, is vibrating with cool assurance, as if she is entirely in control of her every thought and emotion and knows exactly what needs to be done to address this disaster.

"Sophia Larkspur, unless you've come to offer some additional insight into what happened here today, I'm going to ask you to move along." She lifts her chin, her gaze sliding down her nose at me from her superior height.

"Just that I'm sure River didn't do this," I say nervously. I don't like the way Godmother is looking at me. "I came to ask Seven to check the security footage."

"Oh, you're sure, are you?" She taps her fingers in front of her. "Are you certain you want that to be the case? You know, if River isn't responsible for that guest's death, the most likely suspect is the person who committed the last two murders. Since that person is supposed to be in Ashgate, I must question whether we imprisoned the right man. Should I remind you what happens if he is not?"

"Excuse me? I'm not sure I know what you're getting it. You caught Chance red-handed."

"Imprisoning pixies, yes, but there was no hard evidence linking him back to the murders. Those were technically committed by Yissevel, and as that creature is dead, he could not be questioned. Needless to say, if you were wrong, and there was someone else involved, our previous bargain was dissolved on the basis of false assumptions. If it turns out that what happened today is in any way related to the first two murders, you will be beholden to me to find the murderer."

I look between them both. "Murderer? But you said he was merely injured and being taken to Elderflame Hospital. Isn't there a chance he'll recover?"

Seven frowns. "That was for publicity reasons. The man is dead."

I gasp. "What about River? What did he say when you asked him what happened?"

"He denied shooting the man, of course," Godmother said. "Claimed he found the human on the walkway bleeding when he came upon him, but without any witnesses, I'm afraid anyone might claim such a thing."

I hug myself against a sudden chill. So the ambulance was just for show. I glare at Godmother. "There's no way River did this, and you know it. He's not capable of it."

"And if you find proof of such a thing, I'd be happy to examine your evidence, Sophia. Until then, I'll be holding River until we know for sure it's safe to release him."

"But—"

Seven steps between us, cutting me off. "There's a simple way to settle this. I'll go pull the security footage."

Godmother rests a hand on her corset and purses her lips. "You do that, Seven. But until we prove otherwise, as far as I'm concerned, River is our perpetrator."

CHAPTER

SIX

"It should be right here." Seven rubs his temple, looking as frustrated as I feel.

We're in the Wonderland Security office, staring at the recording of the spot in front of River's Tavern where the shooting happened. Seven scans backward second by second. Several minutes are missing. At two p.m., all we see is the brick walkway in front of River's, but then the video skips forward to 2:15 p.m. and River appears in the space, hunched over the dead man.

"Someone's tampered with the video," I say breathlessly, pressing a fist to my forehead. "Again! How is this possible?"

"It shouldn't be." He grits his teeth. "Our system keeps track of everyone who accesses these recordings. Very few employees have the clearance to delete video." He navigates to a command prompt and types a few lines of code. The system returns a string of characters around a single name we both recognize.

I brace myself on the desk, my heart pounding with the implications. "Chance Delaney? How?"

Seven scowls. "This says the change was made from the IP address of Chance's desktop computer."

"How? He's in Ashgate Prison." No one has ever escaped from Ashgate. Then again, has any prisoner ever been as powerful as Chance? My stomach aches at even the thought that he might be free again.

"It's *not* possible that he did this himself." Seven runs a hand down his face. "After he was arrested, his office and everything in it was sealed off. We plan to demolish it eventually but didn't want to destroy any evidence Godmother might need."

That made sense. The legal system in Devashire works similarly to the one in the US. The difference is that our regent, Godmother, can sentence criminals to Ashgate without a trial in extreme circumstances like murder or treason. In those cases though, her verdict can be challenged up to a year following imprisonment. It's supposed to allow for a check on Godmother's ultimate power. In reality, she uses the privilege so rarely that her judgment has never before been questioned. In Chance's case though, with him telling us he wasn't working alone, I can see where Seven would want his bases covered.

"What if he wasn't bluffing, Seven?" I whisper. "What if someone was helping him back then and is still helping him now? Someone with access to his things." I wrap a strand of hair around my finger and pull it tight, anxiety rising in me like a swarm of insects and crawling across the inside of my skin. The base of my neck prickles with it.

"There's no way into that office. The only two people on the payroll with access are me and Eva."

"What about remote access? Maybe someone hacked it?"

He frowns. "Possible but unlikely. I'll get one of my tech guys on it." He fires off a quick email.

"Seven, did River say anything about what happened?"

Seven leans back in his chair. "There wasn't time for him to tell us much. Godmother couldn't wait to get him and the victim out of there. He said he heard a scream and ran toward it to find the victim lying on the sidewalk with a bullet wound in his chest. At that point, he knelt next to the body and tried to keep him from bleeding out. Godmother didn't buy it though. Not with the gun right beside him."

"He admitted to touching the gun?"

"Not exactly. He said he didn't remember seeing it before but it's possible he moved it out of the way. He was focused on the victim. Godmother believes that he made it up to explain why his fingerprints will be on it."

"Aargh!" I grab the sides of my head. "How is it that no one else saw this?"

"Half the park was at graduation. There were people in the restaurant, but no one will admit to seeing anything."

"Fuck. What are the odds that that patch of sidewalk would be completely abandoned aside from River? It's almost like—"

He catches my gaze. "Like a leprechaun was involved. Someone wanted River to take the fall for this."

I groan. He turns back to the video and reverses it again. For a good twenty seconds before the skip, no one is visible in the camera's range. "I don't like this. Someone uses my father's computer to tamper with the security cameras, and then the scene is cleared in a way that screams leprechaun. If I didn't know he was in Ashgate, I'd think he was behind this."

"What if he escaped somehow?"

Seven shakes his head. "It's impossible. Trust me on this, Sophia. He's there."

I take a deep breath. "He told me he wasn't working alone." Our eyes meet. Gods, Seven looks exhausted. "We need to find out who the victim was. Maybe that's the clue to all this."

"Already on it. We didn't find any identification on him,

but I have someone down the hall going through the Wonderland admissions logs and comparing pictures."

"Good." I push my chair back and stand. "I'm going to visit River wherever Godmother is holding him. Maybe he knows more than he was able to share given the circumstances."

He shakes his head. "You can't. They're holding him in Ashgate."

"Ashgate! Why? Godmother knows he didn't do this, Seven. She all but admitted she knows."

"She also told you that he did it until we can prove he didn't." Seven rubs the back of his neck. "The politics around this is bigger than any of us. She needs a scapegoat. She will never let him out of that cell unless we have someone else to put in it."

"I'll just have to go to Ashgate then."

He blinks at me as if I just said I planned to cut off my wing and donate it to science. "You can't just walk into Ashgate. You have to petition Godmother, and then they give you a specific time. There are procedures."

"I'll go to her office and fill out the forms now."

A muscle in Seven's jaw dances wildly, and his body tenses like a loaded spring. "No, Sophia," he finally blurts. "You absolutely cannot go out there. I'll go." He pulls out his phone and stares down at a calendar that has no white space.

I spread my hands. "Even if you went instead of me, it wouldn't be the same. River and I are friends. He'll share things with me that he won't share with you. The two of you have never exactly been chums."

Seven rubs his jaw as if remembering the time River slugged him. "He'll answer my questions if he wants to get out of there."

I tip my head to the side and shoot Seven a disappointed look. "Isolation is torture for a satyr. River thrives on in-person contact. I can't just leave him in there. He's my friend. I need to go to him and tell him that he's not alone and that we are doing all we can to get him out."

"Right. Because he's your *friend*."

"That sneer isn't attractive, Seven, and you're acting childish." I place my hands on his chest and lean in until my face is close to his. "Are you jealous?"

He shrugs. "Why would I be jealous of a man who can walk down the street holding your hand without everyone and their brother losing their shit over it?" His emerald gaze drills into me, brutal in its intensity. I guess when he puts it that way, it makes sense. He's the luckiest man in Devashire. I'm the thing he wants most, and yet he can't have me. It's making him crazy.

I take his face in my hands. "River was there for me the night of the Yule ball. He was a friend to me before that, but he truly supported me then in a way no one else could. And he's been a good friend to me since I returned to Dragonfly."

"Yeah, River's an all-around great guy." His tone is wooden, and he blinks up at me slowly.

"I'm not interested in River and never will be. I'm in love with you."

The corner of his mouth tugs upward. His hands land on my face, and he kisses me gently. "I know why you want to go," he says. "But this isn't about jealousy. Ashgate is a dangerous place. We should go together."

"I don't think so. I think River will be more open with me if you're not around. He doesn't trust you the way he trusts me."

He squeezes his eyes closed. "You're not going to be talked out of this, are you?"

"No."

"Can I convince you to take my personal security with you?"

"Would it ease your mind?"

"Yes."

"Then yes."

"Fine." He flashes me a disarming smile. "Will you join me tonight for a late dessert?"

"I do like to end the day with something sweet." I kiss the corner of his mouth. "I might be able to stop by after graduation dinner, but it will depend on Arden. She's probably freaking out after everything that happened today." I give an exaggerated sigh.

"That reminds me. I have something for her." He reaches in his pocket and pulls out a jewelry box. "Something from my collection."

I balk. "Not your secret collection? A charm?"

He nods. "Tell her not to use it until I have a chance to talk to her about its... properties."

"Is it safe?"

"For her? Yes." The intonation on that *yes* holds a slight question, as if he's not entirely sure about his answer.

I shoot him an exasperated look. "What are you giving our daughter, Seven?"

He leans back in his chair. "Hopefully one more reason to stay in Devashire."

THE FORMS TO VISIT ASHGATE PRISON ARE FIVE PAGES OF bureaucratic hell. They ask for my name, address, income, and highest level of education, and there are no less than fifty questions about why I want to visit the prisoner. As the cherry on the shit sundae, they must be completed in triplicate, each form only slightly different than the last. Mercifully, the pixie at the window of the administration building is a friend of River's. She speeds my application through. My phone rings before I even reach home, and she informs me she's cleared me to visit in two days' time.

Poor River. Two more days seems like a long time to be locked away without a friendly face. But it's the best I can do.

"Mom!" Arden meets me at the door, still dressed in her gown and laurel. I hug her and kiss her cheek.

"I'm sorry it took so long. River is in real trouble, and I'm trying to help him."

"I can't believe he killed that man." Arden's eyes widen.

"That's because he didn't."

Mom chooses that moment to walk into the room. "Sophia! Oh good. I wouldn't let Arden change until you got home. We need a family picture."

I push all thoughts of the tragedy aside. Today is Arden's day, and she deserves far better than what's happened. "Great idea," I say, hooking my arm around Arden's shoulders. "No more talk about the incident that shall not be named. For the rest of the night, it's just us and our pride over this amazing girl."

"Hear! Hear!" Grandma yells from the living room.

I peek at her around the corner. She's knitting something that looks like a sweater for a hamster. I don't ask.

I use a little illusion to spruce my hair and makeup and then follow my parents to a spot in front of the fireplace where Dad has the camera set up on a tripod to take our picture. We time a photograph, all of us smiling as the flash goes off again and again. Afterward, we huddle over the screen, laughing about who has their eyes closed or is making a face.

Mom claps her hands together. "Dinner will be a few more minutes. Let's do gifts first."

"Yes!" I squeal, excited to give Arden the gift I am sure will be her favorite.

I sprint upstairs and retrieve the giant box I've had wrapped for her from my desk and bound back down the stairs to present it to her.

"For the girl whose every dream I pray comes true."

She grins and pecks me on the cheek. Carrying the huge box to the dining room, she rests it on the table before pulling off the bow and lifting off the top. "Oh, Mom!" She draws the cobalt dress from the box and holds it against herself. It's strapless with a formfitting waist and a full, floor-length skirt embroidered with crystals that deepen the color depending on the light. It sparkles under the glow from the dining room chandelier.

"When you first came here, you asked about my dress. I realized you've never had a fairy dress of your own. And since you're half-pixie, that had to be rectified. No matter where you go in life, you should always have a princess dress in your closet. And there's a tiara, necklace, and shoes in there to add to the ensemble."

Only the two of us know how accurate my description of her as a princess is, or how when I mention where she might go in life, it includes fairy society. But Arden knows. And whether she wears this dress here in Dragonfly or in the human world at some future event I can only dream of, she'll always know what it means. Deep down, she's lucky. She's fae. She's the only person like her on the planet. And she deserves this dress to prove it.

"Oh, Mom, I love it." As she hugs me, I feel wetness where her face touches mine. She pulls back, and I wipe away her tears.

I reach into the box, grab the tiara, and replace the laurel leaves on her head with it.

"Beautiful," my mom says.

We all bask in the glow of my perfect gift for a moment, and then Mom pulls a box the size of a coffee mug from the china cabinet behind her and places it in front of the dress box. It's all wrapped in green paper with silver cords to match her school colors. I have no idea what it could be. "The rest of us went in together on this. Happy graduation."

Arden repacks the dress in the box but leaves the tiara on her head. "Thank you all," she says sweetly, then rounds the table to hug Mom, Dad, and Grandma before she even opens their gift. My heart swells with pride. She's a good kid. I've done my job.

Returning to her seat, she unwraps the box. Inside is a metal toy car—a blue Kia Soul. She laughs. "It's adorable!"

I look between the car and my mom, who is wearing a devious grin. "There's more. Look in the wrappings. It's in there."

Arden digs her hand into the tissue paper and pulls out a key.

"You didn't," I mutter.

"We did!" Mom's eyes twinkle impishly .

Grandma squeals.

"What is this?" Arden shakes her head, her eyes expanding to the size of saucers. "Did you... Did you buy me a car?"

"We did," my dad says proudly. "It's used and you'll have to wait until after dinner to see it because it's parked in the guest lot, but it looks just like that one." He points at the toy.

I'm speechless. I glare at Grandma, who flutters her eyelashes at me. "We just hope you like it," she says. "I knitted you a steering wheel cover too, but it wouldn't fit in the box. I'll give it to you later."

"I don't even have a car!" I toss up my hands.

Mom shrugs. "So get a car, Sophia. You're making enough now."

True. I should get my own car, but that's not the issue here. I focus the full weight of my stare on my three elders sitting across the table. "Oh. My. Gods. You did this so that you'd win at graduation gifts!" I point at each of them. "You intentionally one-upped me with the car."

"Don't be silly, Sophia. You can't *win* at gifts," my mom says, but Grandma is nodding her head, mouthing *we won* through a wicked smile.

Arden laughs. "I like both your gifts equally," she insists. "Thank you so much."

I give an exaggerated sigh and straighten her tiara. "Who would take a car over a crown anyway," I mumble. "Oh! I almost forgot." Grabbing my bag, I dig out the brown-paper-wrapped box from River and the small jewelry box from Seven. I hand her the one from River first.

"River made sure I had that this morning before everything happened. He wanted me to tell you congratulations."

The mood in the room sobers, but she tears into it. It's a framed photo of her and a bunch of kids her age in their Bailiwick's uniforms, in front of River's Tavern. All the teens have their arms around each other, but the handsome dark-haired boy who might be a leprechaun next to Arden is kissing her temple. She's beaming, her eyes shifted in his direction. Three dark-skinned girls, one with gorgeous bright red hair that matches her wings, are on her other side. All pixies. A satyr stands behind them all, hands on Arden's and the redhead's shoulders. It's a fun memory of what must have been a memorable moment.

"This is so sweet," Arden said. "I forgot about this day."

"When was that taken?" I ask.

"About a month ago. We had a half day at school and went

there for lunch." She sets it on the table. "This is the only picture I have with my new friends. It's gone by so fast. I never thought to take more." Another tear slides down her face, and I rub her back.

"We'll make sure to thank him for it when he's back among us," I say, forcing cheerfulness into the words. I follow it up by handing her the jewelry box. "One more gift, from Seven."

Grandmother's brows shoot up. "How thoughtful of him."

"He's a friend of the family, Grandma. Friends of the family give gifts."

"Sure they do," she says through a tight smile.

Arden tears into the paper and lifts the lid.

My dad leans forward a little to see and gives a quirky smile. "A gold acorn? Hmm." He shrugs.

Beside him, Mom is squinting at the charm. "You just never know with leprechauns."

Grandma scratches her neck. "I'm sure it's valuable, and the folklore says they're lucky."

Arden takes it from the box by the chain and stares at the charm. "Well, I love it. Put it on, Mom." She hands me the chain. Our gazes lock. I can sense the power in the tiny object from a half foot away. This is no ordinary acorn.

As I hook the chain around her neck, I whisper in her ear. "He said not to use it until he has a chance to talk to you about what it does."

She nods once to indicate she understands.

"Thanks, everyone," Arden says. "This is the best graduation day I've ever had."

Grandma laughs. "It's the only graduation day you've ever had."

"Not true. I graduated from eighth grade," Arden says. "Mom watched as I walked across the stage and shook my principal's hand. No robes though, and Rudy Fenton kept nudging the back of my chair. Also, the gym smelled like Fritos."

"It was a moment." I fold my hands on the table.

A buzzer goes off in the kitchen, and Mom pops out of her chair. "That would be dinner. Arden's favorite lasagna."

"I've got to change before we eat. I'm supposed to return this robe to the school, and I don't want to get sauce on it." Arden heads for her room.

I glare across the table at my father. "I can't believe you bought her a car without talking to me first."

The dad stare slides right down his nose at me. "You're surprised we splurged on our one and only granddaughter when this might be our last time to be a family with her? When she goes away to school, we want her to have something to remind her of us."

The sound of Arden jogging down the steps from her room meets my ears and it hits me. Dad's right. This is it. This might be the last time we're all together in this house, living under the same roof. Even if Arden decides to stay, she'll go to Elderflame and sleep in the dorms at the university there. Since the day she was born, we haven't spent more than a night or two away from each other, only for the occasional sleepover or camp. Now only a month or two separates us from her crossing the abyss into adulthood.

I swallow down a seed of anxiety that rises in my throat and cough into my hand. My face feels cold, like all the blood has drained from it.

"Ah, it's just caught up to you." Dad reaches across the table and squeezes my hand. His eyes fill with tears. "It'll be all right. We're all under the same moon after all."

Grandma blots the corners of her eyes with her napkin and taps the table. "You people are a barrel of laughs tonight. Stars above. Should I knit us some Kleenex? I haven't cried this much since Antoine left Juanita on my favorite telenovela."

Arden breaks the tension when she sails into the room in jeans and a T-shirt and plops into the chair beside me. "I've got a great idea of what we can do after dinner."

"What's that?"

"Trivial Pursuit. I saw it in the cabinet next to the fireplace."

"It's the fairy edition."

She shrugs. "Maybe I'll learn something."

Grandma rubs her hands together. "I'm totally going to win." She leans toward Arden and whispers conspiratorially, "I know everything."

Once Mom arrives with the lasagna, I pull out my phone and text Seven.

> Sorry, can't work tonight. Important family stuff.

> Understood. See you tomorrow.

> She loved your gift.

THERE'S A LONG PAUSE BEFORE HE RESPONDS.

> Someday.

I know Seven well enough to know what that someday means. All the thoughts I just had about running out of time, about this being my last chance at experiencing Arden's childhood... He feels the same way. Only he's already missed most of it.

A lump forms in my throat. It's not fair. She's his, and no matter what, he doesn't deserve to miss this night with her. I swallow hard and steel my spine.

No. Come. Bring the papers you need me to sign.

We both know there are no papers.

Twenty minutes later he shows up at our door with a stack of documents that have nothing to do with me. I have no idea what they say, but I sign them anyway. Then I politely ask him to stay and join us for the game, and Arden enthusiastically demands his participation. My parents have no choice but to duplicate my invitation.

To my delight, he stays and for three glorious hours, we are a family.

When we play Trivial Pursuit, he's the blue piece.

Grandma wins.

CHAPTER
SEVEN

Saul arrives at my parents' door two mornings later, ready to escort me to Ashgate. "Ms. Larkspur, if you'll follow me. I have a car waiting."

"Let me grab my bag." I slip my feet into my shoes and my purse strap over my shoulder, yell my goodbyes to Arden and my parents, and follow him out the door.

We're halfway to the parking lot when Saul looks down at me from his considerable height and asks in his deep, serious voice, "Can you run in that outfit?"

Per Dragonfly policy, I'm wearing a dress—a strapless, tea-length light blue ball gown and silver heels. All pixies and satyrs have to appear in character anytime we might be seen by humans, which we definitely will be while leaving the park. Leprechauns run everything, which means they can appear in regular clothing, usually suits for the guys. Since I've been back in the fold, I've gotten used to living in princess dresses. It's as comfortable as anything else to me now, and that includes the shoes.

I flutter my wings in a devil-may-care sort of way before

responding lightheartedly, "Pixies are light on our feet." Not that I haven't tripped and landed on my face before. It's happened, usually when I'm too distracted to remember to compensate with my wings, but it's rare.

He points his chin at me. "Good. Ashgate is a dangerous place, Ms. Larkspur. I can carry you if I have to, but it's good to know you can run."

"Call me Sophia. Why is Ashgate so dangerous anyway? The criminals are sealed inside the mountain. They can't get to me."

He frowns. "It's not the criminals you need to be worried about."

"Then what?"

He opens the door to the Mercedes for me, and I climb into the back seat. "The cells are guarded by unseelie creatures."

"What sort of unseelie?"

He looks at me in the mirror and grins. "Does it matter?"

I shake my head. There isn't a single unseelie creature I'd want to meet in person. For the first time, my stomach gives a fearful twist at the thought of visiting Ashgate, but I push it aside. River's a good friend and he needs me.

It takes us about an hour to reach the mountain and another twenty minutes to pass through three modern security checkpoints. But when we arrive at the prison itself, it feels like we've gone back in time. No sliding metal gates or video technology is anywhere in sight, just a cave-like opening at the top of three flights of stone steps.

"What now?" I ask Saul.

"We visit the gate warden. She'll tell you what to expect."

"You don't know?"

"No. I've never been."

"But you told me it was dangerous and guarded by unseelie.

How could you know that if you've never been inside?" My words come fast and furious, that niggle of fear in my gut now a raging anxiety that threatens to expunge my breakfast.

He turns to me at the base of the stairs. "Jules Strickland, a fellow leprechaun, visited in 1985 and was never seen again. Went in but never came out. By the time anyone tried to investigate, all they found was a pile of bones and his signet ring. It's dangerous."

My stomach churns. "Great. I wish I didn't know that."

He cuts a judgmental glance in my direction and shrugs. "I tried to keep things vague. You insisted on details, Ms. Larkspur."

"Call me Sophia."

I follow Saul up the stairs to the entrance. The gate warden is a satyr with tattoos covering all her exposed skin and a wild mop of curly gray hair. Silently she hands us both a flyer with instructions.

"Only one visitor may enter at a time—" I begin to read aloud, but she grabs me by the arm and holds a finger to her lips. I continue reading to myself. *Remain absolutely silent until both feet are in the circle outside the cell of the prisoner you wish to speak with. You will be given a maximum of ten minutes with each prisoner you wish to visit. When you are finished, place an offering on the platter beside the door and step out of the circle. Remain silent until you reach the exit.*

"I didn't bring an offering," I say to the woman.

She answers me in sign language.

Oh, so she's mute. I shake my head. "I don't understand ASL," I whisper.

She frowns and points at a bowl of fruit on the table, then at a cup for donations. I dig in my bag for a few dollars and exchange them for a shiny red apple.

"I'll be here if you need me," Saul says, backing against the wall across from the gate warden.

I stare into the dark passageway, fear turning my hands cold as I cradle the apple in front of my chest. I can't get my feet to move. Saul said the guards are unseelie. Is that what eats the apples? I take a deep breath and let it out slowly. I've now been standing here so long things are getting awkward. Saul is watching me with a suppressed smirk, like he's just waiting for me to yell "oh hell no" and head for the car.

But River is down there. He's shown up for me on more than one occasion when I really needed him. As frightening as it might be to visit him, it must be exponentially more frightening to be imprisoned here.

With that thought held tightly in my mind, I start forward in the only direction I can go. The stone walkway slopes down and curves until the natural light is snuffed out, leaving only flickering illumination cast by candles that burn in wall sconces lining the tunnel. I've walked for a good five minutes before I reach the first cell and realize I have no idea which one River is in. Worse, there aren't bars on the doors like a human prison. The openings are blocked by giant stones. You can't see in or out.

However, the circles referred to in the instructions are outside each stone, and when I step near the first one, a name scrawled in blood across the stone glows to life—Crawfoot Gallery—a rather infamous unseelie fae who was responsible for a mass killing before I was born. I shudder to think how long he's been in there.

I move forward, my gaze drifting over each name as it surfaces with my nearness. My skin pebbles from the cold, solemn atmosphere. It feels like I'm in a crypt, and I realize why. This isn't so much a prison as a place where fae are buried alive.

My heart aches for River. The restaurant isn't just his liveli-hood. He lives for social interaction and thrives on physical touch. This isn't just prison for him—it's torture. The longer I think about that, the faster I walk. I've got to get him out of here.

A familiar name flashes on the stone to my right, and I pull up short. Chance Delaney—Seven's father. The leprechaun kept six pixies prisoner in his own personal sex dungeon and ended up murdering one of them along with two humans. Just seeing his name brings back horrific memories of the night I confronted him. He deserves to be behind that stone.

I hurry on, relieved when I see the name River Foxwood nearby. Drawing a deep, fortifying breath, I step into the circle and wait. Almost immediately, a beam of light with no clear origination surrounds me. The stone melts away. River is sitting on a lumpy-looking cot with a thin blanket wrapped around his shoulders. He lifts his face, and I can tell he's been weeping. I've never seen him like this before. My heart pounds. I decide right then that I will clear his name no matter what it takes.

"Sophia?"

"I'm here, River."

He stands and rushes toward me, stopping when he reaches the invisible barrier between us. "Oh gods, it's good to see you. You have no idea—"

"We don't have much time, Riv. You need to tell me about the murder."

"I didn't do it."

"I know. I plan to prove as much and I'm going to get you out of here, but I need you to tell me exactly what happened."

He shakes his head. "I don't understand. Shouldn't there be video? There's a camera right outside my restaurant."

I lower my chin, hating to tell him. "It's been tampered

with. Fifteen minutes are missing. It goes from empty walkway to you hunched over the victim."

He tips his head back and curses. "Damn it. Who the fuck is messing with me?"

"Help me find out. Tell me exactly what happened."

He sighs heavily. "After I left you, I went to the restaurant to make sure everything was handled for the after-party. I helped my staff get all the food to the tent. But a burner on one of our warmers went out, so I headed back to the restaurant to get a replacement. That's when I stopped to talk with a... friend."

I analyze the way he says *friend* and draw some conclusions. "Friend with benefits?"

He nods once. "One who'd left for home directly from my place that morning, along with another friend who sometimes joins us."

"Oh!" I'm not sure why that surprises me. River's never hidden the fact that he's pansexual or occasionally entertains multiple partners. I just didn't think his sex life would be relevant to this case.

"I heard a shot and a scream and ran toward the sound. There was a hole in the victim's chest, and he was covered in blood. I yelled for help, then went to his side to put pressure on the wound. I held his hand while he died." River's eyes glaze with unshed tears, and I can see the memory deeply affects him. "I never even knew the human's name."

Hand on my heart, I say, "That must have been horrible, River, but we don't have much time. Tell me the name of who you were with that morning. If the victim was already shot before you entered the empty walkway, you were likely still with them at the time of the murder. Maybe they can vouch for you. I'm surprised you haven't already brought this up with Godmother."

River balks, his eyes shifting to the side. "I can't... reveal who it is."

"What? I understand wanting to be discreet, but this person could prove your innocence!"

He runs a hand over his face. "The person in question would suffer greatly if it was widely known they participated in a threesome with two satyrs. I promised to keep our affair a secret, and I won't break that confidence."

My hands ball into fists. "This is the exception. Whoever this person is, if they cared for you at all, they'd want you to tell me their name."

He swallows hard. "You don't understand. I *can't* say. I... bargained. I'm *bound* to keep their confidence."

"Fuck! Can you tell me who the other participant was then? The third."

River smiles excitedly. "Yes. It was Patrick."

"The satyr? Patrick Fawnear?" Patrick was always the class clown in school and is a brilliant musician. I hadn't expected he was River's lover.

"Yes. The three of us were together all night. He can confirm that."

"But he wasn't with you before the murder."

"No."

"Can he tell me who was?"

River's face falls. "No. He made the same bargain."

"For fuck's sake! Give me a clue. Work around the bargain. This person isn't worth protecting if they left you in here!"

"You don't understand, Sophia. We *all* made the bargain to hide our arrangement. They can't come forward. They are also bound."

It feels like I've been punched in the gut. "Are you telling me that even if the person wanted to help you, they couldn't?"

"If it involves admitting that we were... together with that person, that's exactly what I'm saying. I can say I was with Patrick. Patrick can admit he was with me. Our third's identity can never be revealed, not even by them." Suddenly unsteady on his feet, River stumbles back and sits back down on the cot, dropping his head into his hands.

"I'll talk to Patrick. I'll figure out a way, River. It just might take me a few days."

He stares at me, and his hands start to shake. His voice sounds tight and raspy as he says, "A few days..."

I check my watch. "We only have a few minutes more. Do you know anything at all about the victim?"

"No," River says firmly. "I'd never seen him before. Nothing odd about that. He was human. They come and go."

"Right. But he didn't say anything to you in his last moments?"

River shakes his head. "He had a bullet hole in his heart and was bleeding out. I think he had a lot on his mind."

"I'm just trying to help."

His eyes narrow and he lifts his chin to look at me, a memory sparking behind his eyes. "He had a rock in his hand."

"A rock?"

"Yeah. It might not mean anything, and I only noticed it because he was gripping it in his fist and I knew the moment he died because his hand went slack and it rolled off his palm."

"What kind of rock? Like a jewel?"

He shook his head. "An ordinary gray rock."

I glance at my watch. We're out of time. "You'll be okay, River. I'll find a way to get you out." The words have to squeeze around the lump forming in my throat.

He raises his red-rimmed eyes to meet mine, and his voice is strained as he says, "The food appears, Sophia. No one comes in, not ever. You are the first living person I've seen since—"

The stone snaps back into place, cutting him off. It startles me and I jump. The light shifts from engulfing me to shining on a silver platter beside the stone. Only then do I remember the apple in my trembling hands. Careful not to drop it, I place it on the platter. My throat is dry and my heart pounds.

River is still in there. He's alone. Truly alone.

A shiver runs through me, and then my breath stops altogether when a pale hand extends from the darkness above the silver tray. Yellow nails tapered to sharp points jut from bony fingers wrapped in pockmarked skin. Round suction cups like sores honeycomb the palm of the hand, and as it wraps around the apple, I hear each of them bite into its flesh like tiny mouths. Juice dribbles from the fist, and then the hand, and the fruit, is gone.

I cover my mouth to keep from screaming and hurry toward the exit. But I slow my steps as I near Chance Delaney's cell. Thinking about Chance twists my gut, as if I've swallowed a worm that's gnawing my insides, wriggling dark and deadly somewhere I can't reach. If he'd had his way, I'd be in a cell in the basement of his hunting cabin, starved, beaten, and likely raped. He's the rot on the underbelly of a diseased snake, and the last thing I want is to see him again.

But I can't shake the thought that this murder has something to do with him. Someone used his computer to tamper with the security cameras. Leprechaun luck cleared the area before the murder. One of the last things he said to me before I put an arrow in his shoulder was that he was working with others to sabotage Dragonfly Hollow. He'd never told me who, just that it was bigger than me. Bigger than all of us.

And then the horrifying suspicion I had before comes to me again. What if he's not behind that stone? He is considered by most to be the most powerful leprechaun alive. What if he figured out a way to escape and he's responsible for the murder? It would be the perfect crime. Everyone would assume he was still here.

I have to know. I have to see for myself that he's in there.

My eyes fall on the platter. I only brought one apple, and I used it for River. Reaching for my purse, I wonder if I could just leave money. That seems like it would pass as an offering. I dig in the center compartment, and my hand falls on a square container of cubes of berry-flavored gum. Hmm. Gum or money. If I had a dozen mouths on my hands, I'd want the yummy gum, not the filthy money.

Gum in hand, I step into the circle. The light turns on, and the stone melts away. What I see inside makes me thankful I haven't eaten today. Chance is there—I take some comfort in that—but he stands at the wall, writing something in his own blood. Gibberish. I can make out letters but no coherent words. His fingers are raw, gripped around a pointed chip of stone. Blood drips from a gash in his arm —his ink.

He stops and slowly turns his head. I'm once again disgusted by his resemblance to Seven. Aside from graying temples and smaller eyes that remind me of a rat's, there's no question they're related, although he's gaunt compared to the last time I saw him and a short beard covers his jaw. His hair is longer too.

"Well, well, well, little bird. How nice of you to visit my cage. If only you could step inside, we could have such fun together."

Eww. Everything about this moment makes me feel sick, but I have ten minutes with this asshole and maybe he knows something that can help us. "Who is responsible for the murder in Wonderland, Chance?"

A dark and wicked laugh bubbles from his chest. He lowers his chin and stares at me like a wolf stalking its prey. "I told you it wouldn't end with me, little bird. The hydra has many heads."

"Give me a name. Tell me who you were working with. Who might have done this?"

He steps closer. "Why would I tell you anything?"

"Because you have nothing left to lose. Maybe if you contribute something useful, Godmother will show you mercy." There is no way in hell Godmother would ever let Chance out of here, but I have nothing else to offer.

"You truly are an accomplished liar," he says through his teeth. "I'm not even sure you realize what a rare and valuable talent that is for a fae. Some of us can't lie at all. We can deceive, we can mislead, but lying like you are to me now, as you look me in the eye—by the gods, I'd say that's as rare as being able to resist a bargain."

I don't bother denying it. I'm running out of time. "Then what do you want?"

"You'd bargain with me?"

"Within reason."

He hesitates, his gaze sweeping down my form in a way that makes my skin want to peel off my body. "Make Seven come and visit me. Don't deny you have power over him. You've had your filthy pixie stinger in him since he was a child. If you tell him to come, he'll come."

"And in return, you'll tell me who's responsible for the murder."

He chuckles. "I've been here, little bird. I don't know who committed the murder you speak of."

"But you have a guess. Someone you were working with who wanted to pick up where you left off."

"Yes."

"You tell me who that is, and I'll ask Seven to visit." I will ask. He'll never come.

"Do more than ask." He sneers. "I want him here."

"We're running out of time, Chance."

"Deal," he says quickly.

I make the gimme motion with my hand.

"Mirror, mirror on the wall, the one you seek isn't *one* at all, but he whose crown is in his bones, and they whose hunger has grown and grown, and she whose hatred is cast in stone. Blood shed by one is blood shed by all."

"What the fuck does that mean?" Based on his earlier comments, I knew more than one person was involved in his scheme, but this poem is utter nonsense.

"You have my answer. You asked who was responsible for the murder, not for a specific name. I told you the truth."

I scoff. "Fine. I said I'd ask Seven to visit. I didn't promise when."

He hisses. "Filthy bird." He pulls his shirt over his head, staining it with blood. "Let me show you what I do with your kind." I cringe as he runs his palm down his swollen stomach and it slithers under his waistband and into his pants. Mercifully, that's when the stone slams into place. My time is up.

The light shifts to the silver tray, and I empty the gum onto it. The only sound is the pounding of my heart in my ears as the pale hand reaches for my offering. This time I don't wait to see what happens. I start for the exit, walking as fast as I can without breaking into a jog; I don't want to call attention to myself or make too much noise. But when a head-splitting screech comes from behind me, I launch into a full-out run.

I'm not fast enough. The creature rushes me from behind, that pallid hand snatching my ankle. I fall, my wings flapping uselessly as I hit the ground hard. My elbows and forearms sting where they slap the stone, but remembering the warning of the warden, I don't make a sound. What will happen if I scream? Will more come? I don't want to find out.

Circular mouths suction to the skin of my ankle, digging in, hurting. I kick at it, freeing myself long enough to flip over. Above me, a faceless thing seethes. At least I think it's seething. It has no mouth and only two indentations where eyes should be. Its nostrils, however, flare angrily. Its body is humanoid but strange, light gray and too long with multijointed limbs. There are holes on the sides of its head but no ears.

It reaches for me with one hand, fingers formed into claws, and I see that the mouths on its palms are lined with tiny sharp teeth. I smell berries and realize my "offering" is stuck and strung between several of the orifices, forming a sticky mess that lowers toward my face. I hold my breath to keep from screaming and turn my head, trying to put distance between me and it.

Out of the corner of my eye, I see the hand stop just a centimeter from my face, and a soft golden glow forms a barrier between us. The thing screeches again in frustration, leaving my ears ringing. Slowly I shift my head and see that the coin around my neck, the one Seven gave me, is the source of the glow. It pulses gently in the hollow of my throat.

For protection. Thank you, Seven! I crab-walk backward, away from the creature.

My foot extends beyond the coin's glow, and it grabs my ankle again. I wince from the pain and pull the coin away from my skin by the chain, directing the glow at the unseelie and trying to get my feet under me.

That's when I hear a thump and another thump. Something red bounces near my hip and rolls toward the creature. An apple. Another one rolls on the other side of us. The creature sniffs like a dog, turns on its haunches, and pounces, taking the apple into its hungry grip.

I use my wings to help me to my feet then half run, half fly for the exit. I'm winded and shaking by the time I reach Saul, who is pointing his gun toward the darkness behind me and holding the empty basket the apples had been in. The gate warden is signing angrily at him.

"I hope you have what you need, Ms. Larkspur," Saul says, "because we've been strongly encouraged to leave the premises."

I nod breathlessly, and we head for the car. My ankle is throbbing, and I have a stitch in my side that makes it hard to breathe.

Once we're inside, I tell Saul what happened. "How was I supposed to know that gum wasn't an appropriate offering?"

Saul hands me the flyer and points at an asterisk at the bottom of the page.

It simply says No Gum.

CHAPTER

EIGHT

"I need you to take me directly to Godmother's," I tell Saul. I've thought about what to do from the moment we left Ashgate. I can't leave River in there. Not for another hour, let alone another day. It will break him. He's too good a friend. "It's important."

"Seven's orders are to take you directly back to his place to debrief." Saul keeps his eyes on the road as he answers me in a tone that's not exactly dismissive but holds a note of resolve, as if the decision is out of his hands.

"Do you need me to call him and have him tell you it's an emergency?" I sit up straighter. "Every minute I don't speak to Godmother is an extra minute that River stays locked up in that hellhole, and let me tell you, Saul, it is the very definition of hell."

His eyes slide to me and then he pulls his phone from his pocket. His thumb flies over the screen while his eyes remain on the road. I'd chastise him to not text and drive, but he's a leprechaun. The chances of us getting into an accident are almost zilch.

His phone dings. Dipping his gaze to the screen for a split second, he frowns. "He says he'll meet us at Godmother's."

I smile smugly and lean back in my seat. Seven trusts me. We've been there for each other since we were children, aside from the time I spent in America, and that was because of his megalomaniac father. I know he's got my back.

At my direction, Saul drops me off under the Wonderland Security office before parking, and I beat feet to Godmother's Tearoom, giving me a few minutes head start ahead of both Saul and Seven. I'm going to need it. A few human patrons are having tea in the gingerbread dining room, but a word with the host and I'm escorted into Godmother's backroom office. To my surprise, it's light and airy, all white wood and delicate furniture. Fuzzy pink throw pillows decorate the white turned-leg sofa. A shiny gold paperweight on her desk reads Boss.

"Sophia Larkspur, to what do I owe the pleasure?" Her deep voice resonates between us, and then her gaze locks on the coin at the base of my throat. Her eyes narrow slightly, but if there's a question in her gaze, she doesn't voice it.

I pretend I don't notice her interest in Seven's gift to me and jump into why I'm here. "River Foxwood is innocent. You have to let him out of Ashgate."

She braids her fingers together and rests her chin on them. "No. I don't have to do anything, Sophia." She points at the Boss sign on her desk, but her gaze shifts back to me.

"Why are your arms all scraped up?"

"I had a run-in with one of the guards at Ashgate."

"Why?"

"Someone tampered with the video surveillance."

"Seven informed me."

"River did not murder that man. The only reason he was covered in the victim's blood is he was trying to help him. The man had already been shot by the time River came upon him outside his restaurant. No witnesses saw what happened because someone used luck to clear the area—likely a leprechaun. You saw that on the video. Who else would be strong enough to do that?"

She drums her fingers on her desk. "Just because a leprechaun cleared the area does not mean they committed the murder. What proof do you have that River didn't do it?"

"I don't need proof." I take a deep breath. "Patrick was with him. He didn't leave his side until he heard the man scream."

Godmother sneers. I can almost feel her scanning me like some sort of lie detector, but I hold my ground, making my expression at once genuine while also showing a hint of shame.

"If that's true, why didn't River mention it?"

"Everything was too... public. Patrick's being with River that morning was a secret because they were discussing something private." I lower my chin. "You see, the only reason that I know about it is because I was with the two of them the night before. But neither of them will be able to tell you it was me specifically. They bargained with me and promised discretion. After everything that's happened since I've been back, I needed it. But it was me who asked Patrick to speak to River, to tell him I was breaking off the affair. That's how I know they were together at that time. I visited Ashgate and River so he could release me from our bargain and I could speak to you about it."

Godmother leans back in her chair and studies me. I get the sense she knows I'm lying, although I'm doing my best to make it believable. Ancient magic nudges me, attempting to taste the lie in whatever I'm made of, or maybe that's just my nerves. She rings a bell on her desk, and a hidden door opens at the back of the room. A redheaded pixie I've never met runs in. Godmother whispers in her ear, and she scampers off again.

"This is a dangerous game you're playing, Sophia,"

Godmother says softly, only for my ears. "I could give you something to force the truth from you."

A chill runs through me. "You could. I'm sensing you won't."

"I don't think River did it any more than you do." Her dark lashes blink at me, and she toys with a quill on her desk.

"Then why is he in Ashgate?"

She taps the pads of her fingers together. "The safety of our guests is my top priority. If River didn't do this, who did?"

I swallow hard, not at all sure how much I should share with Godmother about what Chance told me. I choose my words carefully. "I have reason to believe that Chance Delaney wasn't working alone and that this murder is part of a master plan that is still being carried out in his absence."

Godmother's brow rises. "And what would give you that idea?"

"I spoke to him in Ashgate, and he admitted it. He is working with others, perhaps fairy or maybe a human." *Maybe both.* At least that's my interpretation of the riddle Chance told me.

The redheaded fairy runs back in and whispers something in Godmother's ear, and her mouth spreads into a wide smile. "It seems Patrick has corroborated your story, although, as you warned, he was not able to identify you. But when presented with your version of events, he was able to affirm them. I have to hand it to you, Sophia. If you are lying, it's a very good lie." She grabs a piece of parchment from a pile on her desk, signs it, and marks it with her seal. It sparkles as she rolls it up and hands it to the pixie. "Have River Foxwood removed from Ashgate Prison and delivered to the safe house in Sagewick Forest."

The pixie nods and rushes from the room.

"Safe house?" She's up to something. I can see the twinkle of some devious idea in her eye.

"I'm going to do you this favor and release your lover, Sophia." I bristle when she says *lover*, then correct myself, shoring up my defenses for whatever comes next. "Mind, it may take up to forty-eight hours to complete the necessary paperwork and procedures."

I cringe at the thought of River enduring that place for two more days, but it can't be helped. "If that's the fastest it can be done."

Godmother points her chin at me. "There is a condition of his release."

"And that is?"

"I cannot allow the general public to know River's been freed, you understand, until this case is solved. So in return for my generosity, I expect you to find the real murderer. The sooner you do, the sooner River can return to his regular life."

My breath halts in my throat. This is beginning to sound a hell of a lot like a bargain, and I never signed up to make another deal with Godmother. All amiability drains from my expression, and I glare across the desk.

"Is this how you did it to Seven?" I ask through my teeth. "Gods, a person might agree to a bargain with you without even trying, without even understanding the consequences."

"Careful, Sophia." Her eyes spark, and power gathers in the small room.

"He came to you, a child—"

"He was almost eighteen—"

"Abused by his father, poisoned with blue iron, he came to you for help—"

"And I helped him." One eyebrow jerks upward derisively.

"Not to escape his father's influence."

"He didn't ask to escape. He asked for you."

"Then you never upheld your side of the bargain."

She gives a wicked laugh. "Oh, I did. Your daughter is proof of that."

"Proof of sex. Nothing more."

"Who do you think you're kidding?"

My lips peel back from my teeth, and I can barely contain my rage as I ask, "What exactly was his side of that bargain? How long does Seven have to serve you until he's free of your control?"

Her nails win over her interest, and she draws the tip of one across the cuticle of another. "Until I release him."

"That's not fair."

"Not fair? Nothing about a bargain need be fair, Sophia. Stars above, you're starting to sound like one of those humans you spent so long living among. Seven was remiss in his terms. He never specified how long he'd have to work for me. I could have taken more. He offered *anything* to be with you. Never specified what that anything was or what being with you entailed. I took his servitude as the head of my security team for as long as I desire it, but I could have demanded far more. So don't test me now, pixie. It's not my fault you can't recognize mercy when you see it."

Mercy. Only a fool wouldn't fear Godmother, but this is the first time in my memory that she disgusts me. From the roots of repulsion, I promise myself right there and then to grow strong enough to force her to free Seven, and I don't wait a single moment to try.

"I'll solve this murder if you free Seven."

She laughs. "I've already done you a favor by freeing River, whom you say is your lover. If that's not enough for you, I can call back my assistant and tear up my order to free him from Ashgate."

I blow out a breath. "Fine. I'll do it, but no bargain. You have my word, nothing more."

"Fine." She grins as if this was more than she was hoping for and points a perfectly manicured fingernail at me. "Your word is all I need. After all, unless you want Fairly Goodweather to feature your threesome with Patrick and River in the *Daily Hatter*, you will do as I wish."

I scoff. If I don't do what she wants, she'll further ruin my reputation and hurt Seven in the process. *Bitch.* "You have my word if I have your silence."

"Done." She brushes her hand across her desk.

No silver threads bind me, but they may as well have. I'm knee-deep in Godmother's crap once again, and River's future and my happiness with Seven are at stake. *Fuck.*

"For future reference, Sophia, that coin around your neck won't work against me. If I wanted to bind you, I could bind you." She looks at her nails again, and I feel the tiniest twinge in my stomach. *She's bluffing*, my instincts tell me, and I try to hide my surprise.

"Now go. I'm sure you have better things to do than take up my time discussing your tawdry personal affairs. I'll text you the address of the safe house. I'll leave it to you to break the news to River about my order that he remain there until the case is solved."

Fuck.

CHAPTER

NINE

I'm leaving Godmother's Tearoom with my phone in hand when the love of my life meets me in the street with a folder under one arm. Both of us light up when we see each other, drawn together like magnets until we realize where we are and stop a reasonable distance from each other. It hurts not to reach out and touch him.

My phone dings, and I look down as a text from Godmother streaks across the screen with the address she promised me.

"Looks serious. Why is Godmother texting you an address?"

"It's a safe house—"

"Why do you need the address to a safe house?" Seven steps in closer, lowering his voice and looking as if he's a hair's breadth away from throwing me over his shoulder and locking me safely within his tower.

"Because that's where she's sending River in two days," I whisper. I glance around me. We're alone, but perhaps not for long. This is a public place. "We should go somewhere private."

He gestures with his head toward the Cast Members Only door, and I follow him back there, through the woods and onto our beach. We used to come here all the time as kids. I fell in love with Seven on this beach.

His luck rises around us like a dragon, the heat from its long body brushing against me and making the leaves on the branches shimmy. "We're alone. Tell me everything."

I do. Everything. I am completely honest, not because I'm forced to be but because I want nothing to come between us. I tell Seven every detail about what River and Chance said, even the promise I made to try to get him to visit. I hold back nothing.

Seven takes it all in stride until I tell him how I got River out.

"You told her you were the third," he grits out. "Is it true?"

I glare at him. "No! But River said he and Patrick made a bargain with this person not to reveal their identity. It could be anyone, and it was faster to tell her it was me than to waste time trying to find the person."

He grunts his understanding but continues to sulk.

"Are you upset I lied?"

"No."

"Then why do you look like someone stole the prize out of your cereal box?"

"I just don't like thinking about you with him... or *them*."

I step in closer. "Then stop thinking about it. You do realize it never happened. I lied."

"I'm trying. I can't help it, Sophia. I'm jealous of every second another man gets to be with you even when it happens in my imagination." His crooked smile tells me he knows it's ridiculous, but he pulls me into his arms anyway and brands me with a deep, hot kiss. I melt into him and only pull away when I need to catch my breath.

"The coin worked, by the way," I say against his lips. "It saved me from a run-in with one of Ashgate's unseelie guards." I tell him about my mistake with the gum.

"Fuck, Sophia! Thank the gods it worked, but did you have to put it to the test so dramatically? How exactly did you think you'd escape?"

I shrug. "Who doesn't like gum? I took a chance."

He tucks my hair behind my ears and touches his forehead to mine. "Can you take fewer chances? After all this is over, I want us to be together. That can't happen if you're not in one piece."

"I promise whatever's left of me is all yours," I joke.

He growls and kisses me again.

"Any leads on your dad's computer?"

He groans. "I confirmed it was still there, in his office. And that the tampering happened from that device, not remotely."

"What? How is that possible?"

He shakes his head. "It isn't. No one keyed into the room. Unless someone has learned to walk through walls, I have to believe a very talented hacker has covered his tracks in the data."

"Great. Sounds like a dead end. Did you ever hear back about the identity of the victim?" Last I heard, his team was still working on it.

"Just today. It took longer than usual because his passport wasn't processed through tickets or park admissions."

"Huh?"

"He was a guest of Bailiwick's. His name is Adam Barker. He's a geology professor from a public university in Illinois." He opens the folder and shows me Adam's picture. "He came last week to do a presentation to the grade one students on the geology of the Appalachian Mountains and decided to tack on a short vacation since his entrance into the parks and accommodations were taken care of."

"Geology? I guess that explains the rock in his hand."

"Rock? What rock?"

"River told me that when the man died, a gray rock rolled out of his hand. He'd been gripping it in his fist."

Seven snorts. "Odd."

"So who would want this guy dead? Did he piss someone off at the Dragonfly Club or something? Did you get any footage on him?"

"Hours. My people went through it all. The guy was as exciting as wallpaper. Didn't drink alcohol or gamble. Talked with very few people. Spent a ton of time by the pool and reading on the balcony of his room."

"What else? Who was this guy? Did he have any known enemies?"

Seven closes the folder and pulls out his phone. He brings up Adam's Instagram and hands it to me. I stare down at a handful of pictures of a man with... rocks. Some are of him holding a rock. Others are of him standing in front of a rock with some geological feature. I thumb through his feed and it's more of the same.

"That's it?" I wasn't aware anyone like this guy existed.

"On every social media channel. And I checked Flutter and Puckers. He didn't have accounts on either of them." Flutter is the app humans use to be matched with pixies. Puckers is the one for humans and satyrs. So Adam didn't have a fae fetish. Going off these accounts, it seems the only thing he was interested in was rocks.

"Gods, he really did have a singular interest, didn't he?"

"His Twitter feed is full of geology one-liners."

I stare at Seven like he's speaking a different language.

"Don't take geologists for granite," he deadpans. "Be patient with geologists, they all have their faults."

I groan. "This man is probably the least notable or controversial person who has ever existed. Why would anyone want him dead?"

He rubs a hand over his mouth. "Maybe they didn't. Maybe he was just in the wrong place at the wrong time."

"Unlucky bastard. But if whoever did this chose Adam randomly, how do we find the killer?"

"Tell me again what my father told you."

I recite the verse again for him. "Mirror, mirror on the wall, the one you seek isn't *one* at all, but he whose crown is in his bones, and they whose hunger has grown and grown, and she whose hatred is cast in stone. Blood shed by one is blood shed by all."

"Hmm. That mirror, mirror part could refer to the passage to Shadowvale."

"I thought so too."

"He whose crown is in his bones sounds like Vissevel, but the bone fairy is dead."

"Any ideas on the rest of it?"

He looks out over the water, then shakes his head. "Not a clue. I have an entire library of books on the unseelie though. I'll do some research."

I move in closer and run my hands up his chest. "I can come by tonight to help."

He heaves a beleaguered sigh. "Can't. We have somewhat of a crisis on our hands at Lucky Enterprises. I need to put out a few fires, and after all this"—he holds up the folder he still needs to share with Godmother—"I have a long night ahead of me."

"Crisis? What's going on?"

He smiles and tugs on the cuff of his shirt. "Nothing interesting enough to talk about. A supply chain issue. How about tomorrow night?"

I check my phone. "I'm supposed to meet Penelope for dinner and drinks."

Seven's eyes turn a brighter shade of green, and his lips curl into a wolfish grin. "Excellent. I'll take advantage of your drunken and lecherous state."

"I'm Penelope's night away from the kids. It will be late and my parents will definitely be suspicious if I stay out all night. Rain check?"

He steps in closer, the electric current between us building. "I waited for you for sixteen years, Sophia. What's a few more days?"

LATE TUESDAY AFTERNOON, I GET THE CALL THAT RIVER IS finally being delivered to the safe house. After the week I've had, it's a breath of fresh air. Seven and I keep missing each other, and there hasn't been a single new clue on the case. We made a date for seven o'clock tonight at his place though. I can't wait.

The safe house is a simple but relatively large log cabin nestled in the woods in a remote section of the Appalachians on the border of Devashire. It took me over an hour to drive here, and the closest neighboring house is fifteen miles away. I scoop the groceries I brought for River from the back of Arden's Kia and think again that I need to get myself a car. I shuffle to the door and give it two hard knocks with my knee. When it opens, I almost drop the groceries. Instead, I close my eyes.

"River! Why are you naked?" Satyrs in their natural form have hooves and a shaggy coat of hair from the waist down that does an excellent job of concealing their, um, considerable members, but they can shift to look human. That includes the ability to mask their horns. For practical reasons though, such as ease of finding appropriate clothing, keeping their fur groomed, et cetera, most choose to appear as River does now, human from the neck down, satyr from the neck up. Which means that before I closed my eyes, I got a clear view of the full monty, and River's monty is incredibly, er, full.

Eyes still closed, I jerk when the groceries lift from my grip and he says, "I just got out of the shower. I was trying to find a towel. Does it bother you?" He sounds genuinely surprised.

I open one eye to see he's in the kitchen, his bare ass mooning me as he sets down the groceries. I avert my eyes, but they catch on his wet hair and the way droplets of water stream in rivulets down his spine. I refuse to follow them and instead fasten my gaze on the tattoo of a phoenix on his left shoulder. I never knew he had a tattoo. "Um, I know it's common for satyrs to embrace nudity, but I'd prefer if you—"

He turns around to look at me, exposing himself again. I wince on behalf of all his former lovers. Every single one of them must have left River's bed with a limp.

My eyes flick toward the ceiling. "*Pants*, River! Could you put some pants on?"

"Sure. All you had to do was ask." He sounds as if the thought never occurred to him before now. I hear him walk from the room, and a moment later he returns in board shorts and a T-shirt.

"Thanks."

"Don't mention it." He looks me in the eye and then at the groceries on the counter, and his expression grows serious.

River is an imposing presence, at least six foot four inches of corded muscle just shy of bulky. Horns of impressive size curl like a ram's from the sides of his head. Usually his cheerful disposition acts to balance out his hulking exterior, but when his face morphs like it does right now, I almost take a step back.

"Thank you, Sophia, for getting me out of Ashgate. I wouldn't have survived much longer in that place. But... how did you do it?"

I scratch the back of my neck, wondering if I should tell him. This is River. He'll understand. "I told Godmother I was the third and it was Patrick with you that morning, and Patrick was smart enough to back me up."

His big brown eyes blink incredulously. "You *lied* to Godmother? You told her that you were our third?"

"I had to. If I'd waited to find your actual alibi, it might have taken weeks."

He peers at me with something close to reverence. "Fuck, Sophia. Thank you. You are an amazing friend and much braver than most, but you shouldn't have done that. What do you owe her for getting me out?"

I grimace. "You might want to hold off on singing my praises for a beat. My price was promising to solve this murder, but I didn't exactly get you out, like in the full sense of the word. There's something I have to tell you."

"What do you mean, I'm not out?"

"Did they tell you anything about this place when they brought you here?"

"Not much. They said I'd have to stay until I got the final okay from Godmother to return home. It sounded administrative." Glancing toward the kitchen, he turns sullen. "You brought enough groceries to last... awhile."

I grimace. "You have to stay here until we find the real murderer."

He balks, then tilts his head as if he doesn't quite understand. "But I have a restaurant to run and a cat to feed—"

"You have a cat? Who's been feeding your cat?"

"Sophia, she can't mean to keep me here indefinitely. I have a life." Sudden horror widens his eyes. "Do people still think I did this?"

Silently, I curse Godmother for making me break this news to River. "She wants them to think you did it until we catch someone else. She's afraid if the public knows the killer is still out there that it will impact park revenue. Godmother released you from Ashgate based on my confession, but she'll return you there if you leave this house or tell anyone you're here."

He scrubs his face with his hands and turns a circle as if he's looking for something to punch.

"I'm sorry, River. I promise you that Seven and I will solve this case—"

"Seven? Godmother is making you work with that asshole again?" Oops, River doesn't know about my relationship with Seven. He still thinks I hate him. I shouldn't have brought that up.

I pick at the side of my thumbnail. "Uh, I'm over it. He's all right. The important thing is that we catch the murderer and get you out of here."

He studies me for a second. "Gods, you're involved with him again, aren't you?"

My brows shoot up. "What makes you say that?" I giggle nervously. Did he just look straight into my soul or what?

"Sophia, you're blushing." He grimaces. "When did this happen? After what he did to you? I thought you hated Seven."

I drop down onto the sofa, and he sits down next to me. "I was wrong about him, River. He wasn't responsible for what happened to me at the Yule ball. That was all his dad." This is where I have to be careful. No one knows how abusive the Delaneys were to their kids, and it's not my secret to tell.

River shakes his head. "He had to be at least partially responsible."

"Well, it was a long time ago. We've... been talking... uh, spending time together."

"Fucking..."

"River!"

"Oh come on, Sophia. We both know leprechaun sex is the stuff of legends. There are hearts floating above your head every time you say his name. You're getting some."

I send him a soft smile. "Well, for reasons I don't need to explain to you, please keep this to yourself."

"Who am I going to tell?" He gestures vaguely around him.

"Seriously, River."

"Your secret is safe with me. But you should give a message to Seven for me."

"Oh?"

"Tell him that if he hurts you again, I'll make him hurt seven times as much, and all the luck in the world won't stop me."

I smile. "You're a good friend, River."

"I'm serious. If I ever have to pick you up off the ground again, that guy is going to pay."

I nod. "I heard you. I'll let him know." I rise from the couch. "I should go. It's getting late."

He stands and wipes his hands on the sides of his shorts, then pulls me into a hug that feels like he's wrapped himself around me twice. His lips press into the top of my head. "Thank you, Sophia, so goddamn much. I can never repay you for this."

"It's enough that you'd do it for me. And I'm sorry you're stuck here."

He snorts. "I'll take the bedroom of this place over that cell."

"I'll come back and visit whenever I have an update or a

free minute. Text me on the burner phone they gave you if you need something. Stay strong, okay?"

"You too. And I'm always here for you if things go wrong with the asshat."

He levels a whiskey-colored stare at me. I've started for the door when I hear him say, "Sophia" softly behind me. His voice is choked with emotion.

"What's wrong?"

He glances at the grocery bags. "I hate to ask this. I know you're busy, and you've done so much for me already."

"Ask, River."

"Can you stay for dinner? I don't want to eat alone." His voice cracks, and he swallows hard before adding, "In there, I was always alone."

Days and days he was in that place without seeing another face aside from my short visit. I'm here, and for now I'm all he has.

"You're the chef. What are we making?" I head for the kitchen and start unloading the groceries.

After a night of laughter and a delicious meal with River, I finally feel he's in a good place with a positive mental state where I can leave him. I promise to check on his cat, then race to Seven's. I've texted him throughout the evening, and he knows I'm going to be late, but his responses have become more and more terse.

I arrive at his penthouse just after nine and am whisked into the elevator by a very high-strung security guard. I'm not sure what his problem is, but he fidgets in silence all the way up to the penthouse. I've been here before and don't need an escort. Weird.

When the doors finally open on Seven's floor, the security guard who's stationed at a desk outside Seven's penthouse is out of his chair immediately. "You can go right in, Ms. Larkspur."

"Thanks, Lucas." There are five men who work on this floor at various times. Lucas is by far the nicest.

I push through Seven's door and immediately feel his power in the room. It paces like a hungry animal, pulsing against my skin with an almost erratic tempo. I stride through the magnificent foyer, over the custom fish tank that creates a river of koi fish through his floor, and into his living room. All the lights are off, but I can see Seven's silhouette on the sofa from the light of the moon through the window.

"You're late," he says gruffly.

"I'm sorry. It took longer than I expected." I flip on one of the lamps, casting the white-on-white decor in a cool glow, and my breath catches in my throat. Seven looks like hell. He's cast off his suit jacket and is nursing a bourbon. "What happened?"

He tosses back the rest of what's in his glass, his emerald eyes focused on me with an intensity that steals all the oxygen from the room. Rising from the sofa, he sets the glass down and stalks toward me until his chest brushes mine. "What happened is I've been denied your company for close to a week."

"You saw me at Arden's graduation."

"Your physical company."

I spread my arms.

He reaches around me, his fingers finding the zipper of my dress. It's off me in seconds. I'm just happy he didn't luck it off me. Seven is capable of making fabric tear or a zipper malfunction with nothing but intention. I've had bras deteriorate right off my body. I like this dress. I'm glad he didn't ruin it, although the way he's looking at me, I'm surprised he didn't.

He lowers his nose to the side of my neck and brushes his lips along my skin. "You smell like him," he says darkly.

I scoff. "I don't see how. I hugged him goodbye. Nothing more."

With a flick of his fingers, my bra comes unhooked and I let it drop on top of the dress. I reach for him but he backs away, leaving me standing alone in my panties. I give him a slow, taunting smile. "Well, Mr. Delaney, what do you plan to do with me now that you have my physical company?"

The corner of his mouth lifts, and the world tilts on its axis. Luck rushes through me, an effervescent geyser that leaves me breathless and dizzy. He catches me before I can fall and whirls me behind the sofa. With a hand at the back of my neck, he bends me over the back until my chest falls against the plush white fabric, and I instinctively plant my hands on the cushions.

His hand rubs a circle over my ass. If he didn't know I was turned on before, he knows now. I'm soaking wet.

"Mmm, Sophia, is this for me?" He moves my panties aside and strokes along my wet slit. A low, carnal sound rumbles from his chest. Heat bubbles through me again, a rush of sparkling luck that makes my body feel as light as air.

"Always," I rasp. It's hard to think, hard to breathe, around the luck he's feeding me. My blood fizzes with it.

He leans over me, pulling my hair gently so he can whisper in my ear. "But you were late, bad girl. You kept me waiting."

I turn my head and flash him a slow, smug smile. "You would have waited longer."

His hand leaves my backside and then smacks against my ass. The momentary sting is dwarfed by a massive amount of pleasure as luck and heat rush between my legs. I moan and spread my feet a little wider.

"I bet you would have waited all night," I say breathlessly.

He spanks me again, then drags his fingers through my wetness and circles my clit before pinching it just short of pain.

"Let's see who's willing to wait." He removes his hand.

I try to stand up, but he grabs my hair to hold me in place and spanks me again, then sends a rush of luck to ease the sting. I moan and try to push into his hand, but he removes it and my panties in one swoop, leaving me cold.

"Seven," I say breathlessly.

"I bet you'd wait all night," he says, throwing my own words back at me.

I most certainly do not want to wait all night. I'm aching with a need that seems to ratchet up by the minute.

I don't say a word. His hands land on my ass and spread me open right before his tongue licks up my center. I cry out from the current of desire that shoots through me. He pulls away.

Frustrated, I try to stand and reach for him, but his hand lands gently on the back of my neck, holding me in place. Palming my breast, he tugs at my nipple while his other hand strokes down my spine and between my legs. He massages my folds, circling, teasing. My legs start to shake.

His finger dips inside, and I try to buck against his hand, but he moves away, never deep enough, never hard enough. It's a torturous tease. And when his thumb presses gently against my asshole, I find myself panting with need. He's still fully dressed behind me, looking cool and collected, and I'm naked and so hot I might incinerate into ash if he doesn't do something about it quickly.

I crack. "Please, Seven. I can't wait. I need you in me."

He leans over me, placing a kiss to the top of my spine. Luck dances across my skin, sending all my tiny hairs standing on end. "Are you begging?"

"Yes," I say enthusiastically.

"Thank the gods," he murmurs.

The sound of his belt and then his clothes hitting the floor has me breathing a sigh of relief. He grasps my hips and jerks me against him. My breath hitches.

He leans over me again, his lips brushing the shell of my ear as he says, "I'm going to fuck you so hard you'll spend every minute away from me thinking about it."

I turn enough to touch my lips to his, my voice heavy with emotion as I say, "I already do."

A strangled sound exits his throat as he fills me in one rough thrust. I take a deep breath, adjusting myself to accommodate the size of him. He barely gives me a chance before he's pounding into me. I grip the couch cushions and unfurl my wings, the feeling heavenly after having them tucked in all day.

"Beautiful," he mumbles between thrusts.

One of his hands strokes along my spine and pets the sensitive base of one wing, making me buck harder against him. He gives me what I need, unleashing himself until I cry out as my body hums like a struck tuning fork. The orgasm hits me, but he doesn't let up. At this point, I'm saturated with his luck. Even my fingers vibrate with it. I keep climbing, another orgasm slamming into me, this one stronger than my first. My entire body clenches around him.

He moans but doesn't stop his assault. One hand wraps itself in my hair, tugging gently, as the other finds my breasts, kneading them, pinching my nipples. I gasp and then scream as the most intense pleasure is wrung from my body like the last drops of liquid from a wet towel.

Hot jets fill me as he gives in to his own ecstasy. *Fuck.* My bones have turned to noodles. I don't fight it but go perfectly limp over the back of the couch.

Still buried inside me, he grabs my ass cheek. "You're mine. Only mine."

"Yes," I say over my shoulder. "Just so you know, there is no way I can walk after that. I'm now a permanent fixture in your living room."

He strokes my hair and nuzzles my neck, threading his fingers into mine where I hold myself up on the cushions. "Nothing would make me happier than having you as a permanent fixture in my life." His lips press against my pulse. "One day I'm going to put a ring on this finger with a diamond the size of the iceberg that sank the *Titanic*. It's going to be large enough to see from space. Even visitors from other galaxies will know you're mine."

I smile sleepily at him. "A simple band will do."

He kisses my temple. "Wait here. I'll get a towel."

When he lifts off me, a waft of uncomfortably cool air takes his place and I wish we were in his bedroom so that I could snuggle under the comforter. He returns quickly with a wet towel.

"Thank the gods for birth control." I used to think that pixies and leprechauns couldn't procreate. It sounds ridiculous now, especially since I learned that Arden was Seven's, but in fae society, cross-species relationships are rare and it stands to reason that leprechauns who take pixies as lovers would use their luck to make sure a pregnancy doesn't occur. Pixies open to such a relationship are also usually on birth control. In any case, I'd never seen or heard of a leprechaun/pixie baby until Arden. Godmother has confirmed she's the first. Until Seven and I take our relationship public, we're not ready for a second.

He sighs. "I can use luck to stop you from getting pregnant if I remember. The problem is, deep down, I'd love to see you round with our baby. I hope we have five more of them."

"Five?" I ask, alarmed.

"Unless you'd prefer six?" He winks.

"Let's start with having a relationship we can tell the world about and then decide." I place a kiss along his jaw. "Hey, that was sex games, right? You weren't really angry with me for being late, were you? I did text."

He barks a laugh. "Sex games. I like that." He studies me for a beat, toying with the ends of my hair. "No, I wasn't upset with you, but I was anxious to see you."

"Obviously." I bob my eyebrows.

His eyes drift from mine, and he snags his shirt from the floor, wrapping it around my shoulders. I slide my arms in, and he starts buttoning it up. He's still naked, and my heart warms to know he's putting my comfort first.

"There is something I need to tell you."

I can tell by his voice it's serious. "What's going on?"

He takes me by the hand and leads me into the bedroom where he pulls on sweats and a T-shirt. "After you left, I went to see Godmother. She told me about your agreement and that you refused to bargain with her."

I scoff. "Oh, I bargained, just not magically. She promised not to ruin my reputation, and I promised to keep River in the safe house and solve Adam's murder."

"The thing about Godmother is she always has a plan B. She told me something, something I think you and I both suspected."

A heaviness gathers in my torso, and I brace myself.

"When you first arrived here, I suspected I was Arden's father, but Godmother told me not to tell you."

"I know. We've talked about this before."

His lips thin. "Until today, I didn't know for sure that I *couldn't* have told you even if I'd chosen to." My blood turns to ice. "When I bargained for you, Sophia, I was desperate. I didn't specify the terms specifically enough. I am bound to Godmother for life, and if she orders me to do something, I can't deny her. She hasn't used that power before, not until it came to Arden, and the scary part is, until she told me, I wasn't even aware that I didn't have a choice. I thought I simply desired to follow her wishes."

"But you did tell me eventually."

"She released me after we solved the murders even though she discouraged it."

I narrow my eyes. "Because she knew I'd find out anyway."

He nods.

"And now she's told you about this because she knows that

she can use you to control me. She knows about us, Seven. We may have kept our relationship secret from the general public, but she made damn sure I knew she wasn't buying it for a second. She knows I love you and that all she has to do is command you away from me and I'll do anything she asks."

He tips his head back and closes his eyes. "Of course. That's exactly it and why she chose this moment to reveal it. She wants us both to know we're under her thumb."

My fingers toy with the coin around my neck, remembering how she'd looked at it. "We have to find a way to break her hold over you."

He snorts. "Breaking a fairy bargain without being released from it is nearly impossible. Breaking a bargain made with Godmother has never been done."

I fold my hands in front of my stomach. "Then we get her to release you."

He laughs and shakes his head. "She's not in the business of being forgiving."

"No, but maybe we can find something she wants and convince her to release you in exchange."

"If you figure out what it is that Godmother wants and doesn't have, you are a smarter fairy than I am."

I cross my arms. The chance that we will ever break Godmother's hold over Seven are close to nil. Even with all his luck and all his riches, he's not even close to as powerful as she is. Clever of her to trap him like she did, at a time when he'd been drained by his father and was at his most vulnerable. If she hadn't tricked him then, she never would have succeeded later. She knew what she was doing, and now he's her own lucky charm. *Bitch.*

"Sophia... I know you don't want to consider it, but it's dangerous for you to love me. As long as she's in control, you can't trust what I do. What if she commands me to do something really awful? What if she commands me to leave you and never return?" The weariness I saw on his face when I first arrived is back again. So it wasn't about me being late. It was about this... guilt over the consequences of his bargain with Godmother and the strong feeling that he was roping me into those consequences by loving me.

"Why would she do something like that?"

"Why does Godmother do anything?"

"Right now she needs me. I'm doing what she wants, and someday we will find a way to convince her to break the bargain. Have faith in that."

He kisses me soundly. "I'll try."

Drawing a deep breath, I blow it out slowly. "Have you spent any time trying to decipher your father's riddle yet?"

He rubs his forehead. "No. And about that... it's going to have to wait a few days."

"Why?"

"That problem I mentioned with our supplier, it's bigger than I thought it was. I have to go to the US for a few days to meet with the CEO and see if we can come to an agreement."

My heart thumps heavier, missing him already. "No one else can go for you?"

He shakes his head. "This was one of the few vendor relationships my dad always handled himself. The CEO is old-school, likes the personal touch. It shouldn't take long. I'll go there for a few days, finish negotiating the new contract, seal the deal, and be back here before you know it."

I can't hide my disappointment, but I can't be unfair to him. His responsibilities have multiplied since his father was imprisoned. He has a company to run. I know Seven wouldn't do this if it wasn't absolutely necessary. "When do you leave?"

"First thing in the morning."

"On a Friday? You'll be there all weekend?"

"This can't wait."

"I'll miss you," I say. "And you'll miss your Saturday lesson with Arden."

He closes his eyes as if my words sting. "I'll text her. Tell her I'm sorry."

"She'll understand, Seven. You have important work to do. No one is blaming you."

"Thanks."

"Will you text me?"

"Of course."

"Will you send me dick pics?"

"Definitely. Does it have to be *my* dick?"

"Yours is the only one I want to see."

He pulls me against him. "Would you like an early-access preview?"

I wrap my arms around his neck and lean the full length of my body against him. "Definitely."

CHAPTER

ELEVEN

The next morning, I wake to the blare of my alarm and slap the machine with one lazy hand. I'm due at the casino in an hour to lead my regular class. Evangeline wants me to stop by her office beforehand to discuss something. It promises to be a full day. Only problem is, I can hardly keep my eyes open. Seven and I stayed up most of the night, making love and talking in between. It's becoming harder and harder for me to leave at a reasonable hour each night, and our late-night interludes leave me feeling like a zombie.

"Need coffee," I whisper, rolling myself off the bed and using my desk to hold myself up while my feet hit the floor. I drag my robe from the back of the chair and wrap it around me. Dressing will have to wait until my worship of the goddess caffeine is completed and her celestial gift of alertness is bestowed.

I'm halfway to the stairs when a sniffle from Arden's room interrupts my zombie trudge toward the kitchen. Backing up a few steps, I peek through the crack of Arden's partially closed door. She's still in bed, but her hands are covering her face. It looks like... she's weeping. Although she's trying her best to remain silent, her chest and shoulders shudder with her muffled sobs.

I push the door open. "Arden?"

She wipes her face with her hands and then tries to hide beneath the covers. "Mom, I'm sleeping. What do you want?"

I cross to her bed and sit beside her, rubbing her shoulder. "I want to know why you're crying, and if there's anything I can do to make it better."

The blanket slides from her features and she blinks wet green eyes at me, the same shade of emerald as her father's. All those years I thought her father was human and that those green eyes had come from some ancestor on his side when the truth of her lineage was right in front of me.

My heart gives a painful squeeze. "I think I know what this is about, Arden. Nothing you say to me will ever make me love you any less. Whatever you decide about your future, I have your back." I stroke her hair from her face. "Is this about you deciding you want to leave Devashire? It's okay if you do. You've known what you wanted to do your whole life. You can still follow your dreams. I would never hold you back." I can feel myself start to ramble, but I can't stop. "We'll still see each other. We'll FaceTime and you'll come here to visit—"

"Mom, stop!" Slowly she draws back the blanket and reveals her left wrist. My breath catches in my throat. A crisp Yule ball red ribbon is tied there. I flash back to the day Seven tied a similar ribbon around my wrist. That ribbon has meaning here. A boy had to rent a sleigh for the Yule parade to get it, and he had to choose her to be his date. Choosing this early in the year is a serious commitment.

"Arden, where did you get that?"

She chews her lip. "His name is Edmund. Mom, he's a leprechaun, and he asked me to the Yule ball."

"The Yule ball is in December. It's June. Will you even be here in December? Are you planning to come back for the event?" My skin feels too tight, and my gut is telling me the other shoe is yet to drop.

Her eyes never leave mine, but a stack of books on her desk falls over and the pen that rested on the top rolls across the floor and stops near the bed. She reaches down and swipes it from the floor.

"You did that?" I look at her with pure awe.

She nods. "I have luck, and I can use it. Edmund has been helping me practice some of the same things Seven is teaching me. We were friends before, but we've grown close the past few weeks. He asked me to the ball yesterday."

Suddenly uneasy, I shift and hold up a hand. "Wait. Did you tell him what you are, honey?" My voice sounds high and tight. Leprechauns do not normally ask human hybrids to the ball. Seven and I were the exception, and that was a disaster. But we'd known each other since childhood. Seven and I have spent so much time and effort protecting Arden's secret. What if she hasn't protected it herself?

"He doesn't know who my father is," Arden says. "He doesn't even know I'm part leprechaun. All he knows is that I just discovered I have luck. I'm sure he assumes it came from you. My teachers did."

"Your teachers know?"

"Before I graduated, I used it in class with the other kids. Anyway, I'm going to need all the luck I can muster if I'm to have any chance of getting into Elderflame University." She hands me the pen, and I stare at the Elderflame logo on the side. "I've already talked to an admissions councilor."

My mouth works like a fish's. "It... it sounds like you've made up your mind already. Are you sure about this? You're not just doing this for some boy, are you?"

She snorts incredulously. "No. Mom, please. I'd never."

"It just seems... sudden."

She shakes her head. "Not really. I was already considering staying before I knew about Seven."

My eyes narrow. "What? Why?"

She pushes herself up in bed and rests her back against the wall. "You don't get it, do you?" She wipes under her eyes. "This is why I was worried about telling you. You hate it here and you think I should too."

"That's not true! I just want you to know you have options."

"But I don't. Not really!" She spreads her hands, her tears coming faster.

I shake my head. "Has something happened?" All my organs clench, and a desperate whisper in my head says, *Please don't be pregnant.*

She tips her head and looks at me. "Yes, something happened. I found out that I have a family. I have a father I hardly know and I desperately want to change that. I have a mother and grandparents and even a great-grandmother. I have a home. And the best part is that I belong here because I am fae. I know you wanted me to be a doctor in the human world—"

"You wanted that. You've wanted that since you were twelve—"

"I'm not twelve anymore!" She scoffs. "I don't want to go back to pretending. I don't miss it. I want to be part of a family. I want to be surrounded by people who know exactly who and what I am and love me anyway. I don't want to worry about disguises or identities ever again. I'm fae. That's what I am. And here, people will love me for it. I'll have you and Grandma and Grandpa and Great-Grandma and all my new friends at school. And I'll have Seven." A wistful smile lights up her features. "I have roots. Do you have any idea how good that feels? How loved I feel here?"

"But what about your friends in Nevada? What about Jayden?"

She sighs. "We were already going our separate ways. She got into a college on the West Coast. We'd likely never see each other anyway."

Everything about her—the bright clarity in her eyes, the square of her shoulders, the way she leans slightly toward me—tells me she genuinely believes every word of what she said to me. Arden wants to remain in Dragonfly. My heart does a little leap. "You want to stay."

"I do." She laughs.

"So why were you crying?"

"Honestly?"

I nod.

"I was afraid how you would react to this. I was afraid you'd be angry." She plays with the ribbon on her wrist.

"Why?"

She looks away as she admits, "I know what happened between you and Seven, Mom. The Yule ball? I know it probably bothers you that I'm going with a leprechaun. It must be hard enough for you, being forced to spend all this time with Seven after what he did to you. This is what I want, but I am truly sorry if it makes you unhappy."

I shake my head vigorously. "No, Arden. Things between Seven and me are better now. We're... friends. Really, really good friends." Our eyes meet, and I see the moment she suspects there may be something more. "I'm not unhappy at all. Just surprised. In fact, if this is your choice, I'm ecstatic."

"Mom, is something going on between you and Seven?"

My cheeks feel hot. I made a vow when Arden was a baby to always try to tell her the truth. I want her to trust me, and that means I want to be a good source of information for her. And I can tell by her face she knows. "It's supposed to be a secret."

A long gasp fills the room. "I thought I sensed something between you, but I thought I must be seeing things. Before, when we first came here, you seemed to hate him."

"I was wrong. About many things. I love him, but we want to wait to reveal our relationship until the right time."

"The Gilded Gala!" she says excitedly. "Seven can announce you as his girlfriend at the same time he announces me as his daughter."

I smile sheepishly. "If that's what you want. I don't want to steal your thunder."

"You wouldn't be stealing anything from me. Just making more thunder."

"So when do I get to meet this Edmund?" I ask. "Do I know his parents? Please tell me they don't own Grandma and Grandpa's store or something. That would be awkward."

"No!" She rolls her eyes. "His dad died when he was younger, so it's just his mom, and she works with her parents at some car place. I wasn't really listening." Maybe his family are drivers like Saul or work at the dealership selling cars. Grandma knows all the leprechaun families, but I don't. "Anyway, he wants to meet you too. I was thinking of inviting him to dinner."

"That sounds like an excellent idea."

She lets out a deep breath. "I'm relieved you're taking this so well. I thought you were going to explode. You've been talking about my leaving since I got here."

"Only because I thought it's what you wanted." I can feel tears pricking my eyes as it all settles in. When Seven gets back, we can talk about going public. We can move forward as a family. My lips twitch into a smile. "I'm glad you're staying,

Arden. The only thing I care about is that you're sure, because there's no going back on this one."

She looks me straight in the eye. "I'm sure."

I hold out my arms, and she dives into them. "Then welcome home, sweet girl."

I can't wait to tell Seven about Arden's revelation, but I'm running so late by the time I leave her room that I barely have enough time to get dressed and make it to After Dark. Saul is with Seven, acting as his personal security while he's in the States, which means I'll need to take the character shuttle. Everything feels like I'm moving through quicksand. Plus, after my talk with Arden this morning, I've added a layer of emotional exhaustion to my already-painful physical fatigue.

When I reach the circle in front of Wonderland, there's a man I've never met before standing in front of Seven's black Mercedes. He's holding a sign with my name on it.

"I'm Sophia Larkspur."

The man holds his hand out. "Jericho. I'm a driver for Lucky Enterprises. Mr. Delaney sent me in place of Saul."

"Oh! I didn't know you were coming."

Jericho smiles. "I got the call around two a.m. Mr. Delaney was concerned about the shuttle's reliability. He said the class you're teaching is essential to the casino's operating plans this year and he didn't want to leave it to chance."

How sweet. "Who am I to argue with Mr. Delaney?"

Jericho opens the door for me, and I slide into the back. Once he's behind the wheel, he turns in his seat. "Mr. Delaney also gave me strict instructions to deliver to you the following."

He hands me a venti Starbucks cup, and my heart pounds with gratitude. "One fairy-spice latte, oat milk, no whip."

"Oh, thank you, the gods, and all that is good in the world."

Jericho laughs. "It's from Mr. Delaney. I can't take the credit. And I'm not done. One slice of River's famous quiche lorraine." He hands me a compostable cardboard box that smells of bacon and eggs, and I practically swoon. I take it along with the fork he hands me.

"I'm speechless. This is possibly the nicest thing anyone has ever done for me," I murmur. I sip the coffee and moan.

Jericho stifles a laugh. "One more thing." He hands me a sealed red envelope. "I don't know what's in this, but he hand-picked it very early this morning. Almost made him late for his flight."

I tear into the envelope and pull out a card with bunnies on the front. Two extra-strength Tylenol slide from between the folded halves. I pop them in my mouth and chase them down with a swig of the sweet elixir of life, coffee.

Inside, the card reads: No BUNNY LOVES YOU MORE THAN ME. On the opposite side is a personal note from Seven.

Sophia, Sorry to keep you up so late. I think we put Devashire's rabbits to shame. I hope the coffee and breakfast help you get through the day. Get some rest. I expect to make up for lost time when I get home. Love, Seven.

A deep contentment passes through me as I close the card and slide it into my bag. I am possibly the luckiest pixie on earth. And soon we'll be a real family. I know it won't be easy for us. People here have their prejudices, and I don't expect anything will change just because of Seven's position, but after my talk with Arden this morning, I'm convinced this will work. We'll be okay as long as we stay together.

I snatch my phone from my bag and shoot him a text.

Thanks for breakfast and for the bunnies. I can't wait for you to make good on your promise. Talk soon? I have news about Arden.

Once I press Send, I dig into my quiche in earnest. It's delicious. I'm glad to see that the management and staff of River's is carrying on well in his absence. I've licked the last crumb and polished off the coffee by the time Jericho parks and helps me out of the back seat. He reaches for the box and cup in my hands.

"Oh, I'll take care of these," I say.

"It's no bother, Ms. Larkspur."

"You're right, it isn't," I say with a laugh. "You have enough to do. And please call me Sophia."

He nods. "Have a good day, Sophia."

I stride toward the entrance, recycling the remains of my breakfast gift on the way in, and check my phone for the fiftieth time. My text has been delivered but not read. He must still be in the air. I should have asked exactly where in the US he was heading. I was too eager to say goodbye in every physical way I could think of.

I make it to Dragonfly Casino just in time to slide into Evangeline's office with a half hour to spare before my class. To my surprise, she looks as rumpled as I felt before Seven's gift. Her usual flawless appearance is gone, replaced by makeup that looks rushed and a messy bun. Her face is splotchy too, like maybe she's been crying. I'm filled with concern at the sight of her. Leprechauns rarely get flustered. Something must be terribly wrong.

"Are you okay?" I ask. "Is this a bad time?"

Eva blinks rapidly, as if just realizing I'm here and wipes under her eyes. "Ah, that obvious." Her shoulders sag. For several long moments she stares at me as if trying to decide what to say. "This... *murder* has really gotten to me. I'm not sleeping well." When she says the word *murder*, it comes out like she can hardly force her lips to make the word. As if she still can't believe it's true. "I thought when they caught my father doing what he did, this would be over."

Odd. Adam Barker's murder happened almost a week ago. Working in public relations might mean she's exceptionally hard hit by the event, but I've never seen her this shaken about anything before, not even her father's arrest.

"It's terrifying that something like that could happen here, but Seven is a genius when it comes to security. We're working with Godmother, and we are going to make sure it never happens again." This is one of those times when I'm happy to know how to bluff. I have no idea if what I'm saying is true or not. I hope it is. But if there's one thing I've learned since I've returned to Dragonfly Hollow, it's to expect the unexpected.

She closes her eyes and gives her head a slow shake. "To think that the killer is still out there somewhere... It's chilling."

I stop, my morning brain grinding on that thought. "You don't believe River is the killer?"

Her lashes flutter and she inhales deeply, collecting herself. "Do you? He hardly seems the type. I know he was over the body and everything, but what motivation could he have for killing that man? He counts on humans for his business."

"I don't believe he did it either. I guess that's why Godmother assigned me to help investigate what happened."

She sighs. "I'm glad you're on this, Sophia. I trust you. You'll sort it out."

"I'm not a trained investigator. I've never shot a gun or served in a security capacity. Even what went down with your dad wasn't completely my doing. I'm not qualified for this really, but Seven and his team are, and I'll do what I can to help."

She leans back, her mouth a straight slash. "You are exactly qualified for this," she says. "You've always underestimated yourself, even when we were children. You have an uncanny ability to read people. You may not be a detective, but you can see right through a lie like no one I've ever met. What is solving a crime anyway but deconstructing the lies around it?"

Great. Eva is the third person to nudge at the idea that my ability to lie and to smell a lie are my superpowers. I don't want to be known as a liar, not anymore. I thought I'd escaped all that when I came back here. Especially now, with Arden deciding to stay in Dragonfly and the life I've always wanted so close I can taste it, all I want is to be seen. I want my life to be genuine.

I glance at my watch. It's almost time for my class to start. "Speaking of bluffing, what was it you wanted to talk to me about?"

She rubs her eye. "This actually. Have any of your students asked about what happened last weekend?"

I shake my head. "None. I'm pretty sure the humans see it as an isolated incident. Honestly, when I was living in America, shootings happened every day. Comparatively, Dragonfly Hollow is incredibly safe, and Godmother did a great job spinning it as a personal squabble between River and the victim even though we both know that's not true."

She frowns, her gaze drifting. "Let me know if it becomes an issue. I can give you talking points."

"Okay," I say, slightly confused as to why this warranted a personal meeting.

She gives me a dismissive smile. "Thanks for stopping in."

CHAPTER

TWELVE

"Mr. Tannenbaum, you had a question?" I brace myself. He hasn't won a hand yet, and none of my lessons seem to be sinking in. He's playing the same way he did on day one.

The elderly man scratches his ear. "You keep telling us to assign a range to each of our opponent's hands, but how is guessing what cards they have helpful? How should we know what they're holding?"

"It's true that unless you're psychic, you don't know for sure what cards are in your opponent's hand until you see them, but you can assume a range based on what's in your hand and what's on the table. There are only four aces in a deck. If two are in your hand and two are on the table, how many does Marjory have?"

"None. But that kind of thing doesn't happen very often," he grumbles.

"No, it doesn't. But keep an eye on your opponent's behavior and you'll have another clue. Do they glance at their chips? Are their fingers trembling? Did the corner of their mouth twitch when they first looked at their cards? Every player has their tell, you just have to learn to watch for it."

He leans back in his chair and narrows his eyes on his wife. "What's in your hand, Janice?"

She laughs. "You can find out at the end of the game or if you pry these two cards from my cold, dead body."

A chill runs through me at the turn of phrase, and Adam Barker's last moments flash through my mind. Adam guarded that rock with his fist until it rolled from his cold, dead body. I wonder if it's still there. Did anyone but River notice it? Why would they?

I'm relieved when class is over. I promised River I'd check on his cat, Jinx. Apparently he's an indoor/outdoor beasty, and River was certain he could fend for himself, but he asked me to change the litter and refill his food and water. Now that I know the creature exists, I plan to stop in every other day and make sure he's okay.

His cottage is just past his restaurant, and the only way to get there is through a winding, wooded trail. I've never been there before, but I find it easily enough. Wind chimes strung from the porch ceiling play a tune welcoming my arrival. Nestled within a grove of oak trees, the yard is a collection of clover and wild violets. The home itself is stone with a chimney running up the south side and a dark purple door with a moon-shaped window.

Before I left him, River mentioned a key in the mouth of a toad near the front porch. I find the statue readily enough and stick my fingers into its laughing mouth. They hook on a key ring, and soon I'm inside.

Cozy. The main room has a fireplace, a plush sofa, and two recliners. A suspiciously misshapen knitted blanket on the back looks vaguely familiar, and I wonder if it was a gift from my grandmother. A driftwood coffee table is weighed down by stacks of books. There's no TV, but there's a four-foot-long fish mounted to the wall where one might go.

A galley kitchen runs along the back of the place. I find two empty bowls there and fill them with water and kibble from a full bin right beside them. I haven't even stood up yet when Jinx appears in the open window behind me, his black fur shining in the sun. He leaps to my side and weaves between my ankles, his purr filling the room as I scratch his back and behind his ears.

The cat's belly is round and his eyes bright. "River wasn't exaggerating. You seem to do just fine on your own."

He meows and arches his back into my hand.

I stand and leave him to his meal, making my way to the bedroom on the north side of the cottage and the bathroom off it where the litter box is supposed to reside. I pause when I see River's bed. It's unmade and there are three wineglasses on the bedside table. River, Patrick, and the mysterious third were here, together, right before his world fell apart. I narrow my eyes on a smudge of red on one of the glasses. Picking it up by the stem, I inspect the perfect bow-shaped print.

Lipstick. So the third is a woman. Good to know. If I can find her, I might be able to coax more information out of her about that day.

I take care of Jinx's box, which is remarkably clean considering how long River's been gone. The cat's likely been doing his business outside. I tie off the bag and head for the door to throw it away in the garbage can on the side of the house.

When I return to the cottage, I notice a coat stand that I walked right by my first time inside, tucked behind the door. A long purple trench catches my eye. A woman's coat. I close the door to get a better look.

The fabric is high quality, a European brand with complicated stitching at the cuffs. But it's the buttons that draw my eye, unusual in their craftsmanship. I turn one over to find VS carved into the back and drop the coat like it's on fire. VS is Valentine Sullivan, a satyr who designs custom accessories for the elite of Devashire. Elite meaning leprechauns—they're the only ones who can afford them at hundreds of dollars a pop.

River wasn't just with a woman. He was with a leprechaun woman. Holy shit! No wonder she required that bargain. If anyone found out a leprechaun was carrying on a sexual relationship with two satyrs, it would be a scandal. A male leprechaun with a female pixie would spark a certain level of social outrage—Seven and I are prepared for that. But a female leprechaun with two male satyrs? The fairy world would go up in flames. Devashire would be shooketh. All other gossip would pale in comparison. And if she was a married leprechaun? Why, the *Daily Hatter* might not report on anything else for the rest of the year.

But who? I check the size. Small. A younger leprechaun then. Luck filled the older ones out over time, giving them powerful curves. I'd have to ask Seven who the most likely candidates were next time I talk to him. I check my phone again, but he still hasn't texted me back. Must be busy.

My mind grinds on the question as I lock up the cottage and then head back toward the restaurant. So a female leprechaun met with River to talk about the night before outside his restaurant. I pause on the pathway behind the tavern. It was here, or around here. River said he couldn't see where the man was murdered, only heard him scream. But this wasn't an overly private place. If the wrong person passed by in front of the restaurant, they might see the two lovers together.

A sudden thought causes my breath to hitch. What if River's lover used her luck to cause the area to empty? If she was the reason for the lack of witnesses, the murderer might not be a leprechaun at all. It could be anyone.

I grit my teeth as I put together the implications. It actually makes sense. The person who messed with the security videos didn't edit out the empty sidewalks because they weren't responsible for them. Which means our search for a leprechaun murderer is way off base. It's someone else, someone who was after Adam Barker.

I round the corner of River's Tavern and revisit the spot where Adam was murdered. Unlike that day, the sidewalk is packed with people coming and going from the restaurant. Concentrating hard, I let my luck bubble in my blood, a tiger that rises at my side. I focus it on one thing, the single clue that River shared with me and the thing that made my blood run cold when I thought of it during my poker lesson.

Why was Adam Barker so protective of the rock he was holding in his hand?

Pouring on the luck, I inspect the cobblestone sidewalk, looking for the gray rock River described. My luck tiger sniffs along the pavers. The man held it firmly until the moment of his death. No one would do that unless they were desperate to keep it a secret. *Why* did he want to keep it a secret?

I spiral out from the area where the murder took place, searching and feeding my luck until my head starts to throb. And then there it is, tucked between a strip of lawn and the cobblestone. River is right—it does look like an ordinary stone, only I know this is what I'm looking for because there're no other stones like this here. The wall is cedar. The grass is thick and green. The cobblestones are red granite, and this rock is different. It's gray, yes, and veined with silver, but unlike any other material in the vicinity. I reach down and pick it up, surprised at the weight of it considering its size.

"Why was he hiding you?" I whisper.

"Sophia?"

I look up to find Penelope staring at me with a funny look

on her face. I smile and slide the rock into my pocket. "Hey, Pen! What's up?"

She laughs. "I think I should be asking you the same thing. You were staring at that strip of grass like you might be ill. Did you eat something bad?"

I shake my head, casting a wide smile in her direction. "No." I lower my voice. "Just taking one more look. I'm helping Godmother again."

"You mean to solve the murder?" she whispers, making a face. "Godmother roped you into working with Seven again! Gods, I thought you were done with that."

"I was, but I volunteered myself to help River. We all know he's innocent."

"Yeah, but isn't it hard for you to work with Seven after everything?"

The look of concern on my friend's face is enough to make a ball of iron form in my chest. I can't do this anymore. I can't lie to her, not about this, not now, not when her friendship has become so important to me.

"I like working with Seven," I mumble. "I like... Seven."

"What?" She's looking at me as if she can't quite hear me.

"In fact, I love him, Pen," I say a bit louder. "And he loves me."

"But... he was cruel to you." All the muscles around her mouth tighten and she scowls.

"No. That was his father, not him."

She shakes her head. "It can't go anywhere, Sophia. He's one of *them*."

I nod. "A leprechaun, yes. It doesn't matter to me at all. It never did."

Maybe this was a mistake. Penelope glares at me like an alien's tentacles are flailing from my mouth. I don't even think she's breathing.

"Say something, Pen."

"How long has this been going on?" she blurts.

"Since right after the hospital."

"Six weeks?" she rasps. "You kept this a secret all that time?"

"I'm sorry. I was afraid of how you might react. And I wanted to be sure. We're keeping it quiet for now. No one else knows."

"I'm the first to know?" She points at her chest, and I see pride flicker across her blue eyes.

Technically she's not the first. River and Arden know, and it occurs to me I haven't done a very good job keeping this secret recently. But then what does it matter? It's not going to be secret for long.

She blinks three times and then grabs me and pulls me against her chest in a relentless hug. A deep breath slowly escapes her lips. "I'm happy for you, Sophia. Truly... *And* I hope you know what you're doing."

A tiny spark of elation ignites inside me. She knows. My best friend knows. And she's accepted it. Accepted us. I hug her back. "You know, I think I finally do."

CHAPTER

THIRTEEN

By Saturday afternoon, Seven still hasn't responded to my texts, and I'm beginning to worry. Worse, Eva hasn't heard from him either. I talk to her after my last session of the day, and she reassures me that it's probably nothing to worry about.

"Our cell carrier occasionally has problems with roaming outside Devashire's borders. We're supposed to have coverage, but sometimes the calls don't go through. I'll have my assistant call his hotel and make sure everything's okay."

"Thanks, Eva."

I haven't slept well since he left. Part of it is that I desperately need to talk to him about what I found at River's. A bigger part has everything to do with our past. For over a decade, I thought Seven abandoned me at the Yule ball, intentionally not showing up and humiliating me. Although I now know that isn't true, my body remembers that grief. The memory resides somewhere in my cells, lurking in the deepest portion of my subconscious. And although I know Seven hasn't abandoned me this time, my unconscious mind keeps telling me he has.

Tension in my shoulder muscles leaves my neck and back sore, and I catch myself gritting my teeth.

Checking my phone for the thousandth time, I barely look up as I walk through the door of my family's house and almost run smack into Grandma.

"Finally!" Her bony fingers wrap around my shoulders and squeeze. As fabulous as ever in a tea-length ice-blue ball gown, she's wearing her silver hair twisted up the back of her head today. She looks at me over navy-blue specs. "I thought you'd never get home! Have you heard?"

"I didn't know you were coming over tonight. How are things in Sunnyville?" Grandma lives in a beautiful home in a retirement community outside the park. Still, since I returned to Dragonfly Hollow, she's been here more than she hasn't. I'm pretty sure that if my parents invited her, she'd move in in a heartbeat.

"Boring and irrelevant." She shakes me by the shoulders in a surprisingly strong grip for a fairy of her advanced years. "This is big, Sophia."

I narrow my eyes. "Is this about the murder?"

"Pishposh!" She waves a hand as if something smells. "That happened ages ago, Sophia. Live in the now! No, this is about—"

"Thank the gods you're here!" My mother runs into the room and grabs my hand. "I need your help in the dining room."

"Okay." I'm utterly confused. We normally eat in the breakfast nook.

Once we reach the dining room, I'm even more confused. The table is decked out. My family doesn't have a lot of money, but my great-grandmother on my father's side, gods rest her soul, left us some silver and fine bone china. Normally we keep the place settings packed away in storage, but Mom has pulled them all out and polished everything to a high shine. Gold chargers are topped with navy-blue-patterned plates with a gold edge. The shiny silver candelabra are draped with multi-colored crystals that reflect the swag of flowers and greenery arranged on the table runner. She's done an expert job. It looks like a scene off the cover of a Pottery Barn catalog. "What's going on?"

"I've been trying to tell you," Grandma says. "Arden's new boyfriend is coming to dinner, and he's a *leprechaun!*" Grandma's fingers fly to her mouth, and she inhales sharply.

I laugh. "I know she's dating a leprechaun, Grandma, I just didn't know he was coming for dinner tonight."

Her eyes grow to the size of saucers. "You knew about this?"

"I saw the ribbon on her wrist this morning and she told me."

"Stars and lightning, I'm always the last to know these things."

I scoff incredulously. "What are you talking about? You're always the first to know everything. You know exactly when ninety percent of the people in this town are due to go to the grocery store for milk."

"It's a very regular occurrence, Sophia, if you pay attention." She smiles broadly.

"I've made Cornish hen. Do you think that's fancy enough, Sophia? You work with leprechauns. Do the Delaneys eat Cornish hen?" Mom worries her hands and chews her lip.

My laugh is high, sharp, and completely beyond my control. "At least once a week, Seven eats a burger from that cart off Main Street that always smells like muskrat. And he gets it with imported government cheese."

"What's government cheese?" Grandma wrinkles her nose.

"It's this cheap processed cheese from the United States.

Sometimes it comes in individually plastic-wrapped slices. It also melts like plastic and has a slight chemical aftertaste. I think it's awful. He loves it. It's not exactly gourmet."

Mom smooths her hair. "I just want to make a good impression."

I pull her against me and kiss her temple. "You will. This is gorgeous, and dinner smells amazing. Besides, Arden would never like a boy who would turn up his nose at anything you put in front of him."

Grandma grips the back of the chair. "Well, I for one am going to position myself in the living room where I have a good view of the door. I want to be the first to see who it is."

"She didn't tell you?" I can't believe Grandma doesn't know the name and family history of this boy by now.

"No! To be fair, I asked her not to. I want to be surprised." Grandma's eyebrows bob, and she takes off toward the family room at a bit of a skip.

My mom squeezes my hand. "She lives for this kind of thing."

I giggle. "Yes, she does. Gods bless me with something to be as excited about as Grandma is with gossip."

We both laugh.

"Are you okay with this, darling?" Mom asks. "After everything that happened to you, it wouldn't be wrong for you to feel some trepidation—"

"I'm fine, Mom. Arden has a good head on her shoulders." She also has a lot more luck than my mother knows about. I wish I could tell them about what Arden is and that her father is actually Seven, but he would want to be here for that conversation and the one where we reveal that we're together again. I may have let the truth slip about our relationship to Penelope, but Seven would want to be part of telling my family about us and Arden. It can wait until he gets back.

"Good." She tugs at my wrist. "Then come help me in the kitchen."

An hour later, the hens have been baked to golden-brown perfection, Arden is wearing a gorgeous green dress that would be at home on either a pixie or a leprechaun, and we're all trying not to stare at the door as the clock clicks past six p.m., the time Arden told him to come.

At 6:05 I have to go into the kitchen and pour myself a glass of wine. If this kid stands Arden up, I will personally go medieval on his ass. I will sit on him and pluck his damn nose hair out one by—

The doorbell rings. I raise my head and set my drink down. Arden's welcoming voice fills my ears as she introduces Mom and Grandma. I turn the corner and see her new boyfriend for the very first time.

"Mom, come meet Edmund!"

I approach, my smile widening in what I hope is a welcoming way that conceals the nasty thoughts I was thinking about him only moments ago. "I'm so glad you could join us. I've heard so much about you."

"Likewise." Edmund radiates politeness. "It's good to finally meet you."

I can picture the pupils of Arden's eyes changing from circular to heart-shaped in my imagination; she looks at him with such devotion. It's easy to understand why she's smitten. Edmund has that inky, dark black hair that takes on blue highlights in the right light. His eyes are an intense royal blue that matches the shirt he's wearing, a fashionable thing with a logo on the pocket I don't recognize. His jeans hang on his tall, athletic form as if they were tailored just for him.

"Come back to the dining room, and I'll get us all something to drink," my mother says.

Arden takes Edmund's hand and leads him toward the table while Grandma and I fall in behind them.

"He's a looker, Sophia," Grandma whispers.

"As long as Arden thinks so." I shrug.

"And a strong name. Edmund is a family name you don't hear too much anymore. What's his last name?"

"You should ask him," I whisper. I want to get this kid talking, and who better to loosen his lips than my adorable grandmother?

I arch an eyebrow when Edmund pulls out Arden's chair for her. *Two points*, Grandma mouths.

My father chooses that moment to reveal himself, and I wonder where he's been all this time. Introductions are made, and we all sit down as my mother fills the water goblets and then brings out a tray of brown-sugar-roasted chestnuts wrapped in bacon. Dad pops one of the hors d'oeuvres into his mouth.

"Matthias!" My mother slaps his hand and glares at him, but he just chews obstinately. "I'm sorry, Edmund. We usually have better manners around here."

"I'm glad you told me, or I might have done the same," he says, then charmingly spoons a few onto his plate before tossing one between his teeth. "Delicious."

"Thank you, Edmund." My mother preens.

"Ms. Larkspur," Edmund says suddenly, and I realize after a few seconds that he's addressing me.

"Oh, you mean me. The only one I think of as Ms. Larkspur is my mother, although I suppose she's a Mrs." I laugh awkwardly, then sit up straighter. "Yes, Edmund, you have my full attention."

Arden curls her lip in a silent plea for me to be more normal. I try my best.

"Arden tells me you're working at the casino. My family is

terribly curious. Can you talk about it? Or has the Delaney family sworn you to secrecy?"

I stymie my surprise at his immediate interest in what I do and answer honestly. "No, I can talk about it. I'm teaching poker classes to humans. It's the first time they've tried anything like this, but so far it's extremely successful. All my classes are full."

"If you don't mind my asking, how did you learn?"

The truth is that Seven taught me, but telling Edmund that would reveal far too much. For one, I'd be admitting to a crime back then and also letting on to a romantic connection between Seven and me. That's no one else's business but my own and could possibly cause more trouble in the wrong hands. Sadly, my newfound flirtation with honesty must be short-lived.

"Self-taught." Not a complete lie. Is there any knowledge we attain that isn't in some way acquired through our own devices? "I developed my skills when I was living in America," I add through a shallow smile, also not a lie. "Although I don't recommend that route. Much safer and closer to family to learn here if you can find someone to teach you."

"Exciting though. It's an incredible opportunity…"

Our eyes meet over the table as he trails off, and I get the distinct impression he was about to add "for a pixie." While I admire him for cutting himself off before he said it, I'm fairly sure he thought it, and my impression of him falls a few rungs. Or maybe I'm putting words in his head. I tell myself to give the boy the benefit of the doubt and snag a bacon-wrapped chestnut from the tray, filling my mouth with it before I can say something I might regret.

Grandma chooses that moment to swoop in and take over the conversation. She smiles sweetly. "Edmund, I didn't catch your last name."

"Faust," Arden answers for him, her fingers threading into his.

Grandma's eyes widen and I lean my chin against my fist, wondering what's going on in that pretty gray head of hers. "You're Alicia and Gregory's son?"

Edmund nods. "Yes... but my father died when I was two. It's just my mother and me now."

Grandmother smooths the cloth napkin in her lap. "Of course. Please forgive an old lady. I think I remember your father, you see, as well as your mother's parents, Vivian and Felix *Armon*, right?"

"Armon?" my father chimes in. "Your family owns Armon Trucking?"

I straighten and dart a glance between Edmund and Grandma. Arden had said his family did something with cars. I'd thought maybe his father was a driver like Saul or owned the Elderflame dealership. Never did I guess Arden was dating an heir to an empire! Armon Trucking is *the* commercial transportation company in Devashire. We have an airport, but all the planes and helicopters in it are privately owned. Trains exist in Dragonfly Hollow to take humans from place to place within the theme park, but because most of our population outside the parks is concentrated in and around Elderflame, there's no need for train service there. Which leaves shuttles and buses to transport people, and trucks to transport goods inside and outside Devashire. The Armons own and run all of it. Every apple, every vehicle, every bolt of fabric in Devashire, with rare exception, has traveled at some point on or in an Armon vehicle.

Edmund takes a drink of water, his lips curling in a proud smile. "Yes, they do. My mother runs it now. Grandma and Grandpa retired some years ago, leaving everything to her."

The table turns strangely silent for a beat, probably just a second or two, but it feels longer. I narrow my eyes on Grandma, who is suspiciously eating a chestnut with tiny bites and lots of chewing like she's trying to keep her mouth busy. She does not look at me.

A niggle starts in my gut. Something bothers me about Edmund. I'm not sure if it's just a prejudice against rich people leaking into my opinion of him now that I know just how wealthy he is or if it's something else, but there's something familiar about him. Something I want to protect Arden from, although I can't put my finger on it.

"Did you play any sports at Bailiwick's?" I ask cheerfully, filling the silence.

"Bowbin. I was a right wing."

My father claps his hands. "It's been ages since I watched the Bailiwick's Basilisks play. I'm sorry I missed this year."

Arden shakes her head. "Wait, I never knew this about you. What's bowbin?"

I try to explain it in human terms she'd be familiar with. "It's like a cross between football, dodgeball, and archery. Instead of a football, the marksman, who is like the quarterback, throws a bright red mark at a player on the opposing team."

"What kind of mark?"

"Like a bright red burr that sticks to their clothing. The marked player then runs for the end zone while the right and left wingmen on the offensive team try to shoot him down with bows and arrows. If he's hit, he leaves the game. The winning team is the one with the most points when the last remaining player of one team or the other is removed from play."

Arden gapes at Edmund in disbelief. "Like real bows and arrows?"

He grins. "The heads are flat. When you're hit, you might suffer a bruise but more likely a bruised ego."

My father laughs. "We'll have to go this fall," he says to Arden, then seems to catch himself and looks toward me with a grimace. He doesn't know she's staying.

"I think that's an excellent idea, Dad." I say softly.

Mom chooses that moment to come in with a giant tray of roast Cornish hens, miniature red potatoes, and honey-glazed carrots. I pop out of my chair to help her serve.

Mom takes a seat next to my father, and I watch her practically hold her breath as Edmund takes his first bite.

"Exquisite, Mrs. Larkspur."

"Oh, thank you, Edmund," she says.

I muffle a frown. What kind of brownnosing teenager uses the word *exquisite*? He's too smooth. Edmund doesn't act like a kid trying to impress his girlfriend's parents. He acts like a boy who is well practiced in the art of making others see in him exactly what he wants them to see.

Beside him, Arden eats her dinner with her left hand while she continues to grip his fingers with her right. *Fuck.* She's never had a crush like this before. I fork a bit of hen into my mouth—*Mmm. Delicious.*—while my mother asks Edmund about his postgraduation plans.

"Business," he says without missing a beat. "I plan to work for the family business—follow in my mother's footsteps as they say."

"I haven't met many young people who know what they want to do at your age," I say to him.

He frowns. "There aren't many Fausts, I suppose. I think it's different being a leprechaun. There are expectations."

I don't hear the snobbery in his tone as much as I feel it. Gods, I wish Seven were here. I bet he'd know a lot about the Fausts.

It's just after seven thirty when Arden and Edmund stand up from empty plates.

"Thanks, Grandma," Arden says. "We have to go."

Edmund offers a practiced but charming smile. "We have tickets for Wonderland Theater."

"Oh? What are they putting on?" Mom asks.

"*A Midsummer Night's Dream.*"

"You've never seen that one until you see it put on with actual pixies and a satyr as Puck," I say, excited for Arden to have this experience despite my reservations about Edmund.

"I'm looking forward to it." Arden moves to collect her and Edmund's dirty plates, but I wave her off.

"Never mind that. I'll clear."

I walk them to the door and watch Arden stride toward the center of town on Edmund's arm. I close the door behind them with a sigh.

When I turn back around, Grandma is right behind me, so close her nose is almost touching mine. "Fucking gods!" I jump, my fist going to my chest.

"Sorry," she whispers. "I didn't mean to scare you, but there's something you need to know."

"What?" I'd noticed how quiet she'd gotten at dinner. She knows something.

She looks over her shoulder, but the hallway is clear. My parents are still in the dining room. "That boy is Alicia Faust's son." She widens her eyes as if that should alarm me.

"I gathered that. I know he's rich, but—"

She grabs my arm and squeezes. "Sophia, Alicia Faust is the one you saw Seven talking to at graduation. Alicia was once *engaged* to Seven Delaney."

CHAPTER

FOURTEEN

I blink at Grandma like a cursor on a computer that's trying to process its last command. I try to say no! and what now? at the same time, and somehow it comes out "Snow, what?"

Grandma gets my meaning. "The dark-haired woman I pointed out to you at graduation... While you were gone, Alicia and Seven were an item for a while. They were matched at that big leprechaun thing they do in the summer."

"The Gilded Gala?"

"That's the one."

My skin prickles at the news. No one but us knows about Arden, but what are the odds her son would take an interest in her? I don't believe in coincidences. I smell a rat, although I can't think of what possible cheese it might be after.

"How long ago was this, Grandma?"

She rubs her chin. "Well now... I'd say at least five years. Maybe six."

"Did the relationship last long?" Do I really want to know? Probably not. But I ask anyway, like I'm prodding a sore tooth.

"About a year, I think," Grandma says. My heart clenches.

"Oh, she always seemed more enthusiastic about the relationship than he did."

"What makes you say that?" It wasn't like my grandmother regularly ran in the same circles as leprechaun society.

"The *Hatter*. In every picture, she's gazing up at him adoringly and he's staring at the camera with a wooden smile and dead eyes."

That bit raises my spirits. "How did it end?" Barreling into the ground in streaming flames, I hoped.

Grandma grinned from behind three fingers that warned me of impending salacious gossip. "Well, I heard from Nancy Buttercup who heard from Auria Singh that Alicia grew tired of waiting for Seven to propose and bought herself an enormous diamond ring. Then she let it slip that they were engaged. Only Seven had never agreed to marry her. She probably assumed the social pressure would be enough to force him to go along with the ruse and tie the knot, but he didn't. Instead, he broke it off. Although he never humiliated her by coming right out and saying what she did, they attended the Yule ball separately and she was no longer wearing the ring. She was forced to give a statement to the *Hatter* that the engagement was called off for personal reasons just to get them off her back."

"Holy shit." I laugh a little too joyously. That was better than I was hoping for.

"I might still have a copy of the *Hatter* where they broke the news if you want to read it for yourself."

"Uh, no, thanks. Frankly, I'd love to forget it ever happened."

Grandma purses her lips, her eyes narrowing knowingly on me. "The question is if Alicia has forgotten, or if it will become an issue. I'd just hate for our sweet Arden to step on a land mine with that one. She has such stars in her eyes for Edmund."

I sigh. "About that, did anything strike you as odd about that boy?"

She snorts. "Leprechauns always strike me as odd."

"I mean he's very precocious and smooth-talking for a teenager."

For a moment she thinks about that, then says softly, "Seven was the same way when he was that age, Sophia. You just didn't notice because you were blinded by your own stars."

Flabbergasted by the assertion, I try to think back. Certainly Seven was always charming, especially when it came to parents and teachers, but it was as if it was expected of him, being who he was. I chide myself for my stupidity. Of course Edmund has the same expectations. He represents the Armon/Faust family line, and his mother has probably groomed him from birth to be as smooth as butter and as sweet as honey in any social situation. *Fuck.* I have a new appreciation for what my parents went through with me and Seven. How could you ever know for sure if a leprechaun's feelings were true when their entire lives were on display as the social royalty of our species?

The sigh I heave is laden with worry. "What do you think I should do?"

She toys with the lacy fringe of one of her elbow-length sleeves. "I'd never tell you how to parent your child, Sophia, but if I were Arden, I'd want to know this information so that I could prepare myself. If you're not comfortable talking to her about it, I could let it slip sometime when she was within earshot."

That would be the easy way out, but I owe Arden more than that. We've always had the type of relationship where we could talk about anything. "No. I'll tell her myself."

Grandma pats my hand and returns to the dining room.

AFTER A QUICK TEXT TO SEVEN TELLING HIM I'M thinking of him. I pack up some leftovers along with a bottle of wine to take to River and head to the safe house. The house is dark when I get there. I knock, but when no one answers, I let myself in through the unlocked door. It takes me a hot minute to make my way through the house and find him on the back porch, staring up at the stars. His horns reflect alabaster in the moonlight.

When he looks at me, he doesn't smile.

"I brought you dinner," I say.

"Already ate. I'm a chef. I don't need you to feed me."

"Okay."

The silhouette of his head sways. "But thank you for thinking of me," he says in a softer voice. "If you wouldn't mind, put it in the fridge?"

"Of course." I turn to take it inside but pause. "Is something wrong?" It's a stupid question. Everything about this situation is wrong, and both of us know it. I'm just not used to him directing his disappointment at me.

"Do you think I'll ever get out of here, Sophia?"

"Of course. I'm going to find who really did this and prove your innocence," I say softly.

He scoffs. "But will it matter? Godmother has a scapegoat. She's wrapped this murder up into a tight little package. So convenient."

"Too convenient." It's crossed my mind before, but I'm not ready to guess what it might mean.

"Now you see what I see," he grumbles.

"I'll make her release you. I'll go public with the murderer. I won't give her an option."

He sighs heavily. "I believe you'll try. I just hope you don't end up in here with me, or worse... in Ashgate."

He turns his face, and his eyes glint in the moonlight. In all the time we've been friends, I've never seen River cry. In fact, I can count on one hand how many times I've seen him without a smile on his face.

"I'm willing to take that chance." When he doesn't say anything for a few minutes more, I add, "I took care of Jinx yesterday. He's looking good. I think he's going to survive this."

That makes him laugh. "He's probably taken over the place. I'll come home to his wife and kittens nesting in my bed."

I shrug. "Probably. He seemed like he was enjoying the place to himself."

He stands and strides toward me. "Thanks for doing that for me. I'm not sure what I'd do without you."

"While I was there, I noticed lipstick on one of the glasses next to your bed."

"Hmm. I can't say anything about that."

"I know. But I also found a purple coat near the door. That coat had custom-made buttons that are almost exclusively used on garments worn by leprechauns."

"You don't say." He steps closer, and I can see his face. He's smiling, his eyes taking on a surprised twinkle.

"Your third is a woman and a leprechaun. That's who you were talking to right before the murder. And I think maybe she's the one who cleared the sidewalk. And the person who murdered Adam Barker, perhaps they took advantage of that."

His eyes narrow. "That's a good theory."

"But you can't confirm or deny it."

He shakes his head.

"That's okay. I think I'm right. I also found this." I pull the rock from my pocket and hold it up in the moonlight.

At first he just stares at it as if he's trying to figure out what it is; then he opens the door for me and ushers me inside, flipping on the kitchen light to get a better view. "You found it! That was in the victim's hand."

I nod. "Why do you think he'd be clutching this rock?"

"I have no idea."

"Neither do I, yet, but Seven says Adam Barker was a geology professor who came here to give a presentation to a Bailiwick's class on formations specific to the Appalachians. I'm going to go to the school tomorrow and ask around, see who invited him and how the presentation went. Maybe there's something we're missing."

River takes the stone from my grip and weighs it in his hand. "It's heavy for its size."

"I thought the same thing."

"I wonder... Have you thought about having it analyzed? Maybe whatever it's made of will give us a clue."

Smart. "I bet if I take it to Elderflame University, someone there could tell me what it is." I turn and slip the food I brought into the fridge. An idea comes to me just as I'm closing the door. "What if it's not what's in the rock but the spell on it? Barker was human... maybe he got his hands on a stone that makes up the wards around the park."

River scratches his cheek. "Do you think someone on the outside wants in?"

I shrug. "I'm not sure. Even if they could deconstruct the magic, which humans can't because they're human, what would they hope to accomplish?"

"An undetectable way in and out," River says simply. "Maybe the murderer is a thief."

Possible, but the idea still isn't coming together for me. "I'll get someone to analyze it."

We stand there in the tiny kitchen, the weight of the past

week settling on our shoulders. "I am going to figure this out, River. I'm on it."

He glances down at his toes. "I'm not meant for this kind of life, Sophia. I appreciate you coming. I do. Without you, I'd be out of my mind. I just need to be back in my restaurant. I need to see the people I love." He leans a hip against the counter. "Do you think...? Can you at least tell Patrick that I'm not in Ashgate anymore? I'd hate for him to try to visit me there only to find..."

"Yes," I say immediately. "I'll find a way to let him know."

"Good." He scrubs his face with his hands. "I bet when you were on your way to confront Chance Delaney over that pixie's murder, you never expected it would lead to this. I know when I heard you'd caught him, I believed it was over."

River is one of the only people in Devashire who knows Seven and I were behind Chance's capture. The public believes Godmother is to thank for the raid and his arrest. Fine with me. I never wanted to draw any more attention than I had to.

"Actually, we didn't think he'd be there, at the cabin. Seven suspected we'd find something inappropriate, something he was trying to hide, but we were convinced someone was blackmailing him over a fetish. No one was more surprised than us when Chance walked in."

"I thought you caught him at his hunting cabin?"

"We did, but he was supposed to have a meeting that afternoon. He wasn't supposed to be there."

"Hmm. What tipped him off?"

I blink at River. It's been a long time since that fateful night, and I blocked out some of the details. I had to in order to feel safe and to heal. But now his question makes me look back on that night with fresh eyes. When Chance caught us in the dungeon under his cabin, he was dressed in a suit and tie...

dressed for the office. Seven confirmed he was supposed to be in a finance meeting at that hour. So how did he get to the cabin so quickly, and how did he find out we were there?

I think I know the answer to the second part—we tampered with the fairy ring in the front yard. We thought we'd dismantled his protective wards, but the one we could see must have been a decoy for one we couldn't.

How he got there as fast as he did is still beyond me. The man was incredibly powerful, the luckiest fae in Devashire aside from Godmother, but that didn't mean he could teleport. That trick is beyond even Godmother's abilities as far as I know. So how did he make it to the cabin so quickly?

"You know, I'm not sure," I tell River honestly. "I've been so busy recovering from that night and trying to get you out of Ashgate, I never even thought to ask Godmother."

"Understandable."

I jump when my phone rings. Hoping it's Seven, I yank it from my back pocket, then frown when I see it's a call from Evangeline. "I have to take this. It's my new boss."

"Go ahead," River says softly, then adds with a chuckle, "Tell Evangeline I said hello."

"I wish I could. She's been worried about you." Everyone misses River, but his freedom is predicated on maintaining the illusion that he's still in Ashgate. I might be able to trust Patrick with a vague version of the truth, but I can never risk telling more people.

He gives me a nod and points toward the living room, leaving me alone to take the call.

"Sophia? Are you there? I can hardly hear you." Eva's voice sounds shaky, as if she's been crying.

"I'm in the mountains. The reception is bad."

"What are you doing in the mountains?"

I hesitate.

"Sophia? Sophia, are you there?"

"Visiting a friend."

"Oh... I..." She sobs on the other end of the line.

"What's wrong?" I ask. "You sound upset. Has something happened?"

For several moments, she seems to hesitate. She starts and stops but can't get the words out.

"Where are you?" I ask.

"I'm at Seven's apartment," she says. "He's back. You need to come right away."

"Well, let me talk to him." I can't understand why Seven wouldn't have called me himself.

"He can't right now, Sophia. Oh gods, this would be easier to explain in person."

I am already jogging for the door. "I'll be there as soon as I can."

CHAPTER

FIFTEEN

I reach Seven's building just after ten, where a security guard I don't know—the place is crawling with them—ushers me up to his penthouse. Evangeline lets me in, looking even worse than the last time I saw her. The circles under her eyes are even darker, and she locks the door behind me before pulling me into a hug.

"What's wrong? Where's Seven?" I ask, extremely worried now.

"He's in bed." A tear trickles from the corner of her eye. "I found him, badly injured and barely breathing, in my office. I don't know how he got in there. I've already called a doctor."

Without so much as a word to Eva, I run for the bedroom, suddenly unable to breathe. All my thoughts turn to Seven. I burst through the door and it's as if someone has punched me in the gut. All my breath rushes from my lungs, and my knees threaten to give out.

He looks dead. His complexion is almost gray where it's not covered in blood. His white shirt is soaked with red. He's still in his suit, but the dark material is torn and discolored with scuffs as if he was dragged behind a truck on a gravel road. I climb onto the bed and start examining him close up.

"How long has he been like this?" I ask Eva.

A sob cuts through the room and she answers, "Since I found him. Jericho helped me get him here."

"Why didn't you take him to the hospital?" I ask, annoyed.

She looks at me like I'm an idiot. "We have a private family doctor. I've already called him. He's on his way."

Of course, like everything in their family, discretion is key. After we battled Yissevel, I spent weeks in the hospital but Seven recovered here. That's how the Delaneys work.

"Help me get him out of this suit. I'm going to clean him up." It will be easier for the doctor to examine him anyway.

With Eva's help, I roll him onto his side and ease his arm from the sleeve of his jacket. I wince when a sickening pop comes from his opposite shoulder, and I quickly roll him onto his back again.

"Fuck, I think his shoulder dislocated." For a moment I just stare at Seven, his shallow breathing, pale skin, frail body. "Oh my god, he's negative, Eva. Why is he still negative?" For a fae, luck is like a bank. We only have so much stored up, and if we overdraw our account, the forces of the universe take the luck back from us by cursing us. When we're negative, walking across the street could be deadly. We attract bad luck and bad circumstances.

"I don't know," she says. "I gave him some on the way over here."

"Well, do it again!" I bark at her.

The look she gives me is positively offended, but her expression morphs quickly from defeat to determination. I feel her luck rise in the room like a great feathered beast. It's fiery, like her brother's that always reminds me of a dragon, but feminine. Instead of wrapping around me like a hot, muscular serpent, what brushes my skin is like a duster warmed by the sun. It soars through the room and fizzles as it reaches her brother. She moves closer and places her hands on him.

"Sophia... there's something wrong. I'm sending luck into him but it's just... dissolving. It's like... It's like..."

My blood turns icy in my veins. "Blue iron."

Carefully I feel his wrists and ankles, looking for manacles like the ones FIRE restrained me with when they captured me, but Seven's limbs are unencumbered. His breath rattles in his lungs, and I quickly unbutton his shirt to give him more air.

"Those fucking evil bastards," I say when I see a row of stitches on his chest. Under the stitches is a raised section of flesh in a misshapen square.

"Gods! Is that what I think it is?" Eva yells.

"Bring me a knife from the kitchen. Quickly! And a clean towel."

She runs from the room and returns with a paring knife. Good enough. I don't hesitate but slice the stitches open and dig my fingers into the wound. Seven doesn't flinch or moan, and I try not to think about what that means. My fingers clamp around a stone, and I drag it from his flesh, feeling all my energy drain away as I do. As soon as it's out of him, I fling it across the room and catch my breath. My luck bubbles up again in my veins.

"They sewed blue iron into him?" Eva shouts incredulously. "What kind of psycho would do a thing like that?"

"I don't know, but if I find out, I'm going to kill them." I press the clean towel to the wound and run my hands over every inch of his body, looking for more. I don't find any. "Eva, try giving him luck again. It's the only way to know that it's all out of his system."

That enormous, fiery bird rises over me again and sinks into Seven as her hands come to rest on his arm. The effect is instant. He draws a deep breath into his lungs and then cries out, fisting the sheets. For a second, his eyes are wild; then they fix on me.

"Sophia? Thank the gods." One arm flops around my neck and pulls me to him. He presses his lips to my forehead.

"What happened, Seven?" Eva is pacing now, her luck fluttering around the room. "For fuck's sake, there was blue iron sewn into your chest!"

He looks at her for the first time, then reaches over to grab her hand. "There's something I have to tell you. It's bad Eva. It's so bad." He tries to sit up, and fresh blood pours down his shirt.

"Fuck. Hold still." I press the towel to his chest again. "The doctor will be here any minute. You need that wound cleaned and probably stitched."

He closes his eyes for a long beat. "This can't wait." When he opens them again, I'm sure his luck is coming back because they're glowing bright emerald. His gaze shifts to Eva. "Dad made a deal with Rayrcore for... stones, something he was getting from Devashire, a valuable mineral. Rayrcore made it extremely clear to me that his imprisonment is no excuse for not delivering the goods."

"What mineral?" Eva spread her hands. "Rayrcore supplies us; we don't supply them."

My head is spinning. "Back up. Who is Rayrcore, and what exactly do they supply you with?"

Eva flashes me a pitying look. "Rayrcore is who Seven just met with. They're an American mining conglomerate run by Alex Hearst. They provide us with rare earth metals, which we use in a variety of our products—anything that can run on a battery, like our slot machines for example."

I shake my head, completely confused now. "And your father was bringing stones to them? What kind of stones?"

"Something called malivite. They claim they've *paid* for a delivery of this stuff. I'd never even heard of it."

"Wait, so your father has a secret mining operation happening somewhere in Devashire, and because he was arrested, he wasn't able to deliver the goods?"

"So it seems," Seven says.

I pull the stone from my pocket. "This was in Adam Barker's hand when he was murdered."

Eva reaches for it and turns it between her fingers. "Is this malivite? I've never heard of it either."

I squint at both of them. "Isn't mining in Devashire illegal? I thought Godmother put a stop to it a hundred years ago because of the environmental impact."

"She did," Seven says. "She knows our bread and butter is getting humans in the door, and none of them want to be breathing in dust from mining activities. They come here for the natural surroundings and for the fun. That's why Rayrcore took it upon themselves to kidnap me rather than take this to the authorities. They wanted to show me in no uncertain terms what would happen if I don't keep supplying them. I just can't figure out how their payment to us slipped by me. There should have been a red flag raised if they paid us for something we never delivered."

Eva's face pales, and she sits down on the edge of the bed. "They did pay us."

Seven grunts with the effort of turning his head to look at her.

"It was the day you found out about Dad—the meeting with the accountants. Dad was supposed to attend, but I filled in for him at the last minute. He grabbed me right before the meeting and said he had to go. That was the day Godmother arrested him. In that meeting, I noticed a large payment from Rayrcore. No one could explain it, and we tabled it to ask

Chance when he was back in the office. He was never back in the office. I've been so busy I forgot about it."

Seven runs a hand down his face. "Well, Rayrcore remembers."

The same niggling questions surface in my brain as when I'd talked to River earlier. "How did Chance get to the cabin so fast that day? We arrived at your father's place at the same time he was scheduled to meet with the accountants. If he was in Evangeline's office right before the meeting to ask her to take his place, how did he get to us, an hour outside of Elderflame, so quickly?"

Seven sighs. "The same way I ended up in Eva's office tonight. There's a secret passage through Dad's old office."

Eva and I stare at Seven disbelievingly. "You came through a secret passageway?"

"We need to go to the casino. There's something—" He tries to push up on his elbows and collapses flat on his back.

I place a hand gently on his shoulder. "You're not going anywhere. You were negative, Seven. You had blue iron sewn into your chest. And I'm pretty sure you have a dislocated shoulder."

He groans. "We don't have time for this."

Evangeline slips her hand into his. "You're home now. That's what's important. I'll fill in until you heal."

He closes his eyes and shakes his head. "You don't understand. They still have Saul. And if we don't bring them what they want in seventy-two hours, they're going to kill him."

It's all I can do to keep Seven in bed. I'm as worried about getting Saul back as he is, but he can hardly sit up. We both know we'll need him in tip-top shape to have any hope of doing what we need him to do. Thankfully the doctor arrives. He's an ancient-looking leprechaun who goes by the name of Felix Bonheur. I don't want to leave Seven's side, but Dr. Bonheur insists. Evangeline ushers me from the room and into the kitchen where she puts on water for tea.

"Sophia, I need you to do something for me," Evangeline says, not meeting my eyes. Something's been bothering her for days.

"Just ask already, Eva," I say flatly. "This has something to do with the real reason you wanted me to come to your office the other day, doesn't it? I feel like you've been meaning to ask me something, but you haven't."

Now she lifts her head and meets my eyes. "You've got to tell Godmother about what's happened here tonight. Rayrcore has to be behind the murder even if we don't have proof yet. You need to lie to her. It's wrong to leave River locked up in Ashgate when we all know he didn't do it." She fists her hands on the counter.

I study her for a moment, her agitation, the dark circles heavy beneath her eyes. Her luck rises in the room, those hot feathers brushing against my skin. It's a bird. No, a *phoenix*.

"He's not in Ashgate," I say softly. I could get in big trouble for this, but if what I suspect is true, she'll keep my secret. "He was moved, but you can't tell anyone. If anyone finds out, they'll send him back."

She reaches across the counter and takes my hands in hers. "Please, Sophia, where is he? Is he okay?"

My throat tightens at the pleading in her voice. "Why are you so concerned about River, Evangeline?" I ask softly. "You know, I've never seen you near River's until the morning of the murder. At the time, I thought you were there for PR purposes, but you got there awfully fast for someone who lives in Elder-flame and works in After Dark."

The teakettle whistles, and she slides her hands from mine to pour the water into the teapot with the loose tea. "Do you take it with sugar?"

"Milk." I continue to stare at her, but she refuses to meet my eyes. "You've been worried about River's fate since the moment of the murder."

No response.

"You haven't been sleeping or eating." I eye the way her collarbones protrude where they can be seen inside the vee of her blouse.

"Tell me where he is. Please." She still refuses to look at me.

"Your luck takes the form of a phoenix. I recently learned that River has a phoenix tattooed on his shoulder. Is that a coincidence, Eva?"

This time she raises her gaze to meet mine and there's fire in her emerald-green eyes, the same possessive fire I sometimes see in her brother's. The room grows warmer as her luck circles it, and she says through her teeth, "How exactly do you know what's tattooed on the back of his shoulder?"

Reaching out, I take her hand and squeeze. "I know you can't tell me directly about any relationship you have with River, but tell me this: are you missing a purple coat?"

Our gazes lock, and tears slip from her eyes and carve down her cheeks. "Please, please tell me he's okay."

"He is. But Eva, you've got to break the bargain with him. You can prove he didn't do this thing."

She sobs openly now, her entire body trembling. "No one can find out. A leprechaun with a satyr is scandalous enough. Two satyrs... I will never live it down. No one will ever take me as a wife after that."

A bad taste floods my mouth. "But it's his life, Eva. If you care for him at all, you have to know that his life trumps any fear you might have about the truth getting out." There's empathy in my voice but also a slight edge of accusation.

She gasps as if I hit her, and her eyes rove wildly around the room. "You're right." She runs a hand down her face. "Maybe I can convince Godmother to keep it a secret."

"For a price, I'm sure you can. But right now you must go to him. You must break his bargain with you so that both of you can help us free him."

"But where is he? How did you get him out of Ashgate?"

I cross my arms over my chest. "I told Godmother I was their third. I said I was you."

She gasps, her fingers flying to her lips. "But—"

"Yeah, she's holding it over my head like an acid bomb. One slipup and my reputation, what's left of it, is toast. I don't need to tell you how unfortunate that would be for Seven and me."

"Fuck, Sophia, I'm sorry. I never meant for you to do that. How... how did you even know?" Her voice comes out breathy on that last part, and her cheeks redden.

"I didn't know it was you if that's what you're asking. Both Patrick and River kept their bargain." Not that they had a choice. A bargain can't be broken, not without killing the fairy who breaks it. And although we are experts at finding loopholes in our deals, River is too upstanding of a person to try. "I went to visit River in Ashgate, and he told me there was *someone*. I knew that someone couldn't come forward, so I pretended to be you. Godmother accepted it and moved him to a safe house."

"It takes all participants involved to break a bargain made by three." She sounds breathless.

"You'll need to find Patrick, then bring him to this address." I pull out my phone and show it to her. "You should go now, before you lose your nerve."

Her eyes widen and she grabs her phone, her thumbs flying as she enters the address. "Thank you, Sophia." She squeezes my hand. "Thank you."

Dr. Bonheur chooses that moment to waddle into the kitchen. "Now, now, no need for tears!" he says when he sees Evangeline's face. "Your brother will be as good as new in a day or two. I've loaded him with enough luck to be sure of that and taken care of those nasty wounds. Nothing to worry about but making sure they don't happen again!" He holds up a hand before Eva or I can say a word. "I don't want to know." He reaches into his bag and withdraws an invoice. "My bill."

I glance at the paper. The header reads PIPES AND THINGS REPAIR AND REPLACEMENT. The line item simply says HOUSE CALL with an amount in the five figures. Discretion is key, Eva had said. If someone found this, they'd never know Seven had seen a doctor.

Bonheur gives as both a little wave and then heads toward the door with his big black bag. Once the door is closed behind him, I move for Seven's bedroom.

Eva grabs my elbow. "Don't tell Seven, okay? Not now. He has enough to worry about."

"Okay. But Eva, I've spent a lot of time bluffing over the years, and the truth is always better."

She holds up her phone with the safe house address, hugs me, and all but runs for the door.

SIXTEEN

By the time I return to Seven's side, his hair is wet from a shower and he's standing in front of his closet in nothing but a pair of green boxer briefs. The blood is gone but there are cuts and scrapes marring the muscles of his back, although they all seem to be healing now. When he hears me come in, he turns to look at me and I notice a gash under his left eye. Nothing is worse than the line of black stitches up his sternum though. I cringe when I see it.

"What are you doing out of bed?" I ask. "You need to rest."

"I need to go to Ashgate and confront my father about what he promised Rayrcore. Where is this malivite mine? How much am I supposed to bring them?" He's thumbing through a row of slacks as if he's trying to decide which to wear or which will hurt the least when he puts them on.

"It's the middle of the night. Ashgate is locked up. You won't get in until the morning."

He pauses for a second, staring aimlessly into his closet. "Right. We'll go to Dad's office instead. There's got to be something on his computer, some clue to what I'm supposed to do."

Seven glances over his shoulder at me. "They didn't believe that I don't know what Chance promised them. I think they thought I was working with him, that we were swindling them."

I close the space between us, and it's a good thing because when he turns back to his closet, he stumbles. I wrap my arms around him from behind, steadying him. "It's late. You're in no condition to face this right now. It can wait until tomorrow."

He heaves a sigh and leans back into me. "They have Saul, Sophia."

"I know. Aside from Godmother, you are the most powerful fae in Devashire... when you're healthy. I don't know how they captured you—"

"It was an ambush."

"It won't happen twice." I grip his shoulder and place a kiss on the bare skin of his back. "Rest. Recover. A plan will come to us tomorrow."

He releases the pair of pants he's gripping and hangs his head. "We don't just need to save Saul; we need to stop Rayrcore. I don't know why they want this malivite, but it must be incredibly valuable if they're willing to kill for it. This isn't going to end with one shipment."

"I don't think so either," I say. "The night we discovered what your father was doing, the last thing he said to me before he passed out was that the murders were part of something far bigger than him. He alluded to the same thing when I interviewed him in Ashgate. This Rayrcore thing, it has to be related, and it wouldn't be a jump to connect it to the murder either."

He shakes his head. "I don't know. I can't put it together, and as hard as I tried, they wouldn't share much about it while they were... b-beating me." His voice cracks slightly, and I hug him tighter from behind, pressing my cheek into his back. It's all I can do not to lose it and melt into a pile of tears over what they did to him, but the last thing Seven needs is to have to comfort me right now.

"I'm here. You're okay," I say confidently.

He places a hand on top of mine on his chest. "Thank the gods."

"Please, Seven, let's lie down. We can talk about all this in the morning. Once we're rested and you've had something to eat, we can make a plan. Things will be so much easier when you're well. I promise."

He turns in my arms and presses his forehead to mine. "Will you stay with me? I don't want to be alone."

No way can I leave him tonight. Not after what he's been through. I pull my phone from my pocket and stare at the screen. I don't like to lie to my family, but can I tell them the truth? Yes. Yes, I can.

I text Mom and Arden.

ME:

Getting late. Staying overnight so I don't drive home tired. See you tomorrow.

ARDEN:

Have fun. Going to a movie with Edmund after school, but I'll see you for dinner.

MOM:

You're working too much! Take care, darling.

I heart both text messages, shaking my head.

"What's wrong?"

"Nothing," I say. "I'm staying. My mother didn't even question me about it."

"That's a good thing, right?"

"Yes. Sometimes I think I underestimate my family. I still think they're going to treat me like I'm seventeen. It surprises me when they don't."

"I always liked your family." He smiles wistfully. "When I was there at your house, sometimes I didn't want to go home."

"Well, it wasn't always perfect, but I know when we go public, we can count on their support. They respect my choices and treat me like an adult. Of course, that also means I have no one to blame for my choices but me, and that's a little scary."

He sighs and sinks onto the bed, looking exhausted. "I really wish your choices were the scariest thing we have to worry about."

"Me too." I help him under the covers, then excuse myself to visit the kitchen. A few minutes later, I return with a club sandwich, a sliced apple, and a big bottle of juice.

Seven props himself up against the headboard and groans. "Thanks. I haven't eaten since yesterday."

My insides sink at the thought of what he endured, but I put the tray on his lap and try not to dwell on it. He lifts the sandwich to his mouth and closes his eyes as he takes a bite.

"Hey, I'm spending the night!" I announce again.

His shoulders soften, and he slants a crooked grin. "We established that."

"I just wanted to hear it out loud. By the way, I thought of something while I was in the kitchen," I say. "Your cleaning lady..."

He nods, then bites into the sandwich again.

"When does she come? It's probably not good for her to find me in bed with you, and I plan to be in bed with you."

He grins around what's in his mouth. "Has the day off tomorrow."

I smile in relief and inch toward the bathroom. "Good. You eat that. I'll shower."

It's a testament to what bad shape Seven is actually in that he doesn't offer to join me.

After a long, hot shower and finding an unused toothbrush

in a bathroom drawer, I climb into bed beside a sleeping Seven, dressed in a pair of his sweatpants and an old Van Halen T-shirt I dug out of his dresser. I'm happy to see there's nothing left on his plate and the bottle of juice is empty. I snuggle into his backside and wrap my arm around him. He's bigger than me, and this would be easier if he were spooning me rather than the other way around, but right now, after what he's been through, I think he needs it more.

"I love you," he mumbles.

I'm not sure he's even awake. His breath is even and his eyes stay closed.

"I love you too," I whisper. And then I drift off to sleep.

I WAKE WARM AND CONTENT. THE LIGHT THROUGH THE window sheers is silvery, and a glance at the clock on the bedside table tells me it's early. Barely six a.m. Sometime during the night we've switched positions and Seven is wrapped around me, his hand tucked under my shirt and splayed across my abdomen. His lips brush the back of my neck, and I hear him draw in a deep breath.

"Are you smelling me?" I ask through a grin.

"You're awake?" He lifts onto one arm, and I turn my head to kiss him. "Smelling you comforts me. A day ago, I wasn't sure I'd ever smell you again." His eyes turn stormy.

"What exactly happened, Seven?"

A dark cloud moves across his expression. "They jumped me and Saul the moment we stepped out of the car at their offices. I wasn't focused on protecting us. I never thought I needed to be. I'd dealt with Hearst before, but I guess my father was involved with a lot more behind the scenes than I ever knew about. I was in blue-iron cuffs before I knew what hit me. They asked me where the malivite was and then tore apart our car looking for it. When I told them I didn't know what they were talking about, they didn't believe me. Claimed Lucky Enterprises had taken their payment and the shipment was late. Accused me and my father of underhanded business practices. Filthy fae, they called us. You saw what they did next. They did the same to Saul. They only returned me because I promised I'd talk to my father and come back with the shipment. Saul was their insurance."

"Shit." I shake my head. "You're lucky to have made it out of there alive. We'll get Saul back. We will. We'll find a way."

He rolls me under him, settles between my thighs. "Facing it... Experiencing that kind of pain and wondering if I'd ever make it back to you... Sophia, I don't want to keep us a secret anymore. You are as much family to me as Eva and of course Arden—the three of you are the only family I have left and the only thing I thought about when I was having blue iron sewn into my chest." His voice turns raspy, and he swallows hard against the horrific memory.

I take his face in my hands. "Then I have good news because I don't want to do this anymore either. Arden made her decision. She wants to stay. She's already applied to Elderflame University. She's only waiting to tell you before she announces it to everyone else."

His face lights up with joy, and his eyes grow wet. "We're going to be a family. A real family. I never believed it could happen. I knew she'd make the right choice though. She's a brilliant girl, just like you. She must have realized it was better staying here and living her truth than hiding what she is from the world."

"That and she's dating a boy," I say. "I'd like to think it's more living her truth than boy, but you know teenage hormones."

Seven's entire body stiffens in my arms. "She's dating a boy? Since when?"

"Since before graduation, although I just found out recently. He came to dinner Friday night. Actually, I wanted to talk to you about him because—"

"Who is it?" he asks tersely.

"Edmund Faust."

Seven scrambles off me so fast I get a chill. "No."

"Huh?"

"Tell her to break up with him, now. Forbid her from seeing him ever again." His jaw clenches.

I give a low, throaty laugh. "Oh, my sweet summer child. It's very clear to me that you have never, in fact, raised a teenager, especially a girl. Telling Arden, who is going to be a legal adult in less than a year and a half, to break up with Edmund, whom she says she's in love with, and forbidding her from ever seeing him again is the surest way for her to instantly become pregnant by him and never speak to us again. It's practically a law of nature. You don't want to go there."

He settles back on his heels. The wound in his chest is already so much better, and some other scratches and abrasions I remember from last night are almost completely healed. Being a leprechaun definitely has its perks.

"There's something you should know about the Fausts."

"That you were once engaged to Edmund's mother? My grandmother told me."

A muscle in his jaw twitches like the memory is horribly uncomfortable. "I was never engaged to her, Sophia. She told the *Daily Hatter* we were engaged to try to manipulate me into marriage."

"My grandmother also mentioned speculation about that," I say softly.

"We'd dated, casually, for a short period." He waves a hand through the air. "You'd been gone a long time, and I was lonely—"

"You don't owe me an explanation."

"We were the talk of leprechaun society because if our houses merged, the empire we could create would be unprecedented. The Fausts rule transportation in Devashire, and we have manufacturing and adult entertainment. You can imagine the opportunities. It was my father's wet dream. He would have married her himself if she would have had him."

"Sounds like you had other plans."

"I wasn't interested. Not only was I not attracted to her, the idea of marrying someone only for the potential they offered to increase my wealth and power made my skin crawl. It's not who I am. I didn't love her. The more I got to know her, the less I even liked her. She's shrewd and completely focused on growing her empire. When I told her I would never marry her, she threatened to increase our shipping costs by sixty percent."

"She tried to extort marriage out of you? Psycho!"

He nods. "I told her she could do that, but then I'd be forced to go to the *Hatter* and reveal that she'd bought herself the diamond on her finger and that I'd never proposed. She decided to let it go."

"Fuck, that's messed up! Wait, but I saw you talking to her after graduation. It looked friendly."

"She wanted to know why I was there. Edmund was graduating, but I didn't have a child in the ceremony."

"What did you tell her?"

"That as a member of the school board, I like to attend to wish the best to the new class. It's not unheard of for me to be there."

"That's right. I forgot you did that."

"Still, she saw me sitting near you and speaking with you. I have a hard time believing that Edmund is an apple that has rolled far enough from the tree to be interested in Arden without any other ulterior motives."

I release a heavy sigh. It *is* suspect. "But Edmund doesn't know what she is. He doesn't know she's your daughter. What could he be using her for?" I shrug. "As far as he knows, she's a half-human pixie hybrid and a shopkeeper's granddaughter."

Seven scratches the side of his jaw and snorts. "She suspects I love you. We talked about it back then, when you were gone. Maybe not directly. I mean, I didn't share intimate details with her, but I talked about you. You came up in conversation. She suspects. And after the kiss and the job at the casino, I'm sure she's speculating that I still have feelings for you. She doesn't know that Arden is my daughter, thank the gods, but that doesn't matter. Getting close to Arden gets her close to you, and if she can get dirt on you, she can manipulate me."

"That's devious. She'd actually use her own son for something like that?"

"Most certainly."

I sit up and cross my legs in front of me, trying to center myself. Everything I've ever done, since the moment I found out I was pregnant with her, has been for Arden's benefit. I left Devashire to protect her from a society who would have pressured me to abort her. I stayed in America so she could have a normal human childhood. I came back to Devashire to protect her from the consequences when I was arrested. I would do anything for Arden, but she's not a baby anymore, and to keep doing things for our children that they can do for themselves is dysfunctional. My job as a parent is to make sure she can fly, to prepare her for leaving the nest, not to make her dependent on it.

"Arden is a smart girl. As clever as any teenager I've ever known. And she's strong and experienced in ways that most kids never have to be because they weren't raised surviving in a world where their very existence is against the law. She can handle herself with Edmund."

Seven works his jaw back and forth. "He's a leprechaun, Sophia. Enough luck can make her feel like she's in love."

"Yep. But you've taught her what luck can do. She knows what it feels like."

"What if he tries to manipulate her? What if he uses her?"

"She'll figure it out. And when she does, we'll be there to help her negotiate the fallout."

"We have to warn her." He rubs his palms on his thighs.

"We will. We absolutely will. But only as a side conversation, not like we're forbidding her or telling her what to do. The fact is, when we go public, when we tell people she's ours, she'll have to deal with the fallout on her own. We'll have each other to lean on, but we won't be able to protect her from it. Not completely. We have to start trusting that she's not a baby. We can help her, we can be there for her, we can try to show her the truth, but we can't make her choices for her."

He nods slowly. "I hate it, but I think you're right." He crawls across the bed to me and kneels in front of my crossed legs. "But if he hurts her, I'm going to cause every capillary in his body to rupture simultaneously. I won't kill him, but I will make sure he suffers." There is nothing flippant about his tone.

I grin. "Agreed. We'll take the little pissant out if he hurts her."

He kisses me soundly.

"When do you want to leave for Ashgate to interrogate your father?"

He stares down at me. "When you talked to Chance, did you think he gave you anything of value?"

"No. The riddle he spewed hasn't helped us at all. I think the torture he endured at Godmother's hand and the isolation has damaged his mind. Plus he asked to see you, made me promise to request that you go. Knowing Chance, that means he hoped for an opportunity to get his hooks into you. He tried to kill you before. Who's to say he'd be honest with you now?"

"I agree. So what if there was a way to deliver what Rayr-core wants and get Saul back without talking to him?" Seven has an idea, and the twinkle in his eye tells me it's going to be good.

"I'm listening."

CHAPTER

SEVENTEEN

S even holds a golden acorn, identical to the one he gave Arden, between his thumb and forefinger, its shell glinting in the fluorescent lights. He's handling the charm as if it's the One Ring. I almost expect him to murmur "my precious."

We're standing in his father's office in Dragonfly Casino, preserved as if Chance just moved out yesterday. A sleek desktop computer rests artfully in the corner of the desk with a pen and a notepad on the blotter in front of it. Bookshelves laden with professional-looking tomes line the walls, note-worthy sculptures breaking up the sets of expensive leather volumes.

Seven's brought an oversized briefcase from his place, and he sets it on the desk in front of us, then pops the top open.

"You gave one of those to Arden for her graduation. What is it?"

"A wish," he says solemnly.

"A wish? Like a genie-in-a-bottle-type wish?"

"Sort of. This is an acorn from a tree no longer in existence, one that had roots they say reached all the way to the cauldron, that mystical place from which it's said all fairies came. It will magnify the luck of any fairy that wields it, and with enough focus, the results are very nearly magic. The man I obtained this from claims that Godmother used one hundreds of years ago to increase her capacity for luck and power."

"Wait, have you told Arden about this? Does she know how dangerous it is?"

He nods. "Graduation night. I pulled her aside before I left your parents' house. She knows."

"Gods, Seven. Next time ask me before you hand our daughter a live grenade."

He snorts. "You can't deny she might need it, given the circumstances."

I can't argue with that logic. "Is that the plan then? Make yourself so strong you can charge into Rayrcore and tear Saul from their clutches?"

He smiles but shakes his head. "What Godmother did was extremely dangerous. This little charm packs big magic. Wish too big and it will drain your luck dry trying to fulfill that wish. Many have died, wishing beyond their capacities."

"Wait, Seven, why haven't you used this to break Godmother's hold over you?" How could he not have considered that first?

He frowns in my direction. "I have another one I've held back for that purpose. If I get desperate enough, I'll try it. But yes, I'm afraid. Breaking a fairy bargain without being released from it is said to be impossible. It's very probable that it will kill me before it works."

"So what's your plan with this one?"

"I think this situation calls for a bit more delicacy. Hand me that malivite."

"Would this be a bad time to remind you that we are only

assuming this is malivite?" I pinch above the bridge of my nose, a headache threatening. "River confirmed this was the stone clutched in Adam Barker's hand when he was shot, and it's logical that the stones Rayrcore is asking for are the same as this one. But we're making a mental leap there. They could be entirely disconnected events."

"I'm feeling lucky," Seven says with a wink, then grows serious. "The timing... I don't believe in coincidences. We are taking a risk but an educated one, and every moment matters if we want to get Saul back alive. Besides, I have a hunch that Hearst might not know what malivite looks like anyway."

"Huh?"

"I've been racking my brain, trying to think what motivation he would have to withhold the details I asked him for about the stones while he was torturing me. It occurred to me that he might not know. My dad was a master at giving just enough information to sell something. He used to tell me, 'Make no promises, Seven. Let them assume the promises. They can't hold you to assumptions.'"

"It doesn't matter if it's malivite or not, as long as he thinks it's malivite."

"Mm-hmm."

"Here's to educated guesses." I hand over the piece I recovered from where Adam Barker was murdered. He takes an ordinary rubber band from Chance's desk and wraps it around the stone, then places it inside the case. He pauses, the acorn resting in his palm. "You have no idea how much it pains me to use this charm. I only had three to begin with, and they're absolutely priceless."

"We could try Ashgate," I propose. "Or search your father's records."

He shakes his head. "I want to give them enough to get Saul back but not enough to use the malivite for whatever nefarious purposes they're planning. This is the only way to do that. Once Saul is home and safe, we can take our time figuring out the details."

"Then make your wish and let's do this." My palms are sweating, and I hug myself against a sudden chill.

Acorn in hand, he closes his eyes and his lips start to move. A wind picks up in the room, swirling around us, sending my hair thrashing against my face. Goose bumps erupt across my skin, and my stomach turns over with the gathering power. Under it all, I feel Seven's luck rise around us, only the fiery dragon that usually accompanies his use of luck is now enormous. I can barely breathe because it takes up every spare inch of space, and still I sense the room itself can't contain it. His luck is as big as the building, maybe bigger.

Clank. Clank. Clank. I peer into the belly of the case, in awe as the malivite reproduces, a stone sounding against stone with each additional piece that pops into existence. It spills into every corner, then reproduces until the case is full.

Seven opens his eyes. "We have our malivite."

I pick up one of the pieces and turn it in my fingers. It is identical to the original—same color, weight, and size. Seven fishes the original stone from the lot, still marked by the rubber band. "How long will the illusion last?"

"Forever. They're not an illusion. They're real."

I gape at the case as he closes it. "I thought the point of using the wish was to not give Rayrcore malivite."

"It is. There's only one actual piece of malivite in this case. The rest are look-alikes. Pretty gray stones with the chemical composition of concrete."

"Do you think they'll fall for it?"

Seven gives me a wry grin. "I think we're going to get lucky."

His phone chimes, and he peeks at the screen. "Hearst got

my message. He's meeting me in twenty minutes." He lifts the case and heads for the bookshelves at the back of the office.

"I'm coming with you." No way am I letting him go back there alone.

"Bad idea. These people are dangerous."

"Exactly why you need backup."

His fingers find a latch at the back of the frame, and the bookshelf swings open to reveal a small elevator, barely wide enough for two. He opens the cage and steps inside. The shelf starts to close.

As fast as I can move, I slip through the narrowing crack and press my chest against his, shoving him to the back of the compartment. The cage closes, and the bookcase seals us in. We begin to descend.

"Sophia..." Seven's cheek presses against mine. His breath softly brushes my ear as he says, "I want you to stay where it's safe. I couldn't stand it if anything happened to you."

"You know what? I can't remember the last time I was truly safe. But I can remember when I was happy. Now. Right here with you. If the choice is without you but safe or with you and in danger, I'll take my chances."

The elevator stops and the door opens. We're in a concrete vestibule. I exit the lift and find myself in a tunnel. We must be in the secret underground garage, but this section appears to only be accessible through Chance's old office.

"This is how they brought you back?"

"Not exactly." He leads me away from the exit, through a tunnel just big enough for a single car. It's a long and poorly lit walk until our surroundings transform. We reach a section that looks positively ancient. The ceiling is arched here and decorated with stone gargoyles and arcane symbols. I sense the ward before we reach it, like prickly burrs scraping my skin.

"It knows my blood. Take my hand." Seven's luck rises

around us, and the prickly sensation fades. He leads me under the arch.

I'm in a chamber that would be at home in an archaeological dig. Stone walls carved with ancient runes surround us, and in front of us, a giant mirror stretches across one wall. I squeeze Seven's hand, temporarily struck mute by the revelation. The silver undulates as if it's merely a pool and fish swim just under the surface. But those aren't fish, they're souls, and this mirror is no reflective surface, it's a portal.

"How?"

Seven swallows. "I don't know."

"And it leads to Rayrcore?"

"The garage under Rayrcore," Seven says.

But my mind can't reconcile that. "But Chance must have used this to get to his cabin the afternoon we confronted him. He had a mirror there. I saw it. Godmother said she delivered it to the hands of the guardians."

Seven's brow creases. "This is how they brought me back... but you're right. I don't know how these silvers work. The one we traveled through was a passageway between Devashire and Shadowvale, and we assumed that portal only went between those two places. Maybe they can be used to travel between any two mirrors?"

"I've never heard of such a thing."

He raises an eyebrow. "Why would we? The guardians own that knowledge."

"I don't like this, Seven. How do you know this can take us where we need to go and won't dump us somewhere else?"

"I don't. I'm hoping to get lucky."

I glare at him.

"There's no reason you can't stay here, Sophia. This is dangerous."

"We're in this together," I say firmly.

He sets down the malivite and lifts a long, hooked staff off the wall. The moment he does, symbols ignite across the stone bordering the silver.

"What language is that?" I've never seen anything like it in my life.

"Interesting. *That* is ancient leprechaun, and it says, 'Where the mind lies, there shall ye go.'"

"So you just think about where you want to travel and that's where it takes you?"

"Let's hope."

He dips the staff into the silver and stirs, muscles bunching with the effort. The silver swirls slowly at first and then picks up speed until it seems to shatter into a million spinning stars, a galaxy trapped in the spin cycle.

With a last grunt of effort, Seven casts the staff aside. I get an eye-popping view of it flying back into its cradle before he grabs my hand and pulls me and the stones into the tunnel. My feet hit a squishy floor as Seven lifts the stones from my grip and breaks into a sprint, tugging me forward. We're surrounded by galaxies of shimmering silver, stars that cascade on either side of us while whispers of the dead drift through the air around us. Unfortunately, I can clearly see them growing closer to our heads with every step. The tunnel is getting smaller!

Seven's luck tingles through my hand, and a rush of energy fills me. Ducking, I move faster. I see the light now too. It's dim but flickering like a candle in a dark room. We leap through the narrowing portal and land in a squat on a rough-hewn stone floor. The same breathlessness and disorientation I'd experienced before floods me, but Seven still has my hand and his luck bolsters me. I pant through it.

"You're late, Mr. Delaney," a raspy voice says.

I raise my head to see an elderly man in a black trench coat, his face deeply lined in a way that suggests he's never genuinely smiled. He bares his teeth and they're stained indigo—he's been drinking blue iron. *Fuck.* Our luck won't work directly on him. Beside him, three brutish-looking men with equally blue smiles surround Saul, whose skin is more bruised than not. He's unconscious and barely breathing.

"For a moment, I thought we might have to send your friend back to you in pieces."

CHAPTER

EIGHTEEN

"Hearst," Seven says through his teeth. "I have what you want. Give me Saul."

"Show me." Hearst points his chin toward the case.

Seven places it in front of him and enters the code to unlock it. As he lifts the lid, he slips his hand inside. He's finding the real malivite, slipping the rubber band off. He does it all so seamlessly. Hearst has no idea what he's dealing with when it comes to Seven. He's not his father. Yes, he's as powerful, but Seven has a heart, and that will always make all the difference.

He tosses the piece to Hearst and then turns the case around to show him the rest of the stones. Hearst pulls a magnifying lens from his pocket and inspects the stone.

"That's more than we agreed upon," Hearst says. "There will be no additional payment until our proof of concept."

I desperately want to know what that the concept is, but I keep my mouth shut. We're so close.

"Consider it an act of good faith," Seven says. "To make up for the misunderstanding."

Hearst nods. "Am I to assume then, that you'll be taking your father's place at the helm on this project while he's indisposed?"

Seven nods slowly, deliberately. That's right, don't say a word. Don't give him anything that might lead to a bargain. "Now give me Saul."

Hearst waves at his three goons, and they unchain Saul and dump him unceremoniously out of the chair.

I run to him and squat at his side, inspecting him for implanted blue iron. I don't find any, but the injuries at his wrists and ankles tell me he's been cuffed and chained with it. "He's clean."

Seven closes the case and pushes it across the stone toward Hearst, then joins me next to Saul.

Hearst lifts the case, a dark chuckle rumbling from his lungs. "Pleasure doing business with you, Delaney. I look forward to a *revolutionary* future."

Only when he's gone and we're alone in the room do I ask Seven, "What the hell does that mean?"

"I have no idea."

Saul groans.

"I'm going to have to carry him, Sophia. Do you think you can stir the silver?"

"There's only one way to find out." No part of me wants to remain in this room, which I realize with a start is in the United States. If Agent Donovan knew I was here, he'd have me strapped to a table in a rehabilitation center in no time. I shiver.

Lifting the staff from its hook, I plunge it into the silver the way I watched Seven do it and try to stir. Nothing happens. It's like trying to stir concrete. I pour on a little luck and throw my back into it, pushing with my legs. Slowly the staff starts to move. Very slowly. I circle it down and around, the push turning into a pull that reminds me of a rowing machine. I repeat the process—push, push, push, pull, pull, pull. My face breaks into a sweat, but the staff is moving faster now. Again and again, I stir until the silver itself gains momentum, carrying my strokes along with it.

"Now," Seven says, "concentrate on returning us the way we came."

I toss the staff aside and bound into the swirling stars, looking back only to confirm that Seven is following me, Saul over his shoulders in a fireman's carry. I race forward, mind picturing the room under the casino. It feels like I'm running into a hard wind. Every step is harder than the last. I'm sure the stars are going to collapse on my head before I can reach the other side when Seven pushes me hard from behind. I dive out of the tunnel and roll across the stone with a pained grunt.

Seven and Saul collapse beside me. The tunnel snaps closed behind us. I lay flat on my back, staring up at the stone ceiling. My head is pounding, and I'm covered in scrapes and scuffs. Seven doesn't look much better, and Saul is out again, barely breathing.

"What do you think Hearst meant about you taking over the helm?"

Seven taps the back of his head against the stone. "No clue, but it looks like I'll be visiting my father in Ashgate after all. I have questions, and he's the only one with answers."

THANK THE GODS THAT BY THE TIME SEVEN AND I ARE strong enough to stand, Saul has come to enough to carry some of his own weight. We put his arms around our shoulders and help him through the wards. Seven calls Jericho to pick us up, and we race him to Elderflame Hospital.

It's late by the time he's safely in a room. Besides being a mass of bruised flesh, Saul's got three broken bones: a shin, a clavicle, and an arm. The doctors are able to revive him long enough to tell him he's safe, and then he passes out again. We stay in the room while they set his bones, then hook him up to an IV drip of saline fortified with liquid luck. Eventually the doctors request we leave so he can rest.

"Is there someone we should call for him?" I ask Seven.

Seven rubs the back of his neck. "His mother. But I'll have to check with Human Resources for her contact information. Excuse me." He raises the phone to his ear and then pads toward the privacy of the stairwell.

I stand there, staring through the glass window into Saul's room, listening to the machine's beep and acknowledging the level of evil it must have taken to turn a leprechaun the size of Saul into the broken, black-and-blue blood bag in front of me. Gods, he looks like hell. But then we all do. My cuts and scrapes are many and healing slowly.

Still, any of us might be in that bed if things happened differently. Someone might have died. Life is short, even for us fae. I think about Arden then, about how our time together is sifting through our fingers. How things will have to change. How I won't be able to climb into bed with her like we used to and watch cheesy movies late into the night. I stare and stare at Saul, this man I don't know well but whom I liked a great deal, who'd guarded me and drove me places and shared about his own simple leprechaun life to make me feel better.

My hands start to shake. All the saliva dries up in my mouth, and my throat tightens. I feel an emotion building in my chest, and I know that if I give in to it, the barbed seed of regret will barrel up my throat. I swallow it down, tears flowing, and make up my mind not to waste a single minute more.

Seven returns, still looking at his phone in his hands. "She's on her way. I told her we were in an accident. I didn't know what else to say."

I launch myself at him, wrapping my arms around his neck and weeping into his chest.

"Shhh. Shhh. Sophia, what's wrong. What happened?"

All the words I want to say get twisted up in my brain, and the only thing that will come out is "I'm so tired."

He rubs my back. "Of course you are. We need to eat and rest. We haven't had anything since breakfast, and it's almost eight o'clock."

That must be why I'm not healing. I'm exhausted and hungry. But what I'm feeling right now is far more than all that.

Seven tucks my hair behind my ear. "Let's go back to my place and I'll fix you something."

I shake my head, clinging to him like he's the only thing keeping me from drowning. "No."

"No?"

He takes me gently by the shoulders and eases me off him so he can see my tearstained face. Out of the corner of my eye, I see a nurse give us a judgmental look, but I don't care. I might never let go of Seven again.

"Where do *you* want to go?" he asks me. "I'll take you anywhere. We can go to River's or one of the restaurants in Elderflame. Wherever you want. I'll clear the place out if you want me to."

I take a deep breath and look him in the eye. "I want to go to my parents' house, and after we eat, I want to tell them the truth."

"Tonight?" He looks down at our arms, covered in bruises and abrasions, then at my rumpled dress.

"What are we waiting for, Seven?" I step in closer and place my hands on his face. A few more nurses pass us and glance in our direction, but he doesn't push me away. "Arden's made her choice. We're here together, and for the moment we're alive and well. I don't know what the future holds. I don't know what's going on with your father or Hearst or anything else. All I know is, we've only got today, and I think it's time we told my family the whole truth. They should know before we announce it to the world."

He breathes a heavy sigh of relief, then pulls me into his arms, kissing me sweetly. "Finally. Yes. Tonight is the night."

Warmth spreads across my torso and grows so large that it turns the corners of my mouth up. I'm so happy I almost can't process it. My lips part as more tears start to fall.

He takes my hand, threading his fingers through mine. "Come on. Let's go relieve Jericho. I'll drive. We don't know exactly how this will go."

I nod. As we start walking to the car, I cough into my hand, and I can't stop the delicate purple seed that follows. Seven looks down at it curiously.

"You probably think its gross, but sometimes I can't control it."

He shakes his head. "Not gross. It's a pixie thing. It's part of you. I was just wondering... what emotion is it?"

I close my fist around the seed and give him a shaky smile. "Hope."

NINETEEN

The moment we set foot in my parents' home, we are bombarded by love. I've texted ahead to say Seven would be coming with me and to be prepared because we're a little beat up. Mom meets us at the door.

"Oh my," she says, glaring at our wounds with a worried frown. "Should I fetch the first aid kit?"

"No. We've come from the hospital. Nothing is bleeding, anymore," I say. "But we're both starving. Do you have anything left from dinner?"

She administers two careful hugs. "Who do you think you're talking to, Sophia? No one leaves this house unfed." She ushers us toward the breakfast nook where she has sandwiches and cookies waiting.

"Oh, Mom, thank you." I actually tear up as I bite into a ham and cheese.

"There's lemonade there too, although you two look like you might need something stronger."

"Definitely," Seven murmurs around a bite. "Please, Mrs. Larkspur."

She nods once, darts into the kitchen, and comes back with a bottle of vodka still frosty from the freezer. I pour a shot into my lemonade and then into Seven's.

"Are you sure you don't need anything else? Bandages? Painkillers?" she asks softly.

"No," I assure her. "We're fine. Just scraped up a bit."

"Good. Then Seven, I'd like you to tell me why my daughter looks like she's been in a fight and why you didn't protect her." An unmistakable edge has crept into her voice that makes both of us sit up straighter.

"It's a long story, Mom, and we only want to tell it once, so you can invite Grandma and the rest of them in here."

My grandmother pops out from behind the door to the living room as if she's been waiting there listening and beams like she won the lottery. "I thought you'd never ask!"

She smooths the skirt of her metallic blue gown and tucks herself into the chair across from Seven, resting her chin in her palm.

I narrow my eyes on her. "Do you actually still live in Sunnyville?"

"It's where they deliver my mail, darling. Now, you were saying?"

"Wait. I want to hear this." Dad enters the room from the kitchen.

"Where's Arden?" I ask.

"Out with Edmund again. I think they were going skating in Winter Wonderland," Dad says.

A wave of nostalgia hits me as I remember what it was like to go ice-skating or sledding in the small section of Wonderland where it always snows but is never cold. I haven't been there since I was a child. I hope Arden loves it.

"All right. I'll talk to her later," I say softly. Arden already knows Seven and I are a couple, but I don't want my family to feel bad that I'm just telling them now, so I leave it at that.

"But you're going to tell the rest of us now, right?" Grandma asks enthusiastically.

"Yes." I turn toward Seven, but he motions with his head as if to say *it's your family. You do the talking.*

Across the table, three pairs of eyes stare at me expectantly. I take a deep breath and just say it. "Seven and I are together again. We're going to take our relationship public. And he's Arden's father."

Grandma's gasp fills the room, but my parents' silence is more concerning. I start to explain. I tell them about Godmother and her bargain with Seven and how none of us knew until Arden and I returned to Dragonfly. I talk about working together and the kiss being real, and how what happened at the Yule ball was all Chance's doing. I only stop when it's clear I'm vomiting words, some of which don't even make sense anymore.

I close my mouth. We all stare at each other, silence cloaking us in its weighty blanket.

Seven clears his throat. "I love your daughter," he says to my father. "And your granddaughter. I want to present them both to leprechaun society at the Gilded Gala, Sophia on my arm as my date and Arden as my daughter and debutante. With your blessing, of course."

My parents say nothing. I think they're speechless. But my grandmother's face goes deadly serious. It's the first time I've ever seen her look worried since I've been back.

"Do you know what you're getting yourselves into going public?" she asks. "I like you, Seven. I've always liked you, and I've suspected for a long time that there was more going on between you two than you were letting on. Sophia's feelings for you have been clear to me since you were children." She gives a raspy laugh. "But relationships like yours aren't a common thing in Devashire. I don't have to tell you that. People will talk. People will always talk. But revealing a serious relationship at the Gilded Gala? It's going to be a nuclear bomb. The gala is televised around the world! The *Daily Hatter* will want interviews. The gossip columns will all comment on it. Social media will overflow with vitriol. Sure, you'll have some supporters, your bravery might be celebrated at first, but many more will hope to see your relationship fail to prove it's unnatural... Impossible."

"It's not impossible," Seven says bitterly. "I love her. I've loved her since we were six years old."

Grandma nods, her eyes going teary. "Yes, you have. Sometimes wars are worth fighting, and if you choose to take up your sword on this, I'm behind you all the way. I'm an old woman. I have very little to lose. But make no mistake, both of you, this will be a war. You, Seven, are attempting to elevate a pixie to your status, and if there's one thing that has been treated as sacrosanct among leprechauns, it is their higher status. Your contemporaries will fear that your relationship won't be the last. They'll fear an erosion of wealth to the lower classes, a loss of privilege and prestige. Fear can turn people into monsters. Do what you must, but sharpen your weapons. The beasts will come."

My father finds his voice. "Betty is right. I don't think anyone at this table is surprised by your relationship." His eyebrows lift. "But you have to know going public will change everything. For all of us."

His words force an icy weight of anxiety in my chest. "You're right. It will affect you too. I can't help that."

"Unless you kept it a secret," Mom says. "Why not continue as you have? Now that we know, we can help you."

I sense Seven tense beside me, and when I look over, his jaw is clenched tight. My heart thumps in my chest. I rest both hands flat on the counter, releasing a giant breath. "I'm sorry if this is disappointing to you. I am thirty-four years old, a grown pixie. I've spent the past sixteen years pretending to be something I'm not, living among people who could never truly know me, spending my days wrapped in deception and my nights terrified of being found out. I did that to protect Arden and myself, and in some ways, it protected you as well. I bore the burden of being no one, of living a pretend existence, for so long. Too long. I can't do it anymore, and with Arden staying, it's to her advantage for the world to know she's leprechaun. When that happens, it's going to get hard for us anyway. It won't be that much harder when the world finds out her mother and her father love each other."

"You hope," Mom says.

I nod. "I do. For many things. We can't control what happens. My hopes and dreams may be ridiculous, but I'm going to do everything in my power to make them come true. Grandma called this going to war. I'm willing to fight. I don't want to hide who I am or who I love anymore." I pause for a moment, dreading what has to come next. I stare at a spot on the table as I say, "But I understand if you want no part in it. I can move out. You can distance yourselves from me, deny that you know anything. Eventually they'll leave you alone."

My mom's hand lands on top of mine. "Not for all the luck in the kingdom. We are in this together."

Dad places his hand on top of Mom's. "If we're going to war, I plan to start sharpening my arrows. Gods help anyone who hurts you."

Grandma laughs wickedly. "You know I'm in! I wouldn't miss it for the world. I live for this shit."

Seven leans back in his chair and threads his fingers across his bottom ribs. "Then it looks like you need to pick out a gold dress, Sophia. You're going to the ball."

Grandma nods and murmurs, "Hurrah!"

"There's just one thing I don't understand," Mom says. "Why are you covered in blood?"

THE NEXT DAY, SEVEN AND I DECIDE TO DIVIDE AND conquer. Since only one person can enter Ashgate at a time, he plans to go interrogate his father without me. Meanwhile, I journey to River's house to feed Jinx and then head back to the safe house to bring him more groceries and give him an update on what's happened.

When I knock, no one answers. I knock again, picturing River on the back porch, as lonely and depressed as the last time I'd seen him. I use my key to let myself in.

"Hello?"

A scuffle of sounds comes from the bedroom. The rustle of bedding. The thump of feet on the floor. Low cursing when something glass is knocked over.

"River?" I call, laughing a little.

A moment later he appears in the bedroom door in a pair of gray sweats and nothing else, his hair suspiciously tousled around his horns. "Sophia, thanks for coming!" He embraces me in one of his warm River hugs and takes the groceries from my arms.

"Is that who I think it is?" I gesture an eyebrow toward the bedroom door.

He smirks. "Who else could it be?"

"Someone you met in the woods and charmed out of their pants."

His laugh is deep and rich. "No. There are only two people in the world I want to charm out of their pants."

My brows inch up a little farther. "Both Patrick and Eva are here?"

He nods. "Just Eva right now. We broke the bargain, then sealed it with a kiss. Patrick left earlier this morning for work."

"You've been 'breaking the bargain' for..." I look at my watch. "A day and a half."

His smirk grows more pronounced. "Mm-hmm."

I don't know what to say, so I mouth, *daaaamn.*

Eva appears a moment later, looking remarkably put together for someone who's spent the past thirty hours or so in bed with two satyrs. In fact, her color is back. Her red hair shines like silk, and her emerald eyes twinkle. She adjusts her navy wrap dress as she clicks across the room to us on a pair of stunning Louboutin pumps. She kisses River on the cheek.

"Hi Sophia," she says shyly.

"Hi." I glance between them both. There's obvious affection on River's face, and I've never seen Eva happier. "So now that the bargain is broken, can you finally tell me what you saw that day?"

Eva nods, growing serious. "I used my luck to clear the area around River's restaurant so that I could speak to him without anyone seeing us. It wasn't hard because so many people were distracted with the graduation. Still, to be safe, we met behind his restaurant. All I wanted was to steal a kiss and tell him I was letting myself into his house to get the coat I forgot the night before. But then we heard the shot and the scream."

River strokes a hand down the back of her head. "I ran around the building and saw a man on the walkway with a bloody hole in his chest. I immediately rushed to him, knelt down, and put pressure on the wound."

"Is that when you moved the gun?"

"I don't remember any gun," River says bitterly.

"And I don't either," Eva adds.

They look at each other as if they've just put it all together.

"But Godmother says your prints were on the murder weapon."

River nods. "She told me that, and I assumed I must have moved it without even thinking when I knelt down. But I don't remember that, Sophia. I never consciously saw a gun until Godmother and her team arrived. I was too focused on the bleeding human in front of me."

A dark pit forms in my stomach. We all know River was framed, but by whom? "The gun was there," I confirm, remembering it clearly a foot or two from River's knee. "Eva, did you see anyone ditch the gun?"

She shakes her head. "When I came around the corner, all I saw was River and the victim, but that's what's weird about the whole thing. I was using my luck to clear the area. So both the victim and the murderer must have been immune to it."

"River, were Adam's teeth blue?"

River snorts. "I don't think I ever saw his teeth, to be honest."

"You think he was on blue iron?" Eva asks.

"Must have been if he resisted your luck, right?" I cross my arms against a growing sense of dread. None of this is adding up. If the murderer left the gun near the body, where did they go so quickly?

Eva nods. "I did notice one other thing, but it's not infallible."

"I'll take anything you've got at this point."

"I *sensed* someone."

"Hmm?"

River puts a supportive arm around Eva's shoulders, and she glances up at him before she continues. "I had my luck up, and I sensed another fae's luck nearby... from the direction of the bank. I sensed there was someone else there, but I couldn't see them."

"What did their luck feel like?"

She sighed. "A spider. Giant and dark. The signature left me cold. The thing is, it might have nothing to do with the murder. It's completely possible that someone just shielded themselves with luck when they heard the shot."

"How strong was it? Another leprechaun could have neutralized your luck just as well as blue iron."

"It could have been a leprechaun, but I didn't recognize the signature. It was strong but different. I'm not sure if that was due to distance or something else."

Strong but different. I shake my head. Maybe a leprechaun. Maybe a pixie or satyr amplifying their luck with a charm. That would be rare, but I'm not ruling anything out at this point.

"I'm still struggling with how the gun got there though. Someone had to leave it behind after the murder." I try to think back to the crime scene and find my memory sketchy on the subject. Godmother was there so fast and cleaned everything up so thoroughly I never got close enough to really inspect the scene. Was there blood spray? In what direction? Is it possible the murderer shot Adam from behind the bank? But then how did the gun get to its spot beside River? I keep coming back to that point, and it's starting to hurt my head thinking about it. Seven was closer. I'll have to ask him what he remembers.

"The one thing all of us know for sure is that River didn't do this. So how do we prove that and get him out of here?"

Eva sighs. "I plan to go to Godmother and tell her what I know."

I cross my arms against a sense of unease at the thought. "Do you think you'll have better luck than I did? I don't think she cares about the truth as much as she wants a scapegoat. Her ego is everything. She'll never admit to a mistake unless there's undeniable proof."

"We've *got* to do something." Eva threads her fingers into River's and slants him a pitying look.

I study them both, desperate for an answer that seems just out of reach. "There are a few details I want to run down. Can you both wait a few days?"

"Depends. What kind of details are you talking about?" River asks.

"Now that I have Eva's perspective, I want to rewatch the security video for more clues. And then I want to do some research into which leprechauns have a luck aura that feels like a spider."

Eva snorts. "How do you plan to do that?"

Eva's phone vibrates, interrupting our conversation. She taps the screen, then turns wide eyes on me. "Why is my brother texting me about finding you an outfit for the Gilded Gala?"

"What better place to meet a few leprechauns?" I grin.

Her mouth drops open. Luck is a strange and wonderful thing.

CHAPTER
TWENTY

Once Evangeline came down from the surprise that I was attending the Gilded Gala on Seven's arm, she was quick to offer her help with styling Arden and me for the event, which, as it turns out, is a far more complicated endeavor than what I expected.

"It's not just that it has to be gold, you two. This year's event is a masquerade! Everyone's outfit will be designed to represent a historical or literary figure. It will take a hell of a lot of luck and influence to have anything ready on time. People have been planning their apparel for months. Some since the last gala!"

I glance at Arden, but she's glued to her phone. Texting Edmund, no doubt. I haven't had a moment alone with her in days. She's been with him every waking minute.

"Are you sure we'll be able to find something appropriate?" I ask.

She flashes an adorably mischievous grin. "Seven has made sure of it."

Jericho parks in front of a glass tower in Elderflame, and

Eva leads me up the elevator to the twenty-fifth floor where a svelte black satyr with gracefully polished horns and a bespoke suit meets us at the door. He's a beautiful man, not just handsome but pretty, with perfect skin and enviable posture.

"Ms. Larkspur, I presume. Valentine Sullivan at your service."

Valentine bows slightly at the waist, and I am struck again by his grace and keen fashion sense, at the way the fabric of his suit reacts to his movement. It's breathtaking, like the man is wearing a silk waterfall.

"Thank you for helping us on such short notice," I say.

A smile dances across his face, bringing out dimples in his cheeks. "You must know that Mr. Delaney is a very good customer. What he wants, he gets. It appears he wants the two of you dressed for the gala, and I have strict orders to make sure every eye is on you."

Eva slides her hands into her pockets. "I'm not sure my brother understands what goes into a gala gown. We'll be happy with anything you can do for us."

Valentine snorts and couples his perfectly manicured hands. "Not what I can do but what I have done. Follow me."

"Arden!" I elbow her in the arm and gesture for her to put her phone away.

"It's Edmund. We're just making plans for dinner. I'm supposed to meet his mom," she whispers as she falls into step behind Valentine.

I close my eyes for a beat. I've put off this conversation far too long. "About that, there's something I need to tell you—"

"Here we are," Valentine says, gesturing toward three chairs as music starts to play. I lower myself into one of them. "We'll start with our sweet Arden. My designers and I stayed up all night preparing three prototypes for you. Come in, girls."

Three gorgeous young pixies stride into the room, only

they've used their illusion to make themselves look exactly like Arden. They approach, turn, walk away. One is in a mermaid gown designed to give the impression of a golden toga, another in a dress with bell sleeves and lace that belongs on an eighteenth-century British queen, and the third wears a delicate, sleeveless wrap dress cinched at the waist by a thick band of gold metal. Two gold bracers cover her forearms, and an ornate golden mask depicting leaves and branches with two golden stag horns rises from her temples. A coordinating bow and quiver of arrows completes the outfit.

Valentine gestures proudly at the three. "I give you Persephone, Queen Anne of the humans, and, my personal favorite, Artemis, goddess of the hunt."

"Holy crap," Arden says softly. "Is that really what I look like from behind?"

I chuckle. "Yes, and everyone should be so lucky. What do you think?"

She stares, open mouthed, at each model. "I can't stop looking at Artemis. Can I try it on?"

Valentine makes a show of taking her hand and the hand of the Artemis model and leading them both to a set of changing rooms. They disappear inside.

"I love when my patrons are so easily suited," Valentine says. "Now, Ms. Larkspur, you were a bit more difficult. I wanted to capture the femininity of your pixie blood but also the inner fire and courage that allowed you to survive so long outside our world." He claps his hands, and I watch three more models walk into the room. They look exactly like me, and I suddenly understand why Arden found this unsettling.

The first outfit is made to resemble armor but in a formfitting dress. It comes with a helmetlike mask with wings along the side. "For you, to fortify you against what promises to be a trying evening, I give you a Valkyrie."

"Oooh," Eva says. "You could be a warrior."

"I don't feel like a warrior," I say honestly.

The next model strides forward, dressed in another toga-like dress with a mask to make her look like an owl. Valentine spreads his hands. "Athena, goddess of wisdom."

I smile. It is beautiful but not really me.

The next model takes my breath away. The lining of the strapless princess dress is midnight-blue silk, but it's covered in a layer of tulle embroidered with tiny cascading gold stars, each with a tiny diamond sewn into its center. An asymmetrical, gold filigree laser-cut mask decorated with diamonds perches delicately on the nose of the model. But the best part of the ensemble is the crown of dark crystals on her head, illuminated by hidden lights.

"Oh," I say, hand splaying across my chest. "That's beautiful."

Eva gapes. "Valentine, you have outdone yourself."

"Titania, Shakespeare's queen of fairies, here displaying her rule over the stars. I believe it will suit you."

I stand. "I'd like to try it."

Valentine's smile lights up the room. Twenty minutes later, Arden and I stand on a small platform in front of a large three-way mirror, expertly pinned into our dresses and assessing our new looks.

"What do you think?" I ask Arden. She is a convincing goddess, the highlights in her auburn hair drawn out by the gold metal mask.

"I love it. But Mom, you look stunning. I still can't believe you and Seven are back together again, but any man alive would stop in his tracks if he saw you."

I smile at her. I've spent a little luck to make my hair darker and my teeth whiter to complete the look, but honestly, the dress itself is so flattering I don't have to do much.

"The dress is designed to accommodate your wings," Valentine says. "I confess, I've rarely had opportunity to design for a pixie, but I am pleased with the results."

I pivot on my gold stilettos and smile down at Eva. "What do you think?"

"I think fifty percent of the attendees at the Gilded Gala are going to be hot and bothered by the two of you, and the other fifty percent are going to have a jealous meltdown. You *must* have that dress, Sophia."

I release a deep breath and look toward Valentine. "How much do I owe you?" I'm sure I can't afford these dresses, but maybe I can rent them for the night.

Valentine spreads his hands. "Mr. Delaney has already taken care of it, Ms. Larkspur. Now, if you don't mind changing, I'll have the dresses tailored and brought to the address of your choosing by the end of the week."

I MEET SEVEN BACK AT HIS PLACE THAT NIGHT. HIS FACE lights up when he sees me. It's easier now that my parents and Arden know about our relationship, and I happily throw myself into his arms.

"Thank you for the dress," I whisper.

I feel him smile against the side of my neck. "I can't wait to see you in it."

Luck coils around me, and I inhale sharply at the pulse that sizzles in my blood. But I shake my head and push him away. "Uh-uh. If we start this, we'll be distracted for the rest of the night."

He looks at me through his lashes, his tongue grazing his bottom lip. "Sounds good to me."

I place a hand on the center of his chest. "First tell me how it went with your father."

With a groan, he turns from me and mumbles something about needing a drink. He pours himself one at the bar, then holds up an empty glass in lieu of asking me what I'd like.

"Vodka and tonic."

He fixes me the drink and hands it over.

"Did you get him to talk?"

"The problem wasn't getting him to talk." Seven sips his bourbon. "The problem was that what he said made no sense, and when he said it, he was entirely naked and writing on the walls in his own blood."

I scowl. "I had a similar experience. So he didn't tell you anything about Rayrcore or where the malivite mine is?"

"He told me that it was my holy duty to bulldoze the wall and free the unseelie."

I squint at him. "What now?"

"Exactly what he said. 'Walls. There are too many walls, Seven. Too many rules. Tear it all down. Let the strongest survive. We are the strongest.'" He does an uncanny imitation of his father's voice, and I shiver at the accuracy.

Blinking away my confusion, I ask, "And this has what to do with Rayrcore?"

He snorts. "Absolutely nothing. I learned nothing about the mine or the malivite. I recorded our interaction if you'd like to watch it. There's an especially poignant moment where he takes a piss in the corner of his cell while he's talking to me."

"Eww. No, thanks. I trust your assessment."

He takes another long drink. "How'd it go with River?"

I straighten, feeling all the blood drain from my face. "There's something I have to tell you. Only maybe I shouldn't. It isn't really my story to tell. But it does relate to this and to you and I did find out here, while you were in with your doctor."

He sits down in the chair across from me and runs his fingers through his hair. "I give you full immunity. I will not shoot the messenger."

"It's not that... It's just..."

Seven arches one brow at me. This is important. Sorry Eva, I need his help if we're going to save River and that means he needs to know now. "Your sister was the third," I blurt.

His eyes narrow to slits. "Third what?"

"Eva was the one with River the morning of the murder. She's the one who made the bargain and why River couldn't say her name. She's broken the bargain now and is prepared to tell Godmother the truth to free him."

Seven's eyes widen. He crosses an ankle over one knee. "My sister is having an affair with two satyrs?"

I nod slowly. "River and Patrick. More than an affair, I think. I met with Eva and River today, and they seemed happy. I believe they have genuine feelings for each other."

Seven's lips press together. "I'm not sure what to think about that."

"Maybe you should talk to her about it."

"I plan to." He swallows hard. "While I'm processing that bombshell, did either of them have any clue about who actually murdered Adam Barker?"

"Not exactly, but Eva said she felt someone's power, probably a leprechaun. Their luck signature was a massive dark spider. She sensed them standing behind the wall of the bank. Do you know anyone who fits that description?"

Threading his fingers, he tenses, leaning forward in his chair. "Maybe. There are a few people who have dark insect-like energy."

"You were there before I was. Did the blood from the victim spray away from that direction?"

He thinks for a minute, then rubs the back of his neck. "You know, the only blood I remember was all over River."

"But the man was shot."

"Godmother cleaned up that crime scene so quickly. It's possible she hid the blood. Equally possible the bullet didn't go all the way though him."

"If that's true, it means we have further proof that River is innocent. The gun was found next to him, but a shot at close range would have gone through the victim."

"Maybe he shot Adam from a distance and then ran to his side with the gun."

"Why would anyone do that?"

"I don't know. I'm just preparing you for what Godmother might say. She's going to use any excuse not to free River."

"If the shot was taken at a distance, it's highly likely the murderer is the fae whose luck manifests as a spider. I don't know how the gun got to River's side, but I do know there's something here. We're close. Can you look at Godmother's records and see what the coroner found out? If the bullet entered at an angle that supports it being fired from behind the bank, we'll have even more evidence to free him."

"I'll do one better. I'll check the surveillance video for that side of the bank. Maybe we'll get lucky and whoever tampered with the security system was so focused on the body they forgot the cameras around the bank."

I inhale sharply. "No. Even if they did remember to wipe those cameras too, that proves they were covering something that happened there, which also proves River's innocence."

Seven nods, then leans his head back on the chair and stares at the ceiling. "We should go down to the security office now and review the video."

He's dressed in slacks and a work shirt, although his suit jacket and tie are strewn across the back of the sofa. The neck of his shirt is open, and I can see the scar where the doctor stitched him up following Rayrcore's torture. He's barely healed, and it's clear the events of the day have wrung him out. "You look exhausted, Seven. We have time."

He sighs. "We don't. There's a murderer on the loose. We should check on Saul. See if he's awake. Maybe he heard something about Rayrcore's motives while he was being held captive. And we haven't even touched on what we should tell Godmother about this mess. She's going to want a status update soon."

I stand. "All of that will still be there in an hour."

Seven closes his eyes. When he speaks, his voice is strained. "I know you don't want to hear this, Sophia, but you should really think twice about this weekend. All this shit, it isn't going away once we go public. Godmother still *owns* me. People are going to harass us. If they find out about Eva, the entire Delaney family name is going to be smeared across the gossip columns." His throat bobs on a hard swallow, and a muscle in his jaw twitches. "You should get out now. What if you change your mind about me? What if your feelings change but it's too late because you've already been caught up in this gilded machine I was born into?"

"What if I leave you when you're at your most vulnerable?"

His body clenches like I've hit him in the gut, and his eyes pop open. I've poked a sore spot that needs to be poked. His mother abandoned him to his abusive father, but I'm not them.

"I'd forgive you, Sophia. I couldn't blame you. I really couldn't." A dark cloud passes over his expression, his fingers digging into the arm of the chair. I've never seen a man drawn limb from limb, but he's doing a fantastic impression. He might come apart at any moment. "My family is a fucking mess. This thing with Godmother is a curse. Leprechaun society is a scourge. I love you too much to see your life ruined because of me. I love you enough to let you go."

My heart gives an anguished thump at the thought, and I cross the living room to stand between his knees. Nothing is going to tear me from this man, not even him.

I lean over and place my hands on his thighs. "There's a problem with that plan."

He looks at me with an intensity that seems to cut straight to my soul. "What's that?"

"I love you. And see, I know what it's like to live with you and without you, and I choose with you even if that means we have to build a castle with a moat and we only lower the drawbridge for nice people who are supportive of our relationship."

"A castle?" He gives a breathy laugh.

"Yes, a castle is what we need. I'll be like Cinderella with her prince at the ball every night for the rest of my life."

"You know what they never tell you about Cinderella?"

Lots of things. I've been pondering the failings of fairy tales for some time now, but I'm curious what he thinks, so I ask, "What?"

"They never talk about how the townspeople treat her once she marries the prince. She has to rule over her wicked stepmother and stepsisters, who probably gossip about her all over town. After the wedding, when the glass slippers are packed away, you've got to wonder what happened to her. She wasn't born to be a princess, and being royalty isn't always what it's cracked up to be. What if meeting the prince wasn't the answer to a wish but a curse?"

I smile down at him, my beautiful, damaged, and selfless man, and I tell him the conclusion I've come to about these tales. "They do tell you the end of the story, Seven. *They both live happily ever after*, and it's not because it's easy or that

Cinderella magically knows how to be a royal. It's not because there are no bumps in the road. They live happily ever after because they're together, and in the end, that's all that matters. Life will always be hard. People will always be cruel. But love and family, it's priceless."

His hands sweep under my skirt and land on the back of my thighs. "I don't deserve you."

I unzip my dress, step out of it, and kick it to the side. "No, you don't," I say through a smirk. I lower myself to my knees and reach for his fly. "But I keep you around for your giant cock."

"Sophia... I'm serious—" His words are choked off by a distinctly male sound as I make short work of his button and zipper and take his dick in my hands. He's already hard, looking down at me with a soul-deep vulnerability. I wonder how long it took him to work up the courage to try to convince me to leave him. I wonder how long it will take me to convince him I'll never go.

I tighten my grip around the base of his shaft and slowly swirl my tongue around the head. His thighs clench and his stomach tenses beneath his shirt. It's a power trip. I work my fingers lower to play with his balls, then leisurely lick from base to tip, adding a swirl of my tongue over the crown again where I know he's most sensitive. His breath quickens, but he doesn't move. I do it again, adding the slightest bit of suction at the tip.

He groans. "Gods, Sophia..."

I stare up into his eyes as I take one more languid lick and then suck him deep into my mouth, repositioning myself until he's all the way to the back of my throat. This time that sound turns into a growl. His fingers claw the back of my head, gathering my hair into his grip so he can watch me. *Good.*

Taking him deep again and again, I suck harder, move my tongue up and down his cock. His grip tightens at the back of my head, and then he finally starts to move, thrusting hard and quick into my mouth. His luck rises in the room, tingling hot against my skin, between my breasts, between my legs. It draws my nipples to tight peaks beneath the silk of my bra.

"You're fucking mine," he says between thrusts, his voice taking on a commanding edge. "Your hot little mouth will never touch another cock, you understand?"

I suck harder in answer and groan as he hits the back of my throat. I'm so hot and wound up I reach between my legs and play with myself as his luck rushes through me. The sight must be enough to push him over the edge because his grip on me tightens and he erupts inside my mouth without warning.

I swallow everything he gives me, my own pleasure building as his luck fills me with hot, vibrating energy. He only lets go of me when I've taken all he has to give. Tugging on my hair, he pulls my mouth off his cock and I pant up at him, eyeing him wickedly.

"Whose are you?" he demands.

"Yours." I wipe my thumb under my bottom lip and spread my knees wider on the carpet. "Always."

He makes a strangled sound, then pushes me until my back hits the carpet. My panties are off in a heartbeat, and the next second, his tongue is licking up my center. Only it isn't just his tongue—hot currents of luck are buzzing inside me like the world's best vibrator. One hand splays across my lower abdomen as the other joins in on the fun. He works one long finger inside me, then two, rubbing circles in just the right place, his breath hot against my clit.

A storm is gathering inside me, low and heavy in my torso. I pant through the intensity, arching against his mouth. "More."

I grab his head and press him into me. He doesn't disappoint.

The orgasm rips through me like a stroke of lightning, but it doesn't stop. His luck chases it, driving it higher. My head is tipped back and I'm blinded by pleasure when he enters me, pitching me over the edge again. His fingers dig into my hips, holding me as he thrusts into my clenching pussy.

"Don't forget you chose this," he grits out. "There's no going back."

I wrap my arms and legs around him as he empties himself into me again, and my body decides to reward me with yet another mind-blowing orgasm. I'm so high I think I might never come down. Slowly, like two feathers dropped from a height, we both return to earth.

"Fuck, that was intense," he says, rising so he can look at me.

"Yeah, it was. And I loved every minute of it."

"Good, because I predict it's going to happen frequently in the future."

I reach up to toy with a strand of his hair. "What makes you so sure?"

He strokes the side of my face. "We're going to need something to do in our castle."

TWENTY-ONE

On the night of the Gilded Gala, I emerge from Seven's room dressed in my perfectly tailored gown and carrying my mask. Valentine was right—this may be the only dress that could make me feel confident tonight. I feel like a queen and I stand up straighter, the weight of the crown light on my head.

Seven stops in his tracks when he sees me, his eyes trailing over me. "Gods, Sophia, I have half a mind to tell Jericho we won't need the car after all." He steps in close and grips my chin, running his thumb just under my pouty red lips. "The things I'd like to do to that hot little mouth."

"You'll smear my lipstick." I give him a wink.

"Oh, if that's your concern, there are plenty of things I can think of to do to you that don't involve your mouth." A firm, hot tingle runs up my inner thigh and settles between my legs.

"Seven," I say breathlessly, my hand rising to hold my crown in place as my knees threaten to give out. "Control yourself!"

The tingle stops, and he brushes a hand down his sleeve. "For now."

"You look incredible by the way." He's opted for a velvet tuxedo in midnight blue that matches the bodice of my dress, with a white vest and tie. Understated by Gilded Gala standards, except that all his trimmings are gold. His watch, his cuff links, the buttons on his shirt, and—most importantly—his mask, which is entirely gold and includes a helmet with two impressive horns. "Loki seems appropriate. You're about to pull the trick of the century."

He slants an impish smile. "You picked up on that, huh? Perfectly choreographed leprechaun society is about to go down in flames and topple into chaos. I think we should try to enjoy it. Loki and Titania seem perfectly appropriate. Thank you, Valentine." He smiles and leans forward to place a kiss on my cheek.

We pull apart when the door to the guest room opens and Arden strides toward us, looking like the living, breathing manifestation of Artemis. She's left her auburn hair down in loose waves that gather at her shoulders, but her makeup is exquisite and Valentine's filmy gold dress hugs her body like a whisper.

Seven groans.

"What's wrong with you?" Arden asks.

"Just wondering why I trusted Valentine," he says through his teeth, eyes rolling.

I chuckle. "He thinks you look lovely, Arden."

A tight smile spreads his lips. "Yes, lovely. Are you cold? I can fetch a sweater."

"Not even a little bit," she says through a laugh.

"Did you bring the wish?" he asks, smile fading.

"Yeah." She moves her hair aside to expose the gold acorn at her throat. "Although, based on how powerful the two of you say it is, I hope I don't have to use it."

I run my fingers over the coin at my neck. "It's only for emergencies. Rayrcore isn't going to be happy when they discover we've tricked them, and this is a very public event. We'll be exposed. Seven and I will both feel more comfortable if you have it with you."

Seven slides his hands into the pockets of his jacket. "It just amplifies your luck with a little magic, Arden. It works the same as we've practiced. Focus your intention, hold it against your skin, and the wish will do the rest. Only if you need it, and keep the wish small so you don't drain yourself."

She cracks her neck. "We're really doing this then? I'm going to be introduced as a leprechaun tonight?"

I look between the two great loves of my life and nod. "We are."

Moments later, we're all in the back of Seven's car, headed for the hotel.

As sure as I am about going public with our relationship, my stomach is a ball of nerves. "All right, I'm a little excited for this, come what may. As long as we're together as a family, it will be all right."

Arden shifts in her seat beside me. "I guess this is a good time to tell you both that I've already broken the news to Edmund."

I stiffen. "You did what? I thought we agreed we were all keeping this a secret before today?"

"I couldn't have him find out at the gala." She spreads her hands. "We're in love. What kind of person would I be if I sprang this on him in that setting?"

All levity drains from Seven's expression. "Does his mother know?"

She shrugs, her emerald eyes flashing. "I told him not to tell anyone, but I mean, it's possible." She folds her arms. "What's the big deal anyway? Everyone is going to know in about ten minutes."

Seven sighs. "It probably doesn't matter, Arden, but you need to understand that Edmund's mother and I have a history."

She nods. "You used to be engaged to her. She told me."

I widen my eyes at her. "What exactly did she say?"

Arden shrugs. "Just that she knew you worked for Seven and that she and Seven had been engaged in the past until you both decided to break it off. That's it."

Both decided. What a creative memory Alicia has.

"Be careful with her, Arden. She's not what she seems," Seven says.

Arden bristles. "Mrs. Faust has been nothing but nice to me, and I like her. I want to be with Edmund, and that means getting along with his family. Whatever went on between you, it's in the past, right?"

There's an edge to Arden's voice, and I watch Seven's jaw harden against it.

The sound of cheering grabs our attention, and we all look out the tinted windows. Thanks to special approval by Godmother, Jericho is able to drive us right up to the edge of the rainbow carpet.

"We'll talk about this later," Seven says.

Arden shoots him a look that makes it clear the conversation is over as far as she's concerned.

"Arden," I say quickly. "There's more to this than you think. The Fausts have a history."

"We're here," Seven says. "Masks."

I tie on my Titania mask and help Arden to do hers. The door opens. Mask in place, Seven steps from the vehicle to a roar of cheers and a storm of flashing lights.

Voices scream, "Seeeeveeen! Seeeeveeen! Oh my gods, he's

Loki!" Crowds of women wave at him from behind the velvet rope. He holds out a hand to me.

"Here we go," I whisper to Arden. I place my fingers in Seven's and use a little luck to gracefully slide from the limo, unraveling my wings as I do so that they are on full display.

The cheering stops but the camera's don't. I smile up at Seven, and we take a step forward. The murmurs in the crowd grow louder as Seven holds out his other hand to Arden. She emerges from the vehicle, careful to straighten her bow and quiver as she takes Seven's hand and steps between us. Jericho closes the door behind us, and then the three of us walk the rainbow carpet, arm in arm, toward the building.

The walk feels long with every eye boring into us. I concentrate on the entrance. Black balloons have been strung together to make the hotel entrance look like the side of a cauldron. There's nothing subtle about it. We are pieces of gold, sliding down a rainbow into a pot of gold.

"Seven!" a woman calls from up ahead. She's standing beside a camera with a *Daily Hatter* badge on the side. "Who is that with you?"

Seven pauses and turns to her, a smile spreading across his face that perfectly fits his Loki costume. "This is my date, Sophia Larkspur, and our daughter, Arden."

We start to walk again as the murmurs rise to a fever pitch, and the woman from the *Hatter* elbows her way through the crowd to keep pace.

"Sorry, but did you say Arden is your daughter?"

Seven stops again, and we all smile for a picture. "Yes," Seven says clearly. "Arden is my and Sophia's daughter. We are a modern family. Now, if you'll excuse me."

We walk again as the crowd goes absolutely wild. We're surrounded by a sea of recording cell phones and snapping lenses, people crying out questions.

"Why are you dating a pixie?"

"Did you pay for Sophia to leave Devashire because of the baby?"

"Why are you legitimizing Arden now?"

All the questions are aimed at Seven, as if Arden and I are mere accessories on his arms.

Eva arrives alone behind us and waves to the crowd. Her dress is evocative of *The Little Mermaid*, making stunning work of her red hair, but no one is even looking in her direction aside from me. They don't stop screaming questions at us. A few charge the barrier, and the security guards have to intervene. We all take a deep breath when we enter the antechamber inside the front doors.

"Wow, that was scary," Arden says, one hand pressing into her stomach. "Did you see how they were shoving the security guards?"

"Stay close," Seven says. "It's going to get worse before it gets better."

An usher directs us up a flight of stairs to a balcony overlooking the gala ballroom.

A sharply dressed leprechaun with a clipboard glances at Seven. "Mr. Delaney, pleasure to see you again. The master of ceremonies wishes to know how you would like to be introduced?"

"Seven Delaney with Sophia Larkspur and, introducing for the very first time, their daughter, Arden Delaney."

The man lifts his head in alarm, frowning at my wings, and glares at Seven as if he smells something bad. "Are you certain, sir?"

"Is there a problem?" Seven's luck barges into the room, the dragon energy spreading its wings. Everyone within a ten-foot radius feels it. Behind us, Eva grins as the landing grows increasingly quiet.

"No, sir." The man taps his earpiece and whispers Seven's instructions into it, then repeats himself... twice.

"Very well, sir. Please proceed forward. The MC will announce you, and then you may descend to the main floor." The man's gaze drifts down his nose at me and Arden, and then he moves on to Eva behind us.

Fingers thread with mine, and I glance down to see Arden taking my hand. For the first time, she looks truly nervous. Her chest rises and falls abnormally fast.

"It's okay," I whisper. "We're together. It's okay."

"Edmund said he'd support me." She glances down at the crowd below. "Do you think he will?"

"If he doesn't, he's an idiot."

Seven takes a step forward as they announce the couple in front of us. Arden releases my hand to take Seven's arm again. I do the same, and we step to the center of a brilliant gold staircase with a plush red runner down the center.

All eyes turn up at us, the masks on the crowd below making them appear less seelie and more monster under the candelabra. A hush falls over the gala.

"Seven Delaney with guest Sophia Larkspur and, for the first time ever, introducing their daughter, Arden Delaney."

Gasps rise from the crowd and we begin our descent, step by painfully slow step. Behind the masks, some of the faces show signs of disgust. Others fascination. And still others are unreadable, as if they are calculating how this strange turn of events might benefit or challenge them and are keeping their options open.

My gaze falls on Edmund, who's dressed as one of the three musketeers. I have to hand it to him—he's the only one smiling, and he's watching Arden as if she's the only source of light in a dark room. He approaches as we reach the landing.

"You do know how to make an entrance," he says, his gaze flicking over the three of us. "Arden, would you care to dance?"

Arden looks at me and then at Seven, who also looks at me. *Fuck.* I'm not entirely comfortable with her being out of my sight in this mob, most of whom seem increasingly angry. *Come on, Sophia, think.* I put myself at the poker table. My heart slows. I look at the choices in front of me, and then I trust my gut.

"Seven and I will go with you. I'm always up for some dancing." I slip my hand into Seven's.

Edmund leads Arden through the ballroom to where a satyr orchestra plays, with us right behind them.

When we reach the dance floor, Seven pulls me into his arms. "Smart move. I didn't think she'd take it well if we said no."

"Absolutely not, especially considering he was the only one with a smile for us when we entered the room." We turn three times and continue our waltz. Seven has to lift me to keep from tripping over my feet. "You're very good at this."

"I've done it every year since I was fifteen," he says dryly. "But never with such an attractive partner." His eyes flick to where Edmund is teaching Arden the steps. "I should have taught this dance to Arden."

I look over my shoulder at her. "She seems to be enjoying herself. I wouldn't worry about it."

"How?"

"How what?"

"How do you not constantly worry? All I've done is worry about her since the moment I found out she was mine."

I meet his eyes—deep, fathomless pools of green—through the holes of his mask. "The truth is, I do worry, or at least I start to. But then I remember that she's my daughter and I've raised her to be savvy about life, to make good decisions but also to know when she's made a mistake and own it."

"You've done a phenomenal job with her. I should trust in that."

I give him a soft smile. "It was you also. Many of the lessons I taught her were things I'd learned from you."

His lips part, but he remains silent.

"Poker, of course. When to bet and when to fold. How to bluff. But also that friends and lovers can come into our lives from unexpected places. That sometimes society is wrong about what should or shouldn't be. That sometimes people might hurt you but that the fight isn't over if you can get back up again."

"I never meant to hurt you."

"I know, but the lesson is the same." I glance back at Arden and watch as she spins across the floor in Edmund's arms. "Your daughter is a survivor. Never underestimate her. She has too much of you in her to be taken advantage of."

He pulls me closer, his nostrils flaring as he inhales slowly. "It's the part of her that comes from me that I'm worried about. Or need I remind you that Godmother still has her chains around my neck thanks to the fool I was at her age?"

"And here I am publicly announcing my love for you. I must be an equal fool. Maybe we *should* be afraid for her." We turn three times, and I spot Arden and Edmund again by a table of drinks. She looks like she's enjoying herself.

"Tell me, Cinderella," Seven says, "now that you've made it to the ball, is it all you imagined it would be?"

I lean in close and say in the most seductive voice I can muster, "Oh, I made it to the ball last night, and I found every inch of it worth the effort."

Seven makes a choking sound, his eyebrows lifting. A rush

of luck bubbles through me, and I miss a step. He lifts me and sets me on my feet again.

We stop dancing, and he leads me to the drink table opposite the one where Edmund and Arden are now talking with Edmund's mother, Alicia.

Seven's expression sags when he sees her. "Is it too early to call it a night?"

"I have until midnight with these crystal slippers." I glance around the room again. "Besides, I'm just starting to enjoy myself. Not as many people are hatefully glaring in our direction as before. I think the shock has worn off. Oh wait. That person looks overly interested."

"That's Fredrick Graceling. He's provost of Elderflame University and rumor has it quite the playboy. I've caught him staring at your ass since we took the floor."

"How charming," I say sarcastically, glancing back at the bearded leprechaun dressed as a wizard. "Although he is quite attractive for a man whose sole purpose is to smoke a pipe and tell others they're going on a quest."

Seven smothers a laugh. "Be nice. He's coming this way."

"Delaney, will you introduce me to your lovely friend?" Graceling flashes a warm smile.

"I can do the honors myself. Sophia Larkspur. And you?"

"Fredrick Graceling."

"Are you sure your name isn't Albus or Gandalf?"

He breaks into a low chuckle. "This one is clever, Seven. Wherever have you been hiding her?"

"In my poker room. She teaches there five days a week," he mumbles.

But Graceling doesn't even hear him. He's studying me, his gaze lingering where my dress meets my skin. I feel his luck rise and circle me like a massive gray owl. "Delaney, do you mind if I borrow Sophia for a dance?"

"Sophia can decide that for herself," Seven deadpans.

Graceling extends a hand to me and I take it.

"It's your feet," I warn him, loud enough for Seven to hear. I catch him chuckling behind Graceling's head.

We begin to dance. Graceling is barely older than Seven but far less nimble on his feet. I try my best to follow his lead.

"The Titania costume suits you," he says. "You might as well be the queen of the fairies for how much attention you're commanding tonight."

"It's not hard—just grow a set of wings."

He gives a light laugh. "I find it refreshing honestly. We at Elderflame have long thought it was time to break the gold ceiling on this gala."

"Oh? It's a wonder I'm the first one then."

"I know what you're thinking, that I sit in my ivory tower talking about it when people like Delaney and yourself do it, but what you don't know is that I've invited a number of pixies over the years and all have refused me. No one wants to open themselves up to the possible backlash."

"Then I'm proud to be the first."

He spins me around and I feel his thumb stroke along my spine. A glance toward Seven and I know he hasn't missed it. The look he's giving Fredrick could bend a silver spoon in half.

"I wonder, are you and Seven exclusive or are you here together to support your daughter, Arden?"

"Exclusive," I blurt. "Extremely. We are as serious about each other as two people can be."

"Hmm. A sad day for me then. One less beautiful fish in the sea."

Stars and lightning, he did not just say that. I stop myself short of rolling my eyes. I focus on Seven and the death glare he's giving the back of Graceling's head.

"Anyway, there's something else I wanted to discuss with you, and it has to do with your dear Arden."

"Oh?" Now he has my full and complete attention.

"I wanted to give you the unofficial news that I approved Arden's admission to our premed program just today. She should receive a letter of acceptance this week."

I grip his shoulder excitedly. "That is wonderful news. Thank you, Fredrick."

"My pleasure. She's a wonderful candidate, and I know we won't be disappointed in the decision."

"Do you mind if I go tell her?" I slow my feet, and we grind to a stop.

"Are you sure your mind is settled on Delaney?"

I slant him a consoling smile. "Forever and always."

He gives a disgruntled huff. "Well then, please." He removes his hands from me and wanders off toward a group of women dressed as muses in the corner of the room. I whirl around, searching for Arden. This is shaping up to be one hell of a night. She's going to flip when she learns she's in!

I cross the room to the drink table where I last saw her talking to Edmund and his mother, but she's not there anymore. I whirl and scan the dance floor. Not there either. Nor do I see either of the Fausts.

Seven is still staring at me like he wants to tattoo MINE across my chest, so I put him out of his misery and join him again.

"Does it bother you that I danced with another man?" I trace my fingers along the edge of his velvet jacket, my knuckles brushing his abs through his shirt.

There's heat in his eyes when he looks at me. "Yes. If he wasn't a leprechaun and we weren't in polite company, he'd have had a very hard time of it. One blast of luck and he'd have fallen on that pointy hat of his."

"Oh, you are grouchy tonight. He was a very nice man—"

"He touched your back."

"He told me Arden has been admitted to Elderflame."

"He did?" Seven's lips twitch upward.

"That was what he wanted to tell me and to welcome me to the gala. Apparently he's an advocate."

"Hmm. A good thing I didn't shove his hat up his ass then."

"Where's Arden? I want to tell her the good news."

"She was right—" Seven's head snaps around to where we both saw her last, but she still isn't there.

"I looked there and the dance floor. I can't find her or Edmund. I can't find Alicia either." I dig my phone out of my purse and text her. "She's not answering my texts."

I feel his luck rise around us.

He takes my hand and leads me toward the back of the room. "Come on."

"Let's not get too worried. She's probably just in some corner somewhere, making out with Edmund."

Seven flashes an annoyed look in my direction and tugs me behind him. We circle the first floor and then the second. I start to worry when I feel Seven's luck burn hotter against my skin. "I can't sense her, Sophia."

"Wait, I just remembered something." I pull out my phone again and navigate to the Find Phone app. We set it up a while back in case one of us forgot their phone somewhere. I locate Arden's. "Seven? This doesn't make sense. It says she's at the casino, but isn't it closed tonight because of the gala?"

Seven's phone rings, and I watch all the blood drain from his face as he brings it to his ear.

"Seven, why is Arden at the casino?" I ask again.

He slides the phone back into his pocket and pulls me toward the elevator. "Because she isn't at the casino, she's under it. They have her."

TWENTY-TWO

When your kid is in trouble, time stops. Everything in you focuses on one thing—doing whatever it takes to get her back. Right now I understand how those stories about mothers experiencing an adrenaline rush and lifting a car off their trapped children might be true. I'd burrow through a wall if I thought it would help right now. There is no morality. I have no boundaries. I will do anything to get her back.

We descend into the tunnels, and Jericho arrives with the car. Seven takes over behind the wheel and tells him to go home for the night, and then we're racing toward the casino.

"What exactly did Alicia say to you?" I ask him.

"They have Arden and if we want her back, we both need to come to the mirror. This has to be about Rayrcore. I wouldn't put it past Alicia to be one of the people working with my dad. She's exactly the type of power-hungry tyrant he'd trust with something like this. I'm just not sure exactly what she wants from us."

"That bitch is going to pay, Seven."

"Yeah, she is."

Seven is driving fast enough to make me nervous we'll collide with something in the narrow passageways but not nearly fast enough for my taste. We arrive outside the tunnel, and I practically dive from the vehicle. I start running for the mirror, then realize I can't get through the wards without Seven.

He's right there behind me, his eyes glowing emerald, his luck growing larger by the second, like a great sleeping dragon waking and unraveling toward its enemy. We've reached the archway, and he doesn't even pause. He grabs my hand and yanks me through.

The wards are a sharp prickle against my skin, and then we're in that ancient room again, panting and slick with sweat. We're not alone. Alicia Faust stands with the staff in one hand and a phone in the other. She holds it up to show me the screen, a picture of Arden and me with the penguins at the zoo several years ago. That's Arden's phone!

"She's not hurt," Alicia says loudly and clearly. "But she will be if you don't do exactly as I say."

Seven's luck snaps at her, an angry beast, but her dark eyes spark and another presence enters the room. A large, dark spider.

"It was you," I say breathlessly.

Alicia pretends I'm not even there. "Hurt me and they hurt her. Do you understand?"

"I understand," Seven says.

I don't understand anything, but I'll do what I have to to make her take me to Arden.

"Follow me." She stabs the staff into the silver and starts to stir.

I glance at Seven. She's vulnerable while she stirs the silver. We could easily take her right now. But I see in his eyes the same concern as my own. I know in my gut she's not bluffing.

Only Alicia knows where Arden is, which means she's the only one who can direct the mirror. And if Rayrcore is behind this and they're treating Arden like they did him and Saul, we can't risk not doing exactly what she says.

The portal opens, and Alicia leaps into the tunnel of falling stars. Seven and I clasp hands and dive in after her. It's more disorienting this time than before, and I wonder if it's because I'm the third in and it's Alicia's consciousness that's directing us. I put my trust in Seven. When we finally topple out the other side onto a stone floor, I feel like I've had the wind knocked out of me and I roll into a ball on my side, hugging myself.

Stone, yes, but not the same as before. I run trembling fingers over the floor, surprised, confused. I lift my face, still half-expecting to see Rayrcore's garage and stare up at a man whose face I only know from textbooks and stock photos.

The only way to describe him is golden and filled with light. His hair is white and his skin sun-kissed where it peeks outside his tunic. He's a tall, large man. But it's the crown of stars that halos his head that tells me exactly who he is.

"Welcome to Thistlebend Castle."

We're in Shadowvale?

"King Kieran," Seven says through his teeth.

My mind races like a swirling top, but my instincts lead me to Arden. She's there, chained but otherwise unhurt, although it's clear she's been crying.

"Mom?"

"I'm here, baby!" I scramble to my feet, but the two unseelie monsters who guard her step in front of her and stab their spears in my direction before I can reach her. They're at least seven feet tall with black skin drawn taut over horrific, wolflike forms. Wolflike if a wolf was shorn of all its hair, stretched and twisted. They stand on two legs but look like they run on four.

"You have what you want. Let my son go," Alicia demands. I notice Edmund then, across the room, chained and guarded in the same way Arden is. Arden is staring at him, but he keeps his gaze locked on the floor.

Kieran waves a hand in the air. "Give her the boy. He's done the task appointed to him and earned his place."

One of the black creatures releases Edmund, and he runs into his mother's arms. The two move for the mirror, but Kieran raises a hand.

"Stay where you are, Alicia. We're not done here."

Seven trades a deadly look with Alicia, and I send my own dagger-filled stare after his. If I ever get out of this, I'm going to make her and her brat pay.

"Release Arden as well," Seven demands.

"Whether Arden walks out of my castle or is carried out in the bellies of my hounds is up to you, young Delaney."

"What do you want from me?" Seven's eyes flash, and I sense him holding back his power. Kieran is rumored to be as formidable as Godmother. She bested him, which is why he's here, but she's the only one who ever has as far as I know. Seven is wise to tread lightly.

I inch toward Arden, hoping Seven is enough of a diversion that I can reach her.

"Stay right there, Ms. Larkspur," Kieran says, pointing at me. "I'm afraid everyone in this room is now part of this. I will need your cooperation as well."

"If you want my cooperation, let me go to my daughter!" I blurt.

"All in good time. I'm sure you're wondering why I went to such great lengths to bring you here, and it's time you understood exactly what role you will play in the future of Shadowvale." He turns to the hound creatures. "Bring them."

Bony black fingers seize my shoulders. I try to make eye contact with Seven, but I'm pushed forward into a dim hallway. Arden is in front of me, and I notice for the first time that they haven't taken her bow. I wonder if it's operational or just a costume prop. Either way, Kieran must not see it as a threat to allow her to keep it on her person. Still, if I could get my hands on it...

The hounds herd us along until we reach a large balcony overlooking Shadowvale. I blink against the orangey light of sunset. When my eyes adapt, what I see beyond the walls of the castle confuses me more than anything that's happened today.

"You're mining malivite here?" Seven is beside me again, and he looks as confused as I am.

Kieran glowers at us. "It's sad really how detached you were from your father's vision, Seven. Allow me to bring you up to speed. Shadowvale is a source of a unique mineral." He holds up a segment of malivite between his thumb and forefinger, similar to the one I retrieved from Adam Barker's murder scene but bigger. "This stone is as dense as lead but far more interesting. You see, it shares properties with both rhodium and neodymium to the extent it can replace those minerals in manufacturing. What I'm holding here is so concentrated an ounce of it is equivalent to a pound of those other elements."

Beside me, Seven shifts with his astonishment. "No wonder Rayrcore wants it."

I can't help myself. "Sorry, what do rhodium and neodymium do?"

Seven turns to me. "They're rare earth elements. They're used in electronic devices and car engines. We use them in our slot machines."

"Rare earth isn't exactly rare," Kieran says, "But it is essential and problematic to mine in your world. We are the solution to that problem. We are going to mine, sell, and ship malivite to Rayrcore from Shadowvale. You, Seven, and Lucky Enterprises are going to be the conduit for that transaction."

"Is that what this is all about? You need me because I own the casino now," Seven says slowly. "Once my father was arrested, I inherited the property the portal is on. You want me to power the portal so you can get the malivite from here into Rayrcore's garage."

Alicia laughs. "You self-important twit. I have access to the tunnels too and can open a portal without you. We need you because Lucky Enterprises' manufacturing subsidiary has the established business relationship with Rayrcore. If you don't carry this through, it could raise a red flag with Godmother or FIRE."

"That's it? This is all about selling malivite? But why did you kill Adam Barker?" I ask.

"We didn't," Alicia says.

"I know you were there." I don't bother explaining how I know that. No reason to bring Eva into this.

She nods. "I *was* there because I was working with Adam. I'd provided him with some malivite, and he came to Dragonfly Hollow to share the results of his analysis with me, results I planned to share with Rayrcore. Someone shot him before we could connect."

She's telling the truth and I glance at Seven, but he just shakes his head. If Alicia didn't kill Adam, who did? Kieran had no reason to want him dead.

Seven struggles against the hound creatures' grip, but they only hold him tighter. "Okay, you have me now. Just let Arden and Sophia go."

I glance over to see that Arden's eyes are rimmed with red. She's staring at Edmund. I've never seen her so heartbroken.

The hounds that guard her barely have to do anything because she's barely there. A ghost among us.

You're going to be okay, I mouth to her. Her next breath trembles in her throat, her tears flowing freely, but she offers me a nod.

"They are as much a part of this now as you are, Seven. We are all in this together, for the good of our kind," Kieran says.

The good of our kind. What a crock of shit. He sounds like *Chance*. Connections spark in my mind as I stare out over the balcony at the creatures pulling carts and carrying axes into the tunnels below. The mine reminds me of something from a Tolkien novel, spiraling into the ground with endless activity, only it isn't orcs doing the work. It's goblins—unseelie fae who are, I've read, normally uncooperative.

"How did you get goblins to work in your mine?" Even as I ask it, the hair on the back of my neck stands on end because I know whatever he's done, it must be dark.

Seven darts a glance toward me and then at the mine, and I see the moment it registers on his face.

Kieran responds with a wicked smile that makes my skin want to crawl right off my body. "I'd heard you were a clever pixie, Sophia. No wonder Valentine dressed you as Titania. You would make a fine queen. You already see where this is going, don't you?"

Beside me, Seven has gone terminally silent. I wonder if Kieran knows how worried he should be right now. The last time I saw Seven look like this, he was bringing down Yissevel's house around him.

"I could guess, but I don't see any prizes for being right. Why don't you save us all some time and tell us," I say dryly.

"Such a smart mouth." He focuses on my lips.

Seven gives a low growl beside me. "What are you up to, Kieran? If you want my help, you need to tell me all of it."

Kieran turns to face the mine and rests his hands on the balcony rail. "Delivering malivite through the silver is only the beginning. For too long Shadowvale has been cut off from prosperity because Godmother didn't have the vision to allow it to grow into what it could be. The goblins are working for me because I've promised them they will be rewarded when we bring down the wall and meld this realm with earth."

My eyes widen. "You're a madman. If you bring down the wall, the unseelie will never respect the peace we have with the outside world. There will be chaos. Once the unseelie start feasting on humans, the only outcome is war."

Kieran nods. "A war we should have fought over a hundred years ago. After the humans' Civil War when Johnson tried to force us from Devashire, I wanted to release the unseelie and put the colonizers in their place. Only Godmother believed a peaceful solution was the most profitable. She gathered enough support among the seelie elders to banish me to this realm. And what has become of you who live on the other side of the wall? Relegated to jesters for human pleasure."

"You were wrong then and you're wrong now." Seven shakes his head. "Devashire is more successful than ever. Our gross national product exceeds that of Germany, and we have power and presence economically in every major industry in North America. Humans flock to our tourist attractions. If the seelie had done it your way, there would be nothing left to rule. The unseelie would have ravaged the States. We'd still be living in forests of claws and teeth, hunting for our meals and battling each other for survival."

Kieran turns his focus on me. "What do you think about that, Sophia? How are things in Devashire for you? Is what Seven says true? Has posterity blessed all fae equally?"

I swallow and answer honestly. "No. Of course not.

Leprechauns have benefited the most from Godmother's arrangement, but—"

"And what about walls? Have walls worked out well for you as a pixie? The barrier between Devashire and the United States proved especially problematic for you, did it not?"

"Yes, but—"

"Did you enjoy being treated as a thing? Being told it was illegal for you to live on land that was once ours? Wouldn't you prefer to come and go as you please? To be treated as an equal to the humans that you now serve? And what about the barrier between you and Seven? That's a different sort of wall, isn't it, Sophia? Oh yes, I know all about you and your relationship." His eyes dart to Alicia, who is still holding her son protectively. "Do you enjoy being considered a lesser class than your lover? Do you think they'll allow you to marry? Is it fun for you to think that Godmother and her laws will determine your future with the man you love?"

"Stop it," I hiss through my teeth. My head pounds, and I'm not sure if it's because he's crazy or because he has a point. It's unsettling, and I find my mind racing from his words.

"The citizens of Shadowvale feel the same way about their captivity as you feel about yours. And yes, it is captivity. If there are walls, there is captivity. You understand, don't you Sophia? You understand in a way that Seven never can how tearing down all the walls, all the borders, all the barriers, is the only fair and equitable future."

"You don't know what you're saying," Seven says.

"There the leprechaun goes again, speaking for you. Stealing your voice."

"I don't need anyone to speak for me," I snap. "What I need is for men like you to listen to me. It is true that walls have consequences and sometimes barriers need to be torn down, but that's where the truth in what you've said ends. A fair and equitable future for the fae is not one where there are no walls and no rules, because in that scenario I'd be dead. It is no secret that pixies are a delicacy to the unseelie."

Kieran shrugs. "Nature must take its course."

"Who decides what is nature and what is brutality? Will it be you who rules over the chaos, Kieran? There has always been a fairy king and queen, hasn't there? Someone has to rule. Someone has to settle disputes. If I remember my history correctly, you came into your position by killing the king before you."

"The strong survive, Sophia. I am the fairy king, and I will rule the kingdom that is to come, alongside Hearst, who has made preparations to help us take back North America in exchange for exclusive rights to this." He gestures at the mines and the goblins toiling below us. "Hearst sees the writing on the wall and is willing to bow to my rule. As I have served as the ruler of this unseelie kingdom, believe me, I am strong enough. Look how even the goblins do my will."

"Then there are still walls. You're still above everyone else. It's true that I wish things could be different between Devashire and the United States and maybe the unseelie should be represented as well, but the answer is thoughtful and controlled change, not war and complete chaos. Not sitting back while an army of goblins feasts on hapless humans."

He shakes his head, and the hounds holding me grip my arms harder. "I expected better of you. I thought you of all people would see that this is how it has to be."

Alicia straightens. "I told you, Kieran, she's dangerous and uncooperative. Throw her in the dungeon. It's the only way you'll ensure Seven's compliance."

Seven struggles against the hounds holding him, his power rising until I can feel its heat on my skin.

"Careful, Seven." Kieran touches his thumbs and forefingers to form a triangle in front of his chest and I watch in horror as the dragon of energy beside me is turned inside out and then fizzles like a snuffed candle. Seven slumps in his captors' grasp.

"What did you do to him?" Arden yells.

Kieran approaches her and pinches her chin. "Don't they teach your age anymore that the king and queen of the fairies have dominion over all fairy powers? I can give them and I can take them."

"Leave her alone," Seven grits out beside me.

I try to reach for him but the black hounds hold me firm.

"Oh, your daddy does love you, little leprechaun hybrid." He brings his face close to hers, and my heart sprints in fear for her. I don't like the way he's touching her. I don't like the way he's looking at her.

"I am the king, little Larkspur, and you've wandered into my realm."

"You tricked me into coming here." She says it to Kieran, but her eyes lock on Edmund, who is pouting like someone stole his puppy.

Kieran laughs. "It doesn't matter how you got here, little girl, only that you are here. And now you are mine, just like your mommy and daddy."

I glare at Edmund, wondering how he lured Arden here. The lie he must have told her. Lies. Kieran has been playing us this entire time. I close my eyes and steady my breathing. This is a game, and I'm Sophia Larkspur. I could rail against Kieran touching Arden and threatening her with the dungeon, or I could remember what I do best. I can play the game. What cards am I holding? What's my position at the table? What's already been played?

"You're right, Kieran," I say, shaking my head as if waking up from a deep sleep. "The wall must come down." My voice is firm and completely convincing. He turns to look at me, eyes narrowing. "I see it now. What you say is true. It's a gamble but the only way forward for our species."

"Sophia, you can't mean that!" Seven cries, and he's almost as convincing as I am, although I can always tell when Seven is lying.

"I do, Seven." I look up at Kieran like he's a juicy hamburger and I haven't eaten in four days. I use the slightest bit of luck to make myself more enchanting. "Is it possible to take down the wall? How do you plan to do it?"

I don't look directly at Arden, but as I stare at Kieran, I casually touch the coin around my neck, the dark charm that Seven gave me as protection. It's my table talk, my signal to her to remind Arden that she has a wish. I can't tell her how to use it. I barely understand how to use it myself, and knowing exactly what to wish for in this situation has me perplexed. It occurs to me that this is where the rubber hits the road when it comes to all the things I told Seven about parenting. I raised her to be strong. I raised her to make good decisions. I let her make her own mistakes. Now she's our only way out of this. I have no way to tell her what to do without calling attention to her charm and possibly blowing our best chance out of this. I have to trust that Arden will find a way to save us.

Kieran studies me for a moment and then blessedly leaves Arden's side to approach me. "I understand now what you see in her, Seven. She does have an unusual fire."

Out of the corner of my eye, I see Seven hang his head as if in defeat, but I feel the slightest spark of his luck beside me. He's readying himself.

I drop my chin, turning my face slightly toward Seven. "It's the only way we can truly be a family."

Kieran grins like a shark in bloody waters. "Listen to reason, Seven. Join us. Take your father's place in the new order."

Beside me, Seven goes perfectly still. "What do you need us to do?"

"Thousands of years ago, the wall was erected by the Light Bearers, the predecessors to guardians, using Odin's magic, the magic of the gods. I've spent a century studying that magic, preparing a way to take it apart. The gods are fickle, and this ancient magic has an ancient antidote. All it takes is blood sacrifice, one powerful enough to appease the gods."

"Dark magic," Seven murmurs.

"Ancient magic was dark." Kieran looks out over the mine. "When our kind ruled this world, our luck was stronger and our society traded in bargains and blood. We will unlock those secrets again. And the first step is to kill the guardians."

"What? All of them?" I ask.

"Edmund and I will do that deed," Alicia says, although sniveling Edmund seems less than enthused about being chosen for the task.

"Excellent." Kieran turns back to Seven. "You will open the portal. The sacrifice must be made inside it, where the blood will drip through the stars and into the hereafter."

"Who exactly is being sacrificed?" Seven asks.

I swallow, a nagging suspicion unsettling me.

Kieran lowers his chin. "I think you know the answer to that." His eyes dart to Arden. "The rarest fairy blood of all our kind resides in that girl. No god would refuse it."

"No!" Edmund cries, backing away from his mother. "You promised you wouldn't hurt her!"

"Quiet, boy!" Kieran snaps his fingers and Edmund's mouth disappears. He claws at his face as his mother tries to calm him down.

"Kieran, my son!" Alicia snaps.

"Shall remain quiet now. Why should he cry when our hybrid waits like a lamb for the slaughter?"

Gooseflesh covers my skin and my blood has turned to ice, but I say nothing. Seven doesn't either. We both know words won't help us now. I look toward Arden, willing her to use the wish. She's eerily calm in a way I've never seen her before. Only... I *have* seen that calm in her father and in myself. Oh Kieran, you do not know what you're in for.

"I have questions," Arden says softly, her hand pressed into the base of her throat, palm over the gold acorn.

"And I will answer them. It's the least I can do to say thank you for your sacrifice," Kieran says.

"Will you, as king of the fae, play a part in the spell to bring down the wall?" Arden asks.

He nods. "I will. It can't be done without me. I will snuff the magic and then use your blood to neutralize it permanently."

"Because you're king of the fae," she says softly. "It can't be done without you."

"That's right," he says proudly.

"My teacher at Bailiwick's said that many people believe Godmother trapped you here because if she killed you, another fairy would rise to your position, possibly someone she couldn't defeat. So it was safer for her to keep you alive."

"Clever theory. Although I'm stronger now. I believe Godmother will be unpleasantly surprised when we bring down the wall and I pay her a visit."

Arden's gaze darts to me and then to Seven, where it lingers, almost apologetically.

"*Fuck*," Seven utters under his breath. What does he know that I don't?

Fingers clutching the acorn in the hollow of her throat, Arden says clearly and with intention, "I wish my father was king of the fae."

TWENTY-THREE

Arden's luck snaps out of her body, but unlike before, it's no cute, lovable raccoon. The acorn amplifies her power into a primordial beast that expands to the size of the castle and roars, blowing back my hair in a gale-force wind.

Kieran raises his hands, forming a triangle with his thumbs and forefingers, and tries to absorb the excess energy. His magic glows orange as a sunrise, but it is nothing compared to Arden's. She grinds his power beneath the heel of the wish.

I raise my arm to shield my eyes from the intensity of the clashing magic. Seven draws me into his chest. "Whatever happens, Sophia, I love you. I have always loved you."

His words scare me as much as the flames of power licking at my skin. It feels like we've been thrust into a kiln. A flash between our bodies draws my attention, and I see the coin around my neck glowing bright. The charm! I spin around, my back to Seven, shielding both of us as much as possible. Seven ducks his head, making himself small behind me as the blast grows in intensity.

Kieran is a glowing ball of fire. He is an orange sun, an exploding star, a detonated bomb.

The hound creatures in the room are the first to go, their bodies incinerating to ash before my eyes. Suddenly Edmund screams. His mouth has returned, which must mean Kieran's power is waning, but the blast coming off Kieran is frying the boy and his mother. Alicia shields him with the giant spider of her luck, but it isn't strong enough. They run for the hall, but it's too late. They both collapse near the exit, their skin blistering, then burning off altogether. I watch them gasp one last time before they stop breathing.

Across the room, Arden's eyes glow like emerald fire, the wish protecting her from the fallout. Her luck feels boundless but not targetless. Every ounce of it is directed at Kieran. The rest of us are simply collateral damage.

The king's face sags and his arms flop to his sides. I stand up straighter, my arms wrapped around Seven behind me, panting in the heat of this magic. It finally wanes, coiling back in on itself. Kieran's knees give out, then the rest of him, flesh and bone. He melts into a puddle of blue liquid, his crown of stars splashing down in the center. It dissolves as if in acid, sizzling until it's gone. A cool breeze blows through the room, and I draw a deep breath.

But behind me, Seven pulls away, grunting in pain. I whirl to find him doubled over. "Arden, stop!" I yell. "It's hurting him."

Her hands are fisted at her sides and she sways on her feet. "I'm not doing it! I want it to stop, but I can't."

I wrap my arm around Seven, trying my best to protect him from whatever is happening. He's leaning on me, hard. I can't let him go. I keep one arm around his waist and hold the other out to her. "Come to me, Arden."

But she can't seem to move.

"Go," Seven growls and shoves me.

I rush toward Arden and reach her just in time. Her eyes roll back in her head, and she tumbles into my arms. I collapse onto my knees from her weight but save her from the worst of the fall. Cradling her, I rock her gently. She's barely breathing.

"You're okay. I've got you. I've got you."

Tears slip down my cheeks and fall on her too-hot skin. I place my fingers on the side of her throat, but her pulse is a weak tap against my fingers.

"Come on, Arden. Fight. You are going to be okay. Just hold on." I wish to every god above that I could give her my luck. My chest hurts.

"She's negative," a deep voice with the hollow tone of a cavernous space says above me.

I glance up and find Seven standing over us, only it's a version of Seven I've never known before. A gold crown of stars hovers over his toffee-colored hair like a halo, and his glowing emerald pupils are ringed in silver.

"Let me give her my luck."

"Seven?" my voice cracks.

"Yeah, it's me, Sophia." He reaches down and takes Arden by the arms. When his luck rises in the room, it's clear something has changed. His dragon is no longer red but gold, and it's massive, at least twenty times larger than before. Long moments tick by. It might be seconds, minutes, hours. Time has no meaning when your child is unconscious in your arms.

Finally her body takes on a golden glow and her lips part on a gasp.

"Oh, thank the gods." I draw her to me, but when her eyes pop open, she reaches for Seven.

"Dad?" It's the first time she's ever called him that, and my eyes burn with emotion. Their hands intertwine. "I'm sorry. I didn't know what else to do."

Seven closes his eyes and the crown disappears, its energy sinking inside him. A line from Chance's poem comes to mind: *He who carries his crown within his bones.* He'd meant Kieran. *Mirror, mirror* had meant the portal. *They whose hunger has grown and grown* must have been referring to Rayrcore and their ravenous appetite for rare earth, and *she whose hatred is cast in stone* was Alicia, who'd hated Seven since her fateful purchase of her own engagement ring. He'd told us the truth after all.

Seven's eyes shift to a normal color again. "It was the only thing you could have done, Arden. If you had wished he was dead, his power might have gone anywhere, even to one of the goblins."

He doesn't say it might have gone to Edmund, but we all must think it because Arden's eyes slip to the boy's body. She starts to sob.

"He must have drugged me. The last thing I remember is having a drink with him and his mother and suddenly feeling woozy. They promised to take me outside to get some air, but instead took me to the mirror. I think I passed out for a while, and then you were there. I wanted to use the wish sooner, but my brain was too foggy to know what to do. I—"

"It's all right, Arden," Seven says. "You did the best anyone could do. It's over."

She sits up between us and hugs her knees to her chest, the tears coming in waves now. I draw her protectively against my side. Seven lowers himself to sit on her other side and puts his arm around her shoulders.

"I really loved him," she says.

I look down and see that the red ribbon is still tied around her wrist. It all makes me want to scream.

Seven and I look at each other, then each grab a side of the ribbon and pull. It breaks, and I cast it aside.

"He didn't deserve you," Seven says.

"But did he deserve to die? I did that." Her eyes drift toward the body, her sobs shuddering.

I hug her tighter. "Edmund made the choice to deceive you. He made the choice to drug you and help abduct you. You didn't do that to him, Arden. Kieran did. But Edmund put himself in Kieran's orbit. He said yes to all this."

She nods and presses her forehead to her knees.

Seven's expression turns dark. "Does this change how you feel about staying in Devashire?"

I bristle and brace myself for the worst. It's too late to go back now. Everyone knows who and what she is.

But Arden shakes her head. "No. I want to be here, with my family." She threads her hands into both of ours.

"Truly?" I ask.

At first she doesn't answer, just stares at her toes and releases a long, shaky breath. "Bad things happen everywhere," she says slowly, "but I think friends and family are the only way to weather the storm. I need Dragonfly Hollow. I need you, Mom, and Dad and Grandma and Grandpa. This place has meant more to me than any of the places we lived in America. It's not that it's better or worse, just different, and it's home."

I kiss the side of her head.

"Can we go now?" she asks.

I look at Seven. There's so much to discuss. Is it safe for him? Once Godmother finds out that he's the new king, will she try to banish him like she did Kieran, or worse, try to control him using their bargain? Does he have an obligation to Shadowvale and the unseelie there? What should be done about the mine and Rayrcore?

But the look he gives me tells me everything I need to know. Our problems will always be with us. There will always be some heavy weight regarding his company, our relationship,

Arden, and now his position as fairy regent. But when we're tired and we've had enough, sometimes it's time for the prince and Cinderella to just go back to the castle, roll up the drawbridge, and enjoy being a family.

He rises first and helps us both to our feet. "Let's go home."

TWENTY-FOUR

It's early the next day when I make my way to Godmother's Tearoom and ask the pixie behind the hostess stand to speak with her. I've come alone on purpose. Both Seven and I agree that him being in the same room as her at the moment is a bad idea. Because of their bargain, if she senses what he is, she'll never let him go. Our only hope is to take advantage of the moment, when no one but us knows what occurred.

I'm shown back to her office and take a deep fortifying breath outside her door before being ushered inside. Dressed in a sophisticated yellow gown, Godmother looks like a queen, sitting behind a delicate curved-leg desk, signing something with her long, feathered quill.

She barely glances my way before saying, "Sophia Larkspur, to what do I owe the pleasure of your interruption?"

I sit down in one of the dainty chairs across the desk from her. "It's time for you to release River from the safe house."

Now she raises her dark gaze and stares at me. "Have you solved the murder then? Will you be giving me the name of the true perpetrator to arrest in River's stead?"

I pull out my phone and queue up the security video. "I can give you a name, but I'm not sure you'll want to arrest them."

"Why not?" She folds her arms.

"Because *you* shot Adam Barker."

Godmother flashes a stern look in my direction and then laughs. "Is this some kind of joke?"

"No. No, I'm not joking. You knew that Alicia Faust was supposed to meet with Adam Barker that afternoon. He'd promised to bring her the results of his analysis of the malivite being mined in Shadowvale. You knew all about malivite and its promise for industrial applications because you wrung the truth out of Chance when you arrested him. I watched you torture Chance, but it didn't occur to me just how much he shared with you that night. But when I visited him in Ashgate, it was clear you'd broken his mind as well as his body."

"You're boring me with this nonsense, Sophia," Godmother says. "I was giving a speech to the graduating class at the time of the murder, in front of half the town."

"No, you weren't. The shooting happened afterward, as the crowd was filing into the tent for the after-party. You disappeared in the commotion and then reappeared to get Seven after the murder. You shot Adam so that he couldn't confirm the properties of malivite to Alicia, and you intentionally did it from a distance and from the direction she was standing. Your true intention was to frame Alicia for the crime, but you didn't count on River. He was in the wrong place at the wrong time with the wrong sense of responsibility to the victim. Although you planned for people to see the direction of the shot and to link the murder back to Alicia, another leprechaun had cleared the area, which meant you had no choice but to pin the murder on River. After all, you needed someone to blame."

"Your analysis is far from accurate, but I'll give you this—if you can prove Alicia was in the vicinity of where the bullet originated, she is a major suspect and I will arrest her immediately."

I shake my head. "Alicia didn't shoot Adam Barker. She was scheduled to meet with Adam. She wanted him alive. She needed the information and the sample he carried to take to Rayrcore. But you knew that already."

She waves a hand in the air. "Preposterous. It's an outlandish theory. What motivation could I possibly have to instigate a death in Dragonfly?"

"You thought framing Alicia would stop her and Kieran's plan now that Chance was out of the picture. The fact that Alicia had tampered with the security cameras so that her meeting with Barker wasn't recorded was an added boon. But you forgot one thing. There's security everywhere, and Alicia didn't manipulate the cameras surrounding the bank."

I press Play. Alicia comes into focus on the side of the bank, striding toward the rendezvous point. The pop of a gunshot goes off, and she cows against the building, looking for the source of the bullet. Then the video changes. A different camera, a different angle. The scene repeats, but there in the corner of the screen is Godmother with a shimmer of purple around her. The pop doesn't seem to surprise her at all.

"So I'm standing beside the bank and Alicia. That doesn't mean I shot a man."

"The noise originates with you, Godmother, and although we can't see the gun, you don't react to the shot. It's almost as if you expect it. But if we watch these side by side, we can see that Alicia turns her face toward you when the gun goes off. The shot originates with you."

Godmother leans back in her chair and couples her hands. "You're confused." Her tone is laced with malice. "Let's call Alicia Faust in, and she can explain her behavior on that video."

"That will be impossible. You see, Alicia Faust and her son Edmund are dead. Tragic accident. But I think the people of Devashire would be interested in this video, which is why I've given it to a friend to share publicly if we can't come to an agreement today."

Her power rises in the room, setting my teeth on edge. When she speaks again, her voice is low and her stare intense. "I think we can agree that Alicia Faust shot Adam Barker. River will be freed, and a statement will be prepared explaining that she and her boy were killed trying to escape authorities. You will deliver the bodies to me, and then you are free of your obligation to me."

"Excellent. Now what about Seven?"

"What about him?"

"You must release him from his bargain as well."

"No."

"I have information about Kieran. Information you'll want to know. But I won't share it unless you release him."

"What about Kieran?"

I remain perfectly silent and just stare at her for a beat. "Your bargain with Seven is one-sided. You can break your hold over him at any time. That's what you need to do now if you want me to stay and share what I know about Kieran and his plan to attack you and Devashire."

"Kieran is banished," she says through her teeth.

"Still, when I saw him last night, he was very clear about his strategy." I pull out the piece of malivite I brought back from Shadowvale and toss it onto her desk.

Eyes wide, she probes me lightly with her power and I let her. I haven't told a single lie. I let her taste the honesty in my claim.

She drums her fingers on the desk, and I toy with the coin

around my neck. She doesn't even bother to threaten me with force. We both know it won't work.

"Fine. I will release Seven from our bargain. Now tell me what you know."

"First release him."

She lowers her chin and glares at me. "You're testing me, Sophia, and I'm very close to transforming you into a ferret and tossing you out of here by the tail. I promise you I'll release Seven as soon as you tell me what Kieran told you."

"And I have your word on that?"

"Yes," she says emphatically, her expression full of annoyance.

I lean forward. "Kieran has found a ritual that can take down the wall and meld Shadowvale to earth. He plans to set the unseelie free. He's garnered help from the goblin kingdom and has been mining malivite to exchange with Rayrcore for their help. When he strikes, you're going to feel it from every direction." I shake my head.

For the first time, Godmother looks nervous. She taps the heel of her foot on the floor, her expression going suspiciously blank. "When is he planning this coup?"

"I'll tell you, but first release Seven."

She hesitates. I stand and start walking toward the door.

"Fine!" she grits out. She snaps her fingers, and silver threads appear around her. She cuts one with her fingers.

I pull out my phone to text Seven, but one pops in from him before I have a chance.

> It's done. OMG, Sophia, you did it.

"Now tell me!" Godmother booms. Her magic stabs at my skin. The coin around my throat glows brighter, repelling it.

"Kieran is dead," I say, adding an exaggerated shrug. "So there will be no attack. Toodle-oo!" I wave my fingers.

"Sophia!" The walls shake with her anger, and I hear the pounding of footsteps that I am sure come from her security team.

I pivot. "Yes?"

"You're sure he's dead?" Her eyes narrow.

"Positive. He threatened Arden and so we killed him."

"Do you know who the new king is?"

"Whoever the magic calls, I assume." I force my face into a careful mask.

"You could have told me he was dead straightaway. You cost me my leprechaun with your scheming. I should have you taken to Ashgate for this," she says through her teeth.

"But you won't," I say. "Because now that you can't control Seven, you need us as allies. And despite what you might think, Godmother, I believe that you are the best person to lead Devashire, and so does Seven. And maybe someday Kieran's replacement will surface, and then you might need us to secure your reign. You want Seven in your corner. Trust me on this. And you won't have that if I'm in Ashgate."

She leans back in her chair and threads her fingers. It's with some measure of disgust that she says, "Very well. I'll expect you and Seven to keep that promise. Now please show yourself out."

CHAPTER

TWENTY-FIVE

Six months later...

"Grandma, when did you get here?" I lean against the side of the couch, watching my grandmother knit a gigantic misshapen blanket from fuzzy white yarn.

"Oh, a few minutes ago. Your mom invited me to dinner before the Yule celebration."

"Oh, is that tonight?" I knew it was coming up, but Seven and I have been so busy I didn't realize what day it is. After my conversation with Godmother, River was freed and returned to his life running River's Tavern. He's still seeing Eva and Patrick, and although there's no bargain between them anymore, they've successfully kept their tryst a secret. Seven and I are the only ones who know.

Although Seven was freed from Godmother's hold over him, we still had to deal with the fallout from going public about our relationship at the Gilded Gala and the announcement that Arden was our daughter. At first the commentary was insulting. The *Daily Hatter* ran headlines like PERNICIOUS PIXIE HOOKS DRAGONFLY'S MOST DESIRABLE BACHELOR and WILL SEVEN DELANEY COME TO HIS SENSES ABOUT FLIGHTY AFFAIR? But as time went on and we continued to appear in public—affectionately in each other's company—people became curious about our relationship.

We agreed to an exclusive interview with Fairly Goodweather for the *Daily Hatter* that was recorded for their YouTube channel. Over the course of three grueling hours, we answered every question Fairly sent our way. Seven admitted he fell in love with me in grade one when I softened the blow of his mother's neglect. I admitted that I was wrong to leave the way I did, that Devashire would always be my home, and that in a way, the luckiest day of my life was being captured by FIRE because it brought us back together. The interview was heart-wrenching, and Penelope told me everyone in River's Tavern cried during the live showing.

After that, things changed for us. Oh, there were still leprechauns who looked down their noses at me, but we had no trouble getting a table for dinner at even the snootiest restaurants in Elderflame. The humans loved our story so much there was even a middle-aged romance author from the Midwest willing to buy the rights to it. We liked her, so we signed it over for free. My parents sell copies in their shop, the Silver Ember, where they also do a booming business in Sophia and Seven action figures.

Our popularity also spilled over into our business venture. Spots in my poker classes fill the moment we open them now. The demand is so great that we've added two other poker teachers, another pixie and a satyr. Talks have resumed on allowing fae to take poker lessons and perhaps try a tournament in the future.

As for Arden, she started premed at Elderflame University and dreams of becoming a pediatrician. Graceling tells me she's at the top of her class. That's why I'm here tonight and not staying at Seven's. She's on her way home for winter break.

"It is tonight," Grandma says. "And it will be Arden's first Yule ball. You don't want to miss that."

"I wouldn't dream of it... if she wants to go that is. After everything that happened with Edmund, she might prefer to stay as far away as possible. It took her weeks to get over that evening. She hasn't dated anyone else since. I think it still holds bad memories for her."

Grandma's blue eyes twinkle. "Arden is a strong young woman. Smart as they come. I think you'll be surprised how thoroughly she's recovered when she's home again."

"I hope so."

My phone buzzes, and I pull it from the hidden pocket of my plum-colored princess dress. It's Seven's favorite color on me, and he plans to meet us tonight. My heart leaps when I see the call is from Arden, and I bring the phone to my ear.

"Mom?" Her voice sounds shaky, like she's upset.

"What's going on?"

"I need help. You know how to drive a sleigh, right?" My phone vibrates again, and I see that she'd sent me a picture of a sleigh in line for the Yule parade.

"Gods, Arden. What's going on?" *Fuck*, Edmund would have had to rent a sleigh to get the red ribbon he tied on Arden's wrist. Did no one think to cancel it after he died?

"Can you meet me at the edge of the Winter Wood?" Her voice cracks again, and my heart breaks.

"I'll be there as fast as I can fly." I end the call and head for the door.

When I arrive at the Winter Wood, panting and almost

crazy with worry, I find Arden waiting for me, dressed in the cobalt princess dress I bought her for graduation. She's standing beside one of the red sleighs in the lineup, but she doesn't look upset at all. On the contrary, she's beaming at me.

"Arden, what is going on?" I ask, more than a little annoyed.

"Get in the sleigh, Mom." Arden laughs and points at a thick fur blanket in the back.

"Why? Honey, I'll drive if we can't get out of this. You can be in the back."

She takes me by the shoulders and gives me a kiss on the cheek. "I love you, Mom. Just enjoy tonight, okay?"

Seven steps out from the shadows, dressed in a deliciously tailored dark suit. "What Arden means is, tonight I'm going to drive."

I can't get my mouth to close as he approaches with a red ribbon in his hand and ties it around my wrist. "Seven?"

"It's long past time we had the night we should have had all those years ago." He kisses me gently, then helps me into the back before lifting himself into the driver's seat.

Arden waves. "I'll meet you in the square." She takes off for the center of the park.

"How long have you been planning this?" I ask him.

He turns on the bench to look me in the eye and gives me a wink. "Sixteen years."

I laugh. "You never fail to surprise me."

"Wait until you see what's in there."

Only then do I notice a small cooler under the edge of the blanket. I open it to find a steaming hot cup of cocoa in a River's Tavern cup. I pop off the lid and see dozens of mini marshmallows and a sprinkle of cinnamon. "I love you, Seven Delaney."

He flashes his most disarming smile. "Good, because that will make this so much easier."

I take a long sip.

The band starts to play, and Seven taps the reins and nudges our reindeer into motion. Snow drifts from the star-filled sky. There's not a cloud above us. This is Godmother's magic. Beautiful.

I wave at the cheering crowd as we drive by, my mind flashing back to the nightmare I experienced sixteen years ago. The memories that flood me are just as painful as they were then, but now they have to war with new memories, joyful ones. I can feel the story I've told myself changing, morphing into a tale of misunderstanding, of redemption, of love and connection, of things working out over time. I let it all wash over me, the good and the bad, and I smile at the sharp edge of emotion it creates in me. The snow on my face makes me feel alive.

By the time we park the sled in the special parking area created for this event, I've finished my chocolate and feel light as a feather, like the past is finally truly in the past. Accepted, part of me, but not any more important than any other moment in our lives. I feel healed.

Seven hops down and helps me out the back, and I throw my arms around him. "Thank you for this."

He presses a kiss into my hair. "We're not done."

Taking my hand, he leads me to the gazebo where a satyr band plays and white lights cast dancing couples in their warm glow. My mother and father are there, as is Arden, who's dancing with River; Penelope, who's swaying with her husband Flick; and Eva, who's taking a turn around the floor with a completely healed Saul, along with a dozen more faces I recognize from Dragonfly. "Are we going to dance?"

He smiles as he leads me up the stairs and nods at the string quartet. They stop playing, and all the dancers pause to look at us.

I turn to Seven to ask him what's happening and find him on one knee. In his hand is a box with a ring. Seven once said there would be a day he'd buy me a ring with a diamond large enough to be seen from space. I can't attest to that, but as I look at the monstrosity he's holding, I question whether I'll get tired carrying it around.

"Sophia Larkspur, for as long as I can remember, you've been my best friend. Then you became my lover, and then when you were gone, the one I thought about when I looked at the moon. Somehow I have you back, and all I want is to be with you forever. You are who I think of when I hear the word *home*. All my life, people have said that I'm lucky, but tonight is the test. Will you make me the luckiest man alive? Will you marry me, Sophia?"

Everyone is watching, but we might as well be standing there alone. My attention narrows like a tunnel until I can see only him.

"Yes," I say. "I guess the rumors are true. You are lucky, and so am I, because I can't wait to be your wife."

He slips the ring on my finger, and the world starts again amid flashing cameras, claps, and cheers. He pulls me into an embrace.

Seven's power wraps around me with his arms, making me feel safe and loved. He's never told anyone that he's the king of the fae, and he refuses to use his new power for fear of drawing attention to himself. But I know and Arden knows. And I pity anyone who tries to get between the three of us. They won't succeed. Not now. Not ever.

"Would you care to dance?" he asks me.

"Oh yes," I say. "And then we must complete the rest of our plan."

He quirks a half smile. "Our plan?"

"Sixteen years ago we planned to ride in the parade, dance in the gazebo, and..."

He arches a brow as he remembers our plan to lose our virginity to each other, and a wolfish grin spreads across his face. He sweeps me into the middle of the dance floor. "In that case, maybe half a dance."

EPILOGUE

Six years later…

Seven fills a glass with champagne and hands it to me. "Congratulations, Mrs. Delaney."

"Don't congratulate me yet. Not until it's done."

"Everything is going to be fine. I have a feeling." He smiles, and his eyes glint with power. "Today is a very lucky day."

Every day is lucky now that Seven and I are on the other side of our happily-ever-after. We wait on the porch of our country estate. It's not exactly a castle, but the two-story white farmhouse with a bright red door might as well have a moat. It rises at the center of acres and acres of land, the border of which is protected by a ward only the king of the Fae could master. We've been happy here in our getaway from the city, although Seven keeps his penthouse for nights he needs to stay in town.

"There she is," Seven mumbles as a Land Rover weaves up the drive. It parks near the house, and Arden leaps from the driver's seat, her doctor's bag in hand.

"If it isn't Elderflame Hospital's newest resident!" I say proudly.

She beams back at me. "I can't believe you're allowing me to witness this."

She jogs up the steps to us, and we each pull her into our arms.

"This is a family matter, and you are family," I tell her.

Together, the three of us enter the house and pass through the massive foyer and family room to the kitchen and the antechamber that leads to our garden. A real pixie garden with vines of blooming roses, bushes of hydrangeas, hibiscus the size of dinner plates, peonies, and butterfly bushes. Some of the most beautiful plants have no names, but their flowers are uniquely beautiful, and the scent flavors the air.

Seven is king of the fae, and as such he holds the powers of every fairy species. It wasn't long after we were married that he started producing seeds as a pixie would, and we've planted them here along with mine. There are so many positive emotions in this garden we rarely have to weed.

But the most important plant is at the center of it all. We make our way there now, to the two spheres of glass, one purple and one yellow, that have grown to the size of large pumpkins.

"Are you ready to meet your siblings, Arden?" I ask.

She nods enthusiastically. Seven and I join hands, then bring our heel down with a careful tap on the yellow fairy glass. Cracks form along the edges, and I easily pull the sections apart. Sap spills into the soil and fog rolls up, obstructing my view, but when I reach inside, I find the chubby body of a baby. I gather it into my arms, stroking back its shock of dark hair and staring into two emerald-green eyes.

"A girl!" I squeal. "Arden, you have a sister." I hold her to me until something nudges my arm. Moving her to my shoulder, I watch as two wings unfurl from her back. "And a pixie!"

"What will you name her?" Arden asks.

I look at Seven and smile. "We decided on Harper."

"Harper Delaney," Arden says before holding a receiving blanket out to wrap Harper in. Together we make a baby burrito and Arden takes Harper from me, cooing down at her sister.

I return to Seven's side, and hand in hand, we bring our heels down on the purple glass. This time Seven reaches through the fog, and when he lifts another child from the birth plant, I notice immediately this one looks more like me with brown eyes and hair.

"Harper has a brother!" Seven says, tucking him against his chest.

"No wings," I say.

Arden steps to his side, handing me Harper, and examines the baby. "He's a leprechaun. You can tell by the pattern of the iris. See?" She gently holds open the baby's eyelid, and I see a gently looping pattern in his iris that is different from Harper's. "That will fade by the time he's a year old."

"I can feel his luck," Seven says, a smile spreading.

"Have you decided on a name for my brother?" Arden asks, pulling another receiving blanket from her bag.

"Everett." I kiss my new son on the head, then stand close to Seven so the babies can see each other and both of us together.

"And just like that, we're a party of five," Arden whispers.

Five. I wouldn't believe there was enough room in my chest for the joy I'm feeling if I weren't experiencing it firsthand. We are a family. A strong one. A real one. There are no lies here. No illusions. No more secrets.

The trouble with fairy tales is they never show you the happily-ever-after. The girl marries her prince, but do they stay together? Does it last? Are they strong enough to withstand the pressures that kept them apart before the magic happened?

I can't speak for Cinderella, but for us the answer is yes. Then again, you might say the five of us are as lucky as they come.

THANK YOU FOR READING A HOUSE OF GOLD AND SHADOWS. If you enjoyed this title, please leave a review wherever you buy books.

IF YOU ENJOYED THIS NOVEL, YOU MAY LIKE **THE TREASURE OF PARAGON!**

Dragon bonds can build kingdoms... or break them!

Three hundred years ago, the dragon shifter heirs to the kingdom of Paragon witnessed the unspeakable at the coronation of their eldest sibling. Overthrown by a wicked uncle in a violent coup, the eight remaining siblings fled to Earth, settling around the globe and blending in with the humans around them.

But when one of them falls in love with a witch, the wheels of fate begin to turn. In Paragon, relationships between dragons and witches are forbidden, but nothing can stop these fated mates.

Everything the heirs have been told is a lie. Destined for love and headed for war, their destinies collide with an ancient prophecy steeped in magic.

Together, they'll face the past and take back their throne, or die trying.

Discover the series here: https://shop.genevievejack.com/ products/treasure-of-paragon-stack

Turn the page to read an excerpt of book 1, THE DRAGON OF NEW ORLEANS.

EXCERPT: THE DRAGON OF NEW ORLEANS

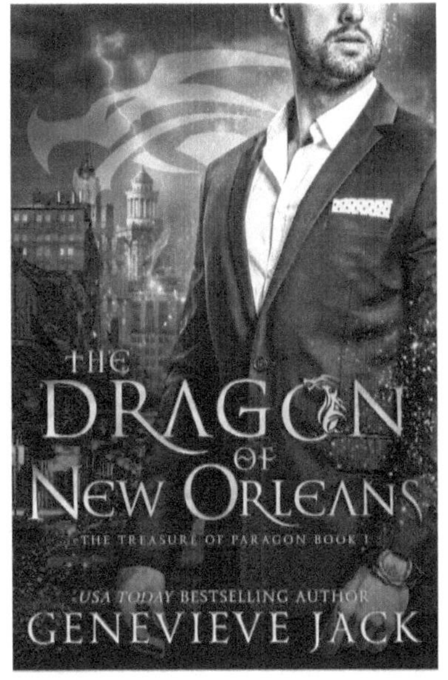

ONE

Gabriel Blakemore was running out of time, which was laughable considering time had never meant anything to him in the past. As an immortal dragon, his life thus far had flowed like an endless river, each new day guaranteed by the last. Not anymore. He thumbed the emerald ring on his finger. Already the curse at its center gave the jewel the appearance of a cat's eye in bright light, a thin black pupil visible at the center of the green. His affliction was spreading.

Hunched over the seventeenth-century Spanish baroque desk in his office at Blakemore's Antiques, he sifted through the stack of papers in front of him, praying for a savior, anyone who had the slightest potential for breaking the curse. None of the candidates seemed powerful enough. He needed more options.

Anxiously, he tugged at the bond connecting him to his manservant. Richard appeared at the door to his office almost immediately, carrying a stack of papers that he squared on the desk in front of Gabriel. "More for you."

Gabriel nodded at the man. Impeccably dressed, as always, in a pinstripe three-piece suit, Richard had proved a crucial asset these days, researching magical options when Gabriel could not. Gabriel had bought the former slave's freedom in 1799, a wise choice. Not only had Richard become a close friend over the centuries, he'd retained a sharp wit and an eye for detail.

The man dusted off his hands before rubbing his sternum. "You don't need to scream down the bond, you know. I'm in the next room. I want to find a cure as much as you do."

Gabriel grunted.

"Are all dragons as friendly and chipper as you, or was I just lucky to be bonded to the best of them?" Richard folded into the chair across the desk, throwing a lanky arm across its back.

"How are sales today?" Gabriel asked, ignoring the man's gibe. He hadn't meant to cause Richard discomfort, but he didn't plan to apologize for it either. Not when the situation was so dire.

"Strong enough that if we all live another year, we can throw one hell of a party," Richard said. "How's that plan coming along? You find a way for us to do that? Live another year? There must be something here. For God's sake, we live in the voodoo capital of America, the home and burial place of Marie Laveau herself."

A whiff of cinnamon and molasses curled off Gabriel's coffee, and he took a long, steadying drink. "Marie would roll over in her tomb if she knew who was running this city now." New Orleans was brimming with humans claiming to have supernatural abilities. Liars, most of them. Unfortunately, the voodoo priestess who'd cast the curse on his ring was the real thing, and she did not take prisoners. Anyone left with true power in the city was either on her side or too afraid to oppose her.

Gabriel snorted. Three hundred years in this realm, only to

be turned to stone by the jealous rage of a woman who couldn't take no for an answer.

The thought made his fingers drum against the desk. Tap-tap-tap. Always in threes. The compulsion to tap was so strong when it hit him, not doing so resulted in pain. Muscle tremors ran the length of his arms and hands. He flipped his thumb against the corner of the paper nearest him, hoping it would curb the impulse.

Richard frowned at his fidgeting. "You should rest, Gabriel. It's getting worse. This is the third time this morning."

"Soon."

"That's what you said an hour ago."

Gabriel pulled the pile of papers toward him. His hands cramped with the effort, and the stack spilled across the walnut desk. He cursed, but the word caught in his throat. A woman's picture had been revealed in the collapse, instantly catching his eye. He lifted the folded newspaper to get a better look.

Enchanting. That was the only way to describe her. He couldn't look away. The woman had eyes the color of deep water and curly black hair as wild as the hint of trouble she carried in her smile. He had the sudden intense desire to kiss away that lopsided grin and further tangle that hair. Where had such an urge come from? A dragon like Gabriel didn't often find himself drawn to human women. He closed his eyes and gave his head a well-deserved shake.

"Who is this?" he demanded.

Richard leaned over the desk in order to get a better look, and Gabriel turned the article in his direction. Richard groaned. "That, my friend, is a long shot."

RAVENNA TANGLEWOOD OPENED HER EYES TO DARKNESS. She blinked and blinked again, but the eyelid flutter didn't seem to help. This was new. While she'd slept, an irregular blotch had formed in her vision, partially obstructing her view. Now it painted itself like black ink against the sterile white walls of her hospital room.

A Rorschach test, she thought. What did she see in it? An oil slick. A dark cumulus cloud. A rough joke told by her brain cancer.

Cancer. That fucking bitch.

The aroma of this morning's half-eaten eggs and the tang of antiseptic brought her fully awake. She was in the exact same place she'd been every day for the past three months: the hospice at Ochsner Medical Center in New Orleans. Only the last time she'd drifted off, there wasn't a stain obstructing half her field of vision.

She rolled her head and the dark splotch followed, blotting out the left side of the room. She closed her eyes again, counted to ten. No change. Damn, that couldn't be good.

Through her working eye, she watched her mother sleep in the chair next to the bed; she at least was the same as Raven had left her. A *Cosmo* was sprawled across her mother's lap as if she'd drifted off midsentence. Though now that Raven looked more closely, the lifestyle magazine was wrapped around a disturbingly worn copy of *Surviving Divorce* by Amy Dickerman, PhD. Raven winced. So her father's pronounced absence had come to this. Or maybe it was a preemptive read, a talisman against the inevitable. As far as she knew, her parents had only separated—the burden of her illness giving rise to separate bank accounts, separate bedrooms, separate lives—in that order. Her care had become an act of full-time charity her father could not abide.

As usual, her mom was bearing the parental weight alone

this morning, although the chair beside her held her older sister Avery's rosary. When had she dug that thing up? Raven hadn't seen the likes of it since their aunt had gifted it to her for her first communion. Avery had never been the praying type. Leave it to death to bring out the inner Falwell in everyone.

Did she think she could pray the cancer away? Raven snorted at the thought. *Pull the plug.* That's what she'd say if she had a say, and if she were plugged in to anything more than Mr. Drippy, her full-time fluid and drug-delivery companion. So far, she could breathe on her own and swallow, unlike the man across the hall. *Stopped the vent,* she'd heard the nurses whisper.

Lucky bastard.

"Hey, beautiful," Dr. Freemont said.

Raven rolled her head back to center, then slightly to the left so she could see him clearly out of her good eye. Dr. Freemont was a balding, portly man whose gray temples gave away his advanced age. Still, he was more fun than his stodgy contemporaries. She liked him.

"Hey, ugly," she responded, although the words sounded choked off and raspy.

His bushy silver brows sank over his bulbous nose. "What's this about? You're holding your head at an angle. Raven, can you look at me straight on?"

"No," she drawled. "Dark." Every word was like lifting a two-ton boulder from the depths of her skull and carrying it through a labyrinth of synapses to finally hoist over her lips. It was exhausting.

Dr. Freemont placed one hand gently on her head, then drew a penlight from his pocket. He swung it in front of her right eye, then her left, where the light disappeared inside the dark fog.

"Squeeze my fingers," he commanded, touching her right

hand. She did as he asked, then wondered why he never placed his fingers in her left, although he'd walked to that side of the bed. Or maybe he had. She could no longer feel that hand.

As Dr. Freemont continued his assessment, she noticed a trend. Her left side wasn't working. Not just her eye, but also her shoulder, her hand, her thigh, all the way to her pinky toe. Numb. Dead. She was dying in halves.

"Why?" she demanded, but she knew.

"The tumor," he said simply. "The pressure in your brain." He kept speaking, but Raven's mind couldn't keep up with his medical explanation. She did catch the word *stroke*. It didn't matter. They wouldn't treat her for it anyway.

"Donate?" she asked.

Half cloaked in shadow, his face turned grim and he lowered his voice. "Yes. The cancer is only in your brain. You'll be able to donate your organs. It's all arranged." His voice was funny, and she wondered if he was lying. Normally Dr. Freemont didn't talk to his patients much about organ donation, but she'd pressed him about it early on. For her, it was a light at the end of the tunnel. Every time he reassured her of her donation status, her heart leaped a little. She'd do something with this life. Leave a part of herself behind that mattered.

If he was lying, she didn't want to know the truth.

"Long?" she asked. He knew what she meant. How long until she died? They'd been at this for over five years on and off. Through railroad spikes of pain that left her begging for someone to bash her head in. Months of chemo that turned her inside out. There was nothing left to try. There would be no more chemo. No more surgeries. Raven wanted to live, but if living wasn't possible, she would settle for being free.

His pale eyes met hers, and he gripped her fingers on the right where she could feel his reassurance. "Not long now."

Not long now. She tried her best to smile. "Good."

Her mother roused, her magazine-wrapped book falling from her lap and clattering to the floor. "Oh! Doctor. Excuse me. I must have drifted off. How is she?"

When he turned to look at her, his eyes glossier than usual, his face changed. A mask slipped into place, clinical and authoritative. Raven rolled her head on her pillow to see her mother, and the dark splotch swallowed most of Dr. Freemont's head. She couldn't see anything above his shoulders when he answered.

"I would never put an expiration date on your daughter, Mrs. Tanglewood... Sarah. We both know how strong she is."

"Yes, I know. This one came out fighting." Her mother still believed Raven could beat this thing.

She was wrong.

"Raven's comfort measures are working. We'll maintain the course." He straightened as if he might leave.

Raven squeezed his hand. "Do it," she said. It was the best part of her day. She wouldn't let him leave without giving it to her.

He turned an impassive expression toward her, half light and half dark as she looked at him straight on. "I have no idea what you are talking about, Raven." The corner of his mouth twitched.

With whatever part of her face was still working, she sent him the sternest glare she could muster.

Raising one eyebrow, he backed up a few steps and glanced into the hall. "You know, I don't do this for all my patients. Only for you."

She smiled lopsidedly.

He removed his white lab coat, cleared his throat, and glanced again at the door. There was no one out there. Ceremoniously, he wrapped his coat around Mr. Drippy, holding the neck in place with one hand and gripping the sleeve with the other. He squared his shoulders.

"I get no drip from champagne...," he began to sing, deep and throaty, in the style of Frank Sinatra. He swayed with her IV pole as much as the length of the tubes leading to the port in her chest would allow. "Mere Toradol doesn't move me at all, but morphine and fentanyl too... Yes, I get a drip out of you." He cradled the screen of the IV pole and dipped it below his round belly, careful not to upset the hanging medications. His lips puckered in an air-kiss toward the screen.

Raven couldn't help it. She started to laugh. Her mother did too, which made her laugh even harder. As always, the sight of that normally stiff and paunchy man dancing with her IV pole tickled something deep inside her, something that bitch cancer hadn't ruined yet. She laughed and laughed until her throat constricted like the valve of a pinched balloon.

Her laugh turned into a cough and then a wheeze.

Dr. Freemont stopped singing.

The next moment he was leaning over her, his pale hands gently shaking her shoulders, and she realized she'd been unconscious. Not long, judging by the look on his surprised face.

"Welcome back," he murmured. He was half dark again.

"That's never happened before," her mother said nervously.

"That's just Raven's body telling us she needs rest," he said. "I'll leave you to it." He removed his lab coat from Mr. Drippy and shrugged it on before nodding his goodbye.

"Well, that sounded promising," Mom said after he was gone. "You just need more rest." She stood up and tucked Raven in, her face positively glowing with denial.

Raven adjusted her head so her good eye was pointed at the door. *Not long now*, he'd said.

That was the day cancer stole her laugh. It was the last time the doctor sang for her. The last time she was awake long enough to ask him to. There were flashes of color and light, the feel of anointing oil crossed on her forehead and wrists as prayers were whispered over her, Avery's rosary dangling from her fingertips above her chest, Dr. Freemont's humorless face as he answered her mother's questions. But most of the following days consisted of darkness.

Until, one night, *he* came for her.

TWO

Death stood at the end of Raven's bed, looming and dark, and she welcomed him with open arms. Open arm. Only her right was under her control. Oh, how she longed to be free of her broken body.

If any part of her had questioned the true identity of her visitor, the skepticism was short-lived. The aura of the supernatural surrounded him. Raven's first clue was his suit, or rather that he wasn't wearing scrubs. An eternity had passed since someone who wasn't a medical professional or close family had entered her hospice room. Her own father didn't come anymore. It was too sad. A lost cause.

Death's miraculous presence aside, there were stranger things about his visit. Her IV had stopped dripping. Mr. Drippy's digital face was frozen, the impossibly full belly of her next drop of morphine hovering by a silver thread at the center of the machine's plastic chamber. She shot a glance toward her mother, hoping for an explanation, but the woman was motionless and rigid, staring, catatonic, toward the darkened hospital windows. The clock had stopped. Midnight.

Raven's time had finally come.

She took stock of the man who must be Death, the new growth of her hair rustling against the scratchy pillowcase as she turned her head. It was the only sound in an otherwise silent room. Under the fluorescent lights, she studied him. This was the one who would carry her home? He wasn't what she'd expected.

Death was a babe.

Dark. Brooding. Heavy boned and unshaven. There was something handsome about him nonetheless, alluring enough for her failing body to send her a flicker of desire, something she hadn't felt in over a year. It was the eyes, black eyes that seemed to burn into her, with flecks of red and mahogany that radiated from pitch-black pupils. His substantial eyebrows were too full to be considered conventionally attractive, but they balanced a generous nose and lower jaw that had no use for frivolity. He was olive-skinned, full-lipped, and big. Really big. Professional wrestler big. Although, based on his sunken cheeks and long, tapered fingers, she got the sense he could be bigger, like he was perpetually hungry.

"Ravenna Tanglewood?" he asked, his voice lined with charcoal and grit. A Clint Eastwood voice. A burning voice. Was he taking her to hell? A whiff of campfire drifted past her nose as he neared. That was one thing cancer hadn't taken from her, her sense of smell. And he smelled like the fall, like oak leaves and pumpkin pie, like smoke and old print.

"Yes." Her voice was nonexistent, mostly lips and breath doing the work.

"You are *this* Ravenna Tanglewood." He removed a folded newspaper from his breast pocket. The pages crinkled in his grip. He thrust it toward her.

A large emerald ring on his right pointer finger glinted in the light, and she had trouble looking away from it to focus on what he was asking her. Eventually though, she zeroed in on the story he was showing her. It was an article by a reporter from the *Tulane Hullabaloo*. PSYCHIC STUDENT SAVES FAMILY. She blinked slowly, confused. Why would Death care about a piece of gossipy journalism?

Before the doctors had discovered her brain tumor, she had experienced a premonition. She'd been doing laundry when a vision of her parents' pub completely engulfed in flames brought her to her knees. Neither her father nor mother took her vision seriously, but for some reason, her sister Avery did. Avery's resulting tantrum led to the purchase of a brand-new fire extinguisher. A few nights later, an inexperienced cook set his apron down too close to the grill and the strings caught fire. Her father reached for the old extinguisher first. It didn't work. Thankfully the new one did, and consequently her father was able to save the pub and the people in it.

It didn't mean Raven was psychic. Dr. Freemont had explained that the tumor in her brain, with its octopus-like tentacles infiltrating her gray matter, was connecting different areas of her mind, making her exceptionally intuitive. She'd subconsciously noticed the expiration date on the extinguisher, and her brain had produced the vision accordingly. It was the cancer, not anything weird or unusual. The newspaper story was a bit of flamboyant reporting by a friend who hoped to use the piece to attract readers to a fund-raiser meant to help with her medical expenses, nothing more.

Death tapped his finger against the newspaper impatiently, the massive green emerald glowing like a star. "Well, is this you?"

She licked her lower lip and nodded. He slid the paper back inside his jacket. Exhausted from the effort of responding, she closed her eyes and prayed silently, *Take me. Please take me.*

GABRIEL STOOD AT THE END OF THE HOSPITAL BED, USING every ounce of willpower he had to restrain himself. When Richard had suggested the girl was a long shot, he wasn't kidding. She was more dead than alive, a porcelain doll he was afraid to startle for fear of breaking her. Still, there was something... alluring about her, the same as when he'd seen her picture. Deep within his chest, a primal urge to heal and protect demanded his attention.

He hadn't felt anything like it in his five hundred years. Not for a human anyway. Perhaps the feeling bore a close resemblance to when he found a rare and priceless item for his collection. Yes, that was it.

She appeared nothing like the picture he'd seen. The only way to describe her now was haunting. The bones of her cheeks protruded as if her skeleton was battling her skin for rights to the surface. Ravenna Tanglewood was death, propped in a bed like a body on display. Above thin lips and a gently curved nose, her blue eyes bulged from her skull, dull and rheumy. Those damned eyes were nothing short of pleading. His chest ached. If she refused his offer, it would haunt him the rest of his days.

He stepped closer to her. Was that night-blooming jasmine? The scent was faint, but he could smell it on her skin. "Is it true you were an anthropology major with a minor in history? Honors student?"

A grunt came from deep within her throat, a warm wet trail of saliva coursing down her lower cheek. Her throat contracted and relaxed, but she seemed unable to form words. He hissed. Damn human hospitals. This was torture. What type of creatures left their females to die like this?

He could wait no more. Already the curse on his ring was weakening his magic. His skin felt thick, like he might turn to stone from the inside out at any moment. He tapped his fingers, exactly three times each against his thumb. Tap-tap-tap. Tap-tap-tap. It was the only thing that helped, the only thing that reminded him he could still move. His magic wasn't completely gone. Not yet.

Still, if he was to save her, he must do so soon.

"I see," he said. "I would like to offer you a job, Ms. Tanglewood. It is hard work. You'll have to learn quickly and take the initiative."

She stared at him blankly. He wondered what she must be thinking, if she could think at all. It was possible her brain was as wasted as her body. From what he'd read, she had brain cancer. Even with magical intervention, there might not be enough left in her head for her to consent. And she must consent. He would not bind her if she didn't. To do so would be to divest himself of any remaining honor he still bore in his wasting body.

He approached her bedside and gently laid his hand on her chest. Those too-big eyes locked onto him. Her heart pounded against his palm. Her expression pleaded for death, but her heart begged for life.

"Ravenna, do you consent? Do you agree to work for me?"

Her eyebrows dipped and her chin twitched as if she didn't quite understand what he was proposing. A tear escaped the corner of her eye. He wiped it away.

"Say yes, little one," he said. "I cannot bear to see you like this a moment more."

Her eyes widened. "Yes," she mouthed.

He smiled weakly. "Praise the Mountain."

As he held her stare, he removed his hand from her chest, the storm of magic brewing within him. His ring glowed brighter as he drew his power to the surface, the dragon within barely contained inside his human form. Opening his jaw wide, he reached deep into his mouth, his large hand wedging itself between his teeth. He heard her gasp as the sound of tearing flesh filled the room. Gabriel grunted. He was likely scaring her, but it could not be avoided. This was part of the transition. The faster she came to terms with what was happening here, the better.

A spurt of crimson blood beaded on his bottom lip as the tooth materialized, clutched between his fingers. He tugged a handkerchief from his pocket and dabbed at the blood, then held the tooth up to the light. It was thin. Pointed. With a long root still bloody from the extraction. Clearly not a human tooth.

"Never gets easier," he murmured.

Beside him, Ravenna trembled. Her arms were covered in gooseflesh. He had to soothe her, to do something to comfort her before she had a heart attack. He closed his hand and drew on the magic of the ring. When he opened it again in front of her mouth, there was no tooth, only a slim white pill.

"Swallow," he commanded.

She must do this now. They were running out of time, her life fading in front of him, his magic sputtering under the weight of the curse. He scooped an arm behind her shoulders and lifted. Her lips parted like a baby bird's, and he dropped the pill to the back of her throat. She gurgled, coughed. He raised her head higher. Her throat bobbed and the choking stopped.

Oh, how beautiful it was shining through her stomach. The red light spread through her torso and to the ends of her limbs, warming her flesh from within. And all the time, she lay helpless against his arm, staring at him with unrestrained wonder, that jasmine scent of hers growing stronger. It made him feel like a god to hold her like this, to know that he'd given her what she needed to heal, to survive.

He watched her chest rise and fall with the first deep breath she'd taken since he'd arrived.

"What did you give me?" she asked, and this time the words were strong and true, more than the breathy whispers he'd gotten before. Good.

His shoulders slumped. The magic had taken its toll. He must get home to rest.

He brought his face close to hers. "Rest. Recover. You're no use to me like this. We are bound now. I will know when you are ready." He pressed his lips to her forehead and lowered her to the bed.

Her mouth worked soundlessly, as if she couldn't find the words for all the questions she longed to ask.

The rhythmic beep of her heart monitor started again, and a drop of morphine fell within the chamber of her IV. As he left her side and the room, he prayed to the Mountain that he'd chosen wisely. Ravenna Tanglewood was his last chance.

MEET GENEVIEVE JACK

USA Today bestselling and multi-award winning author Genevieve Jack writes wild, witty, and wicked-hot paranormal romance and romantic fantasy. She believes there's magic in every breath we take and probably something supernatural living in most dark basements. You can summon her with coffee, wine, and books, but she sticks around for dogs and chocolate. Her novels feature badass heroines, fiercely loyal heroes, and fantasy elements that will fill you with wonder. Learn more at GenevieveJack.com.

Do you know Jack? Keep in touch to stay in the know about new releases, sales, and giveaways. https://www.genevievejack. com/newsletter/

facebook.com/AuthorGenevieveJack

instagram.com/authorgenevievejack

bookbub.com/authors/genevieve-jack

tiktok.com/@Genevievejackbooks

x.com/genevieve_jack

MORE FROM GENEVIEVE JACK!

The Treasure of Paragon

The Dragon of New Orleans, Book 1

Windy City Dragon, Book 2,

Manhattan Dragon, Book 3

The Dragon of Sedona, Book 4

The Dragon of Cecil Court, Book 5

Highland Dragon, Book 6

Hidden Dragon, Book 7

The Dragons of Paragon, Book 8

The Last Dragon, Book 9

The Angel of Paragon, Book 10

The Three Sisters Trilogy

The Tanglewood Witches

Tanglewood Magic

Tanglewood Legacy

Knight Games

The Ghost and The Graveyard, Book 1

Kick the Candle, Book 2

Queen of the Hill, Book 3

Mother May I, Book 4

A Game of Hearts

The Wolves of Fireborn Pack Trilogy

Fated Bonds

Feral Instincts

Forever Mated

www.ingramcontent.com/pod-product-compliance
Lightning Source LLC
Chambersburg PA
CBHW030834190726
48285CB00004B/1216